DISTRACTION

CLUB DESTINY

BY NICOLE EDWARDS

THE WALKERS

ALLURING INDULGENCE
Kaleb
Zane
Travis
Holidays with The Walker Brothers
Ethan
Braydon
Sawyer
Brendon

THE WALKERS OF COYOTE RIDGE
Curtis
Jared
Hard to Hold
Hard to Handle
Beau
Rex
A Coyote Ridge Christmas
Mack
Kaden & Keegan

BRANTLEY WALKER: OFF THE BOOKS
All In
Without A Trace
Hide & Seek

AUSTIN ARROWS
Rush
Kaufman

CLUB DESTINY
Conviction
Temptation
Addicted
Seduction
Infatuation
Captivated
Devotion
Perception
Entrusted
Adored
Distraction

DEAD HEAT RANCH
Boots Optional
Betting on Grace
Overnight Love

DEVIL'S BEND
Chasing Dreams
Vanishing Dreams

MISPLACED HALOS
Protected in Darkness
Salvation in Darkness
Bound in Darkness

OFFICE INTRIGUE
Office Intrigue
Intrigued Out of The Office
Their Rebellious Submissive
Their Famous Dominant
Their Ruthless Sadist
Their Naughty Student
Their Fairy Princess
Owned

PIER 70
Reckless
Fearless
Speechless
Harmless
Clueless

SNIPER 1 SECURITY
Wait for Morning
Never Say Never
Tomorrow's Too Late

SOUTHERN BOY MAFIA/DEVIL'S PLAYGROUND
Beautifully Brutal
Without Regret
Beautifully Loyal
Without Restraint

STANDALONE NOVELS
Unhinged Trilogy
A Million Tiny Pieces
Inked on Paper
Bad Reputation
Bad Business

NAUGHTY HOLIDAY EDITIONS
2015
2016

DISTRACTION

CLUB DESTINY

NICOLE
EDWARDS

NICOLE EDWARDS LIMITED
A dba of SL Independent Publishing, LLC
PO Box 1086
Pflugerville, Texas 78691

DISTRACTION
Club Destiny, 11
Nicole Edwards

COVER DETAILS:

Image: © Pink Ink Designs
Cover Model: Alfie Gordillo
Design: © Nicole Edwards Limited

INTERIOR DETAILS:

Formatting: Nicole Edwards Limited
Editing: Blue Otter Editing | www.BlueOtterEditing.com

IDENTIFIERS:

ISBN: (ebook) 978-1-939786-76-0 | (paperback) 978-1-939786-75-3

BISAC: FICTION / Romance / General

DEAR READER,

If you're a fan of the Club Destiny series, you'll probably say this book is long overdue. Well, you're right. It is. But there's a reason for the delay. If you're familiar with the story, you know that Dylan Thomas suffers deeply from depression, one that consumed him after the death of his wife years ago.

Now, the reason for the delay:

I suffer from depression. This is not a secret. I have made it public knowledge and I am not ashamed of this fact. Is it hard? Absolutely. There are times when I wonder what is wrong with me. Why can things be going well and all of a sudden, I'm living beneath a dark cloud? There isn't a day that passes that I'm not affected, but I'm aware of my illness. I know what it means. I know what the symptoms are. I know what it feels like. I've sought professional help and I have learned to cope—as well as anyone can cope with this disease.

I struggled for a long time as I attempted to write Dylan's story, trying to figure out how to get him in the right mind frame to move forward. Well, it all came to me on a particularly bad day in February 2016. I was under a dark cloud and I didn't understand why. Things were going well. My children happy, my husband healthy, no particular stressors that should've set me off, so I didn't understand.

It wasn't until I was sitting at the dinner table and I told my husband that I didn't know what was wrong that I saw the fear in his eyes. Yes. Fear. You see, my husband has stood by my side through this illness, suffered as much as I have, only in a different way. That's when I realized, I would write this book with that in mind. Seeing things from the viewpoint of those of you who love someone who suffers from depression. I will never forget that fear in his eyes. He worries about me and I love him all the more for it. That doesn't mean it's easy for him.

So, while you're reading this, keep in mind that there are two sides to this story. The one who suffers from depression and the one who is indirectly affected by it.

~Nicole

PROLOGUE

Three years ago, November...

"TELL ME WHAT HAPPENED."

Sarah Fulton paced her therapist's oversized office, past the small settee where hundreds of butts had been planted over the years, her hands flexing repeatedly—open, closed, open, closed—nerves rioting uncontrollably. As she made another hasty turn on the beige shag carpet, she shrugged her shoulders in an attempt to release the nervous tension that had consumed her ever since last night.

Last night. Had it really only been hours, not days or months, since her entire world had been altered once again?

"Sarah?"

"I'm trying," Sarah muttered. "Give me a minute."

"Take as long as you need."

Right. As long as it was within the allotted hour, then she was golden. Otherwise, she would have to come back and relive this again until she was ... cured? No, that couldn't be the right word because Sarah knew that she would never be cured of all the jumbled emotions that had been warring within her for years.

Recent events certainly hadn't helped steady her in any way.

Taking a deep breath, Sarah dropped onto the edge of the forest-green cushion and stared at her hands. "He called me last night."

"He who?"

Sarah looked up into the compassionate brown eyes watching her intently. "Dylan Thomas."

"Your friend," Elaine, Sarah's longtime therapist, confirmed.

"Yes." Though after last night, Sarah wasn't so sure that was an apt description of their relationship.

"Did you expect this?"

She shook her head. "He was the last person I expected to call me." Heck, she would've sworn the president of the United States would've called her before Dylan did.

"What did he say when he called?"

Leaning against the too-firm cushioned back of the sofa, Sarah attempted to get comfortable. It wasn't easy. Hell, this conversation wasn't easy.

"He sounded sad," Sarah explained, looking anywhere but at Elaine's face. "There was something in his voice. A longing, I guess. It was so intense my heart cracked open at the sound."

"What do you think made him sound that way?"

Well, that was easy. "Yesterday was the anniversary of his wife's death."

"I'm sorry to hear that. Was it recent?"

"No." Sarah shifted. "She's been dead for eight years."

"And he's still sad?"

The question was merely an inquiry, Sarah knew. Elaine wasn't suggesting that Dylan should or should not still be sad after all these years. Since Sarah understood the grief he experienced, she knew there wasn't a specific amount of time for wounds like that to heal. They scabbed over eventually, became less painful over time, but there would forever be a scar, a reminder.

"He's had a really hard time with it, yes." Elaine didn't say anything, so Sarah continued, "I should've known better, but when he asked if he could come over, I said yes."

"Were you bothered by the fact that he called?"

"No." Surprised, yes. Bothered, no.

"What was the first thing you thought when you saw it was him on the phone?"

Sarah studied her short nails. She'd been biting them again, a nervous habit she'd picked up several years ago.

"I was...happy?"

"Is that a question or a statement?"

Sarah shrugged. She honestly didn't know.

"Do you think that's why he wanted to come over? Because he's having a hard time?"

"Yes. No. *Maybe.*" Sarah sighed heavily. "Originally I kinda thought so. It was the anniversary of his wife's death. Maybe he needed someone to talk to, or just needed to be around someone."

Although eight years might've seemed like a long time to some people, Sarah could see how the memories that still lingered could be enough to make even the strongest person feel desolate. So, Sarah had come to the conclusion all on her own that Dylan's dark mood had to do with that.

"If he wasn't sad, would you have said yes to his coming over?"

"Probably." Sarah fidgeted, her gaze snapping to Elaine's. "Okay, yes. I would've said yes. I've always had a soft spot for him, even though I know I shouldn't."

"Always is a long time," Elaine noted.

"We dated in high school," Sarah added, swiping her hand over her frizzy blond hair. For whatever reason, she hated her hair today, wished it was longer, less curly.

"You care for him."

It wasn't a question, but Sarah found herself nodding. She did care for Dylan.

"But you don't think you should?" Elaine questioned.

Sarah shook her head. "He's broken, and the absolute last thing I need is to try to help someone else when sometimes it's all I can do to keep myself together."

"Have you been thinking about Paul?"

Sarah studied her fingernails, fighting the urge to fidget at the mention of her dead husband's name. "Yeah. More so since last night."

"And what are you thinking about?"

This was the part Sarah hated. Talking about Paul. Remembering her life with Paul. Even three years later, she still wondered why her husband had ... killed himself. Why he'd left her.

"I feel guilty," Sarah admitted.

"Because your friend called?"

"No." Not exactly.

Elaine jotted something on her notepad, then looked up at Sarah. "And did Dylan come over?"

Sarah nodded. And that was the reason for her guilt. She remembered waiting for him to arrive. Every minute that passed had felt like an eternity.

"Was that what you wanted?"

"Yes." That was the simplest answer. Even looking back on all that had happened, Sarah knew in her heart that she'd wanted Dylan to come over.

"And what happened when he got there?"

Sarah relaxed as best she could and closed her eyes, reliving the night before all over again. She couldn't give Elaine all the details, but that didn't stop the memory from overtaking her.

A sudden knock had Sarah's breath lodging in her chest as her gaze slammed into the wooden barrier of her front door. She studied it momentarily, as though she could somehow see through the varnished wood to what lay beyond. No matter how much she wished she had x-ray vision, Supergirl she was not.

Knowing it would be rude to leave Dylan standing outside in the cold and drizzle that'd descended upon them unexpectedly, dropping the temperatures of the late November evening, Sarah willed her heart to slow and leisurely made her way across the room, wiping her sweaty palms on her leggings and exhaling sharply. Her cold fingers fumbled with the deadbolt, but she managed to turn it, her hands trembling as she reached for the knob. Another deep breath and Sarah slowly pulled it open.

And there on her front porch, just beyond the glass storm door, was the incredibly attractive man she'd been expecting, looking just as sexy as the last time she'd seen him a little more than a week ago at the surprise birthday party Dylan's family had thrown for him.

Sarah sucked in a shaky breath. With his angular jaw sporting days' worth of beard growth and his narrow nose, his bronzed skin and dark hair glistening from the rain ... Dylan Thomas was breathtaking. Even when there was a desolate sadness in his gaze, making him look out of sorts, he was still too handsome for words.

His molten chocolate eyes lifted to meet hers. The same sorrow Sarah had witnessed on multiple occasions was glowing brilliantly, and she instantly knew this was a mistake. What would happen when he crossed over the threshold into her house was anyone's guess, but Sarah had a feeling she already knew what the outcome would be. Part of her welcomed it, but the wiser part was attempting to warn her.

She ignored that part.

"Can I come in?" he asked, the deep thunder of his voice like rough velvet against her nerve endings. Dylan cast a quick glance behind him toward the street, as though there might be someone watching, but she doubted her elderly neighbors were still awake.

With a jerky nod, Sarah pushed open the glass door and took a step back, motioning for him to follow. When he stepped inside, his sheer size instantly overwhelmed the room, making her modest house feel small. While she stood there staring at him, he closed the door behind him and Sarah took another deep breath.

All common decency fled her mind, leaving her unable to greet him properly. She didn't even respond when he mumbled a brittle, "Hey." Instead, she stood there, bare feet rooted to the floor as she unabashedly ogled him, steadily drawing air into her lungs while they stood less than a foot apart.

Every one of her senses was inundated by his presence. He filled her line of sight, and she admired his perfectly imperfect face. All the hard angles, the narrow slash of his nose, his sexy mouth, the beard growth that shadowed his jaw. She could smell the fresh scent of laundry detergent mixed with a subtle spice from his cologne. The only sounds she heard were the rapid thump of her own heartbeat and the labored breaths that filled her lungs. Her mouth felt as though she'd been gargling sand, so dry she struggled to swallow while her palms were still sweating. Simply put, she was a hot mess.

On top of that, she couldn't stop staring. His broad chest, covered in the soft, black cotton of his T-shirt stretched snuggly across his impressive pectorals, drew her gaze and held it.

He stole her breath.

For half a second, Sarah mentally considered what she must look like. It was late and she'd been getting ready for bed when he'd called, so she'd had only enough time to brush her teeth, pile her unruly blond curls on top of her head in a clip, and pull on the first thing she'd found in her closet. She wasn't wearing makeup, and she knew that without it she looked all of fifteen years old.

Then again, she felt like a teenager, too. Young, naïve, aching for something she didn't understand.

Remembering that Dylan was standing directly in front of her, Sarah forced her eyes away from his massive chest. She had to look up to meet his gaze. He was so much taller than she was, so much bigger, broader. It made her think of high school and how he'd been larger than life, such a great, overwhelming presence in her world.

Now, nearly twenty years later, though still just as handsome, Dylan was nothing more than a shell of the man he'd once been, and she knew that was because he'd lost his wife all those years ago. Sarah also knew that that sort of overwhelming, gut-tightening, heart-shredding grief lingered for years, far longer than she thought herself capable to handle. Her wounds were more recent—three years to his eight—but no more or less significant.

Remembering her manners, Sarah cleared her throat. "Can I get you something to drink?" she offered, her voice cracking because of her nerves. "Coffee? Tea? Water?"

Dylan didn't respond, he simply stared, his heated gaze sliding over her, leaving chills on her skin with the slow, seductive perusal. Whatever was about to happen—and she had no doubt that something was brewing between them—could never be undone. They'd been walking this line for a few weeks now, teetering on the edge, but neither of them had given in.

They'd been smart.

Now ... not so much.

Her heart cracked as she fought the memories, the emotions, the heart-wrenching feelings that she'd battled for so long. This wasn't supposed to be happening, but she couldn't stop it. Didn't want to stop it.

Everything she'd endured these past three years had led her here. To this black hole of despair and emotional chaos. The only thing she wanted to do was forget. Just for a little while. And now she could. She could ignore everything else and focus on this man who was giving her the only thing she needed at the moment.

A distraction.

As though watching in slow motion, Sarah's breath shuddered in her chest when Dylan lifted his hand, hesitantly cupping her face, his callused thumb making a few gentle swipes across her cheekbone, then slipping lower. The rough pad caressed her bottom lip and she knew she was doomed.

The warning bells were clanging loudly in her head, yet she didn't pull away from him. His touch was ... warm, tender. That affectionate gesture was enough to kick her heart into overdrive, and that yearning she'd been filled with took over.

It'd been so long since a man had touched her.

Three years. Three long, painful years.

Not since Paul. Not since before her husband's death had rocked the very foundation of her world, leaving her nursing a broken heart as she tried to understand what had caused the man she loved, the man she had vowed to spend the rest of her life with, to take his own life.

But Sarah didn't want to think about Paul right now. He had abandoned her, and the irrational side of her still hadn't forgiven him.

There was a different man here. One she didn't worry about falling in love with, didn't worry about having her heart broken by. Not this time anyway.

Dylan Thomas.

A different type of ghost from her past.

And Dylan was touching her. The soothing sweep of his fingers over her jaw was almost too much to bear. When his other hand released the clip from her hair, allowing the curly strands to fall past her shoulders, Sarah swallowed hard. The intensity in his dark brown eyes was enough to set her insides ablaze.

"Sa—"

She cut him off, putting her fingers over his lips. She didn't want him to say her name; she simply wanted to feel. She didn't want to be that broken, sorrow-filled woman anymore. She wanted to let go for a while, give in to the impulses that she'd denied for so long. Nonetheless, there was a desperation in his tone that she felt echoing inside herself. He needed this as much as she did, and neither of them was strong enough to resist.

Sarah shook her head. Whether she was saying they couldn't do this or simply telling him that words weren't necessary, she wasn't sure. But then he was leaning down, his long, strong finger curling beneath her chin to tilt her head back. His eyes studied her face briefly and she wondered what he was thinking about.

Before words had a chance to ruin the moment, his mouth was on hers, and nothing else mattered except for the light brush of his lips against her own, the subtle yet determined slide of his tongue along the seam, a silent plea to allow him entry.

With hardly any hesitation, she opened for him, meeting him halfway, her hands fisting into his T-shirt as her tongue tentatively skimmed his. For all of a second, the kiss was hesitant, an uncertain exploration. Sweet. Almost reverent.

But in the next instant, the world ignited into a fiery conflagration of passion and need. Their bodies collided, hands and mouths seeking, searching for that something that would calm the riot of emotions churning within them. Separate, but similar.

All the pain she'd been consumed by shattered, leaving her feeling free for once. Free to lose herself in this man, this moment.

Dylan's dark growl sparked the dry kindling that had been so much a part of her for so long, sending her up in flames almost instantly. Her arms went around his neck as he tore at the buttons on the oversized shirt she wore over her leggings, sending the tiny discs flying, pinging off the wall and hardwood, in his heated attempt to get closer to her.

"All the things I want to do to you..."

She didn't need him to finish the sentence, which was good because he clearly had no intention of doing so. There was no mistaking where this was headed, and Sarah couldn't find it in herself to put a stop to it. She tried to rationalize her actions, but that became too much when his bristled jaw scraped along her chin.

Too many clothes.

When he had the front hook of her bra unclasped, he forced her back a step, his eyes lingering on the skin he'd unveiled, and the unbridled approval in his molten gaze sent warmth coursing through her. His callused hands abraded her naked breasts, leaving tingles in their wake and a yearning ache building inside her. Without finesse, Sarah wiggled out of her shirt and bra, allowing them to pool at the floor near their feet.

Naked from the waist up, she reached for Dylan, pulling him to her as her back met the wall with a thud, one of his large hands palming her head at the last second, keeping her from slamming against it.

He was warm and solid, his strength evident. She wanted to absorb some of it into her body, to feel whole one more time in her life. Sarah doubted it would ever happen, but she wished it just the same.

"I need you," he whispered against her mouth, his warm breath fanning her face, the scent of spearmint tickling her nose. "Need. You."

She didn't respond. There was nothing to say. She recognized that need, that overwhelming desperation to do something that would make her feel like she wasn't about to crumble into a heap. At least for a little while.

Tugging at his T-shirt, she helped him to remove it before he worked on pushing her leggings down, her panties disappearing with them until she was standing naked between his solid body and the wall. Her fingers fumbled with the button on his jeans until she finally managed to release it, her lips grazing the hard planes of his smooth, bare chest, while he dug something out of his pocket.

The distinctive rustle barely registered, and she watched as he tore open the condom, forced his jeans and underwear down past his hips, then sheathed his long, thick cock. It wasn't until he was lifting her off her feet so that she was practically wrapped around him that she realized this was really happening.

Her breath lodged in her throat when he pressed the head of his cock against her entrance only seconds before filling her completely in one desperate thrust of his hips.

"Dylan," she cried out breathlessly, her fingers latching on to the flexing muscles in his shoulders. Pain, sharp and bright, had her holding her breath. It'd been so long; her body took a moment to adjust to the thick intrusion. Then, just as quickly as it'd come, the discomfort disappeared, leaving nothing but glorious pleasure as he slid deeper. "Yes."

Dylan pushed into her a few inches before retreating, only to push back in again, her body stretching to allow the invasion. He was big, thick, filling her so ... perfectly.

"You're so fucking tight," he groaned, his voice rough. "Warm ... wet... You feel so fucking good."

Finding his mouth with hers again, Sarah kissed him, wanting to get lost. No thought, no justification. No regret or remorse. No fear of what would happen after. The only thing she knew was the intense, overwhelming ecstasy of him filling her, his rough hands gripping her thighs as he held her against the wall, his hips thrusting forward, and the glorious friction that ignited dormant nerve endings.

He impaled her, a slow, sensual grind at first. Then faster, harder, deeper. His hips driving forward, retreating, forward again. It wasn't sweet, it wasn't romantic, but Sarah didn't care. They were seeking release, both of them, and she knew there was no turning back now.

He never let up, fucking her wildly, the desperation that outwardly consumed them both nearly palpable in the still, warm air that surrounded them. Her body clenched around him, tightening, pulling him in, and she knew she wasn't going to last. Self-induced orgasms didn't hold a candle to this.

"Dylan," she panted. "Oh, please, yes. Don't stop."

Holding on to him, Sarah sought his tongue with her own, her fingernails digging into his scalp as her body hummed with satisfaction. The waves of her release built, driving her higher until she was hovering on a razor-sharp edge, eager to go over.

"Dylan ... I'm ... gonna ..." She couldn't complete the sentence before a firestorm of sensation consumed her, starting in her core and rippling outward in a ferocious rush as her orgasm crashed through her.

Dylan's hips never stopped, his hands gripping her ass tightly as he continued to hold her, thrusting deep, his fingertips digging into her flesh until...

He slammed into her one last time, his cock pulsing with his release, an animalistic roar vibrating from him. "Fuck. So good. So fucking good."

And then the muscles in his body went rigid, and it was over.

He held her close, breathing hard, his eyes tightly shut, chest heaving, body trembling as he leaned into her. When Dylan dipped his face into the crook of her neck, Sarah cupped the back of his head, her fingers brushing his short hair, holding him and pressing kisses against his cheek.

And that was when she realized ... Dylan was crying.

Her heart broke for him. For herself. For lost love and shattered hearts. For that empty spot deep inside that felt as though it would only continue to be a dull, aching void without that one person who'd given you something to live for. Without them ... it was just unbearable.

Even as she soothed him, Sarah knew she couldn't blame him for what they'd done. She'd been just as needy. He'd managed to push the demons that haunted her away for a little while, and for that, she was grateful.

"I'm sorry," he muttered, pulling out of her and helping her back to her feet, never once meeting her eyes. "Fuck."

While she stood there, unsure what to say or do, Dylan rolled the condom off and disappeared into the kitchen. She quickly grabbed her discarded shirt, forcing her arms into it and wrapping it securely around her naked body. When he came back a minute later, his jeans were buttoned, his expression still sad. He looked a little worse for wear, sweat dotting his forehead, his eyes red-rimmed and puffy, and that was when she accepted what would come next.

"I'm sorry," he whispered sadly. "So fucking sorry."

She nodded. She was sorry, too.

He grabbed his shirt from the floor beside the door, and she realized that was the only article of clothing he'd removed. He had even kept his boots on.

"I should go."

She offered another nod.

"I'm—"

"Go," Sarah ordered before he could apologize again. She suddenly didn't want to hear it.

Dylan's haunted gaze lifted to hers, and Sarah saw the pain and the grief, along with something else. He was genuinely sorry.

And so was she.

"Sarah," Dylan began, reaching for the doorknob while she white-knuckled her shirt, keeping it closed.

She cut him off, not wanting to hear his excuses. "Just go. No apologies necessary. I know what this was."

Surprising her, his thick, dark brows lowered, his pain-filled eyes narrowing as though he was waiting for her to explain it to him.

"A distraction," she said sorrowfully. "That's what this was."

"A distraction," he echoed, then turned and left her standing there, feeling just as she'd felt all those years ago, back in high school, when she'd lost Dylan the first time.

Strange how history repeated itself.

"Do you think you were ready for that?" Elaine asked after Sarah had been quiet for a while.

Sarah knew Elaine was referring to the intimacy she and Dylan had shared. Since she'd left out the part where Dylan broke down and cried, the woman would never know how devastating it had really been.

Rather than elaborate, Sarah shook her head, her gaze darting around the room, taking it in. The celery-colored walls, the rows of diplomas framed and perfect, the contrasting curtains covering the window. She wasn't in the past anymore. She was here...in this office, spilling her guts to someone who was supposed to help her overcome the sadness that had consumed her for so long. "I don't think either of us was ready for that. What transpired between me and Dylan will never happen again."

"Why is that?"

"Because we're broken."

"And that means you can't find happiness?"

Sarah met Elaine's questioning gaze. "It means neither of us is whole enough to pull the other through."

"And you think that's a requirement?"

She shrugged. It seemed logical.

"And how do you feel today? After you've had time to process what happened between the two of you."

"I know I'll never be the same." Sarah swallowed hard, still holding Elaine's steady gaze. "I know that the second Dylan walked out my front door, I wasn't the same woman anymore."

"What do you mean by that?"

"I mean..." Sarah dropped her gaze to her hands and took a shaky breath. "I only *thought* I was broken before."

"And you aren't now?"

Sarah lifted her gaze, allowed the imaginary walls to fall in place around her heart once again. "Oh, I am," she said with certainty. "But I refuse to let it own me anymore."

"What do you plan to do about it?"

That was a good question. One Sarah didn't know the answer to. Not yet.

But the one thing she did know...

21

She was tired of being broken.
Damn tired.

Chapter One

Three years later, January 7
Present day

Dylan Thomas kept his gaze fixed on the horizon, watching the storm clouds roll in. For the past ten minutes, he hadn't been able to move, transfixed by the desolation from the coming storm. Long gone were the thin white clouds and in their place, heavy dark ones that blocked out the evening sun, stirring slowly as they rolled closer. There was something eerily familiar about the scene before him, but he knew it had nothing to do with the place.

The churning water, the darkening sky... It was the same as the emotions that had warred within him for years. Only he was a little more than three years sober now, and the uncomfortable feeling he'd once had when the gloomy, roiling emotions pulled at him was no longer present. He wouldn't say he was whole again—wasn't sure he ever would be—but Dylan knew he wasn't quite as damaged.

He'd been standing here as the outdoor patio filled with people, conversation and laughter pushing away the sound of the water lapping several yards below them. The warmth from the heaters held the chill at bay while the music playing in the speakers overhead drifted softly on the breeze. Every now and then he could make out the familiar words of the Eagles.

"How're you doing?"

Dylan glanced over to see his sister, Ashleigh, coming to stand beside him, a huge grin on her face. His baby sister looked good. Healthy, happy, despite the tension he could see at the corners of her eyes.

He shifted slightly so he could see her better. "Good. You?"

He had to give her credit, the look on her face said she wanted to believe him. He knew it would take time before Ashleigh truly trusted his words, but it was evident she was trying. It didn't matter how many days, weeks, or even months had passed, Ashleigh seemed to live in a constant state of fear where Dylan was concerned. Rightfully so considering the hell he'd put his family and friends through over the course of the last decade. He didn't remember a lot of the incidents his family had told him about, but Dylan knew that the alcoholism had made him do and say plenty of things he wasn't proud of.

Although he was working his way back to the land of the living, he suspected his sister expected him to relapse at any moment.

"I'm good," she replied, placing a gentle hand on his shoulder. "A little tired from all the prep work. But we've had a good turnout. Don't you think?"

"Not bad." The yearly CISS company party had been scheduled for months in advance, and though this was a bittersweet event, Dylan was still glad he'd come. And yes, the turnout had been better than expected, considering the rumors that were currently winding their way through the company, some true, some speculation.

"Hopefully the weather will hold up," his sister said, taking a step back and leaning against the railing, facing the others while Dylan continued to watch the choppy water of the lake beneath them.

"We might get lucky," he stated, although he was beginning to have his doubts. Far off in the distance, he could see the rain bands.

"Let's hope."

He felt the tension every time she spoke to him, and he knew she was probably wondering if he was going to fall apart. Or perhaps she thought he already had and he was once again trying to pretend otherwise.

He wished he could tell her that wouldn't happen again, but hell, Dylan wasn't even sure himself. Sobriety happened one day at a time, and he was on day 1,156, yet sometimes it felt like day one.

With that said, he was here at the party to show that he was back in the game. It was another of his many efforts to convince his family and friends that he was working to keep himself out of the deep, dark hole he'd spent most of the last decade in.

He was trying at least.

"Glad Alex picked the restaurant over the boat," Ashleigh tacked on, obviously realizing he had nothing to say.

Dylan's business partner and brother-in-law, Alex McDermott, had wanted to have the party on a boat out on the lake for old time's sake, but Dylan had convinced him to change it at the last minute. For one, it was January. Although the temperatures had been relatively mild, the wind had a bite to it, and it was not the time to be out on the water. The weatherman had been predicting storms all week, and the last thing he'd wanted was for them to be stuck out on a boat, so they'd settled on the waterfront restaurant where they'd had the party last year.

"How is Alex?" Dylan asked, glancing over at Ashleigh briefly. He'd yet to see Ashleigh's husband since he'd arrived half an hour ago.

"He's okay." She let out a deep sigh. "I think it's finally sunk in that this is a reality."

And by reality, his sister was referring to the fact that the company her husband had worked so hard to build was in fact having financial hardship. One that, no matter how hard they'd tried over the last year, they weren't able to recoup from. This would likely be the last company party for CISS, which was why Alex had been so adamant about having it.

"How'd the meeting go yesterday?" Ashleigh asked. "He didn't tell me much."

Dylan rested his booted foot on the bottom rung of the rail and shifted his stance to a more comfortable position. "Sniper 1 Security is willing to buy us out," he told her. "It's not a done deal, but Alex is finalizing the negotiations."

Not that they had much room to negotiate. Dylan knew he played a big part in their company's failure over the years thanks to his depression and the downward spiral from the booze. He'd accepted that responsibility, but it didn't change anything. Alex didn't seem angry, though Dylan knew his closest friend had every right to be. They'd gone into business together, had planned to do great things, and Dylan hadn't lived up to his end of the deal, so yeah, Alex should've been pissed.

"I figured as much," Ashleigh told him. "I hate pushing him on the subject because I know how hard it is for him right now."

It was hard for all of them. They were trying to be as transparent as they could with their clients and their employees, while still working the logistics out with the owners of Sniper 1 Security, the largest security company in the nation. CISS had a lot to offer, especially when it came to corporate security, and that had caught the attention of Sniper 1, a company that focused more on personal security. The discussions had been slowgoing—nine months, in fact—but they were all finally accepting their fate. It was inevitable.

"Where's Riley?" Dylan asked, looking around to see if Ashleigh had brought his niece to the party.

"She's with Sierra and Hannah," she told him. "They're sittin' this one out at home."

"Needed a break, huh?" Ashleigh's daughter was a handful. She was probably the cutest kid he'd ever laid eyes on, but she was at that age—having turned three in December—where she wanted to get into everything and didn't appreciate anyone trying to rein her in.

"A little," she said with a small smile. "I love her so much, but..."

"No need to explain." He chuckled. "I get it. I've got two of my own, remember?"

Granted, his two were all grown up and on their own.

Sort of.

Neither of his kids were technically on their own yet, nor making their own way, for that matter. Stacey, twenty-three—not to mention rebellious like he'd been at her age—would be graduating from UTD in May and currently didn't know what she intended to do past that. And Nate had decided at twenty-one that his associate's degree from the University of North Texas was enough for him. Regardless of their education, both of them still lived at home with Pops, Dylan's eighty-four-year-old grandfather, but, if you talked to either one of them, they were making it on their own.

Yep. Uh-huh. If on their own meant living in a ten-thousand-square-foot mansion, all expenses paid, including their tuition and brand new cars that Pops had insisted they have for Christmas last year.

Spoiled was what they were.

But Dylan accepted it for what it was. He was blessed with two intelligent children, and he wouldn't change a single thing about them even if he could.

"So, have y'all shared the news with the teams yet?" Ashleigh asked.

"Not yet. We'll be working on that in the coming weeks."

"Does Nate know?"

Dylan nodded. "We sat him down last week and explained what was going on. Alex has informed Sniper 1 that it's imperative they bring Nate and Jake on in the current roles they're in."

"And you?"

"I'll be leaving the company," he informed her. It had been a tough decision to make, but one that he needed to follow through with. It wasn't that he enjoyed his job at this point, but he still had reservations about making big changes in his life. Dylan wasn't fond of change, and starting over in his career at the ripe old age of forty-two gave him pause. But it had to be done.

"You haven't changed your mind?" she asked, her smile once again forced. "I'm sure Sniper 1 could take you on if you wanted them to."

Dylan shook his head. "I think having them take Nate and Jake on is enough."

"How is Jake anyway?" she asked, briefly glancing his way, then back to the people around them. "I haven't seen him in a while."

"He's—" Before he could get his response out, Ashleigh cut him off.

"Holy shit. Is that...?"

Dylan felt eyes on him and he turned in time to see... *Holy shit was right.*

He swallowed hard, standing up straight and placing one hand on the rail as he peered behind him into the ocean-blue eyes of the woman who'd haunted his dreams for the past three years.

"Wow, Sarah looks different," Ashleigh whispered, her voice being carried by the wind.

Different was an understatement, Dylan thought, never looking away from the woman he hadn't seen in ... far too long. Previously Sarah Fulton, now Sarah Davis since she'd taken her maiden name back, was standing less than ten feet away, her expression reflecting every bit of the surprise Dylan felt.

But Ashleigh was right, the woman looked like an entirely different person than the one he remembered from that night so long ago and the months leading up to it. The innocence he'd once seen in her eyes was long gone, replaced by something darker, more resolute.

Sure, she was just as beautiful as he remembered, possibly more so standing there in a short off-white dress that hugged every curve and knee-high brown boots that made his fucking mouth water. The blood-red lipstick on her succulent mouth made his dick thicken, his jeans becoming far too tight. The tattoos that decorated her arms beneath the sheer sleeves of her dress were probably the most notable difference aside from the fact that she'd lost weight and no longer had the perfect hips he'd once held in his hands. Also gone were the short, silky blond curls she'd once sported, and now the wind teased her long golden locks. He could practically still feel the silkiness against his fingers.

"Who is that with her?"

Dylan forced his gaze away from Sarah and over to the man standing at her side. He shrugged, although he had an idea. He'd heard Jake mention that his aunt had started dating someone recently. A fact that Dylan had done his best not to dwell on.

"Are you gonna go talk to her?"

Jerking his attention back to Ashleigh, Dylan fought to keep himself anchored in the present, rather than drifting back to that fateful day when he'd last seen Sarah... The night he'd fucked her up against her living room wall.

"Dylan?" Ashleigh nudged his arm with hers.

"No," he answered abruptly, turning his attention back to the water. "I doubt she wants to hear from me."

"Why?"

Dylan shook his head. He was not going to go into the details, not even with his sister, who'd become one of his closest friends in the years since his wife had died. As much as Dylan wished he could talk to her about that night, he was too embarrassed to admit what he'd done. It was just a damn good thing Sarah had come to her senses and sent him on his way. Otherwise...

Damn it. He didn't want to think about it.

Ashleigh moved off the rail and touched his arm again. "Well, I've got to go find Alex. I'll talk to you later, 'kay?"

He offered his sister another nod, grateful for the reprieve.

For some reason, he needed a minute to collect himself, and he didn't need any witnesses to the meltdown he felt coming on.

"YOU OKAY?"

Sarah yanked herself back to the present at the sound of her nephew's voice, forcing a smile while she willed her heart to stop pounding against her chest. A mere few seconds of looking at Dylan Thomas had brought the memories of that long-ago night back in full force.

She could practically still feel his hands on her, his mouth, the way he moved inside her body. Three years had done little to help her forget.

It took a moment to remember where she was, who she was with. Finally, she forced a smile and glanced at her nephew. "Good. Why?"

Jake passed her a glass of wine and handed Bill, her date, a bottle of beer. "You look like you just saw a ghost."

Well, that was because she had. She'd seen a ghost from her past, a man she thought she would be able to handle seeing again. For nearly two weeks, ever since Jake had asked her to accompany him to this party, Sarah had attempted to mentally prepare herself for an unavoidable reunion. Hence the reason she'd invited Bill at the last minute. Though he wasn't her boyfriend, they'd gone on a few dates and she'd thought he would be a good distraction.

Yeah.

That hadn't worked out too well.

In fact, she hardly noticed that Bill was there now that Dylan was standing ten or so feet away from her. So much for mentally preparing for this. Apparently, *thinking* about seeing Dylan again and actually *seeing* him were two very different things.

Being that Dylan was part owner of the company her nephew worked for, running into him tonight had been inevitable. As much as she'd wanted to avoid this event for that reason alone, telling Jake no wasn't in her nature.

As it was, Jake was the closest thing she had to a son. A child of her own wasn't in the cards, but Sarah was okay with that. She'd spent most of her adult life as a teacher, getting the opportunity to frame the minds of other people's children, and she'd never been left wanting more.

Granted, in recent years, Sarah had shed her old life, making some major changes in an effort to make herself whole again. Not only had she sold her house and bought a new one, reclaimed her maiden name, decided to get healthy, changed the way she dressed, and invested in some self-expressive body art, she'd also changed everything else about herself that she could. She'd cleaned out the metaphorical clutter and transformed her ... whole life. Some might call it a mid-life crisis, but Sarah liked to think of it as self-preservation.

Yet, as she stared back at Dylan, she felt like her old self—sad, broken, uncertain, miserable—and that wasn't a good thing. Sarah had decided she despised the woman she'd once been, hating how vulnerable she'd allowed herself to be, and had purposely reinvented herself. It had worked.

Or so she'd thought.

Her gaze strayed to Dylan once more. He looked almost exactly as she remembered. Tall, broad, and obscenely handsome wearing a pair of dark blue Wranglers that hugged every glorious inch of his impressive lower body. The scruff on his face was sprinkled with gray; his once short, dark hair had been shaved almost completely bald. She wondered if that was because it had been receding or if he merely preferred it that way. Whatever the reason, he looked good. Rugged yet distinguished. Better than before, for sure.

What surprised her the most was that the hard years he'd had didn't show in the beautiful lines of his face. And she'd heard all about his struggle back from the dark side—his battle with depression and alcohol—thanks to the fact that her nephew worked for him and because, at one point, Dylan's sister had asked her to help.

Remembering Bill and Jake were standing there, watching her intently, Sarah forced another smile and looked up at her nephew. It still surprised her that he was so tall, registering somewhere close to six one. He definitely got that gene from his father and not his mother, being that she and Sarah hadn't even broken five feet.

"Aunt Sarah?"

"Sorry. Just a little cold, I guess."

It wasn't true. With the heaters planted randomly around the outside area, it was rather warm, almost cozy.

"Do you want my jacket?" Bill offered, referring to his ill-fitting suit jacket.

Touching his arm, she smiled at him. "I'm good. I'll just go back inside in a minute."

"You sure?"

Since she wasn't really cold, she nodded her head, doing everything in her power to keep her attention riveted on Bill's face and not wandering back over to where Dylan was still standing. From the instant she'd stepped outside and noticed him, she'd been doing her best not to think about the last time she'd seen him. It'd been ... God, it'd been so long ago that that incredible night was merely a fuzzy collage of images in her head at this point, so she wasn't sure why she was even affected by him.

But she was.

"Dinner's gonna be served in about ten minutes," Jake informed her. "Do y'all need anything else?"

"No, I'm good. Really."

"Thanks," Bill stated kindly.

"Okay."

Her nephew's eyes strayed in Dylan's direction, and Sarah prayed that he wasn't going to want her to go over and talk to him. She prided herself on being strong, but having to deal with him so soon after seeing him for the first time since...

Yeah.

Sarah wasn't sure she could handle that right now.

It had taken every single second of the last three years to get her world in order, to discover who she really was after spending so many years walking in the shadows of the people who had derailed her life. Her deadbeat sister. Her dead husband. Her overbearing but well-meaning mother. Dylan.

You're not that woman anymore.

No, she wasn't. Gone was Sarah Fulton, the sweet, innocent schoolteacher who had mourned the death of her husband until it had consumed every part of her. She was Sarah Davis once more. The new and improved version. Strong, confident. Unbreakable.

"I'm gonna go talk to Dylan. You wanna come over and say hi?"

She shook her head quickly, realizing her adamant rejection probably looked rather suspicious, but she couldn't help it. For the past three years, Sarah had stayed away from these people. Thankfully, being that they lived in the Dallas-Ft. Worth metropolitan area, that wasn't difficult. As the area had a population of over seven million, randomly running into them was highly unlikely. She spent time with her family and her closest friends, talking to Jake on a daily basis but choosing not to venture into any social settings until she could sort things out in her head. Based on the way Dylan had looked at her when she'd walked out onto the patio just now, she'd succeeded in reinventing herself.

"You sure you're okay?" Jake asked again, his blue eyes searching her face, and she could see the worry creasing his brow.

Smiling up at the young man she'd practically raised after her older sister had abandoned him when he was just a child, Sarah recognized the concern on his face. They were close, always had been. But right now, she wished he didn't see as much as he did because she wanted—no, she *needed*—him to drop the subject.

"Go talk to him," she encouraged. "We're gonna go back inside. There's someone I want to talk to."

"All right," Jake agreed with a curt nod. "We're at a table on the far wall. They've got name cards out. I'll see you in a few."

Nodding in understanding, Sarah started for the door, her gaze once again drifting over to Dylan as her nephew walked up to him.

His dark eyes met hers and she fought to keep her breathing under control.

Shaking off the memories of a time best forgotten, Sarah stepped inside and glanced around at the many familiar faces. It had been a long time since she'd seen these people. Probably the last time had been at Nate's high school graduation a few years ago, back when she'd been starry-eyed and stupidly infatuated with a man she could never have.

Luckily, that had lasted all of a minute.

"Who're you looking for?" Bill asked from beside her.

"Oh, just an old friend," she told him as though that was the most natural answer in the world. Truth was, she wasn't looking for anyone; she had simply used that as an excuse for Jake.

"Would you like to find our seats?" Bill questioned.

Because she didn't have anything else to suggest, Sarah nodded and resigned herself to dinner. As kind as Bill was, it was awkward to be with him. He was such a nice guy, but no matter how hard she tried, she couldn't seem to feel anything for him.

"That'd be great," she told him, tossing back the rest of her wine.

Before she turned to follow Bill, Sarah looked over and caught Dylan standing a few feet away, still watching her intently. She noticed the way Dylan's eyes locked onto her empty glass. Then she remembered that he was a recovering alcoholic and she felt bad—

Wait.

No. She didn't.

She did *not* feel bad for drinking wine. She did *not* feel bad for accompanying Jake to this party or for bringing Bill. She did *not* fucking feel bad for any of it. She was damn tired of feeling bad for everyone else.

Sarah instinctively ran her fingers over the tattoo on her forearm. She'd gotten the intricate phoenix design as a reminder that she wasn't that same broken woman anymore. The fact that she'd been so easily sucked back to a different time only pissed her off.

Knowing these people didn't deserve her wrath, Sarah fixed a plastic smile on her face and turned to follow Bill.

She damn sure wasn't going to let two minutes in Dylan's presence destroy years' worth of effort.

CHAPTER TWO

THE REST OF THE EVENING WENT EXACTLY as Dylan anticipated it would. He managed to speak when spoken to, smile when prompted, and even endured the pity glances he'd received from some people. As much as he hated the way people watched him—as though he was a wild animal about to break his chain—he understood. A lot of these people had been around long enough to have seen his downward spiral, but it appeared that no matter how hard he tried to redeem himself, most people didn't believe he was working himself out of the hole he'd dug.

However, that was exactly what he was doing. He'd picked himself up by his boot straps and made something better of his life. It had taken time. A long damn time, but Dylan was confident in who he was now. He'd made some serious mistakes, he had a lot to atone for, but that didn't mean he wasn't comfortable with who he'd become and the path he was on. And the good news was that he was the only person he had to convince of that.

His attention was drawn across the room when he spotted Sarah getting up from her chair and walking away from her table. He noticed the way her date peered up at her, the gleam in his eye lecherous. Dylan wanted to punch the smarmy bastard for even thinking about Sarah that way. Not that Dylan had any right to do so, nor could he deny that he'd had those same lascivious thoughts every time he looked at the woman.

Especially tonight. From the instant he saw her, Dylan's mind had wandered to places it had no business being. However, the mere thought of Sarah and this guy together… Yep, it had the green-eyed monster rearing its ugly head. Whether he had the right or not, Dylan felt something darkly possessive in his soul. He wanted to insert himself between the two of them and insist that Sarah stop smiling at the asshole.

"Excuse me," he muttered to those at his table, though no one seemed to be paying any attention to him.

Without stopping to chat with anyone else, Dylan wound his way through the tables and toward the narrow hall that led to the restrooms. He caught a glimpse of cream as Sarah disappeared inside the ladies' room. Rather than go in after her—though rather tempting—he leaned against the wall a few feet from the door and waited for her.

Several minutes later, after two other women slipped by him, Sarah emerged. She was smiling … right up until her gaze met his.

"Dating car salesmen?" he said by way of greeting, unable to hold back the bite of jealousy that had ripped through him the instant he'd seen Sarah with another man. He knew it wasn't fair to her that he'd been disappointed to see that she had a boyfriend, but he couldn't help but speak his mind.

Her blond eyebrows darted downward. "Do you know him?"

Well, hell. It had been a joke. "No." Dylan pushed up from the wall. "Is he really a car salesman?"

Sarah watched him warily, nodding. She circled him, as though trying to keep from getting cornered. Dylan pretended not to notice.

"You been dating him long?"

"We're not really dating," she blurted, but her lips slammed closed as though she hadn't meant to say that. The words that tumbled out next confirmed it. "Actually, yes. Yes, I have. We're dating. Officially. For a few months. Many dates."

When she glanced toward the ceiling, he wondered if she worried that lightning was going to strike her where she stood because that had been one whopper of a lie if he'd ever heard one.

Dylan stared at her for several seconds, their eyes locked. Memories of that night so long ago flashed through his mind. So many emotions he'd suppressed since then flooded back, stirring things up inside him. A mixture of anger and jealousy, longing and desire settled deep in his gut.

He had known this woman for what felt like forever, and at one point they'd even been friends. Of course, he'd gone and ruined that by introducing sex into the mix. That night, so long ago yet still fresh in his memories, was probably his biggest mistake. Not that he hadn't enjoyed it, because he had. Immensely. However, it had drawn more emotion from him in the few short minutes he'd been with her than he'd expressed in years before that. Quite frankly, his reaction to Sarah had scared the shit out of him. Not since his wife had Dylan ever felt something like this. Hell, not since Meghan had Dylan felt much of anything at all.

Until Sarah.

And here she was again, a beautiful temptation that he couldn't seem to resist.

There was some sort of magnetic force that drew Dylan closer to the sensual being still eyeing him cautiously, causing him to close the distance as he backed her up against the wall. To his surprise, she was watching him the same way she'd watched him the night he'd come over to her house and...

He smiled at the memory of how her body had clasped his so perfectly. Damn, what he wouldn't give to bury himself in her heat once more. Right here. Right now. To feel that bone-jarring intensity one more fucking time.

If the woman only knew all the devious thoughts he'd had where she was concerned.

Sarah Davis had an innocence about her that she would never be able to shake. No amount of tattoos would be able to dim that naïve glow that lit her pretty eyes. From her heart-shaped face to her plump, cupid's-bow lips and the look of wide-eyed wonder in her dark blue eyes, the woman was purity reincarnate. Red lipstick, smoky eyes, and jet-black eyeliner did nothing to disguise that. He could still remember all the things he'd wanted to do to her, all the ways he'd hoped to have her. It had been about sex at the time. Pure, untainted lust.

And he knew his lust ran deep and hot. If he was alone with this woman for any amount of time, he'd strip her of her innocence and ruin her for eternity.

She deserved so much better than him. Both then and now.

"What do you want, Dylan?" Sarah's sweet, raspy voice was barely a whisper. "I really need to get back to my date."

Okay, so maybe she wasn't looking at him exactly the same way as she had all those years ago.

He lifted his hand, and before he knew what he was doing, he slid his knuckles over the smooth line of her jaw. For the past 1,156 days, Dylan had thought about this woman. Hell, even before then. Ever since that night ... the night that had changed him in so many ways. The night he'd fucked her up against the wall, giving a piece of himself to her without even realizing it.

Although she probably didn't know, that night had been a turning point for him. He'd spent a few more days spiraling completely out of control before he hit rock bottom. But it had been what he'd done to her—the way he'd used her—that had made him wake up and realize the shit storm that had become his life.

"Dylan ... don't."

Pulling back, he realized what he was doing and saw the anger etched into the soft, smooth lines of Sarah's face. Apparently what they'd shared that night hadn't lingered with her the way it had with him. Then again, he wouldn't know because he had walked away and never looked back. He wanted to believe he would have, had it not been for the fact she'd said he was a distraction, but he wasn't sure. Maybe that was just his excuse.

Without another word, Sarah moved around him, still watching him closely before turning and disappearing from his life once again.

"Fuck," he muttered, leaning up against the wall, anger churning in his gut. Anger at himself mostly.

What the hell had he expected to happen just then? Had he really thought the woman would forgive him? That she'd run right into his arms and tell him she'd be open to his deepest, darkest fantasies? He doubted his overbearing attitude would get him far, even if she had considered it.

Sighing, he pushed off the wall and headed back out to the party.

He knew exactly what he'd been hoping for. The same thing he'd been hoping for since the night he walked out of her house.

A do-over.

Fuck being a damn distraction.

Dylan wanted to be this woman's everything.

SARAH WASN'T SURE WHAT HAPPENED BACK IN that hallway, but it took a few seconds before she could get her breathing under control. Coming face-to-face with Dylan like that... It had caused the memories and emotions to rush back, leaving her feeling as psychologically wrecked as if it had been yesterday.

Three years and two months wasn't enough time to forget something that had altered her in ways she hadn't expected. Made her want things she never thought she'd want again. Dylan Thomas had shattered her world more than it already had been. Worse, the man had left her feeling more alone than ever.

Sure, Paul held the award for damaging her beyond recognition. For destroying her world, stealing her dreams, eliminating her hopes. But Dylan wasn't too far behind. He'd put the nail in the coffin, so to speak. Just when she'd become hopeful that there was life after the painful mourning of her husband, Dylan Thomas robbed her of that.

And it was her own damn fault.

Paul wasn't here for her to punish for hurting her so deeply. Sometimes Sarah pretended he was, shouting into the empty house, cursing him for leaving her. She knew she had no recourse when it came to Paul. One day, if they saw each other in the afterlife, she vowed to give him a piece of her mind. Until then, she had to come to terms with it.

But Dylan...

He'd walked right back into her life as though that night had never happened. But the man was delusional if he thought they could pretend that he hadn't walked away. He'd used her that night, the same as she'd used him. Not once had she ever blamed him since; however, she damn sure wasn't interested in going back there, reliving it. Although she didn't hold it against him, that didn't mean she hadn't hoped he would show up on her doorstep again.

Not now, though. He was three years too late.

"Hello, lovely."

Sarah forced a smile as she looked up at her date.

Bill Kasin. Car salesman of the year for two years straight.

God, what was she thinking?

She wished she could've felt something for this guy, but it just wasn't working for her. Sure, he was nice. And she genuinely liked him. As a friend. Ever since he paid for her coffee at Starbucks all those months ago, she'd entertained the notion of dating him. However, more often than not, Sarah had turned down his advances, made up excuses as to why she couldn't go out with him, instead staying home with her cats like a crazy old lady with absolutely no life. If it weren't for her monthly visits to her therapist, her daily phone calls with her mother, and her once-in-a-while girls' nights with her best friend, Jenny, Sarah would've long ago been institutionalized.

Apparently, she'd gotten a burr in her butt tonight because she'd called Bill at the last minute and asked him to come with her. Truthfully, she'd thought he would be busy—she'd *hoped* he would be busy—and unable to attend. Instead, he had sounded far too excited to accept her offer of a dinner date. Not that she thought of this as a date, but it seemed he certainly did. The guilt she felt was overshadowed by her need to keep herself busy. With her mother always on her butt about how she needed to get out there and date, Bill had been a saving grace for a while.

Yes, she was using him. Yes, she felt guilty about that. No, she didn't intend to do anything about it either.

Not yet. Not until she could get her head on straight.

Unfortunately, coming here tonight didn't help at all. Seeing Dylan again... Sarah wasn't sure how long it would take to get over him this time. No one knew that she'd spent months trying to forget about him because no one knew what had happened between them. And she had no desire to tell anyone, either.

Dylan Thomas was a ghost from her past, one that she fully intended to leave there. In the past.

"You ready to go?" Bill asked sweetly.

"Let me say good night to Jake."

Taking Bill's proffered hand, Sarah moved around the room to where Jake was standing in the corner talking to Dylan's son, Nate. She felt eyes on her as she walked, but she resisted the urge to see who or where they were coming from. She had a good idea.

In a matter of a few seconds in Dylan's presence, something intense had passed between them. The same unspoken emotions from so long ago. Lust, need, desire. Something that she didn't want to experience again. It had taken her changing her entire life to forget the men from her past, and now that she'd accomplished that feat, she had no intention on back tracking. Ever.

Hating to interrupt but needing to get out of there, Sarah stepped up to the two men who appeared to be in a heated conversation.

"Hey, Aunt Sarah." Jake's attention flew to her as he stood up straight. He looked like a kid who had just been caught with his hand in the cookie jar.

Cocking an eyebrow, she stared between the two men for a moment. Nate was making a point not to make eye contact and succeeding.

Clearing her throat, Sarah smiled. "I just wanted to let you know that we're gonna go."

Jake smiled, but it looked forced. He leaned down and hugged her tightly, thanking her for coming.

"My pleasure."

"I'll talk to you tomorrow?"

Sarah nodded. "Of course." Glancing between the two men again, Sarah tried to figure out what was up. When it was clear she wasn't going to be able to, she nodded. "Good night. You boys be good."

"Yes, ma'am," Jake said with a wicked grin.

"Nice to meet you," Bill added. "I promise to get her home safely."

Sarah rolled her eyes. She was a complete idiot. The guy standing beside her was a good one. One she'd be smart to keep around for a while.

But that didn't explain why her gaze instantly—and against her wishes—strayed all the way across the room and landed on the one man she could never have, the one man she knew would never belong to anyone ever again because the woman who owned his heart had died holding it, eleven years ago.

Half an hour later, Bill pulled up in front of Sarah's house. As hard as she'd tried, keeping up a conversation with him had been futile. The man preferred to talk about cars and work, and since she had no input on either, she usually kept her mouth shut. Because they had very little in common, they never managed to get to know one another, no matter how many times they'd tried.

When he put the car in park, Sarah had the overwhelming urge to bolt, but she knew that would be rude.

"Sarah?"

Turning her attention to him, she pasted another smile on her face. She was getting tired of pretending, tonight more than most nights.

"Are you okay?"

She nodded. "Fine. Just tired."

"Would you like me to come in? We could watch TV, have some wine?"

God, that was the last thing she wanted. "I think I'm gonna go to bed."

His eyes lit up as though she'd offered him an invitation.

"Thanks for coming with me," she blurted, reaching for the door handle.

"Lemme walk you to the door."

"No, you don't need to do—" That was as far as she got before Bill was out of the car and walking around to her door. She waited patiently as he helped her out.

When he took her hand, she fought the urge to pull away from him, allowing him to lead her to the door.

Sarah took her time searching for her keys in her purse. When she finally found them, she looked up at Bill. "Thanks again ... for going with me. For walking me to my door." She glanced at the door.

His desire to kiss her was written on his face, and the mere thought of his lips touching hers made her stomach churn. She turned away quickly, shoving her key in the lock.

"I'll call you tomorrow," she said and then darted inside, talking to her cats before Bill could get another word in. She managed another smile at him before closing the door in his face.

What in the world was wrong with her? How could she possibly be so rude?

Uggh.

Despite the fact that she wasn't proud of her behavior, Sarah didn't open the door to see if Bill was still standing there.

Sure, she was disgusted with herself, but she wasn't crazy.

Not entirely anyway.

CHAPTER THREE

Monday morning

DYLAN WOKE EARLY, BUT HE REFUSED TO get out of bed immediately. Rather than heading to the gym, then making his way over to the CISS office, he remained right where he was, staring at the ceiling as his thoughts overtook him. No matter how hard he tried, he couldn't get Sarah off his mind. Nothing he did allowed him to escape the events that had taken place three years earlier.

Standing in Sarah's house, Dylan realized he was about to cross a line he would never be able to uncross. He was going to do something that would forever alter the course of their friendship, yet he didn't want to turn around and leave.

He couldn't seem to look away from her, couldn't stop himself from touching her. When he'd asked to come over, Dylan hadn't known why he needed to see her, but he had. A desperate, all-consuming need had clawed at his gut until he'd forced himself to call her.

And here he was, touching her, the back of his finger sliding over the smooth skin of her jaw as he reached to remove the clip from her hair. He watched the silky blond ringlets bounce down around her shoulders. God, she was sweet. Too sweet. Too innocent for what he wanted from her.

"Sa—"

Dylan didn't even know what he wanted to say, but she cut him off before he could, her fingers brushing over his lips. He couldn't stop looking at her, noticing the way she shook her head. Fearful that she would tell him to leave, Dylan made his next move, tilting her head back by curling his finger beneath her chin. He caught her gaze briefly, silently urging her to want him as much as he wanted her.

When Sarah's lips parted, Dylan tentatively met her tongue with his, the breath lodged in his lungs when she fisted his shirt in her small hands. He tried to stay calm, tried to keep his body under control.

That lasted all of three seconds.

Unable to stop himself, Dylan plundered her mouth, crushing his body to hers as he sought all that she could give him. The woman was fire in his arms, obliterating his mind, all his good intentions up in smoke. A growl rumbled up from his chest, her arms wreathing his neck as he gave himself over to the sensations. Sensations he hadn't felt in years. He tugged at the sides of her shirt, sending the tiny buttons flying. He needed to get closer, needed to feel her soft skin on his. It was all he could think about. Quenching the overwhelming lust that had consumed him. He hadn't been with a woman in years, hadn't wanted to.

Not until Sarah.

"All the things I want to do to you..." He didn't get to finish his sentence, needing her mouth on his again.

Jesus H. Christ.

There were so many fantasies racing through his head. He imagined Sarah straddling Chris while Dylan's cock tunneled in and out of her mouth. It had been years since he'd thought about sharing a woman with his best friend, but now it seemed to be all he could think about.

He could practically feel the warmth on his dick, the lust fizzing beneath his skin as his friend gave her so much damn pleasure she couldn't stand it. He wanted to share her, to see another man pleasure her. It was something he'd longed to do again, and he needed that as much as he needed this.

But Sarah wasn't that woman. She didn't strike him as the kind who would enjoy that sort of intimacy, the eroticism of having two men inside her at the same time...

Dylan shook off the thought, burying it deep.

His hands groped, fumbled to unclasp her bra, while his tongue thrust against hers in a heated mating that was slowly taking over him. When her breasts were free, Dylan released her mouth, forcing her back as his gaze raked the smooth swell of her breasts, the sweetly puckered nipples. His hands had a mind of their own, roaming over her, desperate for more. He fought to hold on as Sarah jerked her shirt and bra from her body, dropping them both to the floor.

Another step and he was pushing her against the wall, his brain coming online long enough to send instructions to his hand to cradle the back of her head, not wanting to hurt her but needing her in every way a man needed a woman.

"I need you," he stated, wanting her to understand how much. "Need. You."

With his eyes still closed, Dylan roughly stroked his dick as he thought about that night. The cool air washed over his overheated skin as he jacked off to those mental images that overwhelmed him. God, what he wouldn't give to feel Sarah's hands on him, her mouth, the tight grip of her cunt wrapping around his dick.

His hand tightened around his cock as he jerked harder, faster. He pretended Sarah was there, her luscious lips wrapped around the head of his cock...

"Fuck, yes," he hissed as his dick jerked in his fist. He came, thick spurts of cum spraying his stomach.

It took several minutes to get his breathing under control. When he did, he forced his eyes open. He was still in his bedroom and there was no warm, willing woman at his side. If he had to guess, Sarah was at work. Hell, he didn't even know what she did for a living these days. He remembered Jake mentioning that she'd quit her teaching job, but the kid never said why or what she was doing now.

Damn, he needed a drink. Something to free his mind of this hellish hold those memories had on him.

Dylan glanced over at his phone, then reached for it. He instantly pulled up Alex's number and typed a quick text.

Dylan: *Hey, man. Gonna be out of the office today.*

Alex: *No worries. It's slow right now. Something wrong?*

Everything was wrong, but Dylan wasn't about to tell Alex that. No reason for him to worry. Dylan had it all under control.

Dylan: *All good. Just need to find an AA meeting today.*

Alex: *If you need anything at all, I'm here. Just remember that.*

Dylan: *I'm good. Swear it.*

Or he would be, just as soon as he found a meeting and figured out a way to banish the thoughts of Sarah.

Without taking a drink.

"SARAH?"

Sarah lifted her gaze and met Elaine's concerned look. "Hmm?"

"How did it feel seeing Dylan after all this time?"

She took a deep breath. It was her own fault she was hashing out these feelings with her therapist. As soon as she woke up this morning, Sarah had called Elaine and asked if she could come in for a session. She needed to talk to someone, and since she wasn't ready to share her feelings with her mother or her best friend, Elaine was her only option.

"Confused," she admitted. "I knew it wouldn't be easy to see him, but I didn't expect to have all these emotions"—Sarah gestured toward her chest—"building up."

"Describe the emotions," Elaine prompted.

"Anger, sorrow, anxiety." She held Elaine's stare. "I realized how much I missed him as soon as I saw him. I thought I was over him."

"It's okay that you missed him, Sarah. He played a significant role in your life."

"But he walked out. He…"

"Abandoned you?" Elaine stated. "The way Paul did?"

"Not the same way, no." Paul had killed himself. He had permanently removed himself from the world, leaving Sarah feeling completely helpless and alone. Dylan had simply walked away and never looked back.

"No, I agree. Not the same. But you still feel as though he abandoned you."

"Yes, I do."

"How do you feel about him? Seeing him for the first time, what were your immediate thoughts?"

"That he looked good," Sarah admitted. "He doesn't look quite so … sad."

"That's a good thing, right?"

Sarah nodded. It was a good thing. No matter how much Dylan had hurt her, she still wanted him to heal from his pain.

"And are you thinking about Paul?"

"No." Sarah dropped her eyes to her lap. "Yes. A little, I guess."

"What are you thinking about?"

"About how he left me. About how he allowed his disease to win."

"Today you're angry with him." It wasn't a question.

"Yes." Through the years, Sarah's emotions had flip-flopped when it came to her husband. Some days she was sympathetic, wishing she could've helped him, hating the disease that had stolen his life. Other days she was angry that he hadn't bothered to tell her what was going on. The fact that he had been diagnosed with bipolar disorder—something she had learned from his doctor *after* he had taken his own life—was something she felt he should've shared with her.

Of course, there were plenty of days she felt guilty. Guilty that she hadn't known what was wrong with him or even how to help him.

"Do you wish you hadn't seen Dylan at the party?"

Sarah shook her head. "In a way, I'm glad I did."

"Why's that?"

"I'm hoping I can move on."

"Do you want to move on?"

Sarah's gaze snapped up to Elaine. "Of course I do."

Elaine's smile was soft. "I wasn't stating otherwise, Sarah. In fact, I think you've made some rather significant changes in your life. Do you feel as though those changes helped you in seeing Dylan again?"

"Not really, no. I was instantly transported back to that night."

"Are there things you want to say to him?"

Sarah considered that for a moment. "Nothing I'd want him to hear, no."

Elaine placed her notepad on the small table beside her and sat up straight. "Let's do an exercise. I want you to pretend that I'm Dylan. I want you to say the things that you don't want to say to his face."

Sarah was familiar with this method of Elaine's. She'd done it numerous times over the years. Oddly enough, it usually did help.

"Okay." She glanced around the room. "Do you mind if I stand up?"

Elaine gestured for her to do as she wanted.

Sarah forced herself to her feet and paced the floor, gathering her thoughts. When she stopped, she turned to Elaine and pretended she was Dylan.

"You hurt me." She swallowed. "Although I don't blame you for what happened between us, you still hurt me by leaving. I wanted to help you. I wanted to be there for you, but you wouldn't let me. If I had known that I wouldn't see you again, I would've done things differently."

"Sarah?" Elaine's tone was soft, comforting.

Sarah lifted an eyebrow.

"Are you talking to Dylan or Paul?"

She thought about what she'd said.

"I want you to do something," Elaine began. "I want you to think about Dylan for a little while. Think about the things he has been through, the things he has done. You told me yourself that he's an alcoholic."

"He is." Sarah took a seat once more.

"You're a fixer, Sarah. But it isn't your place to fix Dylan. If he wants help, he will ask for it. I want you to remember that he's not Paul. You told me yourself that there wasn't a commitment between the two of you."

"There wasn't. I was a willing participant."

"Then don't hold that against him. You need to focus on you."

She knew that.

"You take so much on yourself, Sarah. But you need to remember that other people are responsible for their own actions. You are responsible for yourself."

Sarah understood what Elaine was saying, but it was hard to agree.

"Do you feel responsible for your sister abandoning her son?"

Sarah swallowed hard. "No. She did that all on her own."

"But you picked up the pieces because you didn't want Jake to go without."

Sarah nodded. That was true.

"And by doing that, you helped that little boy grow into a fine young man. And you learned early on that you couldn't change Tara. You couldn't make her want to be a mother. You couldn't *fix* her, Sarah. The same way you couldn't fix Paul and you can't fix Dylan. But you can take care of yourself. You can do what makes you happy."

"I know that."

"Good. Then let's work on that, shall we?"

Sarah nodded. It was the only thing she could do.

CHAPTER FOUR

Four days later, Friday

"HI, MOM," SARAH GREETED WHEN SHE SAW her mother's number on her phone screen.

"How are you?" Jillian's chipper tone reflected the smile she likely had on her face.

"Good. You?" Sarah moved away from the large picture window she'd been staring out of, no longer lost in the inky darkness laid out before her.

"No complaints here," her mother said. "Just checking on you."

"Yeah?" Sarah loved that her mother still called every single night to see how she was. It wasn't a new thing, either. Since the day Sarah had moved out of Jillian's house, venturing out on her own her freshman year of college, Sarah had looked forward to talking to her mother. If someone asked who her true best friend was, Sarah would without a doubt say her mother. They were close. Always had been. Sure, there were times Jillian Davis could be overbearing and blunt, but that didn't change the fact that Sarah loved her beyond words.

Growing up, Jillian had been Sarah's, and her sister Tara's, sole provider. Ever since Sarah's father decided he needed more adventure in his life back when Sarah was in kindergarten and Tara was in second grade, Jillian had been a single mother. Oddly enough, Jillian didn't seem to harbor any ill feelings toward Sarah's father, but Sarah couldn't say the same. She resented Geoff Davis for leaving them, even if she did look forward to what little time they spent together, usually at Thanksgiving, sometimes at Easter. Since he had quite the adventurous job traveling around the globe as a wildlife photographer, Sarah didn't get to see him much. Even without her father, Sarah's childhood had been a good one, and she knew that was all thanks to her mother. Jillian had doted on her two daughters, providing everything they needed, although she couldn't afford much more than that.

"I figured since it's Friday, maybe you had a date," Jillian stated, a question in her voice. Her mother was nothing if not curious.

Sarah barked out a laugh. "Not tonight, no."

"What happened to Bill?"

Sarah's nose scrunched up at the mention of his name. She hadn't seen Bill since Jake's company party last weekend. After he'd driven her home, walked her to her door, and she'd rudely slammed it in his face... Sarah refused to think about how Bill had wanted to kiss her, about how he'd made her feel like a cheat and a fraud, because no matter what, she didn't want his lips on hers ever again.

A shiver raced through her.

She needed to talk to Bill, to let him know that this wasn't working between them. That she wasn't in a place in her life for that kind of relationship. She knew he wanted more from her. What exactly he was looking for, she didn't know. He was always trying to kiss her, to cop a feel, seeking intimacy although that was the last thing on Sarah's mind.

He was a distraction, pure and simple.

Granted, they hadn't been dating in the formal sense of the word, but they had gone out a few times when they'd first met. Their interaction had waned after about their third outing because she just wasn't interested in him that way. However, she seemed to be tossing out mixed signals at every turn, and she knew she was the one making this harder on herself. Whatever they were doing, it was going nowhere fast. She felt absolutely zero attraction to the guy, and trying to convince herself she might one day was no longer working, either.

"I haven't heard from him in a while." It was a lie, but her mother didn't know that.

"He went with you to Jake's party, right?"

Okay, so maybe she did know. "Yes."

But that wasn't the *last* time. Sarah had heard from him this morning, actually. Bill had sent her a text message, asking if she wanted to spend the weekend with him. He told her that there was some sort of party—for the upper crust of the Dallas business world—and he'd received a highly coveted invitation and he was hoping she could attend as his plus one. His words.

Seriously. The guy was a car salesman. He wasn't the owner, or even the general manager of the dealership, so she wasn't sure where he came up with upper crust of the Dallas business world or how he factored into it at all. But what did she know... He had informed her he was salesman of the year two years running. At least three dozen times.

"Hmm."

"What does that mean?" Sarah inquired, walking back to the window. The ripples in the pond behind her house were glittering in the moonlight. It was starting to rain again. With the temperatures dipping below freezing at night, it was possible they'd have ice to deal with tomorrow.

"Nothing," Jillian offered with a chuckle. "Just sounds to me like you're not telling the truth."

Her mother had always been able to detect when Sarah was lying. Didn't mean she was going to cop to it, though. "No lie," she lied. "It's not serious between us."

And *that* was the truth. In the four months since she'd first gone out with Bill, Sarah had agreed to only five dates, one of which she'd invited him. Last weekend. But they'd shared dinner every time, nothing more. Well, except for the time he'd taken her to a movie. Not once had there been a single spark between them, so why she hadn't simply broken it off with him, she couldn't say.

"I hope you've given him a chance at least," her mother said, her tone softer.

Ever since Paul had died, Jillian had been worried about her. Sarah understood that. It hadn't been easy losing the man she'd thought she would spend the rest of her life with. In fact, before her mother had called tonight, Sarah's thoughts of Paul had been making her feel the loneliness that had pretty much consumed her for the past six years.

"Sarah?"

"Sorry," she replied. "Yes, I've given him a chance."

"But?"

"But nothing. I just don't ... feel anything for him."

"What about that New Year's resolution you made? I thought you were going to see it through?"

Sarah chuckled at the memory. She'd been at her mother's house on New Year's, drinking sparkling apple juice while her mother and her mother's friends played Cards Against Humanity in the kitchen and downed shots of whiskey. Sarah had opted for the alcohol-free night in an effort to keep an eye on the crazy ladies. When it got close to midnight, they'd all decided to make one resolution for the year and they had to say it aloud. Sarah's had been a promise to go that extra step this year, to meander out into the world, to shake off the melancholy and get back to living life to its fullest. After all, what was the point of a complete physical overhaul if she was going to keep herself locked up in the house?

Well, she was nearly two weeks into the new year, and it felt as though time was quickly passing her by, and she still had no clue as to how she would fulfill that one simple resolution.

"I'm workin' on it." Another lie. The proof that she hadn't followed through was the fact that, six years after her husband's death, she was sitting at home on a Friday night. Alone.

"How'd that party go last weekend anyway? Jake hasn't said much about it."

"It was good," she lied. Okay, so this conversation was going nowhere. One more lie and lightning might strike her where she stood.

"Good? That sounds boring." Jillian chuckled. "What are you hiding? Did you see Dylan?"

Oh, crap. Her mother would have to go and bring him up. The one man Sarah had been trying not to think about for the past three years. One of her biggest downfalls was that she'd spent too much time living in the past, and Dylan Thomas was definitely her past.

Unfortunately, it took little effort for her to vividly remember that heartbreaking night when Dylan had needed a shoulder to lean on, a night she desperately wished she could forget but secretly prayed she never did.

"Yeah," she confirmed. "He was there."

"How is he?" Jillian inquired.

At one point, she would've said sad and broken, but the Dylan she had seen didn't look to be either. He actually looked ... good. "Fine," she said.

There was a brief pause, as though her mother was weighing her options on which direction to take the conversation. Thankfully, Jillian opted to change the subject.

"So, do you have any interviews lined up?"

"Not yet." Although she'd been putting in applications at various places ever since she quit her teaching job and opted to change her life, Sarah hadn't landed a permanent gig. Truth was, she didn't even know what she wanted to do, so she'd been getting by with various temp jobs—waitress, receptionist, a week as a bookkeeper, a hotel clerk for two days and plenty of computer jobs in the interim. Nothing had held her interest, so she kept looking, kept waiting for the perfect opportunity to arise.

Her mother laughed. "You're the only person I know who can sound happy when they say that."

Sarah smiled. There were days when she worried that she wouldn't be able to pay her bills if she didn't figure it all out, but for the most part, she was enjoying herself. She traveled on a whim, if she had the urge, although never too far and never to anywhere exotic. Plus, she focused on learning new things and figuring out what she wanted to do with the rest of her life.

The downside to all of that was her lack of a routine to keep her busy.

With nothing to occupy her time, Sarah was left with too much time to think. She had yet to completely move on with her life, despite her efforts. Her social life had flourished there for a while, but as her therapist repeatedly informed her, she continued to allow the past to hold her back.

Her past being the people in her life who'd ridden roughshod over her heart.

Her father.

Her sister.

Paul.

Then Dylan.

"I know, Mom. I'm my own worst enemy."

"You should go out more. You spend too much time at home."

"I know." Her mother wasn't telling her anything new. She'd been harping on the same subject over and over for years now, to no avail.

Jillian sighed. "Well, I'll let you get back to it."

"To what?" Sarah asked, grinning. "I wasn't doing anything."

"No, but I figure you're looking for something to clean as we speak."

Her mother knew her too well. "Okay, fine. I *am* looking for something to clean. You're welcome to come over and help if you'd like."

"There'd be nothing for me to do," Jillian said with a giggle. "I've seen your house. Spotless. But you're welcome to come over and have a go at mine."

She couldn't deny that. Her house was spotless, but Sarah knew there was always something to do. "I might take you up on that if I run outta stuff here."

"Like that'll ever happen." Jillian chuckled again. "Well, kiddo, don't work too hard. I'll talk to you later. And, Sarah...?"

"Yeah?"

"Quit thinking so much. I know it's hard, but you've got to keep putting one foot in front of the other."

"I know, Mom. And I am. I promise," she said reassuringly.

"Okay. If you need anything, just call."

"I will. Love you."

"Love you, too."

After the call disconnected, Sarah set her cell phone down on the table and stared around the room. She did need something to do. Which, as her mother had guessed, usually meant something to clean. Didn't matter that it was after ten and she would do herself a favor if she simply went to bed. That never happened anymore. Sleep was overrated as far as she was concerned. With sleep came dreams, and those dreams always brought an uneasy feeling in the morning.

At least if she found something to occupy herself with, she might be able to rid herself of thoughts of Dylan. Namely thoughts of the way he had looked at her that night when he'd come by her house and ruthlessly (and beautifully) fucked her up against her living room wall. That night—probably the most memorable of her entire life—had happened all too quickly, hitting her like a boxer taking down his opponent. And she was the one who'd been KO'd.

Not that she'd been pining over the man all this time, because she certainly hadn't. That would've been pure insanity.

Quite frankly, had it not been for the CISS party last weekend, Sarah might've believed she was over Dylan. However, the second she had walked out on the deck of the waterfront restaurant, her gaze straying to him, she'd felt it take root in her soul.

But that was done and over with. She had no reason to see Dylan again, so it would be in her best interest to move forward.

Too bad she couldn't get him off her mind now.

DYLAN CLIMBED OUT OF HIS TRUCK AND nudged the door closed with his hip after snagging the flowers he'd purchased earlier that day from the passenger seat. He'd been putting this off for hours, but he'd finally relented, knowing that if he didn't, he'd hate himself tomorrow.

Pulling his hood up over his head to stave off the bitterly cold wind, he made the grueling trek toward his destination. With every step he took, the constriction on his heart tightened. It had been three months since he'd been here, and yet it felt as though he'd made this same journey only yesterday.

Taking another deep breath, he willed his feet forward, clutching the flowers in his fingers. When he finally arrived at Meghan's grave, he took another deep, cleansing breath, ignoring the cold drizzle that added to an already gloomy evening.

"Hey, honey," he said aloud. He'd long ago stopped worrying whether or not people thought he was crazy for talking to his dead wife, but he knew at this time of night, it didn't matter anyway. No one was out in the cemetery after dark. "I'm here."

Not that she would ever answer him, but Dylan liked to pretend it was possible Meghan could hear him. He wanted her to anyway. It was the very reason he still came here three times a year to spend a little time with her, to tell her what was going on with his life. The same things he'd talked to her about when she'd been alive, only back then, his heart hadn't been so heavy.

Glancing around, he confirmed the surrounding gravesites were absent any visitors, so he decided to take a seat. Lowering himself to the wet grass, he crossed his legs and rested his elbows on his knees after arranging the flowers in the vase set in the stone. The only light came from the randomly placed light posts, but it was enough for him to see.

"It's not much," he muttered as he straightened one of the drooping flowers. "Last minute and all."

He could still remember the few times he'd brought Meghan flowers back when she'd been alive. It hadn't taken but one time for him to realize that the simple gesture was the easiest way to put a sparkle in her eyes. He could admit that he hadn't been the most romantic man on the planet, but he'd tried to show her how much he loved her. Sometimes he wondered if he'd done enough.

The pang he was all too familiar with feeling in his chest was less agonizing than it used to be, although there was still a slight ache. A longing that he couldn't seem to outrun. Even after eleven years, Dylan still wished he could turn back time and save his beautiful wife from the vicious disease that had stolen her from him. But the cancer had been brutal, taking her away from him without giving them a choice.

Since going back in time wasn't an option, he settled for thinking about her often, and for these visits, though they were becoming more infrequent as time passed. For years, he would come out to the cemetery multiple times. Meghan's birthday, their anniversary, Stacey's birthday, Nate's birthday, even his own. He'd made it by for holidays, and sometimes just because. But with every passing year, those visits had lessened, and now, he forced himself to come on her birthday, their wedding anniversary, and the anniversary of her death because he didn't want her to think he'd forgotten about her.

So, thinking about her was exactly what he did for the next half hour, sitting there alone. His feet finally went numb, and he had to reposition his legs to get the blood pumping again. Leaning back on his hands, his legs stretched out in front of him, Dylan stared up at the moon. The clouds parted enough he could see the ominous light shining through.

Glancing down at her headstone, then back up at the sky, he said, "I'm just curious, honey ... am I supposed to be as fucked up as I am? I mean, it's been more than a decade since you ... died." He swallowed hard. "I've heard the pain would fade, and yeah, I can see that it has. But, Meghan, tell me why I can't move on. Damn, honey..." Dylan took a deep breath. "I'm so glad you don't know the man I've been all these years. I can't help but think you would've hated me. At the very least, you would've been disappointed. I wouldn't blame you, either. I've let everyone down."

He wiped away a tear with the back of his hand. He knew he was acting strangely, and surprisingly, he hadn't had a single thing to drink for the past three years thanks to his single-minded determination and a shitload of support from the AA meetings he'd started to attend. It hadn't been easy, but he was making a valiant effort to pay attention to the important things in his life. Work, kids, family. Himself. All the things he'd put off for so long while he'd drowned himself in booze and memories of the one woman he'd never imagined he would have to live without.

"Maybe you should just tell me to move on," he muttered. "It would be so much easier to hear you say it. I can't seem to let go, babe. I can't and I know I need to. The kids look at me funny, on the rare occasion they even do that. Nate's pissed off all the time. Stacey's too busy with her own blossoming social life to notice me at all. And instead of embracing life, I've pushed everyone away because I don't know which way is up anymore."

Dylan knew that time would heal his wounds and it had. They weren't as fresh, not nearly as painful, but sometimes he did wake up in a cold sweat, reliving the day that Meghan died all over again.

Eleven fucking years later.

He was torturing himself. No doubt about it.

"I'm still going to the AA meetings. Minimum of once a week, sometimes more. Not my favorite thing in the world to do, but I'm trying. I know it's important. And they help."

Several more minutes passed as he continued to stare up at the sky, the drizzle making it difficult. His thoughts drifted to other things he wanted to tell her about. And then he remembered the CISS party last weekend.

"I saw Sarah again," he said, casting a quick look around. "Remember her? She was the girl I'd been dating before you and I started going out." He smiled at the memory, but that quickly faded and he was brushing away another stray tear. "I know I've never talked about her since high school, but a few years ago..."

No. Dylan stopped himself before he could go on. The last thing he wanted to do was to rehash that night, to bring about the memories of Sarah and all that he'd denied himself. It had taken everything in him to stay away from her for these last few years. But he'd done it for her. Or so he told himself. Sarah deserved so much better than a fucked-up cowboy like him.

That didn't mean he didn't want her. He simply knew it would never work out between them, even if the sex had been fucking phenomenal. And it had been that. But the thoughts that had run through his head that night... Sweet Sarah Davis couldn't handle what he would want from her. And since Meghan died, Dylan had promised himself that he wouldn't hold back, wouldn't cut that part of himself off anymore.

He barked a laugh. He was pathetic. He *had* made that promise to himself, yet he'd spent the past eleven years grieving. Drunk and focused on no one but himself. Okay, so maybe he hadn't been drunk for eleven years, but sometimes it felt like it. In fact, the drinking hadn't started until Nate's senior year of high school. At that point, Dylan's hopelessness had taken over. Without kids at home to take care of, he felt the loneliness creep in, and he found that drowning himself in a bottle had helped.

"Meghan," he said with a heavy sigh. "Tell me to go away. Tell me to stop buggin' you and I will. But if you don't, I'm only gonna keep comin' back. I'm lost without you, babe, and I know that's crazy. Pops and Ashleigh are worried about my mental state. Still. After all this time." A small smile tipped the corner of his mouth. "Ashleigh told me she'd go to AA with me if I wanted her to. I think she still has her doubts. Not that I blame her. She's dealt with me at my worst, and I was pretty good at pretending there for a while."

When his sister had first suggested it, Dylan had told her she was fucking crazy. He hadn't had any intention of spilling his guts to a stranger, much less a room full of them, but he certainly wasn't going to do it with his family present. Truthfully, Dylan needed those meetings, needed to be able to voice the issues he was facing, know there were others going through the same thing. After years of denial, Dylan accepted that he had a serious problem.

His nostrils burned with unshed tears as he stared at the engraved letters on the stone in front of him. Meghan Ann Thomas. January 13, 1975 – November 9, 2004. His beautiful wife had died less than three months before her thirtieth birthday.

God, he needed a drink. Something to settle his thoughts, to numb the ache in his chest. Whenever he allowed himself to drift back into the past, he felt the little pieces he'd worked so hard to restructure just fall apart again. He wasn't whole; hell, he wasn't sure he ever would be again. But yes, time was dulling the pain. Except for days like this. The horrible fucking days when the memories would invade, taking over his world, reiterating the fact that he would never get to celebrate anything else with the woman he'd loved more than life itself. It was cruel that he did it to himself, but as he'd told Meghan, he didn't think he could move forward.

No matter how desperately he now wanted to.

His throat burned and a sob racked his chest, but he refused to cry anymore. He'd done more than his fair share over the years.

"Honey," he whispered, "I need you to tell me it's okay to let you go. I need you to tell me that it's okay to be me again. I can't keep hiding from everyone. I need something ... some*one*. I know Sarah doesn't deserve the hell I'll likely inflict on her, but ... I want her in my life. There. I said it. It's true. I want to feel alive again and ... God, Meg ... she makes me feel that way. I didn't think it was even possible."

The next thing Dylan knew, despite the effort he put forth to avoid them, the tears were coming, but so was the rain. The sky had opened up, and fat, cold raindrops began falling on him until he could hardly see more than a few feet around him. But rather than run back to his truck to try and escape, he remained right where he was and used the rain as another excuse to let the emotions go.

One day, he was sure he wouldn't be able to cry anymore, and maybe then he'd figure out a way to move on. But until then, Dylan feared this was his destiny.

CHAPTER FIVE

ONCE SHE'D HUNG UP THE PHONE WITH her mother, Sarah had immersed herself in housework. She'd pulled out the vacuum and run it over every inch of her two-thousand-square-foot house. Not only on the floors but the corners of every room, the ceiling fans, the couch, and the baseboards. Did she have a problem because she did this at least three times a week? Perhaps. Then again, Sarah knew that having two cats made vacuuming a requirement, so she wasn't going to apologize for it.

After that, she got the broom and the mop and took care of the tiled floors, then ran the Swiffer duster over all the shelves throughout the house.

But now, as she looked around, she wasn't sure what she was supposed to do. Truth was, she was trying to outrun her thoughts by cleaning, but for the first time in a long time, it wasn't working. Her mind continued to drift back to the one person she shouldn't have been thinking about in the first place. No matter what she tried to tell herself, Elaine was right. Sarah was still searching for a way to help others even when her help wasn't needed. Dylan had made it this far without her interference, so she needed to figure out a way to move on.

Still, she had to wonder if he was still broken. It seemed possible. She didn't know him anymore, wasn't even close to his family or friends to really know the truth. Was that what he wanted from her? A friend? Someone who could help him?

Damn it. Sarah hated that she wanted nothing more than to help him, to *fix* him.

Yep, that was something she'd come to accept thanks to years of talking through her problems—she was a fixer. That might be somewhat true, but Sarah knew what her real problem was. By focusing on everyone else's issues, she didn't have to focus on herself. Plus, she didn't want anyone to suffer the way Paul had. Sarah didn't want anyone in the world to have to come home after work to find the person they loved most dead because they'd overdosed on pills in an effort to extinguish the pain completely. And although Sarah now understood Paul's illness, and she'd reached a point where she could accept that it had happened, she knew she would never forget. Granted, forgiving him wasn't entirely possible.

Was she still angry? Sure. At times irrationally so. But she knew deep down that it had been the disease that killed Paul, and she fought tooth and nail to believe that he wouldn't have left her if he could've helped it.

Her therapist had told her time and time again that she needed to work on herself and not everyone else, but Sarah had a hard time accepting that. It was a wonder Elaine hadn't thrown up her hands already. Then again, the therapy Sarah had been undergoing for the last five years—that and the once-a-month grief-support group she still met with—had been a way for her to deal with the painful loss of her husband.

Only the sessions had unearthed a shitload of issues she hadn't realized she had in the first place. She had a deep-rooted anger toward her father and her sister, which had festered inside her for most of her life. Not that she wanted to, but deep down, she still blamed Paul for the many years she'd lost to grief and overwhelming heartache even though she knew it wasn't his fault.

He'd suffered from an illness that no one had seen. A disease that he'd hidden so well Sarah hadn't known about it. Not entirely anyway. Sure, she'd been aware of his drastic mood swings, thought perhaps he'd been depressed a few times, but who wasn't? Never had she suspected he had bipolar disorder, or that he would find himself feeling so hopeless that he would end his life, demolishing Sarah's in the process.

So, in a sense, the years of therapy she'd forced on herself had worked. In the beginning, she'd spent months trying to learn more about Paul's disease, wanting to help, desperate to find a way to get others to recognize what she'd found out too late. There for a while, she'd even felt worthwhile, content with focusing her energy on others. However, devoting herself entirely to the cause had repercussions of its own. With the help of her therapist, Sarah had realized—three years *after* Paul's death—that she had been neglecting herself, her own well-being.

"And then Dylan walked into my life," she mumbled. "Again."

And that had been a turning point for her. The straw that broke the camel's back.

Before he'd reappeared in her life, Sarah had attempted to get back on the horse, so to speak. That year, she'd been focused on living and not merely existing. She'd been proud of the progress she'd made, too. It had been a turning point for her. Or so she wanted to believe.

Then she'd started getting closer to Dylan. As friends.

Without meaning to, Sarah had unearthed a wealth of feelings that she'd had for the man back in high school. In a short period of time, at that. Months of casual conversation and she'd been hooked on him, causing her to do things that weren't in her heart's best interest, leaving her right back where she'd started. Alone. Heartbroken.

Her therapist was right about one thing ... when Sarah gave a part of herself to someone, she didn't get those pieces back, leaving her not quite whole.

And the spiral had repeated itself for a year while she'd rekindled that friendship with Dylan, resulting in the fiery end to what had started out as a hesitant companionship.

Now, with another three years behind her, she was finally back in control.

Kind of.

Maybe.

Turned out, she had never managed to forget that night or the man she'd come to refer to as her distraction. Dylan was the first boy she had ever kissed back when she'd been a hope-filled freshman in high school, the last man she'd been with back when she had all but accepted that all hope was gone. Unlike high school, when she'd been a naïve teenager, she had no excuse for that night. She was old enough to know better, but still, she'd allowed her hormones to lead the way.

Nope, they weren't in high school anymore, and he definitely wasn't a boy, nor was he the sexy jock every girl swooned over, every boy wanted to be like, and no matter who you were, you just wanted to be near. Sarah had been one of those girls, the ones who'd fawned over him, worshipped the very ground he walked on, although she had done her best to hide it. And for the briefest moment, Dylan had been hers.

Back then.

Yep, that was until he had fallen in love with the beautiful, kind-hearted Meghan Carpenter, who would later become Meghan Thomas. Ever since stumbling upon Dylan, and his son, Nate, at a school function—the last place she would've expected to see him—Sarah hadn't been able to completely shake her thoughts of him. No matter how hard she tried.

"Thinking about him is not helping," she said aloud. "Not helping *at all*."

Pulling her thoughts out of the clouds, Sarah peered down at her feet.

"What?" she asked, looking down at her two sweetly mischievous cats when they wandered into the room. "It's just a little rain."

The sound could be heard on the roof, and Smokey and Blue had never been fond of storms. The weatherman had been predicting it for the past couple of weeks, and it appeared that Mother Nature was finally coming through for him.

Her thoughts instantly drifted back to Dylan as she peered out the window once more. For a brief moment, she wondered what he was doing right that minute. Was he at home? Was he out with a woman? Was he happy? Was he sad? Dylan Thomas might be tall, dark, and obscenely handsome, but the man was more than just a little cracked—he was irrevocably broken.

Though she'd reluctantly accepted her therapist's diagnosis that she was a fixer, Sarah knew deep down, there was no fixing Dylan. When he was ready, when he found the right woman, he would move forward. Of that, she had no doubt.

Which meant...

"I'm not the right woman." Sarah shook her head. "Nope," she told her cats, "I'm not her. Never will be. He made sure I understood that."

Sure, Sarah knew what Dylan saw when he looked at her. Well, maybe not the woman she was now, but before. He'd seen a sweet, innocent schoolteacher with short, curly hair and a petite, curvaceous figure. Although her hair was longer now, and she'd shed the sweet-and-innocent vibe she'd been plagued by, along with the extra fifteen pounds she'd been carrying around since college, Sarah still wasn't the leggy, dark-haired bombshell like Meghan had been. Nor was she graced with exotic beauty like the women married to the men Dylan worked with.

The truth was, men had never looked at her and thought *sexy blond*. They'd never fantasized about her, never imagined wild monkey sex.

She snorted.

Despite the outer appearance, she damn sure wasn't Sandra Dee. Sweet and innocent, she definitely was not. Only no one had ever really noticed. Instead, the men from her past—startlingly few that there were—had always wanted to coddle her, protect her.

No, not only did she still get carded for alcohol though she was thirty-eight years old, she was also blandly plain despite the tattoos and the makeup. Oh, and then there was the fact that she was short, which, unlike the way the romance novels depicted, didn't mean she fit nicely into the crook of a man's arm, it simply meant she wasn't tall enough to do anything without a damn stepladder.

A gruff snort escaped her as she made her way to the kitchen, noticing the stepladder stuck in the narrow nook between the refrigerator and the wall. Yep, at four foot eleven and three-quarters inches, Sarah couldn't reach the second shelf in the upper cabinets. Paul used to enjoy making fun of her, even though he hadn't been but a few inches taller.

"I wish you were here to laugh at me now, Paul," she whispered into the otherwise silent house.

And he would have. Every time.

But unlike Paul, Dylan was tall. And although she had liked the way Dylan had towered over her, making her feel incredibly feminine by comparison, other than at that moment in time, being short didn't do much for her.

"Ugghh." She really had to stop thinking about him.

Attacking the few dishes she'd left in the sink that morning, Sarah tried desperately to forget about the man who had somehow wormed his way back into her brain in the last week. But it wasn't because she lusted after him.

Although there was that.

No, Dylan had caught Sarah's attention again, all right, but he wasn't the strong, sexy boy of yesteryear whom she'd had some hot and heavy make-out sessions with during high school. The man she had glimpsed at that company function was the same man she'd given in to three years ago—quiet, reserved, and still very damaged. A man who had lost his wife yet had never gotten over it. A man who had stopped living his life because he was too busy feeling as though he didn't deserve to live it to the fullest.

At one point, Sarah had thought they were kindred spirits. Now, she knew they weren't. She wasn't the sad, broken-hearted woman she'd been back then. She had reinvented herself, forced herself to move on. They were too different to ever work. No matter how hot she found him.

Gone was the Sarah who sat idly by, waiting for life to come to her, or befriending every single lost soul because she wanted to give them some sunshine in their lives. That girl was gone forever, and there were too many reasons that woman had been chased out of town, told to never return, and in her place was the new Sarah. The go-after-what-you-want-until-you-get-it Sarah.

At least that was the woman Sarah was striving to be, even if it killed her.

Drying the last dish, Sarah placed it in the cabinet before looking around her kitchen. Nothing left to do. Yet there was so much pent up energy lurking just beneath her skin and no way to release it. And it wasn't just energy stored up from an idle day. This was the type of energy that had been building for years, ready for an outlet, and the new Sarah needed a plan.

In walked Smokey and Blue, as though they could sense the shift in her mood. Wild, rambunctious and, most of the time, the only two who would listen to her rant, although she was pretty sure they ignored her all other times, the two kittens she had rescued had grown into independent, sweetly mischievous cats. And now they were looking at her like she was the crazy cat lady she feared she would become.

"What?" she asked them both as they sat on the floor at her feet, staring up at her as if they could figure out what it was she was thinking as long as they looked at her long enough. "I'm not crazy, I promise." She smiled. "Okay, fine. Maybe I am. A little. But at least I'm not talking to myself."

Clearly feeling the building excitement, Smokey and Blue wound themselves around her feet, batting at one another before rolling around on the floor like they normally did, ready for her to give in and rub their bellies.

Staring down at the pair, Sarah knew exactly what she needed to do.

And with her mind made up, she made a mad dash for her cell phone, desperate to make the call before she lost her nerve.

"WHERE'S EVERYONE AT?" DYLAN CALLED WHEN HE walked into his grandfather's house at eleven thirty that night. The sound of voices had him heading toward the living room, stopping just inside the room, surprised to see his son, Nate, there, talking to Sarah's nephew, Jake.

It was Friday night, and from experience, his kids generally had plans that involved friends, clubs, bars, and the like, not sitting at home doing nothing like these two appeared to be doing. Then again, they looked to be in a rather heated conversation, one that Nate didn't seem too happy about.

Dylan crossed his arms over his chest and leaned against the wall, watching them. They clearly hadn't expected him to show up, nor had they heard him. Clearing his throat, he pushed off the wall. There was a brief pause as the two men stilled, then one at a time they turned to look at him.

"What are you two up to?" Dylan waited patiently for one of them to answer, his head pounding behind his eyes. It'd been a long day, one that he wanted to soothe with a bottle of Jack but knew he couldn't. Not only because he'd dumped every last ounce of alcohol he owned years ago but also because he didn't want to go back there. For the first time in what felt like forever, he was feeling as though he was more than a shadow in the darkness.

"You look like shit," Nate offered, a scowl on his face. "You seriously need to shave."

Dylan ground his molars together, trying not to lose his temper. It seemed that over the course of the last couple of months, Nate had changed from the good-natured young man Dylan had raised to a mouthy, irritated version. Something was going on with him, but Dylan had yet to figure out what.

"Good to see you, too," Dylan grumbled, his eyes darting back and forth between them. "What's goin' on? You two talkin' about work?"

Both young men had voiced their concern for the changes taking place, but neither of them had gone into detail. Not with him. If they'd talked to Alex, Dylan didn't know about it.

"No," Jake stated, obviously feeling the tension increasing in the room. "I was just tellin' Nate that I wouldn't be able to go out tomorrow night because I've got to cat sit."

"Cat sit?" Dylan was confused. Who the hell did Jake know that had cats?

"Yeah, my aunt Sarah called a few minutes ago and asked if I would check on her cats tomorrow night. Apparently she's got weekend plans. She doesn't expect to be back until late Sunday."

Just the mention of Sarah's name made Dylan's chest ache.

The sad truth was, he missed her.

Despite the fact he wanted to hear the sweet lilt of her voice—something that had recently started tugging at his conscience again—his pride hadn't allowed him to pick up the phone to call her, or even attempt to make amends last weekend at the CISS party.

"You don't have to stay with the cats," Nate stated, his tone laced with frustration. "They're independent. If you check on them, they'll be fine."

Jake didn't respond.

"Seriously, Jake," Nate continued. "She's not leaving till tomorrow morning. And she'll be back on Sunday."

Dylan waited, hoping one of them would add a few more details. Clearly Nate was up to speed. But Dylan wanted to know where Sarah was going, who she was going with, what they were going to do. Not that it was any of his damn business, but he certainly didn't like what his brain was conjuring up: her going away with Bill the Douchebag for the weekend.

He'd managed to pound the final nail in the coffin that was their friendship long ago, but that didn't stop Dylan from wanting her.

Jake's eyes shot from Dylan to Nate and then back.

Fine, if he wasn't going to come out with it... "Where's she goin'?" he asked, trying to sound as though he weren't all that interested, but the huff he got from Nate said he'd failed.

Jake shrugged. "No idea."

"You don't know?" Okay, so he sounded stupid interrogating Jake about something better left alone.

It's not your business.

"She's been seein' this guy. Bill something or other. You know, the one who came to the company party," Jake went on to explain.

Bill the car salesman. Yep, Dylan definitely remembered. He also remembered how Sarah had said it wasn't serious, only to backtrack quickly.

"Sounds like he's invited her to some fancy party somewhere," Jake added.

Was it serious?

Did she love this guy?

There were plenty more questions running amuck in his brain, but Dylan held his tongue.

Stop! Just fucking stop!

Despite the annoying voice in his head, Dylan couldn't let it go.

"Do you know this guy well?" Dylan asked, again trying to keep his tone neutral. Just small talk, nothing more. It wasn't completely out of left field. Jake was close to his aunt; everyone knew that. She'd practically raised him.

"I've talked to him a couple of times," Jake said cautiously. "I didn't think it was serious, but..."

Yeah, *but* she was going away with him.

Jake continued, his brows downturned, "She said somethin' about not holdin' back any longer." Jake glanced around the room, obviously seeing that Nate was gone.

"How did they meet?" Okay, so now he just sounded pathetic, but so fucking what. There was a spark of something darkly possessive that had just taken complete control of him, and Dylan couldn't stop the questions.

He seriously needed a drink.

"I don't really know. She doesn't talk about him much. He works at a car dealership, that's all she's ever said." Jake was now looking at him funny. "Is everything okay?"

Shit no. But he wasn't about to tell the kid that. "Fine. Just ... curious. So, cat sitting? Tomorrow night?"

"Wow, Dylan." Jake narrowed his eyes at him. "You've been out of the game way too long, man. That was in no way subtle."

No, he didn't think it was, but fuck. Sarah was going away with a guy. For some strange (and clearly selfish) reason, the idea did not sit well with him.

Not at all.

But his brain was too damn foggy for him to think rationally. *Three fucking years, dumb ass.* In all that time, he hadn't made one single attempt to talk to her. Not once. Why should he care where she was going? Or who she was or wasn't with?

His mind instantly flashed back to that night when he'd gone to her house after he'd been at the cemetery visiting Meghan's grave. He'd known as soon as he called her that he was making a horrible mistake, but he hadn't been able to help himself.

Dylan forced himself back to the present when he heard Jake clear his throat. He met the other man's curious gaze.

"Is there somethin' goin' on between you and my aunt?" Jake questioned directly.

Dylan shook his head. "No. Why?"

Jake shrugged. "It's just..."

"What?"

"It's just that she was acting kinda funny ... when she saw you last weekend."

Funny how? He wanted to know but didn't bother to ask.

"Look," Jake said, hands on his hips. "I don't wanna overstep, but..."

"She's your aunt," Dylan filled in for him. "I get it."

"She's more than that," Jake countered. "She's the woman who raised me when my own mother wouldn't stick around." His eyes dropped to his hands. "I don't wanna see her hurt."

By him? Or by Bill? Dylan couldn't bring himself to voice those questions, either.

"I've seen the way she looks at you," Jake said, his eyes not quite meeting Dylan's. "So, if there's somethin' goin' on..."

"There's not," he assured the kid.

"Just don't hurt her, okay? These past few years, she's been different. She's been through enough."

They both had, Dylan thought. Instead of arguing, he nodded, understanding Jake's words as the warning they were meant to be. But now, he couldn't stop thinking about Sarah, couldn't help but wonder if it was possible for the two of them...

As he fought back that strange emotion that whirled in his chest, threatening to pull him under, Dylan had to wonder whether Sarah was the reason he needed to keep moving forward.

More importantly, if that was the case, was he finally in a place to tell her that she was?

"One more question..." Dylan had to ask, otherwise he would never know.

Jake cocked an eyebrow.

"I know she moved. What's her new address?"

CHAPTER SIX

"ARE YOU READY?" BILL ASKED, STANDING IN the doorway of Sarah's house the following morning, looking at her with so much hope in his eyes.

If she wasn't mistaken, his eyes were a little puffy and he'd started sneezing the instant he stepped foot in her house. The tissue he kept swiping across his nose wasn't ramping up his attractiveness, either.

"Do you have … allergies?" she inquired, already knowing the answer.

"Just a little," he said, sniffing once more. "Nothing serious, though. Probably something in the air."

Right.

Sarah observed him again, praying he wasn't having a major allergic reaction to something. He seemed to be playing it off, but he didn't look as though he was having too much fun at the moment. He looked…

Bill wasn't handsome in the traditional sense, but he wasn't ugly, either. He was thin and short for a man—probably no more than five six, if that—with clear blue eyes, a clean-shaven jaw, and perfectly styled medium-brown hair. All in all, he was well-dressed, polite, quite plain, and … sweet.

And therein lay the problem.

Bill was sweet.

And boring.

What the hell had she been thinking when she'd called him up last night and agreed to this? Clearly she'd been inhaling toxic household chemicals or something. It was the only excuse she had as to why it had ever even remotely sounded like a good idea.

Staring back at him, Sarah tried to hide her disappointed expression. "I ... uh... Just give me a minute, please?"

He sneezed, then blew his nose.

Yuck.

"Sure." *Sniff.* "I'll be rearranging the minivan." *Sniff.* His smile brightened up his entire face. "It's one of our newest models. It's a beaut." *Sniff.*

Beaut? Who the hell said that?

Better still, who drove a minivan? Last Sarah had checked, she was thirty-eight and single. Not a soccer mom. And Bill... The man was forty-five, never married, no children. What the hell did he need with a minivan?

Oh, God.

Okay, so maybe it wasn't just the chemicals. Had she been drinking, too? She didn't think so, but surely there was a good reason for her spur-of-the-moment lunacy, a.k.a. agreeing to a weekend away with this man. Why had she thought this was a good idea?

Damn.

She couldn't do this.

Sneaking back to her bedroom, Sarah shut herself in, leaned against the door, and pressed her hands to her chest. She was having a panic attack. She'd been an idiot thinking she could go through with this. Bill was a nice guy, but ... well, there was absolutely no chemistry between them. The second she opened the door to see him standing on her porch, she'd remembered that. No matter how hard she had tried to play him up in her mind, it never seemed to work. The mere thought of getting naked with the guy...

Uggh.

And now they were off to... Shit, she didn't even know where they were going. He'd told her it was a surprise, a chance to see something she'd never seen before. He'd gone on and on about how this was the opportunity of a lifetime, about how they would be immersed in a group of uber-wealthy people who would want to get to know them on a much deeper level. His boss had offered Bill the invitation, since he'd been unable to attend because he already had plans or something like that. Bill even went so far as to say that this could further their careers, the opportunities endless. And though she'd been skeptical, Bill had assured her she'd have a good time.

Because Sarah was spontaneous like that.

Right. The guy clearly didn't know her all that well. She had a routine so strict she rarely deviated from it. Grocery store on Sunday, water the plants no later than seven o'clock in the morning, spaghetti for dinner every Wednesday. In fact, she even had certain scents of body wash designated for each day of the week. Definitely *not* spontaneous.

But this was clearly a business thing for him. How bad could it be?

A soft knock sounded on her bedroom door and her heart went into overdrive.

She had to tell Bill this was a mistake.

"Uh ... Sarah ..." Bill's timid voice sounded through the door. "There's a guy here. He said he needs to talk to you."

A guy?

"I'll be out in a sec," she called back, taking a deep breath.

When she didn't hear his footsteps, Sarah knew Bill had decided to wait for her.

Great.

"You can do this," she muttered to herself. "You *have* to do this. It would be rude not to."

Hesitantly, Sarah reached for the knob and twisted. Inching the door open, she peered through the crack. Sure enough, Bill was standing in the hall, his eyes puffier than before.

Steeling herself, she opened the door fully and stepped out, offering him a smile. "Did he say who he was? Is he sellin' something?"

"No, he's not selling anything," Bill answered, snorting. "Do you have cats?"

Sarah glanced at him, trying to catch up with his change of subject. "What?"

"Cats?" *Sniff.* "I'm allergic."

Well, that explained it.

He didn't even wait for her to respond before he said, "Anyway..." Bill glanced around. "He's the big guy Jake was talking to at that party you took me to last weekend."

Big? What did that mean? Tall? Fat? Muscular?

Sarah didn't know any big guys, regardless of the definition. None who would make a house call anyhow.

As she made her way back to the living room, she saw that no one was in the house. She cast a confused glance over at Bill. He nodded his head toward the front door.

Stepping outside, Sarah came up short when she saw Dylan pacing the sidewalk that connected her front porch to her driveway. "Dylan?"

His head jerked toward her, his feet stilling. He didn't smile, but she felt the warmth of his gaze as it traveled down to her feet and back up.

"Hey," he greeted, his eyes darting behind her.

That was when Sarah realized Bill was standing there, watching them.

"Could you ... uh ... give us a minute?" Sarah asked him politely.

Bill nodded, but he didn't look pleased with the request.

When the front door closed behind her, Sarah casually took two steps down, stopping on the bottom one when Dylan came to stand in front of her. Even with the added inches from the step, she had to look up at him. "Is something wrong? Is Jake okay?"

Dylan's gaze slid to the front door, then back to her. He nodded. "Yeah, he's fine."

Silence.

And it wasn't the comfortable kind where it was obvious they were both thinking. This was the unsettling silence that made Sarah want to fidget. She fought the urge.

"Why are you here, Dylan?" A hint of frustration edged her tone and she couldn't help it.

Dylan's eyes dropped to his booted feet briefly before lifting.

It was her turn to look at him. He was wearing a black hoodie and a pair of dark Wranglers. His hands were tucked into his pockets, and he was shifting back and forth from one foot to the other. He looked nervous.

When he met her eyes that time, there wasn't an ounce of apprehension in his gaze. No, what Sarah saw was ... something that looked a lot like desire.

"Why are you here?" Sarah repeated, suddenly suspicious.

"I don't know." The honest confusion in his tone tugged at a soft spot in her heart, but Sarah pushed it away.

"I'm headin' out for the weekend," she informed him, although she figured he already knew that. It couldn't be a coincidence that he'd shown up on her doorstep today of all days. If she had to guess, her nephew had shared the news with him, and now she was going to have to call Jake and tell him to keep his big mouth shut. Dylan might be Jake's boss at CISS, but that didn't mean he had to know the details of *her* life.

"With him?" he asked bluntly, chin tilting toward the house.

"Yes. His name's Bill."

"I remember." His tone was hard. "Where?"

"Where what?"

"Where's he taking you?"

Sarah shrugged.

"You don't know? Or you don't wanna tell me?" He sounded more like a parent than a man she hadn't seen or talked to in years.

"I don't know. It's a surprise," she said, hands going to her hips defiantly.

Who did he think he was?

Dylan nodded, but that awkward silence descended once again.

"Look, Sarah..." He didn't continue, merely stood there, staring at her.

She wished she could read his mind. Why was he here? What was on his mind? And why the hell had it taken three freaking years for him to make a move if that was what he was doing?

"I..." Sarah glanced behind her at the house. "I really need to go."

His dark eyes pinned her in place, and that time she was certain she saw heat. Her insides smoldered, the same way they did every time Dylan looked at her like that.

Something was definitely going on with him, but Sarah reminded herself that she wasn't interested. He'd made it abundantly clear that he hadn't wanted anything to do with her.

"I honestly don't know why I'm here. I couldn't help myself."

That didn't tell her a damn thing, but it did succeed in pissing her off.

"You should leave."

Dylan nodded again. "I'll go. Just tell me one thing."

Sarah lifted her eyebrows in question, waiting for him to continue.

"Is it serious with you and...?"

"Bill?"

"Yeah," Dylan said with a nod.

It wasn't serious and she knew that it never would be, but she told Dylan, "I don't know yet."

"I can live with that," he replied, another spark of heat igniting in his dark eyes.

"What does that mean?" she asked, knowing she shouldn't.

"Nothin'," he said with a smirk. "Yet."

"Dylan..."

"You'll be back on Sunday?"

She nodded.

"Good. I'd like to come over."

She frowned.

"To talk."

Sarah stared at him, not sure what she was supposed to say, if anything. Luckily, Dylan cut the strained silence with a small smile and a wave as he took two steps back.

"I'm leaving, but I'll be back on Sunday."

Her heart cracked at the sound of his voice, but she bit her lip, holding her thoughts back.

When he turned, she took a deep breath.

Watching him walk away made her stomach hurt. She wanted to call after him, invite him in for something to drink. But she couldn't. Not only was Bill inside, but she knew she had to keep those feelings for Dylan buried deep. He would only hurt her emotionally, and that was the last thing Sarah ever wanted to endure again.

She remained on the porch until Dylan drove away. She didn't turn back even after the taillights of the sweet '65 Chevy truck he drove disappeared out of sight. It was the same truck he'd been restoring in high school. Interesting that he'd held on to it all this time.

"You okay?"

Crap. She'd forgotten about Bill although she wasn't sure how that was even possible.

Turning to see her weekend date standing on the porch behind her, Sarah forced a smile and decided right then that she would go with him. Even if things didn't work out between them—which she knew was going to be the case—she needed something to keep her mind occupied for the weekend. They were friends, after all.

And at that moment, she desperately needed a friend.

DRIVING AWAY, KNOWING THAT SARAH WAS GOING on a weekend getaway with that jerk-off made Dylan's gut churn. Seeing the confusion on her face when she'd realized he'd stopped by had been worse. It'd been a reminder of what had happened between them the last time he'd been at her house.

Something that constantly weighed heavily on Dylan's mind.

Ever since that night, while he'd immersed himself in alcohol and his own grief, pretending Sarah didn't matter, he'd realized what a sad fucking case he was.

She mattered.

So much so that it had been his embarrassment over the fact that he'd fucked her and walked away that got him to open his eyes. What made it worse was the fact that Sarah was the only woman he'd had sex with since Meghan. The *only* one.

Granted, it had taken a couple of weeks of reliving that night over and over in his head before he finally decided to do something, but if Dylan was honest with himself, she'd been the real reason he had decided to stop drinking.

And maybe that was what scared him shitless.

Sarah had always mattered. Even back in high school before he'd fallen in love with Meghan, he'd felt something for her. And when they'd ... fucked ... against her living room wall ... well, he'd felt it again then, too, which had scared the fucking hell out of him.

That night, when he'd broken down and cried after they'd... Yeah. *After.* It still embarrassed him to think he'd fallen apart so easily in front of her. He hadn't cried because of his loss or because he missed Meghan. He'd lost it because of the guilt he felt. His feelings for Sarah confused the shit out of him, and he'd felt remorseful, as though he'd cheated on his wife. His *dead* wife.

To think he might be too late with Sarah now ... that bothered him more than anything.

But she'd said she wasn't sure things were serious. That meant there was still a chance. Right? Surely she wasn't in love with that Bill guy. He didn't even seem her type. He drove a fucking minivan, for fuck's sake. Christ. Dylan was forty-two with two kids, but he didn't drive a damn minivan.

He never would, either.

But Sarah hadn't batted an eyelash when she said she was going away with the guy.

With his foot to the floor, Dylan reached the highway, his thoughts going a million miles a minute as he merged, guiding the truck into the fast lane. It wasn't until he passed a familiar exit that he realized he'd gone too far. He'd passed his house. Instead of pulling off at the next one, making a U-turn, and heading home, Dylan kept going. Maybe he'd drive until he ran out of gas. Driving around aimlessly didn't sound like fun, but he couldn't think of anything else to do. It sure beat going back to Sarah's and insisting that she send Bill packing.

He'd been putting the miles behind him for roughly ten minutes when his cell phone rang. He hit the button to answer the call. "Yeah?"

"Dylan?" his sister greeted.

"Hey, Ash," he replied hoarsely.

"You okay?" Ashleigh asked, her tone wary.

Dylan didn't know the answer to that, nor was he sure if she was referring to something specific.

"Where are you?" she questioned when he didn't say anything.

"Driving."

There was a slight pause before she spoke again. "Why don't you come by?" He could hear his niece in the background, sputtering on about something. "Riley'd love to see you."

"Yeah, okay," he muttered. It wasn't like he had anything else to do.

"Perfect. See you in a little bit?"

"On my way. Fifteen minutes or so." Dylan hung up and took the next exit to make a U-turn back toward Ashleigh's. He'd go spend time with his niece and hope that he could calm down. He wouldn't allow his emotions to control him anymore, even though it would be so easy. And when he was done there, maybe he'd go find a meeting.

Yeah. He'd definitely be doing that.

Roughly twenty minutes later, he pulled up in front of Ashleigh and Alex's house, the one Ashleigh had moved into before she'd started seeing Alex several years back. Dylan still remembered helping her get set up, noticing for the first time the awkward tension between Alex and Ashleigh. Needless to say, he'd been blindsided to find out one of his best fucking friends had been crushing on Dylan's little sister for years. Something he still tried not to think too much about even though they were married with a child.

When he climbed out of his truck, he saw his niece standing at the front door, nose pressed up against the glass, waving her little hand furiously, a huge grin on her sweet, cherubic face.

"Hey, sweetness," Dylan greeted when he pulled open the glass door and stepped inside.

"Unca D!"

Snatching her up in his arms, Dylan squeezed her and blew a raspberry against her neck, making her laugh. With a sweet little chuckle, she started squirming, ready to be put down. Dylan set her back on her feet and watched as she sped off toward the living room.

"Hey," Ashleigh acknowledged with a surprised look on her face, peeking around the corner as she dried her hands on a dish towel. "That was fast."

"Where's Alex?" Dylan questioned, glancing around the house. It still looked the same as the last time he'd been there, expect for possibly more toys scattered on the floor.

The scene reminded him of when Stacey and Nate were little. There had always been toys scattered from one end of the house to the other. He'd worked tirelessly to keep them put up while Meghan had laughed at him, telling him it was pointless. She'd been right. No matter how many times he'd put blocks back in a box or packed Hot Wheels cars into a bin, they always seemed to find their way back onto the floor.

"He should be back any minute," Ashleigh answered. "He ran to the store to grab a gallon of milk."

"I coulda picked it up on my way," Dylan told her, following Ashleigh into the kitchen.

She nodded toward the bar, and he took a seat while she pulled a pitcher of tea from the refrigerator. "I think he needs to get out of the house sometimes. Riley's definitely daddy's girl and she doesn't give him a moment of peace."

Dylan knew that Alex would move heaven and earth for both Ashleigh and Riley, but he understood needing a minute to breathe every now and then. Dylan had depended on his grandfather for so long, needing someone to help with Stacey and Nate after Meghan had died... Thinking back on it now, he realized he'd probably leaned on Pops more than he should have.

"So, how are you?" Ashleigh inquired, carrying the pitcher to the counter.

"I'm ... good." Maybe not great, but he would survive.

Pouring the tea, she smiled up at him, then grabbed a glass. She slid the back of her hand over his scruffy jaw after she set it in front of him. "You need to shave."

"Nate told me the same thing," he groused, rubbing his fingers over the bristle on his face.

He did need to shave. It'd been at least two weeks since the last time he'd picked up a razor.

He wondered what Sarah had thought when she'd seen him. He hadn't thought much about his appearance when he'd crawled out of bed and headed right for his truck as soon as he woke up. His conversation with Sarah's nephew last night had kept him up most of the night, and he'd needed to see Sarah for himself.

Now, he wasn't sure that'd been the best idea.

"You talk to Sarah lately?" he found himself asking before he could think better of it.

Ashleigh stopped as she placed the pitcher back in the refrigerator, her head swinging in his direction. "Jake's aunt?"

Did she know another Sarah?

Ashleigh closed the refrigerator door and turned away from him.

"Did she say something?" Ashleigh asked, her gaze sliding toward the window over the sink.

"No." Staring back at his sister, he realized something was going on that he didn't know about. "Should she have?"

Before Ashleigh answered, the door leading to the garage opened, and Alex stepped into the kitchen carrying a gallon of milk. His sister's attention immediately slid toward her husband, and Dylan knew she wasn't going to answer his question.

"Hey, man," Alex greeted after kissing Ashleigh and shoving the milk into the refrigerator. "What brings you by?"

"Daddy!" Riley hollered, racing into the room and running right into Alex's legs.

"Hey, short stuff." Alex smiled, then swept Riley up into his arms and swung her around. Alex's gaze met his once more.

"I was out drivin'," Dylan said. "Ash called, said I should stop by to see Riley."

"Goin' somewhere?"

His thoughts instantly drifted to Sarah and her impromptu weekend trip. He couldn't help but think he should've put up more of a fight, convinced her not to go with Bill. Hell, he should've offered to take her somewhere. Anywhere. Just the two of them. That would've been the smart thing to do. Letting her go—before he ever actually had her—didn't sit well with him, and he didn't like thinking this could've been his last chance. What happened if she went away with Bill and came back engaged?

The universe couldn't be that cruel, could it?

"I'd thought about it," he told Alex. It wasn't a complete lie. When he'd been driving around aimlessly, he'd given some thought to where he might go. Obviously he hadn't come up with a plan.

But with Sarah gone, he knew he'd do nothing but think about her all weekend if he sat around and twiddled his fucking thumbs. Which was why a trip of his own wasn't necessarily a bad thing. Alex's question only encouraged him to give it more consideration.

"Where're you goin', Dylan?" Ashleigh asked, suddenly incredibly interested in the conversation. "And when will you be back?"

"Don't know. I was thinkin' Shreveport," he said simply. It was the first place that came to mind. He could gamble, drink, and ultimately give in to all of his vices.

Only he *couldn't* drink.

No way was he going to Shreveport.

"Shreveport? What's in Shreveport?" she asked, her eyes widening.

"Nothin' specific. Just need to get away for a bit."

Alex and Ashleigh both stared at him and he could see the concern in their gazes. He'd seen that look so many times over the past few years.

Her voice lowered when she said, "Dylan, have you been drinking?"

He huffed a laugh, then held up his tea glass. "Not yet."

"Have you been to an AA meeting lately? Since Monday?" Alex propped his hip against the counter.

"Twice last week," he confessed.

"Is it helping?"

Watching his sister closely, Dylan shrugged. "I'm still sober. I swear." Even if he wished otherwise, the years of sobriety he'd logged were important to him. Sure, as his sponsor said, it was something he should be proud of, but Dylan was still living one day at a time. It was the only way he could make it through.

When she didn't pelt another question at him, Dylan knew his sister was getting worked up. Ashleigh had been worried about him for a long time. Hell, she had even put off her own wedding to deal with him and his bullshit. Granted, Dylan hadn't been at all happy about that, nor had Alex. The fistfight he and Alex had gotten into would forever be a reminder of how shitty he'd treated the important people in his life.

"Are you sure you should go? I mean…" Ashleigh paused. "Are you going there to gamble?"

"Maybe," he told her. Seriously, if he did go to Shreveport, what else was he going to do? He wasn't much of a gambler, but then again, these days he wasn't much of anything. He'd been simply existing for over a decade, and the moment he'd heard about this Bill guy and Sarah, he'd felt the first real spark of life. He just didn't know how to deal with it. Yet.

When Ashleigh didn't say anything, Dylan filled in the silence. "It's good, Ash. I promise. If I go, it'll be a quick trip. I'd be back on Sunday. You don't need to worry about me."

"But I do," she said softly.

"I know." It saddened him how much he'd caused her to worry. "I'm not gonna do anything stupid. Trust me."

He thought for a moment that his sister was going to cry. He was about to reassure her again, but she turned and fled the room, not looking back when Alex called out to her.

Dylan waited for Alex's wrath. Surprisingly, it didn't come.

"She's a little emotional right now," Alex explained with a heavy sigh.

It took a moment for Dylan to catch the meaning. "She's...?"

A slow smile took over Alex's face as he glanced at his daughter, still in his arms. "Yeah. We're gonna have another baby."

"Holy shi—" He cut the curse off when he realized Riley was staring at him intently. "That's awesome, man. I'm happy for you."

"Thanks. She's worried after..."

Yeah, Dylan understood just what Alex was saying. Ashleigh's first pregnancy hadn't been an easy one. She'd been confined to bed rest for quite some time, and he couldn't help but think he'd been responsible for a lot of her stress.

"Is there a specific reason you're goin' to Shreveport?" Alex inquired.

"No," he admitted.

"What if I had another suggestion for you?"

"Like?"

"Luke and Cole are puttin' on some fancy thing at Devotion tonight. Kicking off the new year and all that. Cole called and tried to convince me to bring Ashleigh. Why don't *you* go by, check it out? I know you've talked about goin' to the club since they opened."

Surprised by the suggestion, especially considering it would be a temptation Dylan wasn't sure he could resist, he tossed the idea around for a moment. It was true, Dylan had been talking about going to Devotion, but he hadn't been able to bring himself to do it. But it didn't sound like a bad idea. If he couldn't have Sarah, he could easily find a way to distract himself with someone else. For a little while anyway.

Right. Like that would ever happen. Even if he convinced himself to pursue another woman, Dylan wasn't sure he could follow through. He wasn't completely dead on the inside, but something had stopped him all these years. His hand had been the only action his dick had received and until Sarah, he'd been good with that.

But he wasn't a damn saint. His little head would eventually win out.

"Are y'all goin'?" Dylan asked.

Alex shook his head. "Not into that scene."

Dylan knew that. And since there wasn't the risk of seeing his sister there—he didn't even want to think about what they would be doing if they did spend time in a place like Devotion—then he might as well go. After all, it would save him gas money and give him something to do. What did he have to lose?

"I like that idea," Dylan finally said.

"But then there's the temptation..." Alex began.

"Of booze? I'm good, man. Swear it." He had too much invested in his sobriety at this point. Too many people were depending on him not falling apart again. It wouldn't be easy, but Dylan wasn't worried. "Just as long as it's not some crazy theme party," he tacked on.

"Optional," Alex said.

"Good."

Alex smiled. "Now that she doesn't have to worry about you leavin' town, maybe you could go in there and talk to her."

"Yeah." Dylan got to his feet. His hand came up to rub the scruffy beard that'd filled in his face. "But then I've gotta head home so I can shower."

"Good idea," Alex acknowledged with a smirk. "You're startin' to look like a grizzly. And the gray... It's taking over."

"Thanks for pointing that out," Dylan said as he grinned at Riley. "Tell your daddy he's an—"

"Watch it," Alex interrupted. "Whatever you say, she's gonna repeat it."

Dylan laughed. He remembered those days.

"Have fun tonight," Alex called out as Dylan headed toward the door. "And don't do anything I wouldn't do."

Dylan peered over his shoulder. "That won't work. You're a fu— prude. I'd be bored to tears if I did nothing."

Alex's booming laugh made Dylan smile. At least he felt a little better.

And if he could settle Ashleigh's nerves a little, he'd feel a hell of a lot better.

CHAPTER SEVEN

BAD IDEA, BAD IDEA. BAD IDEA.

It had become her mantra and Sarah couldn't stop the constant repeat in her head.

When they had pulled up to the hotel roughly forty-five minutes ago, Sarah hadn't been sure what she was supposed to say or think. It seemed awfully presumptuous of Bill to assume she would willingly stay at a hotel with him though they'd never been intimate up to this point. Although she was confused, Sarah had kept her initial thoughts to herself when Bill had pulled the minivan around to the front of the monstrous resort hotel, where they were greeted by the hotel's valet.

Baffled, Sarah had even allowed Bill to take her hand and lead her inside as a million questions zipped through her head, none of which she could seem to voice. But when they'd approached the check-in desk, she hadn't been able to hold her tongue any longer. To her absolute shock, before she could tell him that she wouldn't feel comfortable staying in the same room with him, Bill had smiled over at her, his clear blue eyes flashing, and informed her he'd reserved two rooms, but he was holding out hope that she would end up staying with him.

Her first thought ... he was considerate.

The second ... there was no way in hell she was staying with him.

But disaster averted.

Now, as she walked through the lavish resort hotel on her way to meet him, she wasn't convinced that this was going to go well. And to think, they'd only been there for an hour. The first part of that hour—as well as the forty-five-minute drive—Sarah had nervously tried to come up with a way to let Bill down easy. If she'd learned anything during that time, it was that she was not a spontaneous person and agreeing to this was the worst idea she'd ever had.

During the drive, she'd listened to Bill ramble on and on about cars, even dropping hints about hot women who came into his dealership and flirted with him. Right. Hot women and cars. Because *that* was a turn-on. It seemed to her that Bill was trying too hard to impress her, and the only thing he was doing was effectively pushing her further away.

Clearly cars were his life, and she'd admired his enthusiasm when she'd first met him, but the droning conversation had nearly bored her to tears. While he'd continued to share his wealth of knowledge about the different types of minivans the various carmakers designed and how his were obviously better, Sarah had known that this outing would ultimately be the end of their dating.

Plus, he was allergic to her cats.

It was glaringly obvious that they had nothing in common, certainly not chemistry. And without a spark...

Everyone knew that was the most important thing, and without that spark, there really wasn't anything to look forward to. Which was why she was grateful that he'd agreed to separate rooms. After they'd decided to get settled in, Sarah had deposited her things in her room, neatly unpacking and placing the items where they belonged, then snuck back down to the lobby and told the woman who'd helped them that she needed to change the credit card on her room. There was no way she would allow Bill to pick up the tab. She wasn't heartless, after all.

And now she was supposed to meet him in the hotel bar so that they could have a drink before an early dinner. The place was bigger than any hotel she'd ever been to and she felt a little out of sorts. The lobby wasn't overly crowded, but there were a lot of people wandering around the atrium, some sitting near the stone fireplace that took up an entire wall near the front desk. After asking someone where the bar was and being pointed in the right direction, Sarah continued on.

Once she found her destination, she realized that Bill was not one of the few people sitting in the cozy area that had been sectioned off as a bar. Spinning in a circle, she scanned the various seating spots just outside, trying to find him, but to no avail. Figuring he had possibly been delayed in his room, she wandered through the glass-enclosed atrium, admiring the various decorations and lush plants that filled the space.

Ten minutes later, after taking it all in, she finally spotted Bill. He was sitting at a completely different bar in a different section of the hotel, a huge grin on his thin, pale face while he talked animatedly to a pretty brunette beside him. The woman had her hand on his arm and was smiling and laughing, as though Bill were the most interesting person on the planet.

Great.

This was not going well at all.

What had she ever seen in him? He did have nice taste in clothes even if he had yet to learn that a tailor would benefit him, and he spoke relatively eloquently, although his conversation topics were lacking. Overall, he was ...

Yep there it was again, the same conclusion as last time. Bill was sweet.

Unfortunately, sweet didn't turn her on, no matter how much she wished it did.

Rather than interrupt him (*and* his blatant attempt at flirting), Sarah decided to tour the rest of the place, hoping he'd be finished with his conversation when she returned. As she strolled through, Sarah noted the different attractions that made the hotel a vacation hot spot. Through a wall of windows, she could see the clear blue water of a huge outdoor pool. At the far corner, which was surrounded by a white stone wall, there was a waterslide as well as what looked to be a lazy river, but she couldn't be sure. The outdoor area was closed, but she could imagine it being full to bursting with people during the summer months.

Overall, it was a nice place; she'd give Bill that. She'd never been in a resort such as this, though she'd checked them out on the Internet before. Due to the proximity of the place to her house, she couldn't justify spending quite so much to stay at a hotel when staying at her own house wouldn't cost her anything extra. If it were in another state, perhaps she'd splurge. One day.

Truth was, she'd always been frugal with her money. Ever since her sister, Tara, had decided that being a mother wasn't something she wanted to do with her life—*after* she'd had Jake—Sarah had been helping their mother raise Jake, financially and physically. Her mother had always had health issues, so much of the responsibility had fallen on Sarah. Not that she'd minded. Jake had always been a good kid. But her sister's abandonment had hurt them all.

That didn't mean Sarah didn't think about Tara. She did. All the time. Now that Tara was married to some biker, living up in Oklahoma, Sarah rarely heard from her. The last time Tara had come for a visit had been when Paul died, six years ago.

Pushing her hand into her pocket, Sarah fingered the plastic key card and considered going back up to her room, packing her things, calling a cab, and then hightailing it out of there before Bill was even aware she was gone.

"There you are."

Too late.

Sarah sighed, then turned around to see Bill strolling toward her, a huge grin on his face. He leaned in and kissed her on the cheek.

"Are you hungry?"

Was she? She didn't know.

"If we go to the steakhouse now, there won't be a wait."

Sarah wasn't sure why that mattered. Based on her surroundings, she wasn't sure what else they were going to do there.

Bill must've seen the question in her eyes because he took her hand in his and tugged. "Come on. Let's eat. Then we can change and we'll go out."

"Out?" she asked, peering up at him.

Another brilliant smile landed on his lips. "You didn't think this was all there was, did you?"

Actually, yes. In fact, she hadn't brought anything to wear to go *out*. She had assumed—obviously incorrectly—that whatever event Bill wanted her to accompany him to would've been at this hotel.

Crap.

Bill chuckled as they approached the hostess stand just outside the steakhouse inside the resort. He rattled off his name, and the hostess graciously grabbed two menus, then led them through the dimly lit restaurant to a table at the back. The waiter quickly stopped by, informed them of their specials, offered the wine list, and then disappeared as soon as Bill made a selection and told him they needed a few minutes to look at the menu.

Sarah wasn't hungry, but she was curious. "Where're we going?" she asked, unable to keep the question to herself. She knew he'd wanted to surprise her, but honestly, this place was much more than she'd anticipated.

"You'll see when we get there. It's by invitation only, I'll tell you that much."

"Can you give me a hint?" she probed. For some reason, she was beginning to get a weird feeling about all of it. Maybe that was her conscience eating away at her for accepting this invitation in the first place when she had no intention of taking their relationship to the next level.

"It's a highly coveted place. Not easy to get an invitation, I assure you. But they know my boss, and I've been assured we'll get the royal treatment. And don't worry, I know you'll have a great time."

She wasn't sure how he knew that considering they'd only been out a handful of times. He knew what she'd willingly divulged about herself, and the sad thing was, she hadn't told him much.

The waiter returned, and Sarah felt obligated to order something, so she selected a small filet and a salad, hoping that wouldn't cost too much. Her guilt was eating at her and she wished she'd never agreed to this in the first place.

But now, it seemed it was far too late to worry about that.

"STACEY, HONEY," DYLAN BEGAN AS HE STARED at his daughter in disbelief and possibly a little horror, "what the *hell* did you do to your hair?"

He was pretty sure she hadn't looked like that the last time he'd seen her, but, shit, he'd been so lost in himself lately Dylan honestly couldn't have said for sure. Truth was, he hadn't paid attention to much of anything in his life for years, certainly not the little details.

"Dad!" Stacey laughed, self-consciously sliding her hand over her dark hair, which now had hot pink chunks blended into it. "Knock it off."

"*What?*" Dylan probed innocently. "Your hair ... was *not* that color on Tuesday when I saw you at dinner." Pink. *Really?* "A father has a right to know when his child is havin' some sort of ... breakdown."

"I happen to think it looks awesome," a gravelly voice countered, pulling Dylan's attention away from his daughter.

Pops came ambling into the kitchen, a little slower these days, a smile on his aged face as he leveled his golden-brown eyes at Stacey. Dylan rolled his eyes. Xavier Thomas was in his eighties. What did he know about fashion statements of college kids?

"Of course you would," Dylan said slyly, forcing a smile as he continued to stare at his daughter's outrageous hairdo before turning his attention to his grandfather.

Pops shot him a glare—his way of intimidating Dylan into keeping his mouth shut. Generally, that look didn't work, because Dylan had spent most of his life rebelling against his grandfather, but today, he managed to keep his comments to himself.

"Thanks, Pops," Stacey crooned before stealing an apple from the counter and disappearing as quickly as she'd appeared.

"That girl," Dylan mused. "I don't know what I'm gonna do with her. Next thing you know, she'll have her face pierced."

"She's twenty-three. What do you expect?" Pops teased.

Before his grandfather could say anything more, in walked Dylan's son, Nate, who, unlike Dylan's daughter, wasn't smiling. Thankfully, Nate's hair was normal, though. Dylan wasn't sure what he'd do if both of his kids went wild. As it was, he was still having a hard time getting used to the fact that Nate was twenty-one years old and more than a couple of inches taller than Dylan was. The kid he'd known had grown into a fine young man.

"Hey, Dad. Pops," Nate greeted coolly. "Have either of you talked to Alex?"

"I stopped by his house earlier. Why?" Dylan questioned.

Dylan watched Nate closely, noticing the way his son didn't maintain eye contact for long. It wasn't a secret that Nate had gone to Alex about making his job at CISS full time and permanent despite Dylan's insistence that Nate further his academics before stepping into that sort of role. But after a rather heated conversation with Alex at the time, Dylan had relented to Alex's request to hire the boy on before the merger so that Nate would have an official position with Sniper 1 Security. Perhaps Nate still wasn't happy with Dylan about his reaction to the situation.

Nate had been working for CISS since he graduated from high school three years earlier. Although he'd only been pitching in part time, it looked as though Nate was definitely interested in pursuing a long-time career in the security business. However, whenever Dylan had attempted to discuss it with Nate, aside from a few brusque responses to Dylan's questions, Nate hadn't talked much.

Seemed Nate was happy with the job, though. Or so Alex had told him.

That didn't mean Dylan liked the idea of his son working for CISS, especially with things the way they were. As far as Dylan was concerned, school was the most important thing for his children, and if Nate expected to make a career in the security industry, Dylan wanted him to graduate from college with a degree that was worthwhile. Seemed that Nate and Alex were content with the two-year degree he'd already accomplished, and they'd brushed Dylan's concerns off.

And yes, Dylan had been called a meddling father on more than one occasion, but he was a firm believer that that was what fathers were supposed to do. Even if their kids were grown and no longer wanted their father interfering in their business.

"Why're you lookin' for Alex?" Dylan asked his son.

"No reason," Nate said curtly before turning and abruptly leaving the room.

Well, hell.

What was it with his kids and their hasty disappearing acts? If he didn't know better, he would have thought they were keeping their distance for a reason. Granted, Dylan knew he had to accept some responsibility since he hadn't been the greatest father in the world—not since Meghan died anyway.

"Wow, *Dad*," Pops teased. "Way to run off the kids."

"It's a skill I've acquired," he told his grandfather.

"I can see that." Pops went to the refrigerator and pulled out a pitcher of tea, then retrieved two glasses from the cabinet. "Goin' somewhere tonight?"

"I was thinkin' about it," he admitted. After leaving Ashleigh and Alex's, Dylan made a quick stop, then he'd gone back to his house—the three-bedroom guest house at the back of his grandfather's vast estate, where he'd been living for the past four years—and showered, shaved, and dressed in record time. Now, as he sat at his grandfather's kitchen table, he was beginning to rethink his decision to go to Devotion.

"You look good, kid," Xavier said. "Whatever you do, don't change your plans. You need to get outta the house."

"You don't even know where I'm goin'," Dylan countered, wondering, not for the first time, if his grandfather could read his mind.

"Doesn't matter. You need to do something."

Dylan nodded, then looked away from Pops.

"Did you...?" Pops' gaze drifted to the door, then slowly back to him. "Did you visit Meghan's grave yesterday?"

Swallowing hard, Dylan nodded. Another trip behind him on a day he dreaded because the memories still brought him to his knees.

Eleven long years of nursing a shattered, brittle heart after the death of his wife—his best friend in the world—had left Dylan feeling like a body without a soul. He had watched Meghan suffer, withering away, her fragile body succumbing to the cancer that riddled it while fighting the chemo the doctors had warned them wasn't a sure thing. Up until her very last breath, Dylan had hung on, praying that God would not take her from him, but in the end, she had died. Right there in his arms, while he was unable to contain the tears as the love of his life was taken from him.

A knot formed in his throat as the memories took root. They hadn't even gotten to celebrate their tenth wedding anniversary when she was taken from him. And through the decade since her death, Dylan had kept himself shut off from everyone, wallowing in his own pain and giving everything he had left—which admittedly hadn't been much—to his two children. It had been on the day Nate had graduated from high school four years ago that something inside of him broke open.

Maybe it had been the fear that he had nothing left to live for because his children were making their own paths in life that had caused him to backslide. Or perhaps it had been due to Ashleigh—the one person who had stood beside him for so many years, never allowing him to fully immerse himself in the black despair that had threatened to drag him under— hooking up with Alex, Dylan's business partner and best friend, that had done it.

Either way, the despair had continued to cloak him like a wet blanket, and he hadn't been able to find his way out from beneath it. He hadn't had a single relationship since Meghan's death. He hadn't been able to bring himself to do it, to try to get close to someone.

But there had been one woman.

Sarah.

Somehow, Sarah had always been able to make him smile. Back when he'd first met her roughly twenty-five years ago, when she'd been a bright-eyed freshman and he'd been a senior in high school, *and* in recent years when he'd run into her again.

For whatever reason, Sarah understood him. Whether it was due to the fact she'd suffered her own loss or because she could see through to who he'd been before his life had been forever changed.

Ever since he'd reconnected with her, he'd felt something that resembled hope. At that time, she'd convinced him to join a grief support group, which he'd been reluctant about but had opted to give it a chance. It hadn't been his thing, but he'd gone a couple of times since she'd asked. But it wasn't until their sexual encounter that one memorable night when he'd stopped all communication with her.

Until that night at her house, they hadn't been intimate, nor had he ever expected them to be, but somewhere along the way, Sarah had become a friend. And he'd taken advantage of that. Until recently, he had tried not to think about her, but there were a few occasions where his thoughts of her had helped to clear the fuzz from his brain, offering him tenuous optimism that there might possibly be something to live for other than his children.

But then, Dylan would feel guilty for wanting to move on, afraid that if he fully dug himself out of the gloom he had become so intimate with, Meghan would somehow feel forgotten. But his sweet Meghan wouldn't have wanted this for him; even he knew that. She would be disappointed to know he'd basically died right along with her.

"Hey." Pops' voice pulled Dylan from his thoughts and he looked up at him. "Where'd you go?"

"Sorry," he said, grabbing his now empty coffee cup before he stood. Figuring one more jolt of caffeine couldn't hurt, Dylan made his way around his grandfather to the coffeepot.

"So, what're your plans tonight?" Pops inquired.

Dylan did not want to tell his grandfather that he was going to a fetish club. "Just goin' out."

"With friends?" Pops asked.

"Yeah." It wasn't a complete lie. Luke McCoy and Cole Ackerley, the owners of Devotion, were technically his friends.

"Good. We're gonna stay in tonight. If you need anything..."

Dylan nodded. These days, Xavier spent his time with the woman he'd fallen head-over-heels in love with years ago. Veronica Sellers. Xavier's administrative assistant. Though she was more than two decades younger than Pops, it was clear she wasn't after his money. From what Dylan had seen, they were genuinely in love.

"Thanks," Dylan muttered as Pops left the room, carrying his tea glasses.

Pops would be the last person he would contact, but he appreciated his grandfather's support. The man had been the most prominent person in Dylan's life since his own parents had died when he was young. Xavier had raised him and Ashleigh, and had been more help than anyone else by assisting with Stacey and Nate after Meghan's death.

But tonight, Dylan didn't need anyone to keep an eye on him. It was high time he got out there, did something to change the course of his life, because otherwise, he was simply existing.

And he knew that was no way to live.

CHAPTER EIGHT

SERIOUSLY?

Sarah wasn't sure her day could get any worse. But this... It merely confirmed for the millionth time that this was by far her most irrational decision ever.

After dinner, when Bill told her it was time to change to go out, Sarah had broken down and informed him that unless she could wear slacks and a silk shirt, she hadn't brought anything to wear. But if she'd thought that would deter the man, she'd been oh so wrong. Instead, he had put his hand at the small of her back and guided her into a store within the resort. And it definitely wasn't one of the department stores she normally shopped at. No, this place was...

It was out of her price range, for one thing. She knew that by the flashy décor and the fact that there were very few items placed strategically around the walls on glass shelves. For another, she wasn't sure half of the dresses they had in there would even fit her. It wasn't easy to find dresses for her petite frame most of the time. But, again, Bill had taken her hand and led her right to the sparkly woman with the perfectly coifed hair and flawless makeup who was standing behind the counter, informing her that Sarah needed something for the evening.

That had been fifteen minutes ago.

The woman had been more than happy to help her find just the right dress. With a quick perusal of Sarah from head to toe—twice—she'd apparently decided what she thought would work for her.

"Now, if you'll jot down your sizes, I'll get to work."

Sarah took the small pad from the woman and scribbled down her sizes. Dress, panties, bra, shoes. Hell, at this point, the woman now knew every intimate detail about her.

After guiding Sarah to a dressing room, the woman headed back to the "salon," as she called it, then returned a few minutes later with several dresses for her to choose from.

The first had been way too short.

The second had a neckline that should've been labeled indecent.

The third one had been a rather unusual shade of lime green that no one over the age of twelve should ever be seen in.

The fourth... As she spun around, looking at her butt and the backs of her legs, Sarah had to admit, it wasn't bad. A short, shimmery gold dress that didn't show too much but was still short enough to be sexy. No, it wasn't something she would've picked out for herself, but she liked it.

"Have you found one, sweetie?" the woman called from the other side of the door.

"I think so," she admitted, eyeing the tag on the back of the dress.

Sarah hadn't bothered to look at the price, but before she could move closer to see it, the woman opened the door and stepped into the room with her as though she'd been invited.

"Gorgeous," the woman said excitedly. "You're gonna need a bra to go with that. That one positively won't work."

No, Sarah hadn't figured it would. The single-shoulder dress would require a strapless bra, for sure. Which meant Sarah would have to fork over more money for that. Not that the woman seemed to mind.

"What size were you again?"

Sarah rattled off her size, her cheeks heating with embarrassment. She had no idea if Bill was close by, but for some reason, she didn't want him to know something quite that personal.

The woman disappeared but returned almost instantly, holding out a sheer gold bra and a matching gold thong.

Sarah stared at her as though she were crazy.

"Come on, sweetie. Don't wanna keep that man of yours waiting."

Sure she did.

First of all, he wasn't her man. And secondly, Sarah didn't mind if Bill waited forever because there was no way this night was going to get any better. For either of them.

"If you'd like, you can change here and we'll have your other clothes sent back up to your room."

"No," Sarah said, peering in the mirror again. "That's okay. I'll change up in my room." It would give her time to weigh the risks of rappelling down the side of the building and disappearing into the night.

The woman got the hint, leaving Sarah alone so that she could get dressed in her own clothes once again. Once she was decent, she took the opportunity to look at the tag on the dress and her heart nearly leapt right out of her chest.

Holy crap.

There was no way she could afford that dress without putting a sizeable dent in her credit card. And she certainly wasn't letting Bill pay for it. Not when she fully intended to end their relationship tonight. Then again, what she should've done was march right out of the store and tell Bill that it wouldn't work but thanks again.

Only she had been the one to call him and agree to his offer, so the guilt ate at her.

With the dress, bra, and panties in hand, Sarah returned to the front of the store, greeted once again by the smiling saleswoman. Before she could say a word, the items were snatched from her hand, put into a fancy clothing bag, and then handed back.

"All taken care of, sweetie. Even have shoes in there for you. Have a fantastic night." The woman winked at her, and Sarah was tempted to toss the clothes back on the counter and run.

"I didn't pay for them," Sarah said, her voice low.

"Your man did."

"I can't allow him to do that," she countered, digging in her purse for her wallet.

When Sarah held out her card, the woman frowned.

"Please," Sarah pleaded. "Return the money to his card and charge mine." *Or better yet, just return it all and let me leave.*

Unfortunately, she didn't have the nerve to say the last part aloud, so Sarah stood there, gripping her purse straps tightly while the woman did something on the register. A few minutes later, her credit card was thrust back at her, and Sarah was regretting every second of the past two days.

"Anything else?" the woman asked curtly.

Never one for confrontation, Sarah shook her head in disbelief and then walked out of the store.

Bill was waiting for her just outside.

"Did you find something?"

She nodded.

"Perfect. How long will it take you to change?" he asked.

She shrugged her shoulders. "Half an hour?"

"Fantastic. I'll be in the bar. Meet you there?"

Sarah offered another nod.

Bill kissed her cheek and then left her standing there, staring after him.

She had to end this. Now. Before it was too late and she got herself in a predicament she couldn't get out of.

What're you gonna do? Go home and play with your cats?

Ugh! Sarah did not like that taunting voice. So what if she spent her nights alone. It wasn't as though she was missing out on anything.

Her mind immediately conjured images of her night with Dylan.

Okay, fine. So yes, that was the type of spark she was looking for. But clearly that wasn't going to happen with Bill, so going out tonight was just a waste of time. Hers and his.

How do you know if you don't try?

Gritting her teeth, she ignored the voice in her head and stormed toward the elevator, dress, shoes, and underwear in hand. If her subconscious thought it knew best, she would just have to show it who was boss.

Nearly an hour later, Sarah made her way back to the main floor of the resort, doing her best not to fall and break her neck on the four-inch stilettos the woman had clearly thought accentuated the dress. They did, Sarah couldn't deny that. But she wasn't good with heels, regardless of their height.

A slow whistle sounded, and Sarah braced herself when Bill got to his feet and joined her as she stepped into the bar area.

"Wow. That dress…"

Sarah forced a smile and allowed him to kiss her on the cheek again. At least there was one good thing. With the heels, she didn't feel quite so short.

"Ready?"

She wasn't, but she nodded anyway.

"The limo's waiting out front."

Limo?

He obviously noticed her distress. "Yes, I went all out, I know. But the extra money was worth it." His smile widened. "*Tonight* is going to be so worth every penny I spent on the rooms and the dress."

That's what he thinks.

Sarah didn't bother to tell him that she was the one who'd sprung for the dress, as well as her room. Bill clearly thought spending money made him a man, so she'd let him go on thinking that. For now.

Crap.

Bill took her hand and led her to the main entrance of the hotel. She couldn't help but notice people looking at her as she passed. She wasn't sure if they were admiring the dress, thinking she was a hired escort, or wondering whether she was going to take a tumble in the heels. The latter was a definite possibility. She attempted to cloak herself in confidence, though she felt like a fraud.

Thankfully, the limo ride was short. Only five minutes alone in the car and they had arrived at their destination.

Devotion.

For some reason, that name sounded familiar to her, but she didn't know why. Commercial, maybe? From the outside, it looked like a fancy night club. If that was the case, then it was obvious Bill knew nothing about her because the last time she'd been to a club... Crap. She'd probably been in her early twenties? It had never really been her thing.

She was more of a homebody. She would prefer to sit at home with a glass of wine and a good book or a cup of hot tea and a chick flick. That was her idea of a good time, didn't matter which day of the week it was. Paul had been the same way, so it had worked for them.

The first clue that something was off was the fact that there wasn't a line to get in, yet there were two huge men standing guard at the front door. They didn't look like ordinary bouncers, and the reception area definitely didn't look like the standard nightclub. Not how she remembered them anyway.

A pretty blond was sitting at a glass desk—the type they'd have in a high-end office building—her perfectly manicured hands clasped together on the top. She smiled up at them as they approached.

"We're on the guest list," Bill noted sweetly.

The woman peered at the iPad screen. "And your name?"

"Bill Kasin."

"Ah, yes. Mr. Kasin. You're Bob Masterson's guest," she said politely, obviously recognizing his name. "My name is Emily if you have any questions. We were sad to hear Mr. Masterson couldn't make it, but glad that you could."

The woman's gaze slowly slid over to Sarah, a warm smile on her face. "And your guest tonight is...?"

"Sarah Davis," Bill offered.

The woman typed in her name on the iPad, then peered up at them both. "I'll just need you both to review and sign a nondisclosure agreement." She pointed to a small seating area as she passed over another iPad.

Sarah couldn't hide her confusion. A nondisclosure agreement? What the hell kind of place was this?

Bill chuckled. "Of course we'll sign it."

Without reading the form, Bill signed his name using his finger, then pointed the iPad in her direction. "Your turn."

Sarah peered down at the device. She started to scan the document, wondering what she was getting herself into, but Bill put his arm around her. "Just sign. It's good. Bob told me everything I need to know."

Knowing it wouldn't make a difference one way or the other, Sarah scribbled what might've passed as her signature and took a deep breath.

"You're good to go in," the woman said sweetly. "There are a variety of masks available in the changing rooms if you'd like. Theme night and all. Have a wonderful evening."

Changing rooms? Masks?

What the hell?

"Thank you, Emily," Bill replied, taking Sarah's hand and leading her to a door on the left.

It was at that moment, when he pulled that door open and escorted her into the main portion of the club, that Sarah retracted her earlier statement.

The night... It could definitely get worse.

Much, *much* worse.

DYLAN HADN'T KNOWN EXACTLY WHAT TO EXPECT when he arrived at Devotion, but he'd heard enough about the place that he wasn't surprised.

In fact, it was exactly how he'd envisioned it. That was probably due to the fact that he knew Luke McCoy rather well. The man seemed to have a certain taste and this place reflected that. Underneath all the chrome and glass, there was a fetish club. A classy, high-end sex club that didn't attempt to hide what they were all about. At least not once you were past the prim receptionist and the two massive guys guarding the entrance.

As he looked around, Dylan realized it wasn't all that different from Luke's original fetish club, simply named The Club. Dylan had only been twice many years ago, back when the darkness was closing in over his head. He'd enjoyed himself—as a natural voyeur, that wasn't hard to do in a place like this—but hadn't been able to bring himself to go back. When that one closed and this one opened, he had resigned himself to never getting to see the inside.

For the first fifteen minutes or so, Dylan slowly toured the main floor until he managed to make his way to the other side, seeing several people he recognized. When Xander Boone waved him over, Dylan pasted on a smile and joined the group.

"Good to see you again," Xander greeted, his deep baritone warm and friendly. "You remember my wife, Mercedes."

"Of course." Dylan nodded toward the beautiful brunette at Xander's side.

Taking a step back, he glanced at the others standing around, chatting and smiling.

"Dylan!" McKenna Murphy called out, stepping up to him when he turned. Her arms embraced him, her fiery-red hair tickling his chin. "So good to see you."

"Thanks," he replied, hugging her back and looking up to see her husband, Tag, staring back at him.

"We missed you at the wedding," she said, stepping back and looking up at him.

Tag and McKenna had tied the knot a while back on a cruise ship. He'd been invited, but Dylan had had to refuse. He hadn't been in the right frame of mind, and the last thing he'd wanted to do was bring the party down.

"Congrats, by the way."

"Thanks." She took a step back, positioning herself beneath her husband's protective arm.

Dylan shook Tag's proffered hand. "Good to see you."

"Surprised to see you here." Tag's tone was cordial. "We thought you'd never show up."

"First time for everything," Dylan said, glancing around. He nodded at a couple of other people he recognized.

"Well, I think you'll fit right in," McKenna said with a smirk. "We know beneath that rough cowboy exterior there's a devious kinky side."

Dylan laughed. She was right about that, but he doubted many people knew that about him. That was a side of himself that he'd buried more than two decades ago, when he'd finally convinced Meghan to marry him. She hadn't been into that scene, and he'd loved her too much to risk losing her, so he'd opted to pretend that part of him didn't exist.

A waitress appeared. "Can I get you something to drink, sexy?"

"7-Up," he said.

The woman's dark eyebrow lifted. "That's it?"

"Yes, ma'am, unless you'd like to toss in a lime."

She nodded, then took drink orders from the others before disappearing again.

A hand came down on his back, and Dylan turned to see Cole Ackerley-McCoy standing beside him.

"So good to see you, man," Cole greeted. "Welcome to Devotion."

"Nice place," Dylan said, glancing around.

"Thanks. We're proud of it."

As they should be. Dylan knew that Devotion was a highly coveted fetish club—one of the few in the area. After Luke had abruptly closed the doors on his last one, he'd opted for something slightly different. Thanks to a blackmail attempt—someone looking to leak the names of the club's members—Luke had done what he had to in order to protect everyone involved. He'd shut the doors and opened Devotion. Needless to say, every member signed an iron-clad nondisclosure agreement as well as paid a hefty fee to attend.

"You bring a date?" Cole asked, stepping back and studying Dylan.

"Not tonight." While he waited for his drink, he looked around, took it all in. There were quite a few single people there. More than he'd expected, actually. To hear Logan, Trent, Tag, or even Xander talk about it, couples seemed to make up most of their clientele, which made sense.

Maybe tonight was an exception. It did seem to be themed, though not many people were in costume, but there were quite a few masks worn. He figured that could've been for anonymity as well.

Once the waitress returned with his drink, Dylan took the glass, clutching it tightly in his hands.

"I don't wanna keep you," he told the others.

"We're just here to hang out. Who knows where the night'll take us?" McKenna said.

"Sounds like the perfect plan to me," Dylan said, nodding toward them. "I'm just gonna..."

"Talk to you later," Cole said, still watching him closely.

Turning away from them, Dylan headed toward an empty table in the far corner, hidden partially in shadow. Not many people were in that area and he wasn't disappointed by that. He needed a little time to acclimate to the place. It had been a long damn time since he'd been out like this. Meaningless hook-ups weren't his thing, no matter how much he tried to make himself believe otherwise.

"Hey, man."

Dylan turned at the deep voice that sounded from his right. He smiled when Luke McCoy approached, holding out his hand to shake when Luke joined him. "How're you?"

"Damn good," Luke said with a smirk, giving Dylan's shoulder a squeeze. "Never thought I'd see this day. Glad you could make it." Luke peered around briefly. "You bring a date?"

That seemed to be the question of the hour.

"Not tonight, no." Hell, he didn't know a single woman who would be comfortable in a place like this. For a brief second, he tried to imagine Sarah here, but he couldn't see it. She was far too sweet and innocent for a place like this.

"Well, there're plenty of singles here tonight."

"I noticed."

The place was packed. Not body to body, but as the minutes ticked by, it seemed more and more people were coming in. He had no idea how many people officially belonged to this club, but he figured probably a couple hundred. Not to mention their guests.

"You doin' all right?" Luke asked, drawing Dylan's attention back to him.

"Yeah. Hangin' in there."

"I was talkin' to Alex. He told me y'all are considering a merger?"

Dylan nodded. "It's a done deal. Inevitable, really," he admitted.

It was no secret that CISS wasn't doing so hot these days. There were quite a few security companies in the area, one in particular that seemed to be choking out the rest of them.

"Sniper 1 Security's not a bad way to go," Luke admitted.

"No, it's not. And if they agree to take us on, which it looks like they are, then we're all set." Although Sniper 1 would consolidate the home-monitoring division, keeping a majority of CISS's employees, they would still have to eliminate a few positions. Dylan knew Alex was fighting tooth and nail to keep every employee they had, though, so negotiations were going slow.

"Glad to hear it. I think that'll take a lot of pressure off Alex."

Dylan was sure it would. Unfortunately, a lot of that pressure had been Dylan's fault. If he hadn't been so selfish over the past few years, giving in to the depression and ignoring everything else, he wanted to believe their company could still be thriving.

But one thing he knew for certain, he couldn't change the past. Moving forward, one step at a time, was his only option.

"If you're looking to invest in something else," Luke began, turning to face Dylan completely, "you might want to talk to Trent Ramsey."

"Your silent partner?"

Luke grinned. "Wish someone would explain the silent part of that to him. He's in the process of opening another club. Cole and I will be involved, but he's looking for someone who can manage the thing when he's not here. His acting career hasn't slowed down, but he's insistent that this is what he really wants to do."

Dylan considered that for a moment. He'd been tossing around a few ideas of his own, trying to figure out what he was going to do with the rest of his life. "Thanks. I'm definitely open to talking to him."

"I'll tell him to give you a call," Luke noted. "Well, I need to go find Cole and Sierra. If you need anything, holler."

"Will do," Dylan said, forcing a smile. "Thanks."

"Anytime, man. Have fun tonight. Let loose a little."

That was the plan, but he didn't tell Luke as much. Instead, he downed the rest of his 7-Up, and then ordered another when a scantily clad waitress stopped by his table.

While he waited, Dylan realized the night was going to be over before it ever started. Even though his body temperature was rising thanks to the fantastic visuals going on around him, he simply couldn't see himself getting involved with any of these women, single or otherwise. Sure, the idea of them was fantastic. Although Meghan hadn't ever been into the adventurous stuff, she'd obliged Dylan's kinky side a time or two before they were married. Not as much as he would've liked, but he'd loved her enough that he'd buried that side of himself.

Didn't mean he wasn't interested in letting it out from time to time. Only he'd been hoping for something a little more than one encounter in front of a bunch of strangers. He still couldn't stop thinking about the night he'd fucked Sarah up against her living room wall. The woman had been so uninhibited it had actually shocked him. That night, no doubt about it, had probably been the most intense sexual experience of his life, and it had been vanilla compared to some of his darker desires.

Which was either sad or scary.

He didn't mind the voyeurism or the public exhibitionism, which Devotion offered plenty of. Those drew his interest. He also didn't mind the sharing. It was something he longed to do again, but he wasn't sure it was in the cards for him. No matter what, he wanted to experience this with a woman he'd wake up next to in the morning, not one who would disappear from his bed—or him from hers—before the sun was up.

Scanning the room once more, Dylan decided he'd give it a few more minutes, then he'd probably head home. The idea of Devotion was obviously more impressive than the real thing. At least for a single guy like him. Now, if Sarah were here, that might be a whole different...

"Bill. Seriously. I can't believe you did this. What were you thinking?"

Dylan's entire body went rigid when he heard the woman's voice. It sounded so familiar. Too familiar. But there was no way that could possibly be...

Turning, he scanned the few couples standing nearby, and his gaze landed on the one woman he never would've expected to see there. Then again, based on the tone of her voice and the incredulous expression on her face, she probably hadn't thought she'd be here, either.

Seriously. What were the odds?

"Come on, Sarah," Bill countered with a self-righteous huff. "We'll stay for a little while. Let's mingle. You'll love it. I know you will. Just let go of some of that—"

"What?" she questioned, her body going stone-cold still.

Dylan couldn't look away, wanting to know exactly what Bill would say next.

The man sighed. "You don't have to play coy with me, Sarah. I've seen those books on your shelf. This is the real thing," Bill said defensively, waving his hand.

"Books?" Sarah's anger appeared to take on a life of its own. "Those books were written by one of my friends. I'm not ... into that stuff. It's fiction."

Dylan grinned. Sarah must have Ashleigh's books on her shelf. It made sense why Bill would've thought she'd be interested at least. His sister wrote erotic romance, and to hear people talk about them, they were rather steamy. Not that he'd ever read any of them, nor did he have plans to.

"Come on." Bill grinned. "I know you can't be that much of a prude."

What a fucking dick. The guy had absolutely no game if he thought that shit was how to win a woman over.

"Look, I forked over the money for the hotel and the limo, even the dress. Plus I got you in here. The least you can do is appear appreciative. You haven't even given it a chance."

"I can't believe you!" she squealed, then pulled away when Bill attempted to stop her.

Dylan was instantly on his feet, moving toward them.

Bill reached for her again, his hand sliding around her bare upper arm.

"I'm not staying, Bill," Sarah hissed.

"Yes, you are." His tone took on a hard edge. "For a little while anyway."

"Let her go," Dylan commanded, his tone hard, a red haze clouding his vision at the sight of Bill's hand on her arm.

Bill jerked away from her, obviously shocked by the rough tone. Sarah spun around to face him, her eyes wide.

"Dylan?"

He offered a smile as he regarded the two of them briefly before meeting Sarah's stunned gaze.

"Come on, Sarah," Bill said, grabbing her arm again.

Sarah jerked away from him, stumbling slightly in her heels. Taking advantage, Dylan placed a firm hand on her shoulder to steady her, then moved closer, his eyes never leaving Bill's. The guy looked rather pissed to see Dylan twice in one day. Not that he gave a damn.

"Dylan? Oh, my God. What are you doing here?" Sarah whispered harshly, staring up at him.

"Some friends of mine own the place," he told her. Not a lie.

"If you'll excuse us," Bill stated, reaching for Sarah again. "Sarah's here with me."

It wasn't Dylan's place to take her away from Bill, but she merely needed to say the word and he'd do just that.

Sarah jerked back from Bill, moving closer to Dylan. "No, I'm not," she argued.

Bill sighed heavily, closing his eyes as though trying to rein in his temper. Dylan didn't move, remaining right next to Sarah.

"Look, Sarah..." Bill opened his eyes and pinned them on her face. "I brought you here with me tonight; therefore, you are obligated to remain with me."

"Obligated?" Sarah squealed. "You're insane. And you're also a jerk. I can't believe you'd bring me to a sex club without even talking to me about it. Why would you think this was okay?"

And call her a prude, Dylan thought. He could testify that she was far from a prude. But he didn't mind that Bill thought so considering that meant they likely hadn't been too intimate. He hoped.

"I can't leave you alone," Bill countered. "You're my guest. Either you're with me or you have to leave," he told her, his blue eyes boring holes into Sarah's face.

Sure enough, the asshole was pissed.

"Then I'll leave."

"She'll stay," Dylan stated firmly, putting his hand on her lower back. "She's my guest now," Dylan added before Sarah could offer a retort. "Problem solved."

"What?" Bill's mouth dropped open. "You can't do that. She's here with me. I took responsibility for her when I signed her in."

Dylan's hand, which had come to rest on Sarah's hip, tightened possessively, but Sarah didn't pull away from him. He considered that a good thing. "Not anymore she's not."

"Sarah, seriously. You can't possibly want to go with him."

"I do." She sighed.

"Please," Bill begged and Dylan rolled his eyes. The guy had no pride whatsoever.

"Bill—"

"Just one night," Bill said pleadingly. "That's all I need. I'll show you how much fun you can have."

"With my clothes off?" Sarah snapped.

"Well... It's just..." Bill hedged, clearly coming up empty.

Dylan chuckled. He couldn't help himself.

Sarah glared up at him and he immediately sobered. "Sorry," he muttered, his smile twitching his lips again.

"Last chance, Sarah."

Dylan met Bill's gaze, narrowing his eyes in warning. The guy needed to get a grip. It was evident Sarah didn't want to be here with him. Or maybe it was the club in general. He wouldn't know until they sent Bill on his way and he got the opportunity to talk to her.

"Bye, Bill," she said softly.

Not waiting for Bill to drop to his knees and embarrass himself more by begging, Dylan turned and led Sarah toward an empty table on the far side of the room, away from the glass enclosures, where some very interesting scenes were playing out right before their eyes.

"I can't believe he brought me here," she said with a huff.

Dylan allowed his eyes to rake over her beautiful body. That gold dress was likely the hottest thing he'd ever seen. Or perhaps she was the hottest thing wearing it. Then he remembered what Bill had said.

"Bill bought that dress?"

Sarah shook her head. "He thinks he did. I wouldn't let him pay for it."

Well, then. He wouldn't shred the thing when he took it off her later.

"This was his surprise?" he inquired, waving a waitress over. Surely the guy hadn't thought dragging the woman to a fetish club was a good way to get into her panties. It might work for some women, but Sarah...? No way.

After Sarah was seated, Dylan moved a chair closer, his back to the wall so he could keep an eye on what was going on around them.

"Yes. The bastard." Sarah rolled her eyes. "It was a surprise."

Dylan smirked. Yep, the guy was officially a douche.

"Why are you smiling?" she asked.

"I'm just tryin' to imagine why this would be the place he brought you to."

The instant the words were out, he could practically see her defenses fall into place.

"I'm not a prude!" she exclaimed.

Leaning closer, Dylan held her gaze, keeping his voice low as he said, "Darlin', I wasn't thinkin' any such thing. I know firsthand, remember?"

A pretty blush suffused her face and her big blue eyes darted away.

"Drink?" Dylan asked Sarah when the waitress appeared.

Sarah turned to face the woman. "Yes, please. I'll take..." Her eyes shot to Dylan's glass. "I'll have what he's having. Only make mine a double."

When the waitress met his eyes, Dylan grinned. "Make that two."

"Yes, sir. Two 7-Ups coming right up," she said kindly and then sauntered off.

Sarah's mouth fell open.

"I'm sober, remember?" he told her, proud for the first time in a long time that he could actually say that.

"That's... Wow. That's right. For how long? If you don't mind me asking."

"Three years."

He noticed that Sarah kept her eyes from roaming around the room, and he wondered if she was embarrassed to be there or embarrassed by what she saw. There were some naked bodies now, several couples, a few threesomes, one foursome if he wasn't mistaken, all in various sexual positions.

"Not your thing?" he asked, finishing what was left of his drink while they waited.

"I don't know," she told him, lifting her eyes to his. "I don't even know what this place is."

"It's a fetish club," he explained.

"So, no holds barred?"

"Sort of. As long as the play is safe, sane, and consensual."

"I didn't know these places even existed."

"So what bothers you about it? The fact that there are naked people? Or that they're fucking in public?"

Her sharp inhale was cute.

"Some people get off on being watched," he explained.

"I kinda figured that out on my own."

"Do you watch porn, Sarah?" he asked bluntly. Figuring this would possibly be his one and only opportunity to talk to Sarah like this, he might as well ask the questions he was most interested in.

"Yes," she snapped. "Of course."

He could tell she was lying. "What kind of porn?"

She shrugged. "I don't know. Regular porn."

Dylan laughed.

"Are you laughing at me?" she questioned, her heated gaze pinned on his face.

"Nope. Just curious."

"About?"

Sarah seemed genuinely interested in the answer, and Dylan had the sudden urge to touch her. Getting to his feet, he walked around the table to stand behind her. Swiveling her seat so that she was facing the room directly, he leaned over her shoulder and put his mouth near her ear.

Goddamn, she smelled good.

"Do you watch *bisexual* porn?" he asked, turning her toward a threesome on one of the red leather sofas. A muscular guy with tats covering a large portion of his upper body was lodged to the hilt in another guy's ass, while that guy had a woman sitting on his face. Quite frankly, it wasn't Dylan's thing—the bisexual part, that was—but it was rather hot to watch.

"No," Sarah whispered.

Dylan cupped her shoulders and turned her more. "Do you watch *lesbian* porn?"

She shook her head as Dylan watched two women making out in a chair near the bar, one woman straddling the other, their lips locked together.

"What about *gay* porn?" Once again, he maneuvered her so she could see the two men no more than ten feet away, one on his knees with the other guy's dick in his mouth.

"No."

Dylan noticed she wasn't looking away.

"*BDSM?*" he asked, turning her toward one of the glass-enclosed rooms where a rather intense scene was taking place. A mistress had her subs strapped to a spanking bench.

Another head shake.

"So what does your *normal* porn consist of?" Dylan spun her around to face him.

He was standing directly in front of her now, looking down into those gorgeous blue eyes, and he wanted to kiss her more than he wanted his next fucking breath.

"Okay, fine. I don't watch porn," she admitted.

Taking a step closer, he pushed her legs apart, insinuating himself between them as he forced the sexy gold dress higher on her thighs. He trailed his fingers up her arms, admiring the ink that covered her from elbow to shoulder. Cupping her face, he held her still while he locked his eyes with hers. "But this turns you on, doesn't it?"

A subtle nod was the only answer he received.

"And you don't want to leave, do you?"

She didn't answer him.

"It's okay if you do," Dylan told her quickly. "I'll be sure you get home safe and sound. You don't have to stay if you don't—"

Sarah surprised him, placing her fingers over his lips. "I don't want to leave. Not yet, anyway."

Dylan swallowed hard. "I'm not gonna pretend to know what you want, Sarah. You have to tell me."

Her eyes never left his. "I want you."

Her admission shocked the shit out of him, leaving him speechless. Before he could respond to that, the waitress returned with their drinks, and Dylan realized he suddenly needed a minute. Being with Sarah again ... regardless of where they were... That sounded like heaven to him.

But he did have one stipulation, one he needed to confess to before they did anything more.

The question was, what was she going to think about that?

Chapter Nine

No doubt about it, Sarah was way out of her league in this club, but she couldn't help but be affected by the carnality of it all.

At first, when it had dawned on her what Bill had been expecting by bringing her here, she'd been exasperated. Then again, that was partially her own fault because she didn't have the same attraction to Bill that he possibly had to her. And she wasn't interested in sleeping with him. Not today, not tomorrow. Not ever. And certainly not here.

But seeing Dylan... Sarah couldn't help but wonder whether a higher power had allowed this to happen for a reason. When she'd first laid eyes on him, she'd been shocked. He was the last person she'd expected to see tonight, but in the same sense, he'd been her knight in shining armor, saving her from an embarrassing altercation.

Her next thought, once Dylan had saved her from Bill, was that she needed to keep some much-preferred distance between the sexy cowboy and herself. Only she'd remembered what Bill had said.

I can't leave you alone. You're my guest. Either you're with me or you have to leave.

Sarah didn't want to leave, as stupid or crazy as that sounded. The old Sarah would've balked, horrified to be here in the midst of such debauchery. The new-and-improved Sarah was eager to grab life by the balls, so to speak. She wasn't sure what she thought she could get out of tonight, but she knew that leaving wasn't her first choice. So, rather than tell Dylan that she would call a cab and go home, she'd been rooted in place, terrified to let this opportunity pass her by.

Although she'd come to a firm decision about staying here with him, it still didn't explain what *he* was doing here. What were the chances that he would've been at the exact same ... sex club?

The chances were highly unlikely, except he was here and so was she.

Unable to contain her curiosity, she turned her attention to him. "Why're you here?" she asked after the waitress placed their drinks on the table and Dylan once again took a seat beside her.

"I needed to get out," he offered, his eyes not meeting hers.

"And this is where you spend your time?"

"First time here."

She got the impression he was telling the truth, although she wasn't sure why. She felt entirely out of place with all that was going on around her, but Dylan... He seemed to fit in. And the way he'd spoken to her a short while ago ... the memory of his words made her insides tingle.

Shrugging off the sexual haze, she asked, "So why tonight?"

His dark eyes lifted to meet hers, and she saw a world of emotion there, things she couldn't quite explain echoing in the chocolate-brown depths.

Dylan took a drink, swallowed slowly, then set his glass back on the table. "You want the truth?"

"Always," she told him.

"I came because I knew you were spending the weekend with Bill."

Sarah frowned. She wasn't sure what that had to do with anything.

He must have noticed her confusion because Dylan added, "I figured I needed a distraction."

That comment brought back the memory of the night they'd been together.

Just go. No apologies necessary. I know what this was. A distraction.

Was he saying that now he needed a distraction from her? Or that he simply used sex as a distraction?

"But you're here now," Dylan said as he leaned closer. "And quite frankly, you're the only distraction I need."

Sarah wasn't sure how she felt about that.

"However, there are some things you need to know about me."

Things? That didn't sound good.

"This place..."

Sarah waited, watching the way his eyes scanned the room. When he didn't continue, she filled in for him. "You like this? You get off on this?"

His eyes met hers. "I do."

"Which part?"

"All of it."

"Do you"—she dropped her gaze to her glass—"engage in these types of encounters?"

He didn't answer, so she was forced to look at him again.

"I have, yes."

Sarah had to look around, wanting desperately to understand what he was telling her. "So, you're into threesomes?" She turned back to him. "You like to be with men, too?"

"No, I don't like to be with men, but yes, I'm into threesomes. Sharing a woman."

Two men?

Her eyes wandered again, and the warmth of Dylan's body pressed against her back once again as he turned her to face the activities taking place.

"Imagine you're that woman," Dylan whispered, his tone dark and sensual. "And that's me on my knees, my tongue buried in your pussy, licking you ... slowly."

A shiver danced down her spine.

"And the other man ...he's a friend of mine. And his sole responsibility is to pleasure you."

Sarah watched as the man kneeling between the woman's legs stood and the other guy traded places with him. It didn't take much effort to imagine Dylan's "friend" slipping between her thighs, his tongue lapping at her clit...

Holy crap.

"And now, while he's eating your pussy and fucking you with his fingers, I'd slide my dick between your soft lips..."

Sarah had to cross her legs to ease the ache that had taken up residence there. Her imagination ran wild, and she found herself wanting it.

"It's okay to experiment, Sarah," he said softly, gently. "Two men focused only on you, eager to make you moan and beg for more."

Okay, so it was hot to watch and she wasn't opposed to the idea. As a fantasy. As for reality ... she wasn't sure.

She turned her attention back to Dylan.

Thinking for some reason that she should be pissed, but finding herself more than a little intrigued, Sarah continued to sit there, ogling the scrumptious man outfitted in a pair of well-worn Wranglers that hugged his tight butt, a snug black T-shirt, and boots. The outfit, when she'd first seen him tonight, reminded her of the night he'd shown up at her house. In fact, it looked exactly the same, the black cotton molded to his well-defined chest and large biceps.

Other memories of that night emerged. Like the reminder that, by walking away, Dylan had told her in no uncertain terms that he hadn't wanted anything to do with her.

She'd been right that night. He'd used her as a distraction, the same as she'd used him. Only she doubted Dylan had thought about her since. Sarah, sadly, had spent too many lonely nights thinking about him.

It would do well for her to remember that Dylan had made it painfully clear that he had absolutely no interest in her. None. Just when she had thought they were developing a friendship, he'd gone and brought sex into the mix.

Okay, so maybe it hadn't all been his fault. Sex had been on her mind a time or two, but it wasn't like she'd had any intention of jumping him when he least expected it. Before that night, Sarah had already known how Dylan felt about the idea. At one of the CISS Friday night gatherings, during a drunken rant, one he'd directed at Alex while Sarah had been talking to Ashleigh nearby, Dylan had stated his true feelings on the matter.

If I have anything to offer at all, Alex, it would be one night. And Sarah... She doesn't quite fit the bill.

Why her name had come up in the conversation at all, she wasn't sure. And at the time, she hadn't cared.

At first, she'd thought it had been an offhanded compliment, but still... It had hurt. In her own warped little way, Sarah had come up with two ways to take that—she wasn't the one-night-stand type, or she wasn't the woman for him. Either way, she had been feeling somewhere between too much and too little for the man. But then he had come across crass, which had both pissed her off and turned her on.

If she wants me to take her out to my truck, bury my cock deep in her sweet little pussy while she rides my dick and screams my name, I'd be her man. Or maybe I'll call up Chris and we'll sandwich her between us, fuck her until she's so far gone she doesn't know her name. Otherwise, I'm not interested.

Alex's response had been: *You're a dick, you know that?*

Looking back on it now, Sarah knew it was the booze talking for Dylan. He'd been so far gone at the time, no one had even realized it. However, by then the image had been planted, immediately taking root, and for hours, Sarah had thought about little else. Hell, she'd thought about that one comment for the few months they'd started to establish a friendship. Not the one-night-stand part. That didn't do it for her. The riding him part wasn't bad, but it wasn't what she'd focused on. It was the being sandwiched between him and ... another man ... that got her all hot and bothered.

Not that it mattered.

Either he'd forgotten what he'd said, been too drunk to remember, or he simply hadn't cared, because when Dylan had shown up on her doorstep that dreary November night, it'd been evident what he wanted from her.

And she'd given it to him. Willingly.

Still, she didn't have any regrets, and she decided long ago to put that incident in the past, where it belonged. But that didn't mean she had stopped thinking about him. Not by choice, though. Actually, she'd spent more than her fair share of time trying to forget about Dylan. Only her lonely, twisted mind couldn't completely expel him from her memories, and she'd spent the past three years thinking about him, about that night, about how she wished she'd had more time with him.

However, she knew he was broken. An empty shell of a man who spent his time drowning himself in sadness and alcohol as a way to forget that he'd lost the love of his life. As much as she'd wanted to help Dylan with his problems, she hadn't been able to bring herself to do it. Not personally anyhow. Fixing herself had become her highest priority. It had required a tremendous amount of effort, but Sarah was happy with who she'd become.

Nothing had changed. She still didn't want the responsibility of fixing anyone else.

Realizing she was still sitting there, in the middle of a sex club with the man who'd haunted her dreams for years, Sarah turned and glanced around. She had no idea how this night was going to go from here, but she couldn't say she was disappointed in the turnout. No, she wasn't thrilled with the way in which it had come about, but here she was, and she knew she needed to make the most of it.

Although, there was a tiny part of her that felt bad for Bill. It wasn't that she liked him, but her compassionate side didn't allow her to be mean to others. Even though, after bringing her here tonight and all but showing her what he really expected, Bill probably deserved it.

That reminded her ... Bill was still there. Ew. The thought of doing any of the things these people were doing and having Bill watch made her skin crawl.

"Somethin' wrong?" Dylan asked, pulling her attention back to him.

"Yeah," she said, resigning herself to giving up before she got in over her head more than she already was. "I think I need to go."

For a brief moment, what looked like disappointment flashed across his ruggedly handsome features, but then Dylan masked his emotions, likely shoving them down deep as he always had before.

"I think I'll catch a cab."

"I've got my truck," he said quickly.

"You don't have to do that, Dylan." Sarah knew he'd come here with something in mind. She didn't want him to leave because of her.

"If you leave, I'm leaving anyway."

"I'm staying at a hotel tonight," she told him.

"Is that an invitation?" he asked, heat glimmering in his eyes, his lips quirking up into a sexy smirk.

Sarah swallowed hard. A burn ignited in her belly, and she desperately wanted to find a way to quell the ache.

"It won't be a threesome," she blurted.

His eyebrow quirked. "I don't require it," he stated, his tone soft, reassuring. "But I enjoy it. That doesn't mean I don't want to have you all to myself."

Oh, God. There was no way she could resist this man.

"Is it an offer?" he repeated.

Sarah considered that for a moment. She swallowed hard and said, "Maybe."

God, what was she doing?

"Good." His eyes leveled on her face. "Then let's go back there. Worst case, I'll get my own room."

Sarah knew she should simply call it a night, not entertain the notion of being with Dylan again, but the thought of walking away from him didn't sit well with her.

"Okay," she finally told him, getting to her feet.

"Did you bring a coat?" he asked when they stepped into the reception area.

"No." She hadn't had one that would've looked right with the dress, so she'd gone without.

"Jesus Christ," Dylan muttered. "You're gonna freeze to death."

Dylan signaled the attendant, and when they handed over what appeared to be his coat, he wrapped the leather jacket around her. It smelled like him, sexy, musky.

When he put his arm around her waist, Sarah sucked in a breath. His touch still did the same crazy things to her, but she knew tonight couldn't happen. Not like this.

But as they walked out into the chilly night air, she wondered whether or not she was strong enough to resist it.

WHEN THE VALET BROUGHT HIS TRUCK AROUND, Dylan smiled down at Sarah. She was eyeing the '65 Chevy the same way he'd seen her do before. In fact, his truck had been what had drawn them together back in high school.

One day after school, he'd been talking to Chris, explaining how he'd been working on the exhaust, when Sarah wandered over. He remembered the look of awe on her face, the way she had admired the truck. He'd never met a girl who was so impressed by it until her.

"You drive," he told her now.

"Me?" Her head turned as she took in the truck. "Really?"

He nodded, then led her around to the driver's side. He tipped the valet, then held the door for Sarah. "I wanna see how hot you look behind the wheel."

The smile she gifted him with made his dick jump. He fought the urge to crush her between the door and his big body; instead, he helped her up into the seat, doing his best to keep from touching the smooth skin of her trim thighs.

He watched as she reached down and pulled off her shoes, setting them on the seat beside her. When she looked back at him, her cheeks were flushed, her eyes wide.

Holy. Fucking. Hell.

"Just like I thought," he whispered loudly enough for her to hear. "So fucking hot."

Closing the door, he made his way around the truck. Dylan felt weird climbing into the passenger seat, but he had to admit, Sarah looked damn fine behind the wheel. In that gold dress, the hem resting high on her creamy thighs, his jacket dwarfing her... His dick was definitely taking notice.

Her small hands caressed the steering wheel somewhat lovingly. "I've always loved this truck. I still remember the first time I saw it. I didn't even know it was yours until a few days later."

"I thought you used the truck as an excuse to talk to me," he said.

Sarah chuckled. "Actually, I used you as a way to get to see the truck."

He laughed. Of course she had.

"Where're you stayin'?" he asked when she pulled out of the parking lot of Devotion.

Her eyes slid over to him briefly before returning to the road. When she mumbled the name of the resort hotel, Dylan couldn't help but laugh.

"What?"

"That guy's a douche."

"Thanks," she muttered. "As if I don't feel bad enough already."

"Why'd you decide to go out with him anyway?"

"I don't know." Her tone told him that she was serious.

"Were y'all dating? Be honest with me this time."

"Sort of. We went to dinner a few times. Nothing more than that." She sighed. "No, we weren't really dating. I was ... using him."

A small growl rumbled in his chest and he couldn't hold it back.

"Not like that," she said, shooting him a sideways glance. "I didn't sleep with him. I couldn't. Didn't want to. But he was nice and he really seemed to like me. Or so I thought."

Dylan couldn't ignore the fact that it pleased him that she hadn't slept with Bill. Not to mention the fact that she'd ditched him tonight. It meant Dylan had another chance with her. Maybe. Still, he couldn't believe Bill had been out with her a few times and thought Devotion, of all places, would be a place she'd want to go. Although, given the right circumstances, he could definitely see her losing her inhibitions in a place like that. But not with a man she didn't know.

Admittedly, when she'd said she needed to leave, Dylan had been slightly disappointed. Not that it wasn't for the best, because spending a night in that club with Sarah... Dylan wasn't naïve. He knew what would've happened. What he *wanted* to happen. But he knew Sarah well enough that he wouldn't have liked the outcome tomorrow. She probably would've ditched him and never spoken to him again.

"And in case you're wondering," she said as she turned onto a side road, "I'm not put off by what you told me." Her eyes darted over to him briefly. "About the threesome."

His dick twitched.

"I would like to go back there sometime. I just..." She gripped the steering wheel hard. "I couldn't see being there while Bill was. It kinda grossed me out."

That made Dylan laugh. It was completely understandable though.

He was shocked a few minutes later when they pulled into the resort, coming to a stop near the front doors. He'd recognized the name but hadn't seen the place before. It was impressive.

A valet immediately came out to greet them as Sarah was slipping on her shoes. She gave him a quick look before passing the keys over to the young man.

Dylan assumed that was her way of telling him that he wasn't leaving tonight. A good thing, since he wasn't sure he could've walked away from her right now if he'd had to.

Once they were inside, Dylan took her hand and started toward the check-in desk. "Just so you're not uncomfortable," he told her, "let me get a room."

"Wait," Sarah said, jerking on his hand.

Dylan stopped walking, then peered down at her. Her eyes darted from the lobby to him and back.

"What's wrong?"

"If they see me with you..."

His forehead creased as he tried to figure out what she was inferring. Then it hit him. He laughed, he couldn't help it. "What do you care what they think?"

Sarah studied him for a moment, then slapped his arm playfully. "I was here with another guy a couple of hours ago."

"So?"

"Dylan." The way she dragged out his name made him want to pull her into his arms.

He didn't.

"So you want me to leave?" he asked.

Her wide blue eyes locked on his face, and Dylan wondered what she was thinking.

"No," she said quietly. "I think it'd be best if you stay with me tonight."

He lifted an eyebrow.

"I have double beds," she added quickly. "So don't get any ideas, hot shot."

Double beds? That was strange considering Bill had invited her.

Unable to stop himself, he smiled as he brushed the backs of his fingers over her cheek. Her skin was so soft, so smooth. He wanted to put his lips where his fingers touched, then he wanted to trail them over every inch of her to see if she was as soft all over.

"Come on," Sarah said, taking his hand in hers. "Let's get some coffee."

Coffee? Well, okay then.

Dylan allowed her to steer him through the massive hotel to a coffee shop that appeared to be open twenty-four hours. Sarah led the way to the counter, her eyes sliding over to him every so often. If he didn't know better, Dylan would think she was nervous. Funny, considering where they'd been a mere hour ago.

While standing in line, it was obvious she was trying to look interested in the menu on the wall, but Dylan knew better. She was simply trying *not* to look at him. It gave him a minute to think about where they were and what he was doing. There was a strange sensation in his gut. Was it nerves? Anxiety? Whatever it was, he didn't like the feeling.

When it was finally their turn and the barista smiled and asked what they'd like, Sarah released his hand and stepped up to the counter. "Just a small coffee, please."

"Two," Dylan noted. "Two small coffees."

"Please," Sarah tacked on, making Dylan and the woman behind the counter smile.

She was so damn sweet.

The entire time they stood there, she never once turned her head to look at him. When she pulled out her credit card, he beat her to it, handing the woman a twenty-dollar bill and then taking his change. He dumped the change into the tip jar beside the register, then followed Sarah.

"Generous tip," she muttered.

Dylan didn't respond.

An ugly part of him wondered if Sarah had come to this exact same coffee shop with Bill earlier. He knew it was a stupid thing to worry about, but he couldn't help himself. He was getting lost in his own head. It'd been more than a decade since Dylan felt any damn thing at all, much less a possessiveness that he couldn't explain. When it came to Sarah, he was assaulted with somewhat foreign emotions. He honestly wasn't sure he liked them all that much. The feelings, that was.

In order to keep his brain occupied, he tried to recall all the things Sarah had said about her and Bill. How they'd met, how long they'd been seeing each other. Why she'd started seeing him in the first place. His thoughts were getting away from him.

"How long have you known this Bill guy?" he found himself asking while the waitress poured their coffee.

Sarah looked up at him for the first time since they'd stepped into the coffee shop, her blue eyes checking him out, probably trying to figure out why he was so curious. Truth was, he didn't even know.

"About five months."

Five months was a long damn time. Hell, it was three months longer than they'd dated in high school. Then again, two months was an eternity to a hormonal teenager.

"But you haven't slept with him?" he asked, taking both cups of coffee the woman handed over before turning toward the small counter holding the various accoutrements for customers to use to fix up their beverage of choice.

"Keep your voice down," she warned, glancing around.

There was no one else there except for the two of them, but he smiled anyway. "I'll try."

"And, no," she replied, a little too defensively. "I haven't slept with him."

"Why not?"

"Are you serious?" she questioned softly.

"As a heart attack."

"I didn't like him like that."

"But you liked him enough to let him surprise you by taking you to a sex club?"

Her eyes narrowed on him and Dylan knew he was pushing too far. Maybe he was the nervous one.

Sarah tore open two packets of Equal, then dumped the contents into her cup. "You really want to get into this now?"

Not really, but for some damn reason, he couldn't help himself. "Yeah. I do."

"Why do you care, Dylan?"

Okay, so he'd definitely pushed too far. He'd gone and pissed her off.

"I don't know," he admitted, sipping his coffee. It was true. He had no fucking clue why he cared, but he did. He cared a hell of a lot more than he'd ever expected to.

Her hands stilled as she poured creamer into her coffee. "He was a nice guy. I thought if I got to know him things might ... progress." After picking up her coffee, she left the small coffee shop and went back out into the main part of the hotel.

Dylan followed. "But they didn't," he muttered. "You were just leading him on?"

"What?" Sarah turned to face him, stopping so fast he nearly stumbled into her.

"You heard me," he said, that strangely jealous feeling gripping his insides. "Was it because of me?"

Shit. He hadn't meant to say that, but he wanted to know. No, the truth was, he wanted her to tell him that, yes, she hadn't been with Bill because of him. It was a completely absurd thing to want to hear, but the primal part of him needed to.

"What do you want from me, Dylan?" There was a banked fury dancing in the pretty blue eyes staring back at him. "Are you trying to piss me off?"

"Maybe."

Damn it. Again, he hadn't meant to say anything.

He was so out of practice when it came to women. Leave it to him to royally fuck up a perfectly good evening.

"Why?" She sounded pissed.

"I don't fucking know," he huffed.

"Well, then don't." She stared at him for a moment. "You know what? I think this was a mistake." Sarah stormed off, rushing to the bank of elevators that led to the hotel floors, but not before Dylan saw tears in her eyes.

Jesus Christ. What the hell was wrong with him?

Just when the elevator doors would've closed, leaving him behind, Dylan stuck his arm between them, keeping them from shutting all the way. He joined her inside, never taking his eyes off her. Regrettably, there were three other people on the elevator, so she wouldn't have to talk to him and he wouldn't get the chance to apologize for his less than stellar behavior.

Damn, he sure knew how to derail a perfectly good night.

The tension in the small space increased with every passing floor. They stopped twice, allowing two of the occupants off, and then finally they reached the twentieth floor. Her floor, he assumed.

Before the doors had even fully opened, Sarah exited, and he said a quick good night to the elderly man still on the elevator before slipping out behind her. By the time she was halfway down the long hallway, Dylan was keeping pace beside her, not saying a word.

"What do you want?" she hissed as she ran the key card through the door reader and then pushed open her door. "I don't have anything to say to you." Without a second glance, she stomped inside, allowing the door to close behind her as she went to the dresser and set her coffee cup down. He was clearly being dismissed.

Or he would've been if he hadn't pretended to ignore her obvious attempt to brush him off. He wasn't about to let her shut him out. Not yet anyway.

Although he'd said far more than he'd intended to tonight, he knew this conversation was a long time coming. What had happened between them three years ago... It was obvious he wasn't the only one who remembered that night. Those emotions she evoked in him weren't easy to push aside, even though he'd been doing so for longer than he cared to admit.

Now, it was time they faced the music and figured out once and for all where, if anywhere, this thing between them was headed. As much as he wanted to indulge himself for one night with Sarah, Dylan knew that wasn't him. He wanted more than one night. A hell of a lot more.

Not making a sound, he allowed the door to close behind him, then set his coffee cup on the bathroom counter. He stood there, staring at her as she inhaled deeply, then released the breath slowly, her shoulders squaring.

He was pretty sure she thought he'd stayed out in the hall.

Dylan watched as she picked up her coffee, took a sip, then turned around. He met her gaze, held it. He sensed that she was surprised to see him standing there, but she didn't say as much. Anger ignited in her eyes, and he knew she was fighting back the frustration. He couldn't blame her.

Yet he couldn't help but think that she was so damn cute when she was pissed.

Then it hit him. Just as she'd mentioned earlier, there were two beds in this room. "Why do you have your own room? Why weren't you staying with Bill?" he asked when he didn't notice anything that could possibly belong to a man.

Glancing around, it looked as though she was trying to figure out how he would know that.

"Only girl stuff in there," he said, nodding toward the bathroom. "Don't forget that you invited me to stay." He glanced at the second bed.

"You're into threesomes, remember?" she countered hotly.

So she was feisty. He liked that. Dylan cocked an eyebrow before stalking her across the room.

Her eyes flared and she took a step backward. Dylan took Sarah's coffee cup from her hand and set it on the dresser, moving closer.

It was now or never. "Have you been with anyone since me?"

Yes, he was fully aware how arrogant the question was, but he wanted to know. It was imperative that he know. He didn't understand the reasoning behind it, but the primal beast inside of him was roaring to life.

That banked fury ignited in her eyes, but Dylan ignored it. He didn't care if she was angry; he wanted to know the answer to his question. He moved closer.

"Tell me," he insisted, closing the rest of the gap between them

Sarah backed up again until she had nowhere to go.

In the next instant, he was up against her, his body pressing into hers. God, she smelled so fucking good. Like roses and sunshine. He planted his palms on the wall on each side of her head and continued to stare down at her, the hard ridge of his erection pressed intimately against her belly as he slid one knee between her legs.

"What are you doing?" she whispered, a sexy rasp accompanying the words.

"What does it look like?" He kept his voice low, even.

"It looks like you're bein' an ass," she said. "I think it's best if you leave."

"I don't want to leave, Sarah." His tone gentled even more, his eyes as well.

"Your mood swings are gonna give me whiplash," she announced, her lips pursed.

Her hands flattened on his chest and she pushed, but Dylan didn't budge.

He couldn't. He finally had her right where he wanted her; the last thing he intended to do was to walk away again.

"Now answer my question."

Chapter Ten

As he stood there, staring down at Sarah's surprised features, Dylan realized this night wasn't going exactly the way he had expected it to.

Eh. He hadn't really known how it would go, truthfully. And never could he have predicted that he'd go to Devotion and end up in a hotel room with a woman he hadn't stopped thinking about for nearly three years.

Amend that—a pissed off woman he hadn't stopped thinking about.

No doubt, Sarah was working up a good mad, but she hadn't yelled at him yet. He was beginning to wonder if she was even capable of it. Lord knew she had every reason to be angry with him. Not only for his recent behavior but also for what he'd done years ago.

He'd somehow let his emotions build up and now he was taking it out on her. She didn't deserve this crap from him, but Dylan didn't know what else to do. Was there a better way to handle this situation? Undoubtedly. Would he change the way it had played out so far? Maybe a little.

The fact that he was in a hotel room with Sarah Davis should've been enough for him.

But it wasn't. Not by a long shot.

Backing away from her when she made another weak attempt at pushing him away, Dylan allowed his hands to fall to his sides.

"Why won't you answer the damn question?" he asked.

"Because it doesn't matter," she snapped.

"What's really goin' on with you and Bill?"

It seemed downright strange that a man would invite a woman on a weekend getaway only to get two separate rooms and then surprise her with an impromptu trip to a sex club. Without ever having sex with her before? Either the dude really was a dumb ass or there was more to this story than Sarah was letting on.

Then again, Dylan was being a special form of dumb ass by continuing to press the issue, but that possessive side of him wanted to know that she was his for the taking. Because he had every intention of taking her. However, he wanted her to confirm that whatever had been between her and Bill was no longer standing between them before he made his move.

Sarah sighed, then moved toward the bed and flopped down on the edge. "You're not gonna let this go, are you?"

Dylan didn't say a word, simply continued to watch her.

Sarah's shoulders sagged a little. "Like I told you, I've been seein' him for a few months. Casually."

"Where'd you meet him?"

"Starbucks. He bought my coffee." She looked up at him, then dropped her gaze to her hands. "We hadn't seen each other for a couple of weeks when I invited him to the CISS party. I knew I couldn't handle seeing you, so it was a last-ditch effort to protect myself. It probably would've been over between us if I hadn't invited him then."

"Did it work?"

Sarah's eyes were sad when she peered up at him. "Not at all."

That made him feel better, in an odd way.

"He asked me to go away with him for the weekend, and I got a bug up my ass last night because I knew if I didn't do something, I would spend too much time thinking about..." She looked at him, but she didn't finish the sentence. Dylan didn't need her to. He knew what she was referring to. "Next thing I knew, I had agreed and he was picking me up this morning." Sarah's gaze lowered to her hands. "I was tryin' to come up with a way to back out when you showed up at my house. But then when I saw you, I knew I couldn't. Back out. I needed to move forward." She sighed deeply.

"So you went because of me?"

"No," she answered quickly. "I went because of *me*."

"So you've never slept with him, yet you decided to go to a hotel with him? For the weekend?"

"I didn't actually know he was taking me to a hotel."

"But you knew he was taking you somewhere. Did you think the guy was gonna get a tent? What the hell, Sarah?"

Sarah rolled her eyes. "Okay, so maybe I knew deep down. I just needed"—her eyes softened—"a distraction."

He swallowed hard. A distraction.

That word was being thrown around way too much for his liking.

At one time, he'd been her distraction and she'd been his. At least in her version of things.

"Not the smartest decision I've ever made, I know," Sarah continued. "When we got here, I told him I wanted separate rooms. He said he'd thought ahead and he got me my own room, but he'd been hoping I would stay with him."

"Did he pay for this?" If she said yes, Dylan was going to march his happy ass right down to the check-in desk and make sure they changed the credit card on file. No way was he sleeping in a room that douche paid for.

"He tried. I slipped down and put it on my card. I didn't want him paying for anything for me, because I was planning to tell him that we could only be friends, but I hadn't gotten around to it. I felt guilty for leading him on." She glanced down at her hands. "I'm a chicken, I know."

"Friends," Dylan muttered. "That's a mighty swift kick to the ego, Sarah. And you were gonna tell him tonight? Before or after the club?"

Her shoulders stiffened. "I didn't know about the club until we got there."

"So it's over between you and Bill?" he asked directly, wanting to get to the point. "That's what I need to know. Are you and Bill over?"

A small smile curled the edge of her lips. "There wasn't anything between us, Dylan. Regardless, if there was, I think it's safe to assume I'm done with him."

Dylan took a step closer to the bed, stopping directly in front of her, then tilting her chin up with his finger, forcing her to look at him. "I don't want you to assume, Sarah. I need you to tell me that it's over."

She frowned, her eyes raking over his face. Finally, Sarah nodded. "It's over. Is that what you want to hear?"

He released a breath, feeling lighter although he wasn't even sure why. "It is, yes."

"Why?"

Dylan slid his thumb over her lower lip. He wanted to kiss her, to put his lips over hers and inhale her sigh. To taste her sweetness on his tongue, to feel the warmth of her mouth. To lay her back and cover her with his body, to slide deep inside her and make her cry out for him and only him. Never again did he want to hear another man's name pass her lips. Certainly not Bill's.

He took a step back. "So what now?"

Sarah shrugged.

All the fight seemed to drain out of him, so Dylan joined her on the bed, sitting a few inches away from her.

The two of them sat in silence for several minutes. Dylan resisted the urge to touch her, to put his hand on her thigh, to lean over and press his mouth to hers. She was still wearing his jacket, and for whatever reason, he found that sexy as hell. He wanted her so fucking bad it hurt, but until he could figure out where they stood and which direction they would be heading, he knew pursuing more was a bad idea.

"Why'd you show up at my house this morning?" she asked, breaking the thick silence.

He weighed his answer before he spoke. The last thing he wanted to do was to lie to her. "Jake mentioned he was going to cat sit for you because you were going away with Bill for the weekend," he finally said, not looking at her. "I got jealous."

The mattress shifted when she jerked her head toward him. "Jealous?"

Dylan nodded.

"*Really?*"

Okay, it wasn't *that* hard to believe.

Wringing his hands in his lap, Dylan thought about all the things he'd wanted to say to her, but he didn't know which part to start with. This was new for him. Confusing as hell to boot. Yes, he'd been jealous. To the point he hadn't slept for shit last night, conjuring up a million images of Sarah with another man. Right or wrong, Dylan didn't want her to be with anyone else.

Sarah flung herself back on the bed, staring up at the ceiling, and the shift in the mattress, combined with her new position, which caused that sexy-as-fuck dress to slide up her thighs, made his jeans suddenly very uncomfortable.

"Is it me, or have we done this all backwards?" Sarah questioned softly.

Dylan figured it was a rhetorical question, but he answered anyway. "More like twisted."

Sarah peered over at him. "Like a detour? The scenic route? From dating in high school to friends to sex to ... whatever this is?"

"Pretty much."

"Do you ever miss high school?"

Dylan swallowed hard. He figured she was talking about a time when nothing else mattered, but Dylan's thoughts immediately drifted to Meghan. He still remembered the day he'd fallen for her. She'd been in several of his classes over the course of their four years in high school, but it hadn't been until his senior year that he'd noticed her. Really noticed her.

The sad part was, his life had come full circle. He'd been dating Sarah when he started talking to Meghan. It might've only been a couple of months, but they'd been having fun. However, with that part of his life coming to a close, he knew that dating a freshman would as well. The last thing he'd wanted to do was hurt Sarah, so he'd ended things before they ever got started. And it wasn't until they were over that he entertained the notion of dating Meghan.

So yeah, full circle.

And look where they were now.

"Yeah, I miss it," he muttered. "More than you know."

When the emotion got too heavy, Dylan got to his feet. He held out a hand, and when Sarah took it, he helped her up.

She was tiny. At six foot one, Dylan knew he was taller than average. However, compared to his friends, who topped out at six six, he was average. But compared to Sarah... She didn't even come up to his armpit.

Tiny.

He liked that about her. It made him feel protective of her, as though he could easily wrap her in his arms and keep her safe. Although he doubted she'd like that one bit. The woman was fiercely independent and strong-willed, so he knew she wouldn't want a man coddling her.

"What do you say we start over?" he questioned, tilting her chin up so she had to look at him.

The question must have taken her by surprise, because she didn't respond right away. Dylan held her gaze, waiting as his chest expanded until he didn't think he'd be able to breathe.

"I'd say yes," she finally replied after licking her lips, "but I can't forget it all, Dylan. As nice as it would be to start fresh, we've both... we've both been molded by our history. Even what happened between us ... before. I can't forget. I don't want to. Not all of it, anyway."

He didn't want to, either. And he wasn't talking about all of the things he'd experienced in his life. He was talking about that one night with Sarah. Those few stolen minutes when he'd buried himself deep inside her, getting lost in the warmth of her body. In that moment, he'd felt complete for the first time in years. But the moment it was over, his world had come crashing back down on him, ripping his heart to shreds.

"So what if we don't forget?" he questioned, studying her face. "What if we ... start again? Maybe do things differently."

"You mean the sex?" Her eyes flashed.

His body instantly hardened.

"Like before?" she added. "A distraction?"

"No," he answered immediately. "Not a distraction. That's not what I want, Sarah. I never wanted that."

"Then what *do* you want?"

This was the stipulation he'd been thinking about earlier. Though a one-night stand with Sarah would definitely quell the urge, it wouldn't be enough. Not by a long shot.

Confused as to how to relay that to her, he turned away and slid his hands over what little hair he had. He paced to the window. The world beyond, though cloaked in darkness, was moving forward, one second at a time, just as it always had. And here he was, trying to find a way to tell this woman that he didn't want her to be with anyone else, but also that he couldn't make any commitments to her.

Sex? Yeah. It sounded like a damn good plan.

But even he knew he wanted more than that.

He could get laid in a heartbeat if he wanted to. Since Meghan, he'd resisted one-night stands, mostly because he knew he didn't care enough to even remember their names if it came to it. He'd reaffirmed that he'd made the right decision after the night he'd been with Sarah. That shouldn't have been a one-night stand. It should've continued. No other woman made him feel the way she did. They never would.

And eleven years without a woman, aside from the too-brief encounter with Sarah... Dylan was coiled tighter than a cobra.

"You know what?" Sarah called from behind him.

Dylan turned to face her.

"Why don't we start with dinner? I know it's late, but I'm hungry. There's a small café downstairs. They're open twenty-four hours. We can grab a bite, then we'll talk about the sex."

His eyebrows lifted. He was on board with that plan. Though he hadn't exactly expected sweet Sarah Davis to be quite so blunt.

"Dinner," he echoed. "Then sex."

Sarah laughed. "I didn't say that. I said *talk* about sex."

"I didn't know you were into that kinky stuff." He was trying to lighten the mood, and the smile she shot him told him he'd succeeded.

"Talk, Dylan. Listen carefully. Process what I'm saying." She smiled. "That doesn't mean we'll *have* sex."

"Maybe not," he agreed. "But you want to."

Her chin jutted out slightly, as though she was thinking about it but trying to reject the idea. A full-fledged grin formed on her pretty pink mouth. "It's not the worst idea in the world."

Closing the distance between them once more, Dylan cupped her face and held her there, simply looking at her. "I'm game. For both. Dinner and sex. Or talking about sex. Whatever."

A laugh escaped her as she pulled back. Dylan allowed his hands to drop to his sides.

"Good, 'cause I'm starving." She removed his jacket and laid it on the bed. "Now, come on, let's—"

A knock interrupted her, and Dylan peered over at the door.

Sarah hightailed it over, standing on her toes and peering through the security hole. When she turned around, her eyes were wide. She backed up against the door, palms flat against it as though she was trying to hold it closed.

"Sarah?"

Bill.

Great.

The little fucker must've realized she'd left the club.

The idea that Bill had brought Sarah to the club with the notion of putting her into a precarious situation pissed Dylan off. It made him want to beat the shit out of the guy. The bastard clearly didn't know how to treat a woman.

And you do?

He hated his subconscious sometimes. It chose the most inopportune moments to speak up.

Fine, he wasn't the best example, but still. When it came to Sarah, he really did want to start over with her.

Moving closer, Dylan didn't speak. Her eyes widened the closer he got, and he knew right then what he needed to do.

"Dylan." Sarah kept her voice low, praying Bill couldn't hear her through the door. "What are you doing?"

He was closing in on her, his eyes determined, his mouth holding a seductive grin, and damned if her body didn't start humming as he neared. He was stalking her, and she felt every ounce of his masculine fortitude right down to the core of her.

When he had closed the distance between them, his hands moved forward quickly, thumbs sliding beneath the hem of her dress, forcing it higher on her thighs as he gripped her hips and lifted her off the floor, her back pressed against the door. Then his mouth was on hers and she couldn't resist, wrapping her arms and legs around him instantly.

Oh, God.

As soon as his lips were on hers, she remembered how easily he could control her body with a simple kiss. Then again, there wasn't anything simple about Dylan's kiss.

A sweet heat filled her belly, her sex clenching as he claimed her mouth. There was something so ... naughty ... about him kissing her while Bill stood on the other side of the door.

Sure, it was a crappy thing for her to do to the guy who'd invited her to this hotel in the first place, but in her defense, he had ruined the night by springing a sex club on her.

"Sarah? Are you okay?" Bill's muffled words sounded through the door. "I wanted to apologize for the things I said. And ... I wanted to check on you. I saw you leave with ... him."

Dylan's lips broke from hers, trailing down her neck, leaving her breathless.

"Sorry," she called out, her voice stronger than she expected. "I..." She couldn't even bring herself to lie to him.

"Are you feeling bad?"

"No," she said. "I'm feeling quite good, actually."

Dylan's low chuckle vibrated against her neck as his lips worked their way back to her mouth.

"Do you want to go get something to eat?" Bill sounded concerned. "It's the least I can do."

"Yes," she said, gripping the back of Dylan's head and pulling him back so their mouths separated. "But not right now." *And not with you.* She obviously didn't add the last part.

"Sarah? Is someone in there with you? Is *he* in there?"

She didn't answer him, crushing her mouth to Dylan's as a desperate ache sent her nerve endings in a frenzy. A flash fire of passion consumed her and she really wanted Bill to go away.

"I ... uh..." Sarah lost her train of thought when Dylan's mouth resumed its trek over her neck. He sucked her skin into his mouth and her nipples hardened painfully. She felt the hard ridge of his erection pressing against her, and she didn't resist the urge to grind her hips, adding a sweet friction to the already overwhelming sensations.

Dylan growled quietly.

"It's okay, Bill," she finally said, letting her head thump against the door as Dylan continued to press urgent kisses along her neck, across her collarbone. "I'm good. I'm just gonna ... go to bed."

Bill didn't respond and she wondered if she'd surprised him.

Not that she cared. Sarah was more worried about spontaneously combusting right there in Dylan's arms. His lips moved up to her ear, his teeth tugging on the lobe briefly before he said, "Send him away, Sarah. It'll be less embarrassing for him."

Embarrassing? Huh? "Why?" she said softly.

"Because when you scream my name"—Dylan's words were a hot rush spoken softly into her ear—"while I'm tongue-fucking your pussy, I'm sure he'll realize exactly who's in here with you."

Sarah couldn't form words. The mental image he'd created had her clit pulsing. If he wasn't careful, he'd make her orgasm from his words alone.

"Okay," Bill called, uncertainty in the single word. "I'll go. Are you mad?"

"Not at all," she said truthfully.

"It's just... I know what I did was ... wrong. But I want us to be friends if nothing else."

She had been mad. He was right about that.

But not anymore. At the moment, she couldn't think clearly enough to sort through the emotions consuming her.

"Okay. Good. We're friends," she assured him.

Sarah bit back a moan when Dylan ground his erection against the apex of her thighs, stimulating her clit through the thin fabric of her panties.

"Well, then, I guess I'll check on you later?" It was phrased as a question.

"No need," she told him. "I'm ... good." Better than good, actually.

Did he leave? Not knowing whether or not Bill was still standing in the hall, Sarah remained quiet as she guided Dylan's mouth back to hers.

She had no idea what it was about him that heightened every one of her senses, but Sarah couldn't get enough of him. Suddenly, food no longer mattered. The only thing she wanted was to feast on him for a while, to trail her lips over every hard angle, every smooth plane of his body until he was the one begging for more.

The thought made her smile.

Dylan Thomas thought she was sweet. Most people did. But what they didn't know was Sarah had a kinky side. She didn't like vanilla sex. Although, it'd been years since she'd had an encounter that had been anything but. Actually, it'd been years since she'd had sex at all.

The last time was the incident with Dylan. Him fucking her against the wall. It hadn't been exactly kinky, but it hadn't been vanilla, either. And those erotic romance novels on her bookshelves... She read them. Of course she read them. And she enjoyed them. Every aspect. Including threesomes, and a wide variety of other intriguing situations.

Sweet she was not. She wanted this man to do dirty things to her.

Based on his admission earlier, plus the way he touched her, the eagerness in the way he kissed her, along with those dirty words he'd whispered moments ago, Sarah knew Dylan would be into it. He'd be just as willing as she was.

For reasons she couldn't understand, Sarah was ready to explore this side of herself.

Who better to take the journey with than the man she'd long ago given her heart to? Even if that exchange had been one-sided. Sarah wasn't looking for love. She wasn't looking for happily ever after. She wasn't that girl anymore. She'd known love and it had been ripped away from her without warning.

But now she was being given the opportunity to explore herself in ways she hadn't expected. She felt safe with Dylan.

And that … for now … was all that mattered.

CHAPTER ELEVEN

CHRIST!

Dylan held still momentarily, his cock nestled perfectly against Sarah's pussy. The only thing separating them was the rough denim of his jeans and the smooth silk of her panties. He prayed Bill had decided to take Sarah's advice and go away because he wasn't sure how long he'd survive this.

Bill's words echoed in Dylan's head.

It's just... I know what I did was... wrong. But I want us to be friends if nothing else.

Not if Dylan had anything to say about it.

Dylan had to give the guy some credit; at least he'd had the decency to come up to check on her. Granted, if he'd been a minute later, he would've found Dylan and Sarah walking down the hall together, and that wouldn't have looked all that good. Not that Dylan would've given a shit. The man didn't deserve her.

Not that Dylan did. He knew he wasn't a saint, and he had his own sins to atone for, but he would've never put her in a situation like that. Not without her permission and complete understanding.

So, Bill's timing had been both good and bad. Dylan was trying to be a gentleman, truly wanting to take her to dinner, share casual conversation.

But this… this was good, too.

"I think he's gone."

Dylan pressed his forehead to Sarah's, his breath still rushing in and out of his lungs. "That's good."

"You can put me down now," she said with a chuckle.

"Don't want to," he answered easily. He wanted to carry her to the bed, strip her naked, and use his mouth to explore every inch of her.

But doing that wouldn't give them the opportunity to move forward. It would simply take them back in time, and though the idea of being lodged inside her was the best one he'd had in a long damn time, Dylan wanted to take this slow.

"Dinner," he reminded her.

"No food," Sarah whispered, her hands sliding up to cup his face.

He pulled back to look at her. Her cheeks were flushed, her lips swollen from his mouth, and her wide blue eyes had darkened, the same heat surging through him reflected there.

"We're starting over, remember?"

"We can start over *after*," Sarah countered.

"After what?" Dylan knew the answer to that question, but he had to ask anyway.

"After," she mumbled, pulling his head forward and crushing her mouth to his.

Dylan was overwhelmed by her. The way she kissed him was unlike anything he could ever remember. Sweet yet eager. Gentle yet desperate.

He knew how she felt because he felt it, too.

"Please," she whispered against his lips. "I need to feel you inside me."

Holy fuck.

Those few words spoken from that innocent mouth would likely lead to his demise.

Sarah squirmed, obviously trying to get back to her feet, so Dylan relented and set her down. When her heels touched the floor, she planted her hands firmly on his chest and pushed him.

Not expecting the move, he stumbled back a step.

Her eyes darted up to meet his. "On the bed."

"Bossy," he murmured.

Sarah continued to stalk him, and he gave her what she wanted, backing up until the bed stopped him. With another gentle shove, Sarah forced him to sit down. Based on the wicked gleam in her eyes, she was enjoying this.

He watched as she easily slipped those sexy heels off her feet and tossed them across the room. Her eyes never left his.

Dylan knew there was no backing out now. Whether they ever made it to dinner tonight was still to be seen. Perhaps they'd have breakfast. He didn't know.

But the one thing he did know was that he wanted to feel her wrapped around him again.

When he'd pressed her against the wall, her soft, pliant body beneath his, Dylan had damn near lost his mind. She smelled sweet, like... Hell, she smelled like some sort of exotic flower. And he'd been drunk on it. The lust she inspired in him was more than he'd known in years, yet he had no fucking clue how to deal with it. Being the barbaric asshole obviously wasn't the way to go, yet he was so overcome with this possessive, nearly blinding desperation, he couldn't see past it.

Gripping her hips, he jerked her forward. When she stumbled, he leaned back, pulling her on top of him. Sliding his hand into her hair, he cupped the back of her head and brought her mouth down to his. The urgent moan that escaped her made his cock swell. It didn't help matters when she adjusted her position so that she was straddling him, her thighs bracing his hips.

He allowed the cool, silky strands of her hair to slip through his fingers as he made love to her mouth with his. He would never get enough of this. Kissing her, tasting her, hearing her soft, sexy moans.

Hell, he was ten seconds away from embarrassing himself, and that was from the gentle friction of her grinding her pussy against his cock.

"The dress needs to go," he told her. "Take it off."

The command seemed to shock her momentarily, but to his surprise, Sarah sat upright.

When she went to jerk the dress upward, he grabbed her hands. "Slowly. Like you're unwrapping a gift just for me."

She glared at him and he smiled back at her.

Resting one hand behind his head, he settled on watching her. As the dress slid higher, revealing the silky gold G-string she had on, Dylan's stomach muscles tightened. While she worked the dress up her body, he allowed one hand to trail up her thigh. Her breath hitched when he slipped his thumb beneath the silky material to find her wet and hot for him. With gentle strokes of his thumb, he teased her clit, keeping his eyes locked with hers.

"You're still dressed," he admonished with a grin.

"I'm a little distracted," she muttered, her eyes closing as he pressed his thumb down a little more. "Dylan..."

He loved the way she said his name, that breathy little sigh making him eager to watch her come apart beneath him.

"Dress," he reminded her.

He choked back a laugh when she practically ripped the dress off, throwing it over into the corner before returning her gaze to his.

"As much as I like the bra, it's gotta go, too," he instructed.

That took less time, and when Sarah revealed her pert little breasts tipped with soft pink nipples, it was Dylan's turn to suck in a breath. She was beautiful. Soft and curvy in all the right places.

"Come here," he said, using both hands to cup her ass and scoot her closer to his head.

As she straddled his chest, Dylan reached up, gliding his palms over her soft, smooth skin, stopping just shy of her breasts. He cupped them lightly, loving the way she watched every move he made.

"So fucking pretty," he mumbled, lifting his gaze back to hers. "Lean forward so I can taste."

Sarah leaned forward, adjusting her position again so that her breasts were at his mouth. Using his tongue, Dylan licked one taut nipple, then the other, enjoying the soft mewling sounds she made.

Though he didn't regret their first time together, Dylan did wish he'd taken his time with her. He'd wanted to explore every inch of her with his mouth, but he'd allowed his need for release to win out.

Not tonight.

Tonight, he fully intended to explore her until she was begging him to let her come.

He only hoped she was ready for this.

SARAH HAD KNOWN THAT IF DYLAN EVER set his sights on her again, she'd be hard-pressed to resist. Sure, she talked a good game, but she knew her resolve was weak at best. The man was intense, he was focused, and he'd turned every ounce of his determination on her. Her body was screaming *hallelujah,* while her brain was trying to keep up with the overwhelming sensations flooding her.

The way his big hands cupped her breasts... Oh, God. Sarah knew she wasn't well-endowed, but that had never bothered her. Based on the grunt of approval and the flame of desire that ignited in his eyes when she'd removed her bra, it didn't appear Dylan was bothered by it, either.

Leaning forward, as he instructed, Sarah sucked in a sharp breath as his lips closed around one puckered tip, his tongue lashing at her sensitive nipple slowly, gently.

Ah, yes!

When he switched to the other, her back bowed, thrusting her breasts closer, eager for him to continue. She fought the urge to grind her pussy against his stomach, but it wasn't easy. Her inner muscles clenched and released, over and over, grasping at the emptiness she longed for him to fill.

"Dylan," she cried out when his teeth clipped the underside of her breast, making her gasp from the pleasure-pain that consumed her.

She sighed when he licked the sting away with his tongue.

Time passed slowly as he focused all of his attention on laving her breasts, to the point Sarah felt she would implode. It felt so good, but she needed more.

She wanted to see him, to run her hands along the muscles of his stomach, his chest, his arms. She wanted to glide her tongue along every dip and valley of his impressive body, but he was still dressed.

Dylan released her breast, his hands gripping her sides as he urged her to sit up. Staring down at him, she planted her hands on his chest and waited to see what would come next.

The naughty grin he flashed her made every muscle in her body tighten in anticipation.

"I'm not done tasting," he said, and the next thing she knew, Dylan pulled her hips again, and she crawled forward as best she could, still straddling his torso.

"What are you doing?" she asked.

"Sit on my face, Sarah. Let me taste you."

Oh, holy mother of...!

She was too turned on to be embarrassed by the idea, so without conscious thought, she scooted forward until she was poised directly above his head, his warm breath fanning the insides of her thighs.

"How much do you like these panties?" Dylan asked.

Confused for a moment, Sarah tried to process his question. Then it no longer mattered because he gripped the thin lacey strip around her hips and tore them right off her body.

Why that was so damn sexy, she didn't know, but she moaned.

"Damn, you're so fucking beautiful, Sarah."

His words were drowned out by the sounds of her panting breaths and cries of pleasure as his tongue dipped into her folds, grazing her clit before venturing lower. The sensual onslaught made her woozy, her chest rising and falling as she fought to suck in air, trying to remember to breathe. It was too much. Way too much.

"Dylan!" she cried out the moment his lips wrapped around her oversensitive clit, suckling her until the ripple of an orgasm turned into an overwhelming churn, crashing through her. As she rode the waves, Dylan didn't let up, continuing to drive her mad, sending her higher and higher until she shattered once again, free-falling into the abyss.

She was vaguely aware of Dylan shifting her, the mattress at her back, his strong hands sliding over her skin. He didn't even give her time to come to her senses before he was over her, his mouth melding to hers. She tasted herself on his lips, and that only fanned the flames again. She fought to get his shirt off, jerking until he was helping her.

"Jeans off," she demanded.

His eyes glittered as he propelled himself off the bed. Sarah watched as he tugged off his boots, then shucked his jeans after retrieving a condom from his wallet. Sweet mercy. The man... Clothed, Dylan Thomas was sexy, but naked... Holy crap. She ogled every glorious inch of him. The hard planes of his chest, the muscles in his arms, the narrow taper of his waist, and his thick cock bobbing eagerly. She heard the rustle of the condom, and she was suddenly glad he'd come prepared, because she wasn't sure she could handle the repercussions if he hadn't. She needed him so badly her body ached to feel him.

All thought of exploring him slowly fled as he crawled back over her. Sarah ran her palms over the muscles of his back, her hips thrusting upward as though that would encourage him to move faster.

"You want this?" Dylan asked, his voice a low, sensual growl.

"So much," she whispered back.

"Then open your eyes."

Sarah hadn't even realized she'd closed them. When she forced her eyelids open, she found him hovering directly above her, his body propped on his forearms. She felt every inch of him touching her.

"Put your legs around my hips," he instructed softly.

She didn't need to be told twice. Slowly, she grasped his hips with her thighs, feeling the rigid length of his erection nudging at her entrance.

"Don't close your eyes," Dylan said, his thumb brushing a stray lock of hair away from her face. "Not once."

Nodding in understanding, Sarah raked her fingernails along his skin, relishing the growl that rumbled up from his chest.

His hips shifted and she felt the head of his cock pushing into her. To her dismay, he didn't slam into her. No, Dylan tortured her with a sensual, slow pace while he continued to watch her, their eyes locked together as he claimed her body with his.

"Sarah."

There was a reverence in his tone that made her briefly wonder where this was taking them. Though she'd been all for the explosive sexual romp they'd had years ago, this was so much more than that.

"Fuck," Dylan groaned. "You feel so good."

He was filling her, stretching her, igniting all the dormant nerve endings that had gone unused for years, and she needed more. Jerking her hips, trying to lodge him in deeper, Sarah huffed when he pulled his hips back.

His strained chuckle made her smile, despite the fact he was driving her to madness.

"More," she pleaded.

"Tell me," Dylan encouraged.

Sarah wasn't sure what he wanted to hear, but her body was aching for the pleasure only he could bring her, so she didn't falter when she said, "I need you to fuck me. Hard."

His eyes flashed, something dark and possessive that sent a shiver of need racing down her spine.

Then Dylan shifted his arm so that he was resting on it while one hand reached for the metal headboard attached to the wall. Then he slammed forward, using the driving force of his hips coupled with the pull of his arm so that he was impaling her deeper. He never pulled out, never withdrew completely, but he managed to fuck her so perfectly Sarah knew she would never be the same.

And for now, she didn't even care.

CHAPTER TWELVE

THE ONLY THING DYLAN FELT WAS THE glorious way Sarah's body hugged his. Her arms around his neck, her legs around his hips, her pussy gripping his cock. It was heaven and hell. The pleasure was so intense he didn't want it to end, but the urge to come was blinding him, making him delirious.

Rolling his hips forward, then back, Dylan continued to glide through her slickness, the smooth walls of her pussy stroking him, squeezing him. He savored every sexy moan, the bite of her fingernails raking down his back, the seductive glimmer in her eyes as she stared back at him.

"Sarah." He wasn't going to be able to hold back for much longer. As much as he wanted this to last all fucking night, he was nearing the edge, ready to launch himself over. "Come for me, Sarah."

With his eyes locked with hers, he saw the passion that swirled in the ocean-blue depths. She was close, but she was holding back the same way he was, wanting to cherish every second. There would be more, he had no doubt, but for now, he couldn't hold off his release.

"Oh, fuck, baby," he growled, his chest tightening, his cock pulsing. "Do that again… Squeeze my dick, Sarah." He growled, the feeling fucking phenomenal. "Oh, yeah. Shit… Gonna … come."

Gritting his teeth, he fought the urge, but when Sarah's thighs tightened on his hips, her pussy clasping down on him, the effort was futile.

Sarah's strangled cry was all it took to send him soaring, his release tearing through him. He grunted and groaned as the pleasure-pain took root, battering him from the inside out. And then, just as fast as it had started, it was over.

Dylan remained right where he was, lodged inside her, staring down at Sarah's beautiful face. She was smiling up at him, her smooth hands sliding up and down his biceps. He was trying to come up with the right words to say when her sweet voice broke the silence.

"That was a good start," she whispered.

He barked a laugh, his cock twitching inside her. And when she began to laugh, her muscles clasping his already sensitive dick, he had to pull out of her.

Dropping onto his back, he stared up at the ceiling as he tried to catch his breath. "What now?"

"I'd say we do that again," she said, propping up on one elbow. "But I think you'll need some time to recuperate. You're what? Forty-two? You need, like, two minutes for every year?"

God, he liked this woman. She made him laugh.

"Just a few minutes," he told her.

"In the meantime," Sarah said, climbing out of bed and heading for the dresser, "I say we grab some food."

"Room service," he muttered, not sure his legs were strong enough to carry him back downstairs.

"Good idea."

Dylan stayed where he was, distracted by the sight of her getting dressed. He watched as she pulled on a pair of pink boy shorts and a T-shirt before bounding over to the small desk and grabbing the menu.

When she crawled up on the bed, he held up a finger. "Hold that thought."

Forcing his legs over the edge of the bed, he managed to get to his feet. Once in the bathroom, he closed the door, disposed of the condom, and then went to the sink. Staring at himself in the mirror, he waited for the regret that he expected to hit him, but it never came.

Unlike last time, Dylan didn't feel bad about what they'd done. He felt ... alive. For the first time in a long time, he felt good. Back to the land of the living, no longer stuck in a time warp of despair and misery. Sarah had brought light back into his life and he wanted more of it. He wanted enough to push out all the shadows that had haunted him for so long. He needed her in a way he hadn't needed anyone. Ever.

That thought scared him because he had needed Meghan. She'd been his wife, his lover, his best friend.

But he wasn't trying to compare the two women. Not even close. Sarah was... Damn. She was beauty and light, laughter and joy. She made him want things he never thought he'd want again. And he couldn't regret that. Not even for a second.

Not wanting to keep her waiting, he splashed water on his face, rinsed his mouth with the mouthwash she had on the counter, and returned to find her sitting on the bed, the menu laid out before her.

"You okay?" she asked, her eyes meeting his. There was concern in her gaze, confusion.

He knew she probably expected him to break down the way he had last time. It still embarrassed him, but he wasn't going to allow the memories of the past to intervene tonight. This was new for them. He wanted to move forward, not go back. And the only way to do that was to start over.

Glancing down at his spent cock, he willed the damn thing to come back to life, but it was clearly tired. Not that he blamed it. Sarah was something else. She made him feel more than he expected, and he wasn't merely referring to the sex.

"Yeah, but now I'm starving."

"Me, too." Her eyes flashed and he could see the relief there.

Flopping onto the bed, he reached for her, pulling her on top of him as she giggled in surprise. Cupping her perfect little ass, he pulled her close.

"Kiss me," he said softly.

She studied him for a moment, but then her mouth hesitantly met his in a kiss so fucking sweet Dylan's heart skipped a beat. This was new and exciting, but beyond that, he knew that there was something more than physical attraction between the two of them. Perhaps that was what made it so amazing.

Whatever it was, he didn't ever want this night to end. But since he knew it eventually would, he decided to make the best of it.

SARAH COULD GET USED TO THIS. LYING in Dylan's arms, feeling the warmth of his skin against hers, the sound of his heart beating against her ear.

After they'd made out a little more, she managed to slip out of his arms and order room service. While they waited for the food to be delivered, Dylan had surfed the channels on the hotel television, finally turning it off when the knock sounded on the door. They then ate while they talked, mostly about what Devotion was and how it had come about. He had informed her that his friend Luke advised him to contact Trent Ramsey regarding another club potentially opening up in the Dallas area. Of course, Sarah had to fangirl a little because Trent freaking Ramsey, hello!

"So are you gonna do it? Talk to him?"

Dylan nodded. "Yeah. What could it hurt? At the very least, it'd be a good investment."

"So, you're really leaving CISS?"

He took a deep breath, let it out slowly. "I need to do something else, to let that part of my past go. The longer I try to hold on, the more I delay the inevitable. Once they're bought out, Alex will be fine. And yeah, I'm interested in what Trent has to say. Luke mentioned he's looking for someone to manage the place as well."

"So you'd invest and work there?"

"If things work out, probably."

Sarah considered that for a moment. "Do you think we could go back to Devotion?"

Dylan's eyes searched her face. "If you want, sure."

There were a lot of things she wanted. Some of which she hadn't even known about, but Sarah wanted to experience these things with Dylan. Who knew where this thing between them was going, and she wasn't even eager to find out. Sarah simply wanted to live life to the fullest, to ride this out for as long as she could.

Once they were all talked out, they had made love once more, and that was how she ended up here, lying beside this man in the darkened room.

"What're you thinkin' about?" Dylan whispered, his lips brushing her forehead.

"Nothing much. You?"

"Too tired to think," he answered with a yawn.

"Am I keeping you up?" she asked teasingly. Sarah had purposely kept her hands from trailing all over his sinful body, not wanting to push for more when they both needed sleep.

"Only because I don't want to close my eyes," he said.

Her heart turned over, loving how open and honest he was. She wasn't sure if Dylan had always been that way, but from what she remembered, he'd never been the kind to open up completely. Not to her anyway. Back in high school didn't count. She didn't recall much about those days, but she remembered the way they'd always talked, laughing, joking, making out. It had been an amazing time in her life.

But this...

She wasn't sure anything compared to this.

Her heart was still wary, her brain trying to remain in control. It was hard to do when she'd always had feelings for this man. He seemed different in so many ways, and she honestly wanted to see where this ride would take them.

Curling up closer, Sarah put one hand on Dylan's chest, holding him close as she closed her eyes. As she allowed sleep to consume her, she made one last promise to herself...

She wouldn't push for more.

If things happened, they happened.

If they didn't...

Well, she didn't want to think about that part.

CHAPTER THIRTEEN

FROM THE MOMENT HE OPENED HIS EYES, Dylan had been waiting. For what, he wasn't sure.

Regret, maybe?

But it never came. And an hour later, after they'd showered and dressed, the only thing he wished was that he had his hat. A weird thing to think about at this point, but he wished he had it, nonetheless. If for nothing else than to shield himself and the emotions he knew were written all over his face. Emotions he wasn't ready to deal with, but they didn't seem to give a shit whether he was ready or not.

Last night had been fucking incredible. Making love to Sarah, falling asleep with her in his arms. Every damn second he'd spent with her had sealed his fate. No way could he fuck this up again.

After opening the door for Sarah, Dylan allowed her to lead the way down the long, narrow hotel hallway, back toward the bank of elevators. Once they made it, he reached around her and pushed the button to take them down to the hotel lobby. He got another whiff of her sweet scent, and he fought the urge to groan. A smart man would've kept her in bed all damn day.

A ding echoed, signaling the arrival of the elevator and as the doors opened, Dylan realized they'd be alone. Once inside, he tried to keep his eyes on the doors, but he continued to glance over at the beautiful woman standing beside him until he was unable to take his eyes off her.

She'd been quiet for most of the morning. They both had been. A little small talk when appropriate was about all either of them could offer. There had been no need to talk in the shower because he'd used his mouth for other things, namely bringing Sarah to orgasm twice before he'd buried himself in her sweet heat and brought them both to climax.

"You're beautiful, you know that?" Why the words came out, he had no idea, but he couldn't hold them back. He'd always enjoyed looking at her. From her silky blond hair to her big, innocent blue eyes and the freckles across her nose. This morning, she looked more like the Sarah of old. Her hair was back in a ponytail and the only makeup she wore was lip gloss. Saying she was cute didn't do her justice because cute was reserved for puppies and babies—and this woman was nothing even close. She stirred his blood in ways he didn't think would ever happen again.

Not after losing Meghan.

When the doors opened on the main floor, he took a deep breath and followed Sarah out into the busy lobby, his hand on her lower back. He let her lead until they were once again in line at the coffee shop. Never once did he stop touching her. If it bothered her, she didn't act like it. But she wasn't touching him back.

No, Sarah stood perfectly straight, eyes facing forward, arms hanging loosely at her sides as she waited for the people ahead of them to place their orders and be on their way. As soon as it was their turn, Dylan once again pulled out money, refusing to let her pay. Once he pocketed the change, he reached down and took Sarah's hand in his as they turned to wait in another line for their order to be delivered.

This time she did react, but she didn't pull away. Instead, Dylan found himself staring down into wide blue eyes. He saw confusion there and he knew exactly how she felt. He was just as confused by his own actions as she was. He hadn't seen or talked to her in three years. A fucking eternity. Yet he'd somehow ended up in her bed last night, woken up with her in his arms this morning. It was fast, but he didn't feel bad about that. He wanted more. Wanted to spend every waking moment with this woman.

And he'd inserted himself in her life all over again, still not knowing exactly what he wanted from her. The one thing he did know ... he felt better when she was around. He couldn't explain why, but whatever the reason, he didn't care. He was tired of feeling empty, tired of not giving a shit whether he lived or died, yet unwilling to take his own life because he'd never do that to his kids or his family. It was a feeling he was ready to let go of.

And he felt like Sarah might just be a way to dig himself up and out those last few inches. Back into the light again.

SARAH WAS PRETTY SURE THAT THIS WAS what *waiting for the other shoe to drop* felt like.

As they stood in line waiting for their coffee and scones, she couldn't help but feel like she was in some sort of alternate universe. One where things happened that weren't supposed to. Like Dylan Thomas spending the night with her after rescuing her from an awkward situation. Not that she'd needed rescuing. She would've handled Bill on her own. Eventually.

But running into Dylan had been a pleasant surprise.

However, it was all unexpected. More so the way she was reacting to him. There was no animosity, no hard feelings. She was enjoying her time with him and she definitely wanted more. Not just a day or a week. A lot more.

Not that she was expecting that, but she felt a welcome churn in her belly. Anticipation? Hope? Who knew.

The question was, what did he want? They hadn't talked about anything, and though she'd come to her own conclusions on how she wanted this to play out, she wasn't sure what page he was on. Sarah figured that was something she ought to know before she got in too deep. She could tell herself all day long that she would take this one step at a time, but she knew her brain wouldn't allow her to go forward without some understanding of how this would play out.

She waited until they'd received their coffee and found a quiet section to sit in before she asked him flat out. "Should we talk about last night, Dylan?"

She was surprised to see a small smile, one that reached his beautiful brown eyes. She hadn't seen many of those from him, even back when they were hanging out all the time. But this time, she sensed there was something he wanted from her, yet he didn't know how to go about asking.

"Talk?" he questioned quietly, his attention focused on the coffee in front of him. "I didn't realize there was anything to talk about."

"There's not," she answered, sipping her coffee before looking at him again. "Unless you want to."

Based on the way he shrugged his shoulders and let his gaze stray from hers, Sarah got the feeling he didn't want to talk. For now, she could accept that. What had happened between them was a lot to take in. It would take some time to figure out where this was going. If anywhere.

Dylan glanced around. "Is this your idea of a getaway?"

Confused, Sarah looked out into the hotel, watching the few people milling about.

"Not really, no. But neither is a sex club," she admitted with a grin.

"If you could go anywhere, where would you go?"

"The Caribbean," she blurted, then shook her head. "I don't know why, but I've always wanted to go where the water is clear and the sand is white."

"Let's go," he said, his eyes locked on her face.

"I'm thinking now probably isn't the time for us to run away. How about we start slow?" She offered him a smile, but there were warning bells clanging loudly in her head. "Maybe breakfast."

"Breakfast is good," he told her, a shy smirk tilting his lips as he sipped his coffee.

Sarah wanted him to smile all the time. It transformed the harsh angles of his face and made him ridiculously attractive.

"What about Vegas?" he asked.

"What about it?" She was clearly lost.

"Have you ever been?"

"No."

"Is it somewhere you'd want to go?"

Still confused, she studied his face. "One day, sure."

"How about Colorado?"

His questions were definitely keeping her off her game, but she chuckled. It was more small talk. "I could handle Colorado."

"New York?" he asked.

"I've always wanted to go," she admitted. "Rockefeller Center, Times Square."

"Me, too."

"Are you looking to travel, Dylan?"

He shrugged. "Sometimes I want to get away, leave all this shit behind, yeah. But I never do. I'm not big on vacationing alone."

"It's not as lonely as it sounds," she admitted. "I've traveled by myself. Had a good time, in fact."

"What places have you visited?"

Sarah wrapped her hands around her coffee cup. "I went to Hershey, Pennsylvania. Last year, I went to Washington, DC. I've been to Florida and California because, you know, Disney." Most of the places she'd gone, Sarah had gone by herself. Safe places. Family friendly. Nothing too adventurous like Vegas or even New York.

"One of these days, we're going to head out somewhere."

Sarah felt her heart leap. She liked the idea of a vacation with Dylan. Some time alone, just the two of them.

She knew she needed to keep the conversation going, so she asked, "What about work?"

Dylan glanced down at his hands. "CISS is in the final stages of the merger with Sniper 1 Security."

"Oh. I didn't realize it was a done deal. I figured it would take awhile."

"It's been in the works for a long time. It's almost over. As I said, I've agreed to stay on to help Alex for as long as he needs me. There's nothing for me to do though. I think he's afraid to let me go, not wanting to send me spiraling. Truth is, I'm ready."

"But you don't have another job lined up?" She knew she sounded incredulous, but she couldn't help herself.

Dylan's lips curved up. "I've got plenty of money, Sarah. And I'm looking into other opportunities."

"The thing with Trent Ramsey. I remember." Sarah shook her head, then held up a hand. "And before you get defensive, you have to forgive me. I'm in no position to ask questions like that. I quit my teaching job almost three years ago and I've been temping ever since. I make decent money and the jobs pay the bills. I've got my savings, too. When you spend so much time at home alone, there isn't much to spend money on." She smiled. "But I don't know what I want to do yet, so I haven't committed to anything. I know where you're coming from."

When Sarah met his eyes again, she noticed his smile was wicked.

"Let's go somewhere, Sarah. A few days. Let's get away from everyone and everything."

Was this his way of escaping reality for a while? Was that what she was? An escape?

Darn it. She did not want to think like that. It didn't matter. They were having fun.

"Tell me you don't think about it from time to time," he urged.

"I do, sure," she admitted.

Could she really do this? Other than her cats, she didn't have anything pressing to take care of. She knew she could take Smokey and Blue to her mother's house and Jillian would take care of them while she was out of town. She always had Jake to help out, but she didn't like the idea of burdening him. He was young, needed to live his life to the fullest and not worry about taking care of her.

"Say yes, Sarah," Dylan whispered, leaning in close.

She studied him for a minute. Being with him last night, here in the hotel... It felt like they were in their own little world. Was that what he was hoping for? To avoid real life for a while longer? Sure, the idea sounded intriguing, but she knew that the real world would eventually intrude once again. When they got back, would he disappear?

"Forget I asked," he said, leaning back and taking a sip of his coffee, the light in his eyes dimming.

"No," she blurted. "I'd..." Sarah sighed. "I'd like to go somewhere with you. I'm not saying no. I just think ... maybe we need to take it slow."

Sarah watched Dylan's throat move as he swallowed, his Adam's apple bobbing slowly several times. He was obviously conjuring up something, but for the life of her, she didn't know what.

"I've missed you," he said, almost too low for her to hear over the muted sounds from the others in the coffee shop.

But she *had* heard him. And she couldn't believe her ears.

"Excuse me?" she asked as she leaned forward, trying to get his attention. His eyes lifted to meet hers, and she was the one who swallowed hard.

"I wanted to tell you that before last night," he stated softly. "Making love to you... It wasn't as spontaneous as it might've seemed. I've thought about it for a long damn time." He paused, staring down at his coffee, then lifting his gaze to meet hers. "I was serious when I said I wanted to start over with you, Sarah," Dylan whispered, his eyes intent. "I'm not good at this. I'm rusty in the dating department. It's been a long time since..." He paused, swallowed. "I want to spend time with you."

God, how could she say no to that? Even if she still doubted his intentions, Sarah didn't want to say no.

"That's it?" she asked, wanting to lighten the mood. "Just spend time with me?" She pretended to be appalled by the idea. "Oh, please don't tell me you're gonna talk me to death."

Dylan laughed, the sound rusty—like his dating skills—as though he didn't do much of it. "If I recall, you're the one who suggested we talk."

"True."

The harsh lines on his face softened. "I promise to do a whole lot more than talk."

"Thank goodness." Sarah laughed, the heavy weight in her chest easing somewhat. "The thought of you droning on and on and on..." Sarah held his stare, smiling. She felt lighter than she had in a long time. This man did that to her. He filled her with hope, something that had been fleeting in recent years.

"We'll see if you're complaining when we get back to the room," he said.

Instead of answering, she nodded in agreement. Her voice seemed to disappear. She was out of sorts, completely confused about what was going on here. Out of the blue, Dylan had shown up in her life again and was offering to take her on a trip. Just the two of them. She hadn't been lying when she said she loved to travel. It didn't matter where. She was all for seeing the sights, learning about new things, experiencing the world outside of Dallas. And to experience that with Dylan...

Whether it was tomorrow or next week, or even next month, she looked forward to this.

Needless to say, Sarah knew she was in over her head this time.

CHAPTER FOURTEEN

Tuesday, January 17

"SINCE WHEN DO YOU PLAY GOLF?" DYLAN asked Chris as he steered the golf cart down the narrow path.

"I don't, but that's my goal this year."

"To play golf?"

"To be good at it," Chris countered with a smirk.

"From what I can tell," Dylan joked, "you're gonna need all damn year for that to happen."

Chris grinned. "Hence the reason we're out here in January. Now get your club and come on."

Dylan groaned, but he climbed out and grabbed a club. He didn't know the first fucking thing about golf, but he figured what the hell. If Chris could get out here and do this, so could he. Then again, it was hard to tell Chris no. The man didn't take kindly to the word, and he'd been known to bug the shit out of Dylan until he got his way.

"So, where were you last weekend?" Chris asked as he lined up his shot.

"Out."

Chris's gaze darted up to Dylan. "Do elaborate."

While Chris took his shot, Dylan considered how much he wanted to tell his friend. Christian Biggs had been Dylan's best friend since high school. Through the years they'd been through every damn thing together. Chris was the one person who'd been by Dylan's side when Meghan died, helping him with Stacey and Nate as they tried to steer through the first dark, dreary months without her. The man was like a brother to Dylan.

"So, who'd you go out with?" Chris prompted.

"Sarah."

Chris frowned, as though racking his brain to put a face with the name.

"Sarah Davis," Dylan clarified.

Chris stopped and turned toward him. "Yeah?"

Dylan nodded, then dropped his golf ball and took a swing. He wasn't sure what he was aiming for and didn't really care, either.

"So, she's talking to you after…"

Chris was the only person who knew about what happened between Dylan and Sarah. Since Chris knew Sarah from high school, Dylan had been reluctant to talk about her, but he'd needed someone. As much as he wanted to share the details with Ashleigh, he knew that wasn't possible. His sister would judge him, even if she didn't want to. She couldn't help herself and it was obvious she only wanted what was best for Dylan.

"And … how'd the weekend go?"

"Better than expected."

They headed back to the golf cart; this time Chris got behind the wheel.

"Where'd y'all go?"

"Devotion." Dylan watched Chris's face as he processed that information.

"Seriously?"

Dylan chuckled. "It wasn't like that. It was a fluke that we ended up there at the same time. I only went because Alex suggested it. She had a date. The douche thought surprising her with a trip to a sex club would get him lucky."

Chris choked. "He surprised her? What the fuck?"

"It didn't turn out well for him if that's any consolation."

"So, you were her knight in shining armor?"

"I only stepped in when I saw the prick manhandling her." That was mostly the truth. Dylan had intended to interfere no matter what, but he didn't mention that part.

"So ... y'all were at a sex club. Did you get busy?"

"No."

"She's not into that shit, huh?" Chris stopped the cart near the ninth hole. His ball had made it to the green. Dylan had no fucking clue where his own had gone.

"She said she'd be interested in going back."

Chris's gaze slammed into Dylan's face. He knew what his friend was thinking. Since Dylan was thinking it, too, he didn't have to say anything.

"Well." Chris sighed, reaching for his club. "This is an interesting turn of events. But I can't say that I'm not happy for you."

Dylan glanced down at the ground. He wasn't getting his hopes up where Sarah was concerned. He wanted to spend more time with her, but he wasn't sure where this thing with them was headed.

"One day at a time," Chris stated, his tone low.

"That's how I'm taking it."

"Good. Now go find your damn ball and let's get this show on the road."

That's exactly why Dylan liked Chris. The man didn't harp on the emotional bullshit, but he made it clear that he was there for Dylan if he needed him.

Funny thing ... if things went well, Dylan knew he'd be needing him in the near future.

"YOU LOOK BETTER THAN THE LAST TIME I saw you," Elaine said as Sarah took a seat on the couch after they'd shared the normal pleasantries.

Sarah smiled. "I feel better, too."

"Did something happen?" Elaine picked up her notebook and set it on her lap.

The instant Sarah got back from her weekend with Dylan, she had called Elaine and left a message, asking if she could get in to talk to her. She had specifically told her it wasn't an emergency, so Elaine had penciled her in for today. Of course, that had left Sarah with plenty of time to go over the events of the past weekend and all that had happened.

"I guess you could say that," Sarah informed her, leaning back and getting comfortable.

Elaine smiled. "Do tell."

Sarah went on to tell her therapist about Bill and their awkward date. She told her how it started at a hotel and ended up at a fetish club.

"A fetish club?" Elaine asked, clearly wanting to make sure she heard right.

"Yes. You know, sex club."

Elaine's expression didn't change.

"Well, needless to say, I didn't take the surprise all that well. We got into an argument and suddenly I find myself looking up at Dylan."

Elaine's thin eyebrows lowered. "He was there? At the fetish club?"

Thankfully, there was no judgment in Elaine's tone.

"Yes."

"And I assume this was a surprise to you as well?"

"It was. Turns out, one of his friends owns the club. We ended up staying for a little while, but then he took me back to the hotel."

"The hotel you were staying at with Bill?"

Sarah nodded. "I insisted on having my own room. I also paid for it myself. I felt guilty because I don't like Bill that way. I never have."

"And what happened after Dylan dropped you off at the hotel?"

Sarah felt her cheeks heat. "He didn't drop me off. I..." Sarah forced her eyes to Elaine's. "I asked him to stay."

Elaine nodded. "Did you get a chance to talk to him?"

Taking a deep breath, Sarah launched into the story of how they'd gone to get coffee and then the awkward confrontation.

"It sounds to me like Dylan cares for you, Sarah."

"Because he doesn't want me to be with Bill?"

Elaine set her pen down. "Because he clearly wanted to know that you were no longer in a relationship with Bill."

Sarah hadn't considered that. She hadn't really considered anything. Although their conversation had replayed in her mind a million times, she never could understand what had prompted his anger in the first place.

"And how did you feel when you got back home?"

This was the hard part. "Good."

Elaine quirked an eyebrow, clearly wanting Sarah to explain.

"I enjoyed my time with Dylan. It seems as though he's interested in seeing me again. He called me last night. We talked for a little while."

Elaine smiled. "No feelings of guilt? Or self-doubt?"

Sarah shook her head. "No. Not yet."

Elaine leaned forward, resting her elbows on her knees. "Sarah, it's perfectly okay for you to enjoy spending time with Dylan."

"I know that."

"So you plan to spend time with him?"

"Yes. I do."

"And why did you need to talk to me about it?" Again, there was no judgment from Elaine, just genuine curiosity.

"I don't know."

"Were you seeking my permission?"

"No."

"Good." Elaine sat up straight. "Because you don't need it. You've got a good head on your shoulders, Sarah. You're inclined to make good decisions, but sometimes you think too much. I'd like to see you take this one day at a time, but give it a chance."

Sarah nodded. "That's my plan."

As long as she could convince her heart to do the same thing, Sarah knew she'd be fine.

CHAPTER FIFTEEN

Wednesday, January 18

THE FOLLOWING MORNING, DYLAN FOUND HIMSELF SITTING in a restaurant waiting for Trent Ramsey to show up for their impromptu meeting. He'd finally forced himself to call the man back, ready to talk about opportunities for a new club. As he'd promised, Luke had already informed Trent of Dylan's interest, so the call had been expected.

Dylan had chatted with Trent very briefly, but he'd confirmed his desire to talk in depth about the opportunity. He had anticipated them getting together at some point, but what hadn't been expected was how quickly Trent wanted to make this all happen. Surprisingly, the man had suggested a quick meeting to go over the details. From the impression Dylan got, this was a done deal despite the fact that Dylan was pretty much out of the loop.

"Sorry I kept you waiting, Dylan."

Dylan looked up to see a man wearing sunglasses and a baseball cap shrugging out of his jacket before tossing it onto the seat. Trent was evidently in disguise. Not that Dylan was surprised by that. The man was one of the most famous people in the world. With his starring role in an extremely popular action movie series, the disguise was likely necessary, even in the small café where Trent had suggested they meet.

"It's been a hectic morning," Trent went on to say as he dropped into the booth, casually reaching over the table to shake Dylan's hand. "Did you order yet?"

Dylan shook his head. "Haven't been here long. Just wanted to make sure we got a seat. Didn't know how long this would take."

"I say we eat while we talk. After all, breakfast is the most important meal of the day."

Okay then.

Ten minutes later, after they'd ordered food and received their coffee, Trent launched right into his spiel about this new club he was envisioning.

"I'm comfortable with the way Luke runs Devotion," Trent explained, "but I'm interested in something a little more ... hip. I know that sounds strange, but I preferred his previous club to this one."

"By *hip* ... I assume you're not talking open to the public."

Trent shook his head. "Absolutely not. But I am interested in something a little darker, more in the realm of bondage and discipline."

"BDSM," Dylan mused.

"Exactly. And right now, there isn't a club in the Dallas area that caters to it the way I want."

"So, you're into that?" Dylan wasn't judging, he was simply trying to get a feel for who this man was. "BDSM?"

"Yes." Trent apparently wasn't going to elaborate.

"What about your ... career?" Surely the man considered the repercussions of owning a BDSM club and the impact it could have on his acting career.

Trent leaned back, resting one hand on the table, the other along the back of the booth. He looked completely casual, not at all put off by Dylan's line of questioning.

"I was just offered a leading role in another movie. After some serious negotiations, I took it. That's going to eat up a lot of my time. So, if you're asking whether or not acting is a priority for me, then yes, it is. It pays the bills, and as long as the roles are still coming, I'm still taking them. But this endeavor is equally important. A lot of actors dabble in producing and directing. That's not my thing. This is."

Good point.

"So what is it you're looking for from me?" Dylan asked, leaning back when the waiter returned to deliver their food.

"Thanks," Trent said to the waiter. "I've got financial backing although it wasn't necessarily needed. I've got more than enough to finance this endeavor, but I was looking for some silent partners who were familiar with the industry. I'm venturing into an area that's outside of a lot of people's comfort zones. I want to have input other than my own. If you're interested in that aspect … as a partner … I can have my lawyer present the information to you." Trent picked up his coffee. "I'm also looking for someone to manage the club. From the highest level. As much as I want to do that, it's not going to be possible. Luke will tell you that I tend to stick my nose in where it doesn't belong, so I need someone strong enough to push back when necessary."

Dylan grinned. He could totally see that from Trent.

"If you're interested, you'd be responsible for hiring people and managing the day-to-day. We will have to vet the clients and work diligently to ensure their safety and anonymity while they're in attendance. I'll get you anything you need."

"You said you're looking for something different from Devotion. Are you modeling it after another club?"

"Have you heard of Devil's Playground?"

Trent shook his head.

"It's an establishment owned by Maximillian Adorite. He resides here in Dallas, but his most successful clubs are in Las Vegas and New York. He does have one here, but it's a basic nightclub. The other two have similar clubs within the walls, but they've also got expansion clubs, which are in the realm of what I'm looking for."

Las Vegas and New York.

"I'm not at all interested in the nightclub aspect. Too many of those to contend with."

"So, a standalone fetish club is what you're looking for?"

"Exactly. And so you're familiar, I think you should go visit one of the other two," Trent stated after chewing. "Get a feel for it. I'm breaking ground in two months. It would be ideal if you were up to speed. Things are going to move fast."

Of course they were. Dylan suspected Trent Ramsey did everything at warp speed. At thirty-four, the guy was young, definitely still a hot commodity.

"I assume since you're breaking ground, you've already got a location in mind?"

Trent nodded, then took a sip of his coffee. "I do. It was critical that I put a little distance between my new club and Devotion. I'm not looking to be in competition with Devotion. After all, I own a stake in it as well."

Dylan understood that. "That's good information to have."

"So, I'm going out on a limb here and trusting what Luke told me," Trent added. "If you want the job, it's yours. I'll get you the contract details so you can look it over. If the money's an issue, let me know. I think it's fair, but if you feel differently, I expect you to speak up."

Straight and to the point, that's obviously how Trent rolled.

"I'm interested," Dylan told him, setting his coffee mug down. "Of course, I'll have to review the contract. And I'll head out to Vegas to check out Devil's Playground to see what I'm in for."

"Perfect. I'll get you a suite at Carnality. It's the hottest fucking place out there right now. Max Adorite bought the flagging hotel/casino, changed the name, and has revamped it into one of the nicest places on the strip. Don't let the name fool you."

Interesting name, Dylan had to admit.

"I can get my private jet to take you out there," Trent offered.

"No need. I've got one of those."

Trent's eyebrow lifted, obviously curious.

"My grandfather," he stated.

"If you don't mind me asking..."

"Xavier Thomas."

Trent grinned. "No need to explain further. I recognize the name."

Dylan figured he would. Xavier Thomas was a billionaire who had worked his entire life to get where he was today. Plenty of people had heard of him.

"Again, I'll get my lawyer to send the information over." Trent glanced down at his watch. "I have to run. I'm heading to California in a couple of hours. Need to take care of a few things first. I'm looking forward to working with you, Dylan."

"As am I," he said, shaking Trent's hand as the man stood. "And I'm covering breakfast."

Trent smirked. "That's probably a first."

Yeah, well, Dylan damn sure wasn't looking for any handouts.

"Call me when you check out the club. Let me know what you think. We'll get together next week and walk through the blueprints and the design."

Dylan nodded. "Will do."

With that, Trent was out the door and Dylan was still trying to catch up with the conversation. He took a moment to breathe before he pulled his phone from his pocket.

Now it was time to call Sarah.

Looked as though a trip was in their immediate future after all.

"VEGAS?" SARAH COULDN'T KEEP THE SURPRISE OUT of her voice.

She also couldn't keep the smile off her face. Standing in her living room, holding the phone to her ear while she danced in place, she knew she looked like a loon. Still, her smile widened.

"Yes, ma'am," Dylan crooned. "You said you've never been, so I figured this would be a good time for us to check it out."

"Is this business or pleasure?"

"Both."

"So you talked to Trent Ramsey?" She still had a hard time believing that Dylan knew the famous actor.

"I did. He offered me the job."

"Wow. That's ... awesome. Did you accept?"

"I did. Well, provided the numbers all work out. But I did agree to go check out a club in Vegas."

"And you want to take me along." It wasn't a question. She liked that he'd called, that he wanted her to go along with him. Even though it felt a little fast, Sarah wasn't above spending more time with this man.

"I do."

There was a strange feeling in her chest. Her heart was swelling, close to bursting. Ever since Saturday night, Sarah had been talking to Dylan every day. They hadn't seen each other since he dropped her off on Sunday evening, but she was partially to blame for that. Once she got home, reality had set in, and she'd needed a little time to come to terms with everything. After talking to Elaine, Sarah felt a little better.

One day at a time.

Those words continued to play over and over in her head. She was trying to ensure she did just that, but it seemed as though things were moving fast.

Then again, they'd started this three years ago, so maybe fast wasn't the right word to use to describe it.

"Say you'll go with me, Sarah," Dylan said softly.

"Yes," she blurted. "I'll go with you. When?"

"Tomorrow morning."

"Wow. Okay. That's a quick turnaround."

Dylan chuckled. "When you meet Trent, you'll see that's his normal speed. Our flight leaves at ten, so I'll pick you up at nine."

"Don't we need to be at the airport early?" She knew there were still heightened security measures in place, which meant the security lines were usually long.

"I've got it all taken care of."

"Okay, then. I guess I'll have to trust you." Sarah glanced around her house. "How long are we going for?"

"Two nights, three days."

That should make it relatively easy to pack. "Okay."

"Do you need me to come over and help you pick out your clothes?"

Sarah chuckled at the seductive note in his voice. "I think I've got it covered." She knew if she allowed him to come over, packing would be the last thing that got done.

"Oh, and Sarah..."

"Hmm?"

"The club we're going to visit..."

"It's a sex club?"

"It is."

She figured it would be.

"I'm good with that." Surprisingly, she really was okay with it. "I'd love to check it out."

"Okay, good."

"I'm even willing to participate," she offered, grinning at the hitch in his breath.

"Yeah?"

"What's the saying? What happens in Vegas stays in Vegas?"

"Baby, it won't just stay in Vegas, I promise you that."

Well, then.

When they disconnected the call, Sarah once again peered around her house. She had so much to do. She needed to clean, do a load of laundry, pack. And she needed to call Jake to let him know she was leaving town. Then she'd have to call her mom, drop the kitties off over there.

Holy crap.

She was going to Vegas tomorrow.

With Dylan.

Shit. What in the world was she going to wear?

CHAPTER SIXTEEN

Thursday, January 19

"A PRIVATE JET?"

Dylan glanced down to see Sarah staring at him, her eyes wide with wonder.

"I'm partial to the private part," he told her, grinning. "Did I mention those jeans look amazing on you?"

Sarah laughed, turning away from him quickly but not quickly enough. He still noticed the blush that crept over her cheeks. God, she was sweet.

Sweet and sexy and fun. And damn, but he couldn't wait to get her alone on this plane. He hadn't touched her since Sunday, hadn't *seen* her since then, and he was itching to get his hands on her.

After they were seated and Jim, the pilot, shared the details of the flight, Dylan poured them drinks and waited for takeoff.

"Sprite," he said, offering her the glass. "If you'd like something else, I'm sure I can find it."

"This is perfect," she told him, meeting his gaze. "I don't need alcohol to entertain me."

Neither did he, Dylan realized. And it was the truth. He hadn't craved anything since the night he saw Sarah at Devotion. Well, he craved *her*, but that was entirely different.

"So, do you fly on this thing often?" Sarah asked, her eyes scanning the interior.

The interior of the jet was all decked out in cream-colored leather and rustic wood. His grandfather had spared no expense when it came to transportation. The jet was used often, so it only made sense that it was the equivalent of a high-end condominium, complete with a large bedroom, an oversized bathroom, and satellite television. All the luxuries of home in the sky.

"Whenever I want to go somewhere, yes." He smiled, then added, "Which is rare."

"It's nice. I've never been on a private plane."

Dylan trailed his finger down her arm. "Don't worry, we'll break this thing in right."

All day yesterday, when he'd been setting up their stay in Vegas, Dylan had thought about Sarah endlessly. More specifically, he'd thought about getting her alone again. It was a wonder he could keep his hands off her now. From the moment he'd dropped her off at her house on Sunday, Dylan had been eager to see her, touch her, to pull her into his arms and never let her go. It was a feeling he wasn't used to. One he'd never expected to feel again, actually. But he wasn't fighting it.

"So, there's no flight attendant?" she inquired.

"There is. Two, actually. Dave and Mindy Burke. Husband and wife who work for my grandfather. But I told them to take a break. They're in their private room, probably reading, maybe sleeping."

"Room?"

"It's small but comfortable. Like a small first-class lounge. With a door. They like it in there."

"Oh."

"I was hoping for some privacy." No reason not to tell her what his intentions were.

Sarah's golden eyebrows rose in question. "Is that right?"

Jim's voice came over the speaker, announcing their departure and asking that they buckle up. Dylan managed to relax a little.

"So, once we're up in the air..." Sarah turned her head, smiling at him.

Dylan saw the glimmer of heat, the way she bit down on her lower lip. Yeah, clearly she was as intrigued as he was where the in-flight entertainment was concerned.

"Are you teasing me, woman?"

"Maybe."

Dylan placed his drink in the cup holder, then unbuckled his seat belt. He quickly changed seats, choosing the one across from her so that he could see her better.

Sarah giggled. "Running from me already?"

If only.

The engines roared to life and the plane shifted abruptly, clearly gearing up for takeoff.

This was going to be one hell of a ride. At least if he had anything to say about it.

For a few minutes, he merely watched her, admiring the sexy woman sitting across from him. She was wearing boots and jeans and a sweater that looked as soft as her skin. Sarah had pulled her hair back in a ponytail, which gave him an unobstructed view of her neck and the hint of a tattoo that peeked out of her sweater, right on her shoulder. He remembered how she'd looked when he'd been lodged to the hilt inside her, so fucking beautiful it nearly hurt to look at her.

He wanted to take his time with this woman, but he couldn't wait to see more of her. It was probably expected that he court her, but he'd waited so damn long for her, he wasn't sure he would survive the wait.

No, he _knew_ he wouldn't survive the wait. The way she was staring at him, as though she was ready to eat him for dessert...

The plane was moving down the runway, bouncing over the tarmac. It wouldn't be long now.

"Why're you looking at me like that?"

Dylan smiled. "I'm imagining you naked."

Her eyebrows lifted.

"Which I fully intend for you to be just as soon as this plane is in the air."

A soft pink glow lit her face.

"Is that okay with you?"

Sarah nodded.

"Good."

Dylan took a sip of his drink as the engines revved and the plane moved forward. It gained speed and Dylan tried to think of anything besides pulling Sarah onto his dick and fucking her until they both couldn't breathe.

When the plane finally left the ground, he released a breath.

"Take your boots off," Dylan instructed, keeping his voice low, his tone authoritative.

Her eyes widened momentarily, and he noticed the way Sarah went very still. She clearly knew what he was up to. Now he simply had to wait to see if she was going to participate.

Keeping his eyes on her, he watched as she sipped her drink, then very slowly leaned down and removed her boots, one at a time. When she'd completed the task, Sarah sat up tall, her eyes locked on his face.

"Now your jeans."

Her head swiveled, her eyes darting in the direction of the front of the plane.

"No one will come back here," he assured her. "I asked for complete privacy, and the Burkes are nothing if not professional."

She seemed to trust him, which he found incredibly hot. Not that he would lie to her. Dave and Mindy weren't coming back here unless Dylan summoned them, which he wouldn't.

His dick stirred to life as Sarah slowly unbuttoned her jeans, then lowered the zipper, a hint of turquoise lace peeking through. He could see the hesitancy on the smooth lines of her face, but he also noticed her desire. This woman would forever surprise him, of that he was positive. Dylan liked that she was willing to do as he instructed.

By the time the plane leveled out, Sarah's jeans were on the floor beside her boots. Her trim legs were crossed, and he noticed the way she was rubbing her thighs together.

"The sweater's gotta go, too," he informed her.

Sarah smiled, but he could tell she was fighting her nerves. It was sexy as fuck. The woman wasn't used to this, but she was clearly willing to experiment. Dylan considered that a good thing because he'd made a vow to himself to rock her world as often as possible during this trip. He wanted to see how far she was willing to go. He'd seen her interest at Devotion, knew there was a devious side to her sexuality, and he wanted to experiment with it, to bring her pleasure like she'd never known existed.

Another few minutes passed while she finished off her drink, but the sweater did finally come off, leaving her clad in a matching turquoise bra and panties.

Hot damn, the woman was fucking sexy. Curvy and tattooed. His dick stirred in his jeans.

Dylan waited patiently until Jim came over the speaker again, informing them they could move about the cabin. He then made a quick call to Dave, reminding the man to give them complete privacy. He wanted to ease Sarah's nerves as much as he could, because in a few minutes, once he got his mouth on her, Dylan knew there would be no stopping him.

He unbuckled his seat belt, then went over to the bar and poured himself more Sprite. It was more to give him something to do than anything. While he sipped it, he leaned against the counter and studied her.

"Spread your legs for me, Sarah."

Her legs slowly separated as he allowed his gaze to rake over every glorious curve of her body. The gentle swell of her breasts, the smooth contours of her stomach. Although he'd liked her body immensely before, he still loved how she looked now. Sure, he would've preferred that she hadn't felt the need to slim down, but that was her prerogative. She was still sexy as fuck.

"Wider."

Her eyebrow shot up, a clear challenge in her eyes. He smiled at her, not moving from his position, wanting to make her burn for him.

"You want my mouth on your pussy, Sarah?" he challenged.

Her sharp inhale sounded above the muted roar of the engines. Dylan had to fight to keep from smiling.

Her knees drifted farther apart.

"Put your knees over the armrests," he told her.

It was obvious she was reaching her breaking point.

Good thing he was a patient man. He could wait her out while he continued to push her out of her comfort zone.

And he had a hell of a lot more pushing to do.

SARAH'S SKIN WAS HOT, AND SHE KNEW she was blushing. With every command that came out of Dylan's mouth, she burned hotter, brighter, her body taking over, driving out all rational thought. It no longer mattered that they were on an airplane, that there were people on board who could easily walk in on them should they choose. The way his eyes slowly raked over her skin made her pussy throb with anticipation, her body declaring that Dylan was in charge and she would do his bidding.

She'd never known anything like this before, and she found she craved more. It made her think about Devotion, about all the things she'd seen in the few minutes she'd been there. The way people were uninhibited, chasing their desires.

She wanted that.

She wanted Dylan to provide that.

Forcing a deep breath, Sarah propped her legs over the armrests, realizing how open it made her, how vulnerable. The thin lace of her panties did little to hide her from his hungry gaze.

"Take off the bra," he instructed.

Oh, heavens. The man was going to make her go up in flames if he kept this up.

With trembling fingers, she managed to free the clasp, pulling the thin straps from her arms and dropping it onto the floor.

His hooded eyes remained locked on her, his voice lower when he spoke. "You slay me, Sarah. You bring out the dangerous side of me. So many things I want to do to you."

Yes! She wanted him to do all of those things and more, but she kept her thoughts to herself.

She watched, her eyes wide, hands trembling as Dylan approached slowly. She could see the ripple of muscle beneath his T-shirt, his solid thighs beneath his jeans. He looked like a jungle predator ready to attack its prey.

When he went to his knees directly in front of her, Sarah stopped breathing. She continued to watch him, his hands as they slowly glided over her bare legs, drifting higher, his thumbs caressing the insides of her thighs, moving closer to where she wanted him.

When his hands stopped at her hips, she forced air into her lungs. And when he jerked her forward, she squealed in surprise. Dylan's mouth lowered, his warm breath fanning her belly, moving south until he was hovering right over her lace-covered sex.

Dylan's teeth raked over her skin, the sheer fabric keeping him from coming in direct contact. She wanted to feel the warmth of his mouth, the rasp of his tongue, but she couldn't form a sentence to tell him as much. Instead, she remained transfixed by the sight, mesmerized by her senses, everything coming together, a storm of sensual ecstasy brewing inside her.

He shifted her panties to the side with one finger before his tongue darted out, sliding through her slit, caressing her labia, making her wetter than she thought possible. Sarah's eyes rolled back into her head, her stomach muscles clenching from the overwhelming sensations battling her body. His mouth was hot, his tongue wicked with its intensity, the way he lapped at her, pressing firmly against her clit before sliding lower.

He jerked her forward again, his dark brown eyes nearly black as he lowered his mouth even more.

"Dylan..." The word escaped on a strangled breath. Electricity pulsed in her veins, shooting out in all directions as he feasted on her, driving her mad with need.

He lifted his head slightly. "I could eat your pussy for hours. Just like this."

His mouth lowered again, her body vibrating, her heart rioting in her chest.

"Touch your tits for me," he ordered, his voice a deep, dark rumble in her ears.

She did his bidding without thought, her hands cupping her sensitive breasts, her fingers pinching her nipples, need slamming into her as he continued to flick her with his tongue. Gone were all her body image issues, her modesty. Sarah had never imagined something like this, or how it would make her feel. Surprisingly, she wasn't focused on hiding from him, or even how she looked in the bright overhead lights that seemed to spotlight her. The only thing that mattered was Dylan and the way he made her body burn.

She needed to come, but she didn't want to. Not yet. She wanted to be swallowed whole by the incredible feelings he bestowed upon her. Sarah didn't want it to ever end.

Dylan added his fingers to the mix. Sarah nearly shot up out of the chair when he pushed one deep inside her. He was diligently stroking her G-spot, obviously aware of just what she needed. When his thumb brushed against her anus, she stilled.

"You ever been fucked here?"

She shook her head, still staring at him, her body in an uproar.

He teased her more, gently probing the sensitive flesh.

"Will you let me take your ass, Sarah? Let me fuck you here?"

She nodded, unable to stop herself. At this point, she would give Dylan anything he wanted. She was putty in his hands.

"I will," he declared, his tone dripping with assurance. "One day, I'm going to bury my cock in your ass, make you beg and plead for me to let you come."

Of that, she had no doubt.

"Have you ever taken two men at the same time?"

Sarah knew she should've been terrified by the idea of having two men touching her, let alone fucking her, but she wasn't. She should've been disgusted that this man would want to share her with someone else. Again, she wasn't bothered by it. In this moment, with him doing these deliciously taboo things to her body, she wanted everything he was willing to give her.

"Pleasure," he stated. "It's all about your pleasure, Sarah."

She nodded, not even sure why she was.

His breath fanned her slick pussy lips as he spoke, his words sending chills racing across her skin.

"I like to watch," he admitted. His eyes darkened even more. "I could never share all of you, Sarah, but your body... To watch as someone pleasured you, your eyes locked with mine... The thought makes my dick harder than I thought possible."

"Yes," she whispered, her pussy clenching around the finger still lodged inside her.

"Yes, what? You want that?"

"Yes. Everything. I want everything you'll give me, Dylan."

A growl vibrated from his chest, sending flames licking at her insides as he once again lowered his mouth, feasting on her. His finger began a rhythmic thrust and retreat inside her as he pierced her asshole with his thumb, his lips wrapping around her clit.

Sarah couldn't hold on any longer. Her body exploded, sensations slamming into her violently, making her cry out his name as she came harder than she'd ever come before.

CHAPTER SEVENTEEN

SHARING HIS ULTIMATE FANTASY WITH SARAH HAD been a gamble, but the instant her eyes glazed over and she agreed, Dylan damn near came in his jeans. As much as he wanted to go on pretending there wasn't a dirty, devious side to his sexuality, he couldn't. He'd restrained himself for years and years, knowing that Meghan would never submit to his secret desires on an ongoing basis. Sure, she'd given in to him once or twice, back before they had children, but Dylan knew if he'd pressed for more, she would've thought he was perverted, probably even sick.

But he wasn't either of those things. Not to say that sharing a woman's body was the norm, because it wasn't. However, it certainly was far more common than a lot of people realized. It was the very reason there were clubs like Club Destiny, Devotion, and Devil's Playground. Those places offered people the ability to explore their sexuality with like-minded, consenting adults. There was nothing wrong with it, as long as all parties involved were safe and agreeable.

And yes, Dylan wanted to explore those more taboo aspects with this woman. What it was about her, he couldn't put his finger on, but he was enjoying the fuck out of figuring her out.

After pulling her panties down her legs and discarding them into the pile of clothes, Dylan forced himself to his feet, then picked Sarah up and carried her over to the couch, perching her on his lap while he kissed her, allowing her to come down from her orgasm. He couldn't resist stroking her smooth skin, cupping her breast, all while he teased her tongue with his own. When she sighed into his mouth, grinding her ass against his crotch, he allowed himself to be more aggressive, pinching her nipples gently, nipping her lower lip.

Damn, but this woman made him absolutely insane with lust.

"I want to feel your pretty lips on my dick," he whispered against her mouth. "To watch you suck me."

Sarah grinned and the gleam in her eyes made his dick twitch.

"Can you do that for me, Sarah? Can you blow me right here?"

She nodded and he reluctantly released her as she slid down to her knees in front of him. Not wanting to wait, Dylan unbuttoned his jeans and forced the denim down his legs while Sarah tugged his boots from his feet. When she pushed his shirt up, he realized she wanted him as naked as she was, so he quickly discarded it while she leaned in and teased the head of his dick with her warm breath.

"Fuck, yes," he hissed, placing his hands on the couch cushion, not wanting to reach for her yet. "Tease me, Sarah. Lick me."

He kept his eyes locked on her face as she wrapped her pretty pink lips around the head of his dick and sucked him, licking, laving, teasing as her eyes remained on his.

She was so sweet. Tentative yet eager. The way her mouth wrapped around him, her tongue curling over his shaft...

"Love your mouth," he whispered encouragingly. "Perfect fucking mouth."

That seemed to spur her on, because she caressed his shaft with her tongue, driving him wild with the soft vibrations from her moans. She seemed as eager to suck him as he was for her to do it.

Reaching between his legs, Dylan fisted his cock. "Lick my balls," he instructed.

Sarah's head dipped lower and the warmth of her mouth assaulted his sensitive sac. Damn. A chill raced down his spine, and his stomach muscles tensed, exquisite sensations rocking him.

He slowly stroked himself, not hard enough to push him over the edge, but enough to keep him hovering on the brink. When he knew he couldn't handle much more, Dylan ordered her to stop.

"Stand up," he instructed.

He assisted her to her feet as he got up. With his dick throbbing, desperate to be inside her, he urged her onto the couch.

"On your hands and knees."

While she got into position, Dylan rolled a condom on, then moved in behind her, one knee on the cushion, one foot on the floor.

"You ready for me, Sarah?"

"More than ready." She wiggled her butt toward him, making him smile.

Drawing on the last of his self-control, Dylan lined up with her warm, smooth cunt, then pushed inside her. He was once again overwhelmed with sensation, consumed by the tight sheath of her body as he plunged in deep.

"Oh, God!" Sarah reached forward and put her hand on the arm of the sofa as Dylan slammed into her. He pulled back, then thrust forward hard. He couldn't help himself. He was staking his claim, taking what he wanted because he needed her with an intensity that scared the shit out of him.

"Don't want to hurt you," he groaned through clenched teeth.

It was a fucking wonder he had enough sense to realize that it was definitely a possibility.

He wanted her that fucking badly.

SARAH KNEW DYLAN WOULDN'T HURT HER. SURE, she could feel the sheer power behind every thrust, but she wanted him as much as he wanted her. Deep down, the man was far too caring to cause physical pain, even if he feared he might.

Pushing back against him, Sarah forced him deeper, loving the way he filled her, stretched her, brushing sensitive nerve endings. "You won't hurt me, Dylan," she said, shifting forward slightly, then back. "Fuck me."

Dylan groaned but slammed into her again and again. Every cell in her body was alive, every nerve tingling. She loved that he was losing control, that he couldn't help himself.

"God, Sarah... Fuck..." Dylan fucked her harder, deeper, faster.

Sarah kept her elbow locked, trying not to let the power of his thrusts push her forward. It wasn't easy, but holy crap, it was incredible. She'd never been fucked like this before.

His fingertips dug into her hips, his cock plunging deeper every time. She was so close ... too close.

"Dylan!" Before she could say anything more, her orgasm ripped through her, stealing her breath as she held on for dear life.

Seconds later, Dylan followed her over.

When his arms banded around her, taking them both down to the cushions, she sighed. This thing between them was shocking in its intensity. Sure, she'd known the sex was good between them, but this went above and beyond good in every way imaginable.

Two hours later, Dylan held her hand as he led her to the waiting limo. Their luggage was quickly placed in the trunk, and they were soon on their way to the hotel. She had no idea where Dylan had opted to stay, but it really didn't matter. They were here and the trip was off to a fantastic start.

Dylan leaned over, his mouth brushing her neck. "Is it bad that I want to strip you again and fuck you right here?"

Sarah chuckled. "You've got more stamina than I gave you credit for."

"It's you," he whispered, reaching for her hand and placing it over the hard ridge of his erection pressing against his jeans. "You do this to me."

She liked that she did, but she could say the same about him. Every minute she was with him, Sarah felt the heat of her arousal throbbing deep in her core. It was a feeling she hadn't felt in far too long; something she had sometimes feared would never return. Yet Dylan Thomas made her body burn. Between the smoldering gleam in his dark brown eyes and the sinful sound of his deep voice ... Sarah knew resisting him was impossible.

However, there was no sex in the limousine because they arrived at the hotel a few minutes later. A bellhop was instantly there to get their luggage while Dylan led Sarah inside to a private reservation desk. A few minutes later, they were heading up to their room.

It was hard to believe she was in Las Vegas. It was true, she'd always wanted to go to see what all the fuss was about. It wasn't that gambling was her thing, but sightseeing was. And to be able to see the beautiful Las Vegas strip at night... She couldn't wait.

At the very least, she knew this was going to be a memorable trip.

Chapter Eighteen

Once they made it to the hotel room, Dylan found he couldn't sit still. Whether it was being confined to a relatively small albeit luxurious space with Sarah and wanting nothing more than to strip her naked and bury himself inside her again or if it was simply having been cooped up on an airplane for the past few hours, there was a restless energy coursing through him. Whatever the reason, he was in dire need of something to do.

"Are you hungry?" Sarah asked when she joined him in the living room after she had unpacked her suitcase.

"I could eat," he told her, his eyes raking up and down her body. She was still wearing her boots and jeans, and he couldn't help but admire the way she filled out the denim. The woman had a body that wouldn't quit. Of course, knowing what she was wearing beneath the denim did nothing to stop the lust from simmering hotly in his veins.

"Good. First we eat, then we can go check out the sights."

"Works for me." Pocketing his wallet, Dylan followed Sarah out into the hall. "We've got all night and tomorrow, too. We go to Devil's Playground Saturday night."

"Devil's Playground?" She smiled up at him. "That's an interesting name. What is Trent going to name his club?"

"Good question. He didn't say."

"I'm sure it's going to be something devious and sexy," she stated, pushing the button for the elevator.

"Probably."

"I do like the name of this hotel. It's intriguing. Definitely makes me want to explore it."

Carnality. Yeah, he could see the intrigue in it. Especially in Sin City. The hotel décor suited the name. Everything from the carpeting to the elegant light fixtures up above was decked out in red, black, and chrome. It set the mood, erotic yet elegant. Dylan didn't know Max Adorite personally, but he got the feeling those two words could be used to describe him. Well, if those two words could be used to describe a mobster.

"Are you a gambler?" Sarah inquired once they were heading down to the lobby.

"Not much, no." With an addictive personality, Dylan knew that it would be too easy to go too far.

"Me neither."

Dylan watched Sarah take in the sights and sounds of the casino floor as they wandered through rows of slot machines, past the gaming tables, beyond the coffee and dessert shops until they reached the café. It wasn't quite lunchtime according to Vegas time, but since Dylan's stomach was still on Texas time, that didn't matter.

As soon as they were seated and ordered, Dylan found himself once again watching Sarah intently. He didn't want to reflect on everything he was feeling as he sat at this table with this woman, but it was hard not to. The depth of what he'd already started to feel for her scared him. He wasn't completely comfortable with it, not sure he ever would be. But he wasn't interested in fighting a losing battle, either. They were here to have fun, to enjoy one another, and that was what he fully intended to do.

"So, tell me more about this club Trent wants to open," Sarah urged, rearranging her silverware.

"It's along the lines of Devotion, but he's looking to cater more to the BDSM community."

Her eyebrows dipped low. "Is that something you're interested in?"

"Me, personally? No."

"But you would be working there?"

"He's looking for someone to manage the club."

"So you'll be busy with the mundane tasks most of the time." Her smile was impish.

"That's the plan. Doesn't mean I won't have time to play." He winked at her. "You would come to visit the club, wouldn't you?"

The huge smile that lit up her face warmed something deep in Dylan's gut.

"If you invited me, I might." Sarah folded and unfolded her napkin. "So what all does managing a club of that caliber entail?"

"Like anything else. It's a club, but it's still a business. There are licenses and permits to maintain, rules to implement. There're employees, vendors, customers."

"Only they're spanking each other," she said, her tone teasing.

"Probably."

Sarah giggled and Dylan felt more warmth course through him.

He wasn't sure what had happened over the course of the past week, but whatever it was, he hoped like hell it was just the beginning.

SARAH HAD NO IDEA WHY SHE WAS so nervous. Ever since they stepped off the plane, she'd been fidgeting. Once they had made it to the hotel room, it had gotten worse, hence the reason she suggested food. Right now, eating was the last thing on her mind although her stomach was rumbling.

And that had nothing to do with where they were, either. Sure, she wanted to check out the sights, explore the underbelly of Las Vegas, but her anxiety came from something else. Something deeper. Something better left alone.

As much as Sarah wanted to enjoy this moment, this man, her thoughts were plagued by her past. Dylan's past. Namely Paul and Meghan. Then again, Paul was never far from her mind. She thought about him constantly. It never seemed to matter how many hours she logged with a counselor, Sarah never felt completely whole. With Dylan, it was easy to pretend, to forget for a little while. Sometimes she could almost believe that love might be in her future.

But would it really?

Was it possible for her to find love twice in her lifetime?

She honestly didn't know.

Once the food came out, they both ate in silence for a few minutes, a million questions bouncing around on Sarah's tongue. She tried to swallow them down, but she found she couldn't.

"Dylan?"

He paused with his fork in the air, his dark brown eyes coming to rest on her face, backlit with curiosity.

Sarah knew she should let this go, but she couldn't. She had a deep-seated need to know.

"Where do you see this thing between us going?" God, she hated herself for asking that. More so that she sounded so insecure. She had promised Elaine she would take this one day at a time, but it seemed her heart was too curious to do so.

His eyebrows furrowed.

She sighed. "I'm not asking for your undying love or even a marriage proposal," she blurted. "But I'd like to know if this is going to fizzle out at the end of the weekend."

Dylan set his fork on his plate, then wiped his mouth with his napkin. Sarah's stomach churned as she waited for an answer.

"I'm hoping we can have fun," he answered, his voice low. "I wish I could promise you more than that..."

Yeah. Just what she'd expected.

It bothered her that she cared. But the truth was, she did care. As much as she wanted to pretend she could handle casual sex, Sarah knew it wasn't in her. Since Paul... Well, since her husband died, Sarah hadn't been with anyone but Dylan. Before him she hadn't been with anyone, either. Yes, she had dated before she and Paul met, but nothing had ever progressed to the point that she trusted anyone enough to sleep with them. Then Paul came along and swept her off her feet.

Taking a deep breath, Sarah forced a smile. "I could use some fun in my life." It wasn't a complete lie.

Dylan watched her intently and Sarah had to look away. She could tell he was trying to read her expression and she didn't want him to.

"You finished?"

His question took her off guard, but she glanced down at her plate and realized she'd eaten more than she thought. Sarah nodded, then placed her napkin on her plate while Dylan signaled for the check.

A few minutes later, they were stepping out into the sunshine. It was chilly, but the sun warmed her face. She started to walk, unsure where they were going, but Dylan stopped her suddenly, pulling her in close to him. There were people everywhere, some going away from the casino, others coming toward it. No one seemed to notice that they were standing there.

Sarah stared up into Dylan's face, her eyes locking with his as she tried to read his mind.

"Nothing has changed," he said softly, his fingertips pressing gently into her back as though he wanted to ensure she didn't get away.

Placing her hands on his chest, she nodded. She wasn't even going to pretend to know what he meant by that.

"Look at me."

Realizing she had glanced down at his chest, she forced her eyes upward.

"I want the next few days to be about enjoying one another. What do you say we wait until we're back in Texas before we try to figure this out? We both deserve this. A chance to get away, to forget about the present and the past for the time being."

Sarah knew that she could never forget her past. There had been plenty of tear-filled nights when she wished she could, but if she was completely honest with herself, she wouldn't trade her life with anyone else. It hadn't always been easy, but she had loved fully and been loved in return. This thing with Dylan... It scared her for the simple fact that she knew she could easily fall in love with him. Did that make her a bad person? That she could move on from Paul? She never thought it would be possible to love someone else. Not until Dylan reappeared in her world.

"Let's take a walk," he whispered. "Then we'll head up to the room, take a nap, and I'll take you out to dinner. Baby steps."

Sarah smiled. "Baby steps."

She could do this.

Didn't mean her heart wouldn't be broken in the process.

Chapter Nineteen

Dylan awoke on Saturday morning with a familiar warmth pressed up against him. It took his brain no time at all to realize Sarah was next to him, soft and sleepy. She was completely naked, at his request. They had spent all of Friday wandering around, and then last night, they had taken in a show—the Jabbawockeez, at Sarah's request—before going downtown to see the Freemont Street Experience. Needless to say, when they'd returned to the hotel, it had been well after two in the morning. At that point, they'd stopped and grabbed a bite to eat. After that, when only the hard-core gamblers were still awake, they had wandered through the casino. Sarah had put some money into a few slot machines and actually made a few bucks back, but they hadn't stayed for long.

Although they had agreed to wait until they were back in Texas to figure this thing out, the tension had still been there, despite Dylan's attempt to put Sarah at ease. It seemed neither of them could fully ignore what was going on between them. As much as he wanted to assure her that they were moving forward, Dylan wasn't ready to get ahead of himself. He wanted to enjoy the weekend, to explore this thing between them.

And in the same instance, he was ready to stake a claim on Sarah. To keep her close and never let her go. He was torn as to how to play this out, but he knew from experience that he needed to think this through, to take his time. The last thing in the world he wanted was for Sarah to get hurt.

"You're awake," Sarah mumbled, rolling closer, her lips gliding over his chest.

"I am." Dylan allowed his hand to slide down her back, easing lower until he was cupping her ass. Damn, the woman had a perfect ass.

But more than he liked the feel of her softness against his hardness, Dylan found he liked waking up to her beside him. It was a foreign feeling, something he hadn't experienced in so long he'd almost forgotten what it felt like to have someone so close, body against body, skin to skin. He could get used to this. Used to her.

"What are we gonna do today?" Sarah asked, her voice raspy from sleep.

"Well…" He dipped his face lower until he could press his lips to her neck. "I thought we'd start with an orgasm."

"For you or me?" Sarah sighed, tilting her head and offering him better access.

"For both of us."

"Hmm. An equal opportunity lover. I like that about you."

"I certainly aim to please." He trailed his tongue over her ear, then gently nipped her earlobe. "I want you to ride my dick, Sarah. Take whatever you need from me."

A tremor ran through her, but Sarah didn't move away. Dylan took that as a positive response.

He reached over and snagged a condom from the nightstand, then quickly rolled it on while Sarah shifted. When he relaxed back on the bed, he watched as she straddled him, her cool fingers sliding over his chest, her fingertips tormenting his nipples.

"I love when you do that," he growled.

"How about when I do this?" Sarah positioned herself over him, taking his cock inside her, slow and easy.

"Fuck..." He inhaled sharply, watching the point where his dick disappeared inside her sweet pussy. "I really fucking love that."

Sarah began a slow roll of her hips while Dylan admired the sexy sway of her tits. Back, forth, back, forth. The silky strands of her hair slipped over her shoulder, obstructing his view. He gently eased her hair back, wanting to admire all of her.

"Oh, yeah... God, Sarah..." He trailed his hands down her arms, her hips, over her thighs, urging her closer, thrusting his hips upward until he was lodged balls deep. "Fuck, yes, baby," he hissed.

For several minutes, Sarah blew his mind as she impaled herself on his dick, her eyes locked with his, her soft moans of pleasure echoing in the room.

"Beautiful," he whispered. "So fucking beautiful."

Sitting up, Dylan wrapped his arms around her waist, holding her still momentarily, loving the way her pussy clenched around him, the way her breasts crushed to his chest, her arms wreathing his neck.

"Put your hands on my shoulders," he urged, his hands gripping the soft, rounded globes of her ass.

When Sarah did as instructed, Dylan began lifting and lowering her, keeping her close as he enjoyed the friction of her body against his. He pulled her down harder and she moaned loudly.

"Like that?"

"Mmm-hmm." Her breath fanned his ear as she held on to him, her nails digging into his skin.

He continued like that until his arms tired, and only then did he shift her onto her back, allowing him more traction to fuck her ruthlessly. Dylan drove deep, retreated slowly, all while watching her face. Her golden hair fanned out over the pillow making her look like an angel.

"Dylan ... I'm close ... so close..."

Giving her everything he had, Dylan fucked her harder, deeper, faster until finally, they both went over together.

Two hours later, after showering and grabbing coffee at the coffee shop in their hotel, they were once again out on the street, moving from one casino to another. Sarah seemed fascinated by the various themes, and Dylan found he was fascinated by her and her reaction to it all. They walked for what felt like days, until finally they stopped in another hotel to have lunch. At that point, they sat for a while, watching as people walked by, laughing, smiling, some still stumbling from a rough night before. Dylan damn sure didn't miss those days, preferring to have complete control of his faculties. It took him a long damn time to get to this point, but now that he was here, he couldn't fathom going back there to that dark, lonely place.

"What're you thinkin' about?" Sarah questioned when the waitress returned with their check.

Dylan shifted his gaze to Sarah and smiled. "I'm having a great time."

Her smile lit up her face. "Yeah?"

He reached for her hand. "Thanks for coming with me."

Her smile was shy as she nodded.

It was true, this woman made him feel things he hadn't expected to ever feel again. He couldn't imagine being here with anyone else. Hell, he couldn't imagine feeling this way for anyone else. Maybe he'd known somewhere deep in his heart that Sarah Davis was a part of his soul. She'd been placed in his path at a time when his world had been the darkest. She was the reason he chose to dig himself out of the hole he'd buried himself in and now, here they were.

"I was thinking maybe we could grab a nap before we head to the club," she told him when the waiter returned to clear away their dishes and give him the check to sign.

"I think that's a brilliant idea."

As he got to his feet, Dylan knew that tonight was going to be a true test for them. Either she would like the club or she wouldn't, they would stay or they wouldn't, they would enjoy themselves or they wouldn't.

But no matter what, Dylan knew that the club did not define who he was. No, he didn't want to hide that part of himself any longer, but if it meant making Sarah happy, he had the overwhelming feeling that he would do whatever it took.

He only hoped he didn't have to make that choice.

AFTER A THREE-HOUR NAP, SARAH WAS up and getting ready while Dylan lounged on the bed, flipping through channels on the television. He was ready, except for getting dressed. She figured it had to be nice being a guy in that regard. A little effort toward showering and they were good to go. Little did the man know but she was slowly losing her mind because for her to get ready meant makeup, lotion, perfume, hair dryer, flat iron, curling iron, a nail file, a lint brush ... and a whole lot more. Plus, a hell of a lot of deep breathing.

They were going to a sex club.

On purpose.

Holy crap.

What in the world did one wear to a sex club?

She remembered the night at Devotion. From her fuzzy memories of that evening, most of the people around her hadn't been wearing much of anything at all, so she couldn't very well get ideas from that experience.

"Not helping," she muttered to her reflection in the mirror.

"Are you talking to yourself?"

Sarah spun around to see Dylan standing in the bathroom doorway, his arms crossed over his bare chest, his jean-clad legs crossed at the ankles. It should be a crime to look that damn sexy without even trying.

"Yes, I am," she confirmed.

"Are you at least getting a response?"

Sarah grinned, then turned and faced the mirror. "Not a helpful one, no."

"What seems to be the problem?"

She shrugged, leaning forward and applying gloss to her lips. "I don't know what to wear."

"What are you wearing beneath that robe?"

"Nothing," she admitted.

"That works for me."

Sarah chuckled. "You're about as helpful as talking to myself."

Dylan laughed. "Wear the black dress that's hanging in the closet."

She met his gaze in the mirror. "Really?"

"Yeah."

She took a deep breath and nodded. If only it was that easy.

An hour later, Sarah was wearing the black dress and her favorite black, strappy heels. She wasn't teetering quite as badly as she had the last time she'd gone to a sex club, which she considered a plus. Then again, she knew she didn't look quite as cool and collected as the sexy cowboy standing at her side, either.

Dylan was wearing a pair of starched Wranglers, black boots, a black jacket over a crisp, white shirt, and his black Stetson. The man made her mouth water when he dressed like that.

When they stepped out of the elevator into the hotel lobby, Dylan took her hand in his, and Sarah willed the damn thing not to tremble. She did not want Dylan knowing how freaking nervous she was. This was something he was comfortable with, apparently. She wanted to be able to give him this, although she had no idea what it entailed. Sure, she was a willing participant, but that didn't mean she wasn't scared out of her mind.

Okay, maybe scared wasn't the right word. More like edgy. Nervous.

The man had mentioned sharing her with another man. Would he do that with a stranger? Would she even be okay with that?

Dylan suddenly stopped, then turned Sarah to face him. His dark eyes locked with hers and she fought the tears that were threatening. She did that when she was nervous.

"We're gonna visit this club tonight, Sarah," he whispered softly, his thumb brushing her chin. "There are no expectations."

"Are you sure?"

His dark eyebrows darted down.

"I mean, you did mention you wanted to share me," she blurted, hating the tremble in her voice.

His smile altered his face in ways that affected her insides. "Not here, baby. Definitely not here."

Was that relief that filled her?

"When and if that day comes, we'll be in a place I know, a place where I know you'll be safe. And it damn sure won't be a stranger touching you."

Sarah exhaled sharply. That made her feel remarkably better.

"Is that what you're worried about?" He looked genuinely concerned.

"A little, yeah."

Dylan's arms wrapped around her and he pulled her in close, his head lowering until his lips were brushing her ear.

"I want you to trust me, Sarah. Implicitly. I will never put you in harm's way. I will never sacrifice you for anything. If you want to explore, you let me know. Otherwise, I'm going to assume we're here to enjoy the evening, and we can do that without sex. I'm more than happy to take you back to the room and strip that sexy little dress right off your body. Doesn't have to be at the club."

Sarah nodded, then patted his chest. When he stood up straight, she went to her toes and kissed his mouth lightly. "Thank you."

"Come on," he urged. "Let's take a look around, see what it's all about. You can decide from there what you're comfortable with."

Taking a deep breath and exhaling slowly, Sarah managed to calm her rioting nerves. Knowing that Dylan didn't expect anything from her tonight made it easier to follow his lead as they headed toward the entrance. They bypassed the long line that wound through the casino. There were people of all different shapes, sizes, and colors waiting to go inside. Some appeared frustrated by the wait; others were making the best of it, joking and laughing.

When they reached the bouncer, Dylan gave the man his name, and they were waved through with instructions to head up to the VIP lounge.

Sarah paused as soon as they stepped into the main club. She couldn't help but look around. It was relatively early by Vegas standards, but the people at the club didn't seem to notice. Then again, there were no windows in there or in the casino, so it was hard to tell what time it was at any point in the day or night. There were hundreds of people scattered about. Some standing at the high tables, drinking and talking. Others on the dance floor grinding against one another. There were two additional levels, both of which had leather seating and people filling every square inch.

"This is the main club," Dylan spoke into her ear. "Let's go to the VIP area."

Sarah nodded, then allowed him to direct her toward an elevator, where another bouncer was standing. Dylan again introduced himself and the man checked a sheet of paper on a clipboard before hitting the button to open the elevator doors.

When they stepped out into the VIP area, Sarah instantly noted the difference. Where the main club was lit with strobe lights, this one had dim red lights throughout. There was a long bar on one side and plenty of available seating. Along the walls there were sections separated by sheer curtains. The music wasn't quite as loud, but the bass was just as deep, reverberating off the walls and the ceiling, making her insides rattle.

Dylan took her hand and led her to one of the sectioned-off areas. It was more like a room, really. There was a long leather couch with chaise lounges on each end and a glass table in front. There was also another bouncer standing sentry at the front, obviously keeping an eye on things.

Once they were seated, a waitress came in and took their drink orders.

"7-Up," Sarah told her. "For both of us."

"Also," Dylan added, "if you wouldn't mind, we'd like to let Isaiah Fontenot know that we're here."

"Yes, sir."

The woman disappeared and Sarah turned to Dylan. "Is he the club manager?"

Dylan nodded. "Trent texted me this morning to let me know Isaiah wanted to meet us."

"Really?"

Dylan smirked. "Turns out, Max Adorite, who owns this place, is a silent investor in Trent's upcoming venture."

"Ah. Okay then."

Sarah managed to relax. If this was going to be mostly about work, she figured she had absolutely nothing to worry about.

Funny, that should've made her feel better.

Surprisingly, she was a tad bit disappointed.

CHAPTER TWENTY

DYLAN KEPT HIS CONVERSATION WITH ISAIAH TO small talk. The man had informed Dylan that he'd been managing the club for a few years now and only recently had Max finished remodeling the hotel and casino. According to Isaiah, he shared the management duties with his twin brother, Micah, and they also worked close with the club managers in New York. If Dylan understood correctly, Isaiah was letting him know that two was better than one when it came to taking on a task that size.

For the full half hour he'd spent chatting, Dylan had watched Sarah. She seemed comfortable here. More so than she'd been at Devotion. He wasn't sure why that was. Perhaps it was because there was the illusion of privacy with all the sectioned-off seating. Then again, there were plenty of open areas where things were beginning to ignite quickly.

"Well, I'll leave you two to it," Isaiah said, getting to his feet. "It was a pleasure meeting you, and if you have any questions, feel free to call me any time."

Dylan took the card that Isaiah held out to him.

"That's my cell phone number and my brother's is on there as well. We'll be glad to help out if you need us, but I'm sure you'll do fine."

Shaking Isaiah's proffered hand, Dylan said good night and then waited until he was alone with Sarah once again.

"What do you think?" she asked when he turned to face her.

"About?"

"About this place? Managing something like this?"

Dylan glanced around.

He liked the idea of managing a club, knew he could handle the task. For one, he needed something to occupy his time, to keep him busy. Something of this nature would definitely do that. It would give him another chance, something he honestly hadn't thought he would get. He was still on the fence as to whether he deserved it or not.

"It seems doable," he answered nonchalantly.

Sarah grinned. "Yeah?" She moved closer. "Do you think you could handle seeing scantily clad women all night and day?"

Dylan nuzzled her neck. "Darlin', there's only one scantily clad woman I care to look at. I assure you that."

Sarah pulled back and stared at him. He could tell she was processing his words and probably wasn't sure whether to believe him or not.

He figured it was best to show her.

Getting comfortable on the couch, Dylan held out his hand to her. "Come here."

She inched closer.

"On my lap," he instructed. "Facing me."

He couldn't hide his amusement when Sarah glanced down at her short skirt. Yeah, she knew what would happen when she straddled him. Which had been his point exactly.

Dylan recognized the heat in her eyes. She was going to accept his dare.

A few seconds later, Sarah was straddling his thighs, the stretchy fabric of her dress still hiding her ass from anyone looking in on them, but it had ridden high on her thighs, revealing the black silk beneath.

"There's something you need to know about a place like this," he explained, sliding his fingers along the sleek column of her neck, trailing over her collarbone. He urged the strap of her dress down her arm, noticing the way her nipples pebbled beneath the fabric.

"What's that?" she asked breathlessly.

"People are here for various reasons," he noted.

"Such as?"

Dylan watched Sarah's face as he freed one breast from the restricting fabric, his thumb gliding over her nipple. She wasn't wearing a bra, which made it easier for him to tease her.

"Some like to come to watch."

Sarah's hand tightened on his bicep when he flicked her nipple with his fingernail.

"Some like to be watched."

"Which do you prefer?" she whispered hoarsely.

"I like both," he stated, leaning in and licking the dusky pink tip, nibbling with his teeth. "The thought of someone watching as I pleasure you... It's an aphrodisiac, Sarah. It makes my dick hard."

Sarah leaned forward, pressing her breast closer to his mouth.

"Is someone watching us now?" she asked.

Dylan pulled back, peering up at her face once more. "I don't know. But that's part of the appeal. If I had to guess, I'd say yes, someone is. Who? I don't know. Don't care, either. I'm not looking for someone to join us, but if someone else can take pleasure from what I'm doing to you, more power to them. As long as they don't interfere."

Sarah drew in a breath when he once again leaned in and sucked her fully into his mouth, his tongue curling around her nipple as he palmed her ass, pulling her closer so he could grind the hard ridge of his erection against the apex of her thighs.

"Dylan..."

He released her from his mouth and leaned back, watching her. "Tell me, Sarah," he encouraged. "What do you want me to do to you?"

Her eyes were shuttered, her lips parted. She looked like sex personified, and he had the urge to fuck her right here and now, showing her what it felt like, the rush that could be had in a place like this.

"I just... I don't understand it," she said, her head tilting slightly.

Dylan finally nodded. "Turn around."

He helped her off his lap, then pulled her back down when she was facing out into the club. Dylan hadn't bothered to fix her dress and surprisingly she hadn't, either. Not that it mattered. When she was once again situated, he pulled her back against his chest and cupped her breasts in his hands, teasing her nipples.

If she wanted the full experience, if she truly wanted to understand, Dylan was more than willing to walk her through the process, to offer her the sort of pleasure that could be had right here. Right now.

And at that point, he would truly know where she stood on the subject.

As well as what that meant for the two of them.

IT WOULD PROBABLY DO HER A WORLD of good to remember that she was in a public place and that, as of this moment, she wasn't entirely clothed. Then again, Sarah was having a hard time remembering her own name, much less anything else.

When she'd been straddling Dylan, she knew that no one could really see her. Sure, they probably could guess what he was doing to her, but she'd had her back to the room, offering her a bit of privacy. That certainly wasn't the case now.

As she stared out into the crowded VIP section, she couldn't tell whether people were watching her or not. Which likely meant they couldn't tell that she was watching them, either. At Devotion, it had been a little more obvious.

Dylan's mouth pressed against her ear, his warm breath fanning her neck.

"Do you like to watch, Sarah?"

Did she? She wasn't sure.

"See the couple over there? To your left?"

Sarah glanced to the left, surveying the people, trying to find the couple Dylan was referring to. It didn't take but a second to see what he was seeing.

"Do you think she even knows we're watching her?" he asked.

No. No, she did not.

"Tell me what you see, Sarah."

Sarah leaned into Dylan more, unsure whether she could actually get her voice to work. She knew he was pushing her, giving her the full experience of the club, but she wasn't sure she could go so far as to explain what that man was doing to the woman.

"Tell me," he urged, his fingers clamping onto her nipples.

Sarah moaned softly, enjoying the way he tormented her.

"He's licking her," she said, although she doubted he could hear her.

"Where? Where's he licking her?"

Sarah pushed against Dylan's hands, urging him to continue his ministrations. Her breasts were overly sensitive and she loved what he was doing. The feeling of being on display was highly erotic. Knowing someone could witness Dylan pinching her nipples while she ground her ass against him. She wanted to feel him inside her, filling her, fucking her, driving her over the edge.

Another pinch had her drawing air into her lungs.

"Her pussy," she replied. "He's licking her pussy."

"Is she enjoying it?"

"Yes."

"Would you be enjoying it? Knowing someone was watching you like this?"

"Yes."

"Why?"

"Because I wouldn't care who's watching."

Dylan's hand left her breast and trailed down between her legs. Sarah instinctively widened her knees, offering him access to where she needed him most.

"What about those three over there?"

Sarah's gaze roamed the room, her eyes fighting to stay open as Dylan's fingers dipped beneath the elastic edge of her panties.

"Tell me what they're doing."

Swallowing hard, Sarah relaxed against Dylan. "Oh, God. Please..."

"Please, what?"

"Put your finger inside me."

Sarah couldn't believe she was being this wanton. They were in a public place, for crying out loud, but she couldn't seem to help herself. She was enjoying this more than she ever thought possible.

"Tell me," he urged.

When his finger pushed inside, Sarah moaned, gripping his forearm and holding on for dear life.

"The one guy... Oh, God..." Her inner muscles clamped down on the two fingers he thrust inside her. "The one guy is kissing the woman's back ... and she's sucking the other guy."

"Sucking what?"

"His ... dick... Dylan!" Sarah cried out when he speared her with his fingers, pumping into her, making her heart race and her blood thrum in her veins.

"Are they enjoying themselves?"

Sarah nodded.

"Do you think they notice that I'm finger-fucking you right here?"

She shook her head. "No ... they don't notice us."

"Would they notice if I pulled my dick out and fucked you right here on this couch?"

"No."

But Dylan didn't do that. He continued to finger her, pushing in deep and slow.

"What about those two over there?" he whispered, nipping her neck. "To the right."

Sarah glanced off to the right, and she stopped moving when she noticed a man and a woman watching them. They appeared innocent enough, the two of them sitting side by side, drinks in their hands as they watched what was going on around them. The man's eyes were on Sarah.

"Do you think he notices how my fingers slide deep inside your warm, welcoming cunt, Sarah?"

Oh, yeah. That guy noticed.

"Will he take his wife back to their room later and do the same thing to her as I'm doing to you?"

Sarah moaned. She realized she was grinding her hips, trying to take more of Dylan's fingers. She was so turned on she could hardly breathe.

"I want you to come for me, Sarah. Come all over my fingers. Then I'm going to take you back to our room, and I'm going to fuck you all damn night. In every position imaginable."

His fingers pumped into her while his thumb circled her clit. Sarah's fingernails dug into his shirt as she held on until the last possible second. When her orgasm crested, the room dimmed, the music was muted, and the only thing she noticed was the vibrant sound of her heart pounding in her ears.

She couldn't believe Dylan had made her come right there in front of those people.

Did it bother her that they were watching?

Surprisingly, no.

Did it make her hotter that they were?

Quite possibly, yes.

What did that say about her?

"Relax for me, baby," Dylan whispered.

Sarah focused on breathing. She felt as though she were outside her own body, watching as Dylan fixed her clothing, covering her completely. His warm hands caressed her, his lips gliding over her neck. She felt safe with him. As though he wouldn't let anything bad happen to her.

And maybe that was why she could let go like she had.

"Are you all right?" he asked, his fingers curling beneath her chin and turning her head so she could look back at him over her shoulder.

"Better than all right," she admitted.

And maybe that was what scared her most.

CHAPTER TWENTY-ONE

"TAKE THE DRESS OFF, SARAH," DYLAN COMMANDED as soon as they were back in their hotel room.

It was a wonder he'd been able to walk from the club. His dick was like a steel rod, eager and desperate for Sarah. The way she'd allowed him to pleasure her back at Devil's Playground had been unlike anything he'd ever experienced. He figured she probably would've been agreeable to anything he'd wanted down there, but truth was, he wanted her alone.

Sarah stared back at him, her eyes still glazed from their make-out session in the elevator. He didn't even give a damn that there were cameras watching every move he made when he'd been sliding his fingers between her thighs. He'd been careful to keep her hidden from view, but he hadn't been able to keep his hands to himself.

"Would you like me to help you?" he asked when she didn't make a move to disrobe.

"Not yet," she said, her voice raspy.

"No?"

Sarah shook her head. "I have something else in mind."

"Do you now?"

When Sarah reached for his hand, he allowed her to lead him over to the chair near the window. The curtains were still open, giving them a glittering view of the Las Vegas Strip.

Before he could sit down, Sarah turned to face him, her fingers deftly unbuttoning his jeans.

"I want you in my mouth."

Fuck. The woman could certainly do some damage when she used that commanding tone. The sexy words that came out of her mouth made his dick pulse.

It didn't take long for her to pull his jeans down to his knees. She pushed him so that he fell back into the chair. Once he was seated, she removed his boots, one at a time, then tugged his jeans from his legs. Dylan helped her out, shedding the jacket and removing his shirt in the process.

"I like you naked," Sarah mused, her eyes raking over him.

"The feeling's mutual," he told her. "Take the dress off, Sarah. But keep on the panties and heels."

Watching this woman undress was the equivalent of sex. Dylan didn't think she even realized how fucking hot she was as she slowly stripped the black dress from her body. So fucking hot he couldn't resist stroking himself, seeking a little relief.

When she had removed the dress, he spread his legs, giving her room to kneel before him. He did his best to keep his composure when she wrapped her sweet lips around the engorged head of his cock. The way her tongue caressed him made the hair on his arms stand on end.

"So fucking good," he groaned, reaching out and sliding his hands into her hair. He guided her head forward, slipping deeper into her mouth. "That's it, baby. Suck me."

For what felt like an eternity, Sarah deep-throated him, the suction making his lungs work harder just to maintain the last thread of his control.

When his balls threatened to erupt, he pulled her off him, then helped her to her feet. Seconds later, he had her on her back on the bed, his mouth fused to hers. She was squirming beneath him, her silk-covered pussy pressing against his aching cock.

"It's my turn now," he told her, pulling back before he worked his way down her body, his lips and tongue trailing over every inch of her skin.

He didn't stop until he was between her thighs. Using his hands, he pressed her knees wide and licked her.

Sarah's back bowed and she cried out, but he didn't stop. Dylan worked her to the edge, then retreated. He wasn't ready to send her over yet. He had something more in store for her tonight.

"Dylan ... please..."

He moved up over her. "Please what?"

"I need to feel you."

He teased her clit with his thumb, then dipped one finger inside her. "Like this?"

She didn't answer, so he kept teasing. When she was writhing uncontrollably, Dylan pulled his finger from her pussy and delved down to her anus. He pushed inside, gently, slowly. Sarah's breath hitched, but she continued to push against him.

"More... Dylan, I need more."

"Here?" He continued to fuck her ass with his finger. "You gonna let me take your ass, baby?"

"Yes... Just don't stop."

"Play with your clit, Sarah," he instructed as he got to his knees.

Her hand snaked down between her legs, and she began rubbing her clit, slowly at first, then faster.

"Don't make yourself come," he demanded.

Unable to wait, Dylan climbed off the bed, located a condom and the lube he'd brought with him before joining her on the bed once more.

"Keep going, Sarah," he commanded. "Show me how you like to be touched."

While he watched her play with herself, Dylan quickly rolled on the condom and coated it with lube, then urged her legs back with his knees. "Hold your knees close to your chest."

Sarah stopped teasing herself and did as he instructed. The position opened her completely.

"Dylan..."

He met her eyes. "Tell me, Sarah."

"I need you..."

"You've got me, baby. I'm right here."

After generously applying lube to her asshole, Dylan pushed in one finger, then two. He leaned over her, melding his lips with hers as he fucked her deep and slow. The last thing he wanted was to hurt her. If he took her now, no doubt he would. When Sarah began rocking against his fingers, he added a third. She bit his lower lip and he pulled back.

"Too much?"

She shook her head. "No."

"Does it hurt?"

"A little." Her smile was slow and seductive. "But in a good way."

"Fuck, woman..." He once again kissed her, wanting to offer a slight distraction while he continued to prepare her. "Turn over on your stomach."

Dylan moved off her and Sarah instantly flipped over.

"Put your ass in the air, baby."

She did as instructed and Dylan sucked in a breath as he lined up behind her.

"I'm gonna go slow," he warned.

Using his free hand, he pushed her shoulders down onto the bed as he guided his cock into her ass. She was so fucking tight he briefly wondered if this would even work.

"Relax, Sarah."

"I'm trying."

Leaning over her, Dylan kissed her shoulder, her neck. He nipped her skin and she moaned.

"You like that?"

Sarah nodded.

"You like that I want to fuck your sweet ass?"

"Yes."

"It makes me so fucking hard, Sarah. Knowing that I'm the first man to fuck you like this." He pushed in a little deeper, the head of his cock slipping past the tight ring of muscle. "Oh, fuck, baby."

"Fuck me, Dylan!" Sarah whimpered as she pushed back against him. "I need more. Now."

Then more she would receive.

SARAH EXPECTED MORE PAIN, BUT IT DIDN'T come.

Sure, there was tremendous pressure.

"Fuck, Sarah… Your ass is so goddamn tight."

Dylan's words were whispered in her ear as he leaned over her. Since he was clearly holding back, Sarah pushed up onto her hands and rocked against the intrusion. It was intense, unlike anything she'd ever felt before.

"Oh, yeah. That's it, Sarah. Fuck my cock."

Sarah loved that he was so verbal, his words brushing along her nerve endings.

"So damn tight, baby. Think about what it'll be like with a cock in your ass and in your pussy. Do you think you can handle that?"

The mental image made her body quiver. The idea of two men pleasuring her at one time…

"Yes," she hissed.

Dylan gripped her hips, stilling her movements. "Don't stop," she pleaded.

"Not stopping, but I want you to be still."

Sarah sucked in a breath and stopped moving.

"Now let me fuck your ass while you finger your pussy. I want to feel your fingers inside you."

Sarah had to drop back to the mattress in order to get her arms beneath her, but she did as he wanted, teasing her clit with one hand while pushing two fingers inside her. Her body clenched tightly.

"Oh, fuck yes," Dylan hissed as he began rocking his hips.

He went slow at first, but finally he worked up a rhythm that had her entire body rocking as he slammed into her, his cock filling her ass, her fingers plunging into her pussy.

"Sarah ... baby..." Dylan panted roughly behind her. "So good. Your ass is fucking perfect."

"Fuck me," she pleaded. Surprisingly, Sarah was close, she could feel the tingles igniting in her core. She was going to come with Dylan fucking her ass. She'd never imagined this would feel like this.

His hips slammed against her ass as he fucked her, picking up speed as his fingertips dug into her hips.

"Oh, God..." Sarah rapidly stroked her clit, faster and faster until she couldn't hold back any longer. "Oh, God, Dylan... I'm..." She screamed, her body exploding, her mind going blank as she was obliterated by sensation.

"Fuck... Coming, Sarah. Goddamn." Dylan roared his release, his hips stilling.

Sarah didn't move. She couldn't. She remained right where she was until Dylan slowly pulled out of her.

"Stay right there," he whispered.

"Not going anywhere," she assured him. "Except to sleep."

Dylan chuckled, but Sarah drifted off. When she came to, she felt something warm between her legs. He was cleaning her, and she appreciated the gesture because she damn sure didn't have the strength to get up.

"Sore?" he asked when he crawled into bed beside her.

Sarah snuggled up against him, her cheek on his chest. "A little."

He kissed her forehead, and within seconds, Sarah once again drifted off.

But not before thinking that this man owned her.

Heart, body, and soul.

CHAPTER TWENTY-TWO

AFTER SARAH STEPPED FOOT INTO HER LIVING room on Sunday evening, she was positive she was dreaming. For the last three days, she'd done so many things. Things she had never imagined herself doing. And not all of them involved sex.

Although Dylan had taken her to a sex club, he'd also taken her to a show, they'd shared some incredible food, done miles of walking to see all that Las Vegas had to offer tourists. He'd taken her downtown, and they'd watched the Fremont Street Experience, and he'd even convinced her to give zip-lining a try—which she would gladly never do again. And after all of that, he'd ushered her back on his grandfather's private jet, and they'd flown back to Texas together. Side by side and sometimes hand in hand.

If she was being honest with herself, Sarah had never felt quite like this. Relaxed, free, optimistic about her future.

However, she still had a few doubts lingering deep down. They seemed to be front and center now that she was smack dab in the middle of her own reality, not on some dream vacation for a few days. It seemed that was when she always started to worry. When she was alone with her thoughts. The notion of someone else abandoning her always became more prominent during those times, no matter how hard she tried to ignore them.

After Dylan had dropped her off a few minutes ago, he had kissed her on her front porch and then left. Part of her had wished he had stayed because she hadn't been ready for him to leave. The other part of her knew that they needed to put some distance between them. She was becoming too attached to the man. More than she'd expected.

But when it came down to it, Sarah knew that she'd done what she'd promised herself she wouldn't.

She had gone and fallen hopelessly in love with Dylan Thomas despite knowing she shouldn't. Despite knowing that he wouldn't love her in return. Not the way she wanted to be loved. Unconditionally. Forever.

Which was rather disappointing, but Sarah had tried to put herself in Dylan's shoes. He was a different man than the last time she'd been with him. Gone was the depression and the drinking. He was quick to smile and laugh, always eager to make love. And she felt as though he genuinely wanted to spend time with her.

But even though he was apparently living his life to the fullest, she still seemed to be waiting for him to backtrack. To retreat into the darkness from which he'd pulled himself. She'd known Dylan for a long time. She'd spent a lot of time with him, as friends. Eleven years was a long time to mourn the loss of someone who meant so much to him. Sometimes she thought he would never get over Meghan and she understood that. The fact that Paul's memory had been pushed back, deep into her heart, made her feel guilty.

Seeing Dylan smile, the tiny lines around his eyes crinkling when he watched her, Sarah hadn't wanted to do anything to take that away from him. From her. And not one time had he taken a drink. Of anything. His sobriety was a miraculous thing and she was so very proud of him. But she didn't want to mention it, afraid if she did, it would make him relapse.

"Blue! Smokey!" Sarah set her suitcase just inside the front door and looked around for her cats. It didn't take long for them to come waltzing into the living room, both of them looking at her as though she'd lost her mind.

They didn't like it when she wasn't home. They usually made that painfully clear. Even when she was just going to work. Her mother had texted her to let her know she'd brought them over that morning, wanting them to be here when Sarah returned. She was grateful because she'd missed them.

"I'm home," she said as she moved forward, bending down until she could scratch them both behind their ears. "I told you I wouldn't be gone long."

"Aunt Sarah?" Jake called from the kitchen and Sarah had to clutch her chest. She hadn't realized he was there. Turning to look out the window, she noticed his BMW parked on the street. Apparently, she'd been so lost in her own head that she'd missed his car entirely.

"Hey," she said by way of greeting. "Sorry, I didn't know you were here."

"I just got here a few minutes ago. Grandma said you were coming back today. I wanted to check in with you."

Sarah looked at Jake and smiled. He was such an incredibly handsome young man. A man she still had a hard time believing used to be a sweet yet lovingly defiant little boy. Not that he didn't have good reason, but luckily, Jake hadn't written off all family after his mother decided she didn't want kids. Jake used to tell people that and it broke Sarah's heart every time.

He wasn't that same little boy anymore. Considering he'd lived with Sarah and her mother—Jake's grandmother—for most of his young life, she figured she could take some of the responsibility for that.

"How was Vegas?" he asked as he pulled a soda from the refrigerator, offering her one as he did.

Sarah climbed up on the stool at the breakfast bar as she watched him. "Interesting is the first word that comes to mind."

"Did you have fun with Dylan?"

"I did. A lot of fun."

He had the decency to blush. "Sorry. It's none of my business. I tend to worry."

"You and me both, kid," she muttered.

He tilted the can to his lips and studied her. Sarah could tell he had something on his mind, but she had no idea what. It could be anything, knowing Jake.

"Did Dylan tell you that they sold CISS?"

Her nephew sounded slightly peeved by the notion, but she couldn't really blame him. From what Dylan had explained to her, he took sole responsibility for the downfall of CISS. She figured he'd probably expressed that to others, which meant Jake likely blamed him as well. Sarah couldn't believe that one man could bring down an entire company. Sure, Dylan probably had to shoulder some of the blame but certainly not all of it.

"Yeah. He told me."

Jake nodded.

"He also told me that Alex is making sure that you and Nate will have a job with the new company."

"Yeah. That's what Alex said."

"And you're not happy about that?"

Jake's gaze dropped to the countertop. "I'm not happy that CISS is having financial problems."

"These things happen," Sarah assured him.

"Well, they probably wouldn't have if Dylan hadn't become an alcoholic."

Ah. So that *was* what this was about. Sarah could understand Jake's frustration. She could also understand his need to lash out at someone. However, she also got the feeling that Jake was likely projecting some of Nate's feelings. Her nephew was the happy-go-lucky kind of guy. He was the one who overcame every obstacle and didn't point fingers when things didn't go his way.

Usually.

She waited, hoping he would elaborate.

"So, are you serious about him?"

Okay, so that wasn't the question she'd expected.

Knowing that she couldn't lie to him, Sarah nodded. "I'm serious, yes."

"Does he feel the same way?"

Sarah shrugged. "We're taking this slow, Jake."

"Slow? You consider a weekend in Vegas slow?"

"It was a business trip for him," she replied defensively.

"And he took you along with him?"

Sarah studied Jake for a minute, weighing her words carefully. She got the sneaking suspicion that this conversation didn't have the slightest thing to do with Dylan or her, but Jake was trying to pick a fight.

"What's going on?" she asked, clasping her fingers together on the bar top. "Talk to me, kid."

He turned away from her, swigging what was left of his drink before tossing the can into the recycle bin.

"Nothing to talk about. I just wanted to make sure you were all right. That Dylan had treated you right."

"Of course he treated me right," she stated firmly. "Why would you think otherwise?"

Jake spun around to face her, and Sarah noticed what looked a hell of a lot like tears in his eyes. She instantly knew this had nothing to do with her and everything to do with him.

Now, if she could only get him to open up.

With Jake, that was usually easier said than done.

DYLAN STILL COULDN'T BELIEVE HOW MUCH FUN he'd had during his mini-vacation with Sarah in Vegas. Although he'd never been able to resist the lust that she stirred inside of him, they'd gotten along seamlessly while they'd been there. More than lovers, more than friends.

In fact, he wished he was still with her now. He found himself not wanting to spend time away from her, although he knew he needed to. Some distance would put things into perspective, and he definitely needed that right now. As much as he enjoyed their time together, he knew that Sarah wanted more from him. At times, he wanted to give her that. To express his true feelings for her and to move forward. But something was still holding him back.

Which was why he'd dropped her off at her house and headed home. Rather than go back to his lonely house, though, he had stopped in at Pops' house to check in.

"It's about damn time you got back."

Dylan spun around and searched for the owner of the voice. He knew who it belonged to, but he didn't know where Nate was. He found his son standing on the stairs, glaring down at Dylan.

"Hey," he greeted, trying to keep his cool.

It was evident that Nate had an issue with him. Dylan had long ago accepted that he deserved his son's wrath, but he'd also known that they would eventually have to talk things through. He hadn't anticipated that chat happening just yet, but he figured now was as good a time as any.

"Let's talk in the kitchen," Dylan prompted, not waiting for Nate to respond before he headed that way.

Footsteps sounded behind him and he took a deep breath, bracing himself for a fight.

Nate's anger had been festering for some time now, and Dylan figured when the kid finally let the emotions out, it wasn't going to be pretty.

"Did you have fun?" Nate snapped, dropping into the kitchen chair, still glaring at him.

"I did."

"At least someone did."

Dylan paused as he reached for a glass. "Something wrong?"

"That's a stupid question, Dad. When has anything been right?"

Okay, so maybe this wasn't really about him like he'd thought. "Want to talk about it?"

"With you?"

Dylan didn't bother to say that he didn't see anyone else in the room. He simply studied Nate carefully, then moved around the bar and over to the table.

"Look, Nate," he began as he took a seat. "I owe you an apology. I haven't—"

"Why do you think everything's always about you?" Nate bellowed, jumping to his feet.

Dylan was up in an instant, his hands on Nate's shoulders. His son was shaking, clearly angry, but at what, Dylan wasn't quite sure. He'd thought Nate had been angry with him, but now he had his doubts.

"What's it about?" he asked softly.

"It doesn't matter," Nate snapped. "It never fucking matters."

Dylan gently squeezed Nate's shoulder. "It always matters. When it comes to you, it does, Nate."

His son's dark eyes met his, and Dylan held his breath, hoping his son would open up to him.

The next words that came out of his mouth weren't quite what Dylan expected.

"I'm gay, Dad."

Well, it was a start at opening up.

"Okay."

Nate frowned, shrugging Dylan's hand away. "*Okay?* That's all you have to say about it?"

Dylan's own anger came bubbling up. "What do you *want* me to say, Nate? Did you have this conversation planned out? Did you write a script that I should know about? You're gay. Fine. Am I supposed to react badly? What do you want from me?"

Nate's eyes widened momentarily. "You're not gonna tell me that I'm not gay? That I must be confused?"

"Why would I say that?" Dylan didn't understand what the hell was going on. "Do you think you're confused?"

"No."

"Well, then why would *I* think you're confused?"

"Because your son is gay," Nate countered hotly.

"So fucking what?" Dylan stared at his son. "Some of my best friends are gay. Does that mean they're confused?"

That seemed to take the wind right out of Nate's sails. He stood there, staring back at Dylan.

When his son's face fell, Dylan finally put all the pieces of the puzzle together. Everything he'd witnessed over the past couple of years, the way Nate interacted with Jake, the way the two men acted toward one another.

This wasn't about Dylan at all. Sure, he probably hadn't helped the situation by becoming a raging alcoholic and ignoring his children altogether, but the weight on Nate's shoulders wasn't placed there by Dylan. He wasn't sure that was a good thing or a bad thing. As a father, he wanted to fix his kid's problems, but this was something he couldn't fix.

"Is this about Jake?" he asked, making sure there was no judgement in his tone.

Nate dropped back into the chair. "He doesn't want to see me anymore."

Oh, hell.

His son was in love.

"Did he say why?"

Nate seemed surprised by the question. "He said we're too young."

Well, Dylan could hardly argue with that, but he knew that wasn't what Nate would want to hear. "Have you been ... dating him for a while?"

"It hasn't been official. More like friends."

"But you wanted more?"

Nate stared at the wooden tabletop. "Yeah."

"And what did Jake say when you brought it up?"

Nate rolled his eyes. "I didn't bring it up. I've been waiting for him to ... accept it."

Shit.

Dylan had no idea what to say to make this better for Nate. Young love was hard, and that was the case whether you were gay or straight. The heart wanted what it wanted, and everyone knew it didn't always work out.

"Talk to me, Nate."

"I don't want to talk," Nate growled, his anger returning. "I'm so fucking tired of talking. I just want..."

Ah, hell.

The second the tears began to fall from Nate's eyes, Dylan's heart constricted. He threw his arms around his son and held him, offering comfort, knowing it wouldn't help.

Dylan hated that he couldn't fix this for his son. He didn't even know how to try.

But he could be there for him the way a father should.

Yes, Dylan had made a lot of mistakes over the years, but the one thing he'd never stopped doing was loving his kids, wanting what was best for them.

So, that was exactly what he did. He kept his arms wrapped tightly around Nate and he hugged him.

Didn't matter that it was as much for him as it was for his son.

CHAPTER TWENTY-THREE

Tuesday, January 24

WHEN THE TEMP AGENCY CALLED HER LATE yesterday afternoon, Sarah had reluctantly accepted a one-day assignment to fill in as a receptionist. Apparently, the company's previous one had bailed on them and they had a lag until the new one started. Figuring it would be simple and easy, she'd opted to do it. More so because she needed something to do rather than sit around thinking while trying to come up with nonexistent things to clean around the house.

The day had gone exactly as she'd expected. Nothing overly dramatic. No pain-in-the-ass boss who drilled her endlessly about stupid shit. No vindictive office assistant who was jealous. In fact, it had been relatively boring.

And once again, after eight hours at the office, Sarah found she was pacing her living room floor.

She glanced at her cell phone, trying to pretend it wasn't the elephant in the room. She hadn't heard from Dylan since he dropped her off on Sunday. Rather than call him herself, she'd been hoping he would make the first move.

That was two full days ago.

It wasn't that she thought he needed to be the first one to reach out. More like she was afraid of appearing too needy. She could admit to having abandonment issues, and that was always the first thing she jumped to. But with Dylan, she knew she couldn't assume the worst. It wasn't fair to him. They'd had a wonderful trip, and she longed to see him again, but Sarah knew she needed to slow things down. For her own sake if nothing else.

But then it dawned on her. Why did he have to be the one pursuing her? Shouldn't she make the effort? What if he was waiting for her to call him? It only seemed fair, right?

"Uggh." Sarah thrust her hand through her hair.

Reaching for her phone, she pulled up Dylan's contact information. Just as she was going to hit the call button, her phone rang. The vibration startled her, and she dropped the phone, scrambling to catch it before it died a painful death on the hardwood.

She managed to grab it just in time.

"Hello?" Hmm. She sounded like she'd just run a mile. And not in a sexy, breathless kind of way, either.

"Sarah? Are you okay?"

Sitting in the middle of the living room, Sarah laughed into the phone. "I'm fine. Sorry. I almost dropped the phone. I was just about to call you."

"You were?" Dylan inquired, his voice dropping an octave or two.

"Yeah."

"Because you wanted to see me?"

Sarah lay back on the floor, staring up at the ceiling. "Actually, yes."

Smokey and Blue were instantly at her side, crawling over and around her, whipping her in the face with their tails.

"Mmm."

God, she missed him. She missed seeing him, hearing his voice.

"How're things?" he inquired.

"Good. Busy. Sort of. I went to work today. One-day deal. It was boring."

"Doing what?"

"Answering phones."

"Sounds … interesting."

Sarah chuckled. "No, it sounds as boring as it was."

Dylan's sexy laugh echoed in her ear. "What else is going on?"

Sarah thought back to her conversation with Jake. "I talked to my nephew. He sort of grilled me when I got back on Sunday."

There was silence on the other end of the phone, and Sarah pulled it back to see if the call had disconnected.

It hadn't.

"Dylan?"

"Yeah." He sighed. "Did Jake happen to mention Nate?"

Well, crap. "He … did. Yes."

"Nate's devastated."

"Oh, no." Sarah sat up. "I'm so sorry. If it makes a difference, I don't think Jake's doing all that hot, either."

"So, you know?"

"That he's gay? Yeah. I know. But I've known that since he was fifteen when he told me."

"Oh."

"You didn't know?"

"Not officially, no," Dylan said softly. "I had my suspicions, but I was leaving it to Nate to talk to me about it."

"Trust me, I get it." And she really did. Had Jake not come to her, Sarah wasn't sure she would've been able to address it with him.

"Maybe I should have gone to him. Made him talk about it."

Sarah chuckled softly. "You do know that wouldn't have changed what they're going through now, right?"

"Maybe."

"No maybes about it," she countered, keeping her voice low. "Whether it's a crush or true love, it would've happened anyway. They'll figure it out. They're young. They're resilient."

Dylan was quiet again, and when he finally spoke, his voice wasn't nearly as strained. "So, what're you doing tomorrow?"

"Nothing," she admitted. "That I know of."

"You want to have lunch with Trent Ramsey?"

Sarah bolted upright, getting to her feet. "Trent Ramsey? *The* Trent Ramsey? Please don't be messing with me right now."

Dylan chuckled. "I'm very serious. He wants to meet, see what I thought about Devil's Playground. Figured maybe you could give him your insight as well."

Sarah's cheeks heated instantly as she thought about her experience at the club.

"Sarah?"

"Yeah. Yes." She cleared her throat. "Yes, I'd love to have lunch with you and..." Did she call him Trent? Or Mr. Ramsey?

"Good. I'll pick you up at ten thirty tomorrow."

"Okay."

"Sarah?"

"Hmm?"

"I miss you."

Her heart turned over in her chest. "I miss you, too."

And just like that, the call was over and Sarah felt her heart growing to ten times its normal size. She hated getting her hopes up, but it seemed to be a moot point. Every time she thought about Dylan, she felt giddy. It seemed as though things were moving in the right direction. Part of her insisted on taking it one day at a time, but the other part wanted to fast-track this. More importantly, she wanted to know how things were going to play out.

Everything was falling into place. Or it seemed to be.

And on top of that, she was going to meet Trent freaking Ramsey.

Oh, crap. What in the world was she going to wear?

How did she even talk to a celebrity of that caliber? Was she supposed to play it cool? Act like she had lunch with famous people every day?

There was no way this was going to end well.

INVITING SARAH TO LUNCH SEEMED LIKE THE most natural thing in the world to do. Dylan hadn't lied when he told her that he wanted her to share her experience with Trent. However, he could've easily told the man himself.

The truth was, Dylan wanted to see her. Hell, he would've gone to her house tonight if it hadn't been for the fact that he was meeting Alex and Ashleigh for dinner. He figured he owed his brother-in-law a heads-up before he finalized things with Trent. The last thing he wanted Alex to think was that Dylan was abandoning him. Then again, he'd done that long ago.

"Hey." Ashleigh greeted him with a smile when she appeared at the front door.

After a quick hug, Dylan stepped inside, shrugged out of his coat, and tossed it over the chair. "Where's Riley?"

"She's over at Sierra's for a couple of hours. She's a total terror these days. We don't get a moment's peace. Never mind trying to have dinner."

Dylan chuckled. "She takes after her mom, huh?"

Ashleigh glared at him, grinning. "I was never that bad."

"I'm sure Pops would disagree."

"Whatever. Come in the kitchen. I've got to pull the pork roast out of the oven."

"Where's Alex?"

"He's taking a quick shower." Ashleigh pulled on a pair of oven mitts. "How was the trip to Vegas?"

Dylan tried to hide his surprise. He wasn't sure how Ashleigh found out, but apparently she was up to speed on what he'd been up to. "It was good."

"And Sarah? Things good with her, too?"

Dylan couldn't stop the smile that formed on his mouth. "She's great."

After setting the pan on the stove, Ashleigh turned to look at him. He could see his sister's brain working, but he didn't have the slightest idea what was running through her head.

"Have you talked to her?"

"Define talk," he urged. Of course he had talked to her, but he figured Ashleigh was referring to something specific.

"About Meghan?"

Dylan looked away instantly. No, he hadn't. Yet.

"Both of you have suffered tremendous loss, Dylan. If you want this to work out..."

"I know," he stated, still not looking at her. "Right now, we're taking things slow."

Leaning back against the counter, he crossed his arms over his chest and forced his eyes to Ashleigh's face. He should've expected this from his sister. She cared about him, he got that. Didn't mean he wanted to talk about it.

"I'm happy for you, Dylan. And for Sarah."

He frowned, confused.

"I haven't seen you this happy in a very long time," she said, tossing the oven mitts onto the counter. "I'm not sure if it's her or something else..."

"It's her," he acknowledged. No reason not to admit it.

Ashleigh grinned. "I thought so. She's sweet. I like her."

Dylan hadn't realized that Ashleigh knew Sarah all that well. They'd been introduced once or twice at various events, but the way his sister spoke of her said she knew Sarah better than a mere acquaintance. "Do you talk to her often?"

Ashleigh's expression went blank. He recalled her doing something similar the last time Sarah had come up in conversation.

"How well do you know her?" he inquired.

"Not well," she answered, shaking her head. "I..."

Dylan waited.

Ashleigh sighed. "I called her a couple of times. A few years ago. Back ... you know. Well, I called to ask her for some help. With you."

"Help?"

"Yeah. She's resourceful. Her husband suffered from bipolar disorder, and she has experience with … depression."

He cocked an eyebrow.

"I wanted her to help me pull you out of your depression," Ashleigh blurted. "But don't worry, she turned me down."

That didn't sound like Sarah.

"I figured it had something to do with what happened between the two of you a few years ago."

Okay, so that grabbed his attention. How the hell would Ashleigh know…?

"She never actually admitted anything to me, but I could tell by how standoffish she became that something happened. When I first asked her to help, she was willing. We talked at length and she gave me all sorts of suggestions. We had lunch a couple of times. But then one day she sort of shut down on me. After she gave me some information about grief counselors and group therapy, I stopped calling her because I could tell that…"

Ashleigh stared back at him, but she didn't continue.

When the silence became too much, Dylan took a deep breath. "I fucked up with her," he admitted.

"I figured as much." Ashleigh's smile was sympathetic. "I'm just happy she's back in your life now. She's good for you. She knows a lot about…"

Dylan did not like the sound of that. "I don't need her to fix me now, Ash."

His sister's eyebrows lowered. "I didn't say you did."

"Is that what you think she's doing?" Dylan hadn't considered the fact that Sarah might be placating him in order to help keep him sober.

"No, not at all." Ashleigh glanced down at the counter. "Yes, I tried to call her after I saw you talking to her at the CISS party, but I didn't leave a message. I just needed her to know that you're recovering."

Anger penetrated deep within him at the thought of Ashleigh interfering. Was she telling him the complete truth? Or had she actually talked to Sarah?

"What's goin' on in here?"

Dylan turned to see Alex standing in the doorway. He was studying them both intently, probably curious as to why their voices were raised. Dylan didn't want to go into details, but he needed to mull over this information for a little while. The fact that Ashleigh had sought out Sarah to help him through his ... problems...

Was that what Sarah was doing now? Did she pity him? Was he some fucking charity case for her?

The idea did not sit well with him.

"Let's eat," Ashleigh stated, drawing him out of his thoughts.

Dylan forced Sarah from his mind, choosing to focus on the here and now.

A few minutes later, after the food was dished up and the three of them were sitting at the dining room table, Dylan took the opportunity to talk to Alex. He explained about his conversation with Trent, about the new club, about his desire to take the position.

"So what's stopping you?" Alex asked, his fork hanging over his plate.

Dylan reached for his tea glass, looking Alex directly in the eye. "You."

"Me? What the fuck?"

"I owe you everything," Dylan said, keeping his voice low. "I let you down in a big way. I damn sure don't deserve to move on to something else if you don't approve."

Alex looked sincerely appalled by the statement. But Dylan continued. "You've stood by me, but I haven't done the same in return."

"Bullshit," Alex barked. "You don't owe me shit. The fact that CISS is having trouble is not your fault."

"Sure it is."

"No. It's not!" Alex got to his feet. "You don't get to take this all on yourself."

That wasn't the reaction Dylan expected. "I fucked up."

"We all fucked up, Dylan. It's over and done. You need to move on. And yes, if you're looking for my blessing to go work for Trent Ramsey, you've got it. I want what's best for you. That's all I've ever wanted."

Dylan didn't respond. He didn't know what to say.

"Look," Alex said, breathing deep, then exhaling slowly. "You suffered a loss that is unfathomable. No one knew it would happen. And you coped with it. Maybe not the right way, but no one blames you for that. The only thing we want is for you to be happy and healthy. That's all that fucking matters."

Dylan nodded.

"Please sit down," Ashleigh whispered to her husband.

Alex lowered himself back to his chair. "I'm sorry," he said to her.

"It's okay. We're all okay. That's what's important."

Dylan agreed with that statement. It was what was important.

But was he really okay?

Or was he now jumping in the deep end? More importantly, was Sarah setting herself up to be his life raft?

CHAPTER TWENTY-FOUR

Wednesday, January 25

SARAH WAS DOING HER ABSOLUTE BEST NOT to fidget, but that was harder than it appeared. She was about to officially meet Trent Ramsey.

"Relax," Dylan whispered in her ear. "He's just a man."

The laugh that erupted from her chest sounded eerily like a frog. "A famous man," she countered. "Like, one of the most famous men in the world."

"Don't let him hear you say that," Dylan told her.

"What? Why?" Sarah stared back at him.

"He doesn't like it."

"Really?"

"No. I don't know." Dylan's smile was mischievous. "He probably does. Go fucking nuts."

Sarah laughed and the tension in her shoulders lessened.

But no sooner had she taken a deep breath than the most gorgeous actor to bestow the big screen stepped up to their table, and she lost her train of thought.

Thankfully Dylan had everything under control. He introduced her to Trent, and when the man kissed her hand, she thought she might faint.

"She all right?" Trent asked Dylan.

Sarah shook her head in answer. No, she wasn't all right.

Trent freaking Ramsey.

Holy balls.

"She will be. She's a little star struck."

"I am not," she stated indignantly, although she was definitely lying.

Trent grinned, his trademark crooked smirk, and Sarah nearly went up in flames. Dylan's hand on her thigh was the only thing that grounded her.

She took a few minutes to compose herself while the waiter delivered drinks and then took their order. Trent and Dylan conversed as though they were old friends, talking about a little of everything.

"So, tell me," Trent prompted, glancing from her to Dylan, then back, "what did you think of Devil's Playground?"

"It was ... nice." *Nice?* Wow.

That wasn't at all what she'd wanted to say.

"Nice?" Trent leaned back and smirked. "I like nice."

Sarah closed her eyes and counted to ten. She heard Dylan chuckle, which only made her face heat more. So much for being calm, cool, and collected around this celebrity. She just wasn't cut out for this. Seeing him on the big screen was one thing, sitting at a table with him...

"So tell me more," Trent said, his attention on Dylan.

Dylan proceeded to give Trent the lowdown on the club, going into detail about the things he liked, the things he'd do differently. He sounded professional and Sarah couldn't help but hang on his every word.

It was safe to say she was falling for this man. Hard.

"The club in New York is similar," Trent noted. "I happen to prefer it over Vegas. However, I'm not interested in doing the same thing. I just wanted you to have a baseline. Something to compare to Devotion."

Sarah picked at her salad, listening to the men discuss their next steps. Meetings coming up, plans to be nailed down, contracts to be signed. Oddly enough, she wished she was part of it. She didn't know why, but it sounded like an adventure, something she could totally see herself doing.

Not that she had management experience. Certainly not in a club of that caliber.

"What do you think, Sarah? Would you be game?"

Sarah's head jerked up and she stared at Trent. He'd clearly been speaking to her, and she hadn't heard a word he said.

The man chuckled, probably thinking she was a complete loser.

"I ... uh..." She had no clue what to say.

"I'm not sure she'd be interested in working for you," Dylan teased Trent.

"Me?" Her eyes widened as she cut a glance at Dylan, then back to Trent. "Work for you?"

"At the club," Trent added.

"What would I be doing?"

"I've got an idea," Trent continued. "Why don't the two of you come to Devotion tomorrow night. I'll give you the full tour, show you the things I'm interested in incorporating into my club."

Dylan's eyes were on her face and Sarah found herself nodding her head. "We could ... uh ... do that."

"Good."

She turned her attention back to Trent. "What's the name of your club, anyway?"

Trent shrugged, as though it didn't matter that he hadn't come up with a name at this point. "I'm still working on that. Why? You have some ideas?"

Sarah shook her head. "Not yet. But I'm sure I could come up with something."

Damn. The longer she sat here, the worse she was making this on herself.

Trent seemed to consider that for a moment, his big hand wrapped around his iced tea glass. "Great. Tomorrow night, you can tell me what you've come up with."

Oh, jeez.

"Now, what do you say we talk about something other than work for a bit?" Trent grinned. "There'll be plenty of time to hash it all out in the very near future."

For whatever reason, that didn't settle Sarah's nerves any. In fact, she was even more nervous now.

"TRENT HAS TO THINK I'M CRAZY," SARAH muttered as they walked up to her front door.

From the moment they left the restaurant, she'd been mumbling to herself. Dylan couldn't help but smile at her rambling. She was so damn cute, even when she was ogling Trent Ramsey. More so when she was trying to figure out how to redo the past two hours. It wasn't possible, but it was cute to watch.

"I doubt he thinks that," Dylan assured her.

Although it had been evident she was nervous, he thought she'd handled things fairly well with Trent. Especially since she'd come face-to-face with the world-famous actor moments before he'd delved into a conversation about business.

"Oh, he definitely does." She unlocked her door and stepped inside.

Dylan followed.

Unable to help himself, Dylan grabbed her and pulled her into him. "Who cares what he thinks?"

"I do," she retorted, a frown on her pretty mouth. "I can't stop thinking about it."

"Well, how about I give you something else to think about?"

He kissed her, pressing his mouth to hers gently before sliding his tongue along the seam of her lips. Damn, he'd missed her.

"Mmm. You're good at distractions, you know that?"

Sarah's comment reminded him of how she'd once referred to their night together as a distraction. In turn, that reminded him of what Ashleigh said about how Sarah had wanted to help him. Dylan found himself pulling back, watching her closely.

"Did I say something wrong?"

"No," he answered without thinking. He didn't want to get into it with her now. "Are you game for going to Devotion tomorrow night?"

Sarah retreated, sliding her hand over her hair as Dylan watched her.

"I'm good with it." Her eyes met his. "But can you do me a favor?"

"Anything."

"Whatever you have planned... Can you let it be spontaneous? At least for me? I'm not sure I can get inside my head and willingly walk into that club knowing that things might..."

Yeah. He understood where she was going with that. Dylan reached for her hand, lifting it to his mouth. "I can be spontaneous. But you have to do something for me."

Her eyebrows rose in question.

"You have to make it very clear what you're willing and not willing to do. I can't make any assumptions. No, let me clarify that. I *won't* make any assumptions. Either you're on board or you're not."

"I'll be sure to make my preferences clear."

"Good." Dylan pressed a kiss to the inside of her palm. "Then I'll pick you up at eight tomorrow night."

Her smile was sweet, albeit a little surprised. "I'll be ready."

As much as he wanted to stay, to spend the night with Sarah in his arms, Dylan needed some time to think. He had a few issues he needed to work out before tomorrow night. No way would he put Sarah in a precarious situation if he wasn't willing to move this relationship forward. What he wanted from her required trust on both sides.

After kissing her quickly, Dylan left. By the time he was in his truck, he was already dialing the phone. There was only one man he trusted when it came to sharing Sarah. And since it appeared she was on the menu for tomorrow night, he needed to get things worked out.

When it came to something like this, spontaneity wasn't always the best option.

"Yo, bro. What's up, man?" Chris answered, his deep voice rumbling through the phone.

"Not a hell of a lot," Dylan told him.

"I was gonna call you. See if you wanted to hang out."

"Yeah? More golf?" Dylan hadn't seen Chris since their last golf outing, but they talked every few days.

Having been best friends since high school, it was hard to believe their friendship had lasted this long. Then again, everyone needed the laid-back friend who didn't pass judgment and didn't try to interfere in every damn thing going on. Chris was that friend.

Oh, sure, they'd had a few falling outs. Chris had been at Dylan's side when Meghan died, and for the years that followed. He had made sure Dylan knew he didn't agree with numbing his emotional pain with alcohol, but as with everyone and everything else in his life at that point, Dylan hadn't given a shit.

"What do you think about them Cowboys?" Chris asked, a smile in his voice.

"It's about damn time."

"You're damn right about that. So, what's up?"

"I wanted to..." Dylan took a deep breath.

"Talk to me, man," Chris urged, his voice lower. The guy clearly caught Dylan's hesitancy.

"I need a favor."

"Anything. You know that."

Another deep breath and Dylan divulged everything that had happened in the past few months. He went into detail about seeing Sarah, about what had happened between them a few years ago, about taking her to Vegas, and yes, about his desire to share her.

"You sure, man?" Chris asked. "This is a serious step. I'm not saying no, but man, I want you to be absolutely sure."

"Why wouldn't I be sure?"

Chris cleared his throat. "If she was just any girl, I'd be all over it."

"What does that mean?"

"Seriously, Dylan. You haven't figured it out yet?"

"Figured out what?"

"Bro, this isn't the first time I'm hearin' about this chick. She's the only girl to have caught your attention in…"

Dylan didn't say anything. He knew where Chris was going with it.

"Look man, I can't see the look on your face right now, but even *I* know."

"Know what?" Dylan couldn't hide his frustration.

"That you're in love with her."

It was Dylan's turn to be quiet.

What. The. Fuck?

CHAPTER TWENTY-FIVE

SARAH SPENT THE ENTIRE NEXT DAY IN a panic.

Well, not entirely freaked out, but mostly.

Thankfully, she had Smokey and Blue to keep her preoccupied. They seemed to be in rare form, wanting more attention than usual. Plus, she spent nearly two hours on the phone with her mother to pass the time and keep her mind off tonight.

"Seriously, Blue," she told her cat. "If he asks me my thoughts about the club, what am I supposed to say?"

No answer, of course.

"It's not like I have any great ideas. Sure, I might have a few ideas, but it's not like I've given it a lot of thought."

Meow.

"Okay, fine, I've given it some thought." She had. She'd thought a lot about this new club Trent was building. She wanted to have an intelligent conversation with the man, after all.

Not to mention, it kept her mind from wandering to other things.

Like Dylan. And what they'd be doing tonight at Devotion.

"Ugghh."

Unfortunately, those thoughts seemed to overshadow Trent's club, which left plenty of hours for Sarah to fret about what to expect when they went to Devotion. Even thinking about it made her stomach churn with nerves. If she'd been smart, she would've insisted that Dylan outline in detail how he wanted tonight to go. But, no. Rather than play it safe, she'd told him to be spontaneous.

As though she hadn't had enough surprises lately.

If she was being honest, Sarah wasn't nervous about what might happen. Every single time she'd been with Dylan, he'd amplified the lust factor with minimal effort. She knew when they got to Devotion, it would be no different. The fact that there would be plenty of activities to watch would help as well. Not that she was a voyeur, but there was no doubt that she'd been turned on both at Devotion and at Devil's Playground simply by observing those around her.

Of course, she'd been turned on by having people watch her as well, which was new and exciting. Maybe even a little disturbing. Sarah had always known that she was a highly sexual person. When it came to dealing with Dylan, her hormones were definitely out of whack.

The loud knock on her front door pulled a squeak from her throat, and she jumped, causing her heart to slam against her sternum.

"Relax," she muttered to herself as she headed for the door.

Proud of herself that she didn't fumble with the deadbolt, Sarah pulled open the door and stared at the sexy cowboy standing on her front porch.

"Hey," he greeted, a warm, sexy smirk on his face.

How was it that every time she looked at him, her clothes wanted to jump right off her body?

"Hey." Stepping back out of the way, Sarah allowed him to come inside.

Before she could turn to get her coat and her purse, Sarah was stumbling into Dylan's arms.

"Damn," he grumbled before sliding his mouth over hers.

The kiss sent molten heat simmering in her veins. And just like that ... lust factor set to boil.

Dylan's hands slid down to her thighs. The warm rasp of his fingers against her skin had Sarah sucking air into her lungs. As he lifted her dress higher, she briefly wondered if they were even going to make it out of her house tonight.

"What do you have on beneath this sexy dress?" His words were said so low she barely heard him. That or her blood was pumping so hard she couldn't hear over the steady thrum of her heartbeat.

"Uhh ... panties?"

Dylan smirked. "Take them off."

Sarah pulled back enough to look him in the eye. One dark eyebrow lifted, as though daring her to argue with him.

"I thought we were going out."

"We are." He grinned. "But you won't need them."

A shiver raced down her spine.

"If you'd like, I can help you take them off."

God, no. If she allowed that, they might never make it out of her house.

Sarah took a step back, freeing herself completely from his embrace. Making sure to keep herself covered, she stripped her panties down her legs. Slowly.

Two could play this game.

She loved the way his eyes tracked her movements.

"Holy fuck." His voice was raspy. "Virgin white." Dylan's eyes lifted to hers. "You tryin' to kill me, woman?"

True or not, Dylan's words made her feel sexy. A newfound confidence filled her as she tossed her panties onto the bar, then grabbed her purse. Dylan helped her with her coat, his hands sliding over every inch of her he touched. Deliberate, no doubt.

Strangely, her nerves had dissipated somewhat. All within the three minutes he'd been in her house.

"Let's do this," he rumbled softly. "Don't want to keep Trent waiting."

And just like that, her nerves were back.

Sheesh.

THE SECOND DYLAN HAD SET HIS EYES on Sarah, he'd been hard-pressed to rethink their plans for tonight. The dress she was wearing—a silky white number that complimented her olive skin and showed off her tattoos—made his dick come roaring to life. Even now, as they left their coats with the attendant at Devotion, Dylan couldn't stop looking at the woman.

Taking her hand, Dylan settled it onto his arm and led her through the doors and into the club proper. It looked much the same as it had last time he was there, though he didn't recall much about that night, either. Seemed that when he was with Sarah, she drew all his attention and held it.

"Now that you're walking in here with your eyes wide open, what do you think?"

Sarah smiled up at him. "I know what this place is, but for whatever reason, it's not nearly as intimidating the second time."

Dylan chuckled. "Would you like something to drink?"

Sarah shook her head. "I'm good right now."

"Let me introduce you to a couple of people."

They maneuvered through the club, past the few people who were already there, most of them still clothed.

Luke McCoy turned, his eyes scanning the room, but Dylan noticed the second Luke recognized him. He headed right for them.

"Damn good to see you tonight," Luke greeted when he approached.

"Thanks for allowing me in," he joked as he shook Luke's hand. "Luke McCoy, I'd like you to meet Sarah Davis. Sarah, Luke is one of the club's owners."

"Nice to meet you." Sarah shook Luke's hand.

"I've heard a lot about you," Luke told her.

Sarah seemed surprised.

"My wife is close to Dylan's sister. You've been a hot topic a time or two."

Sarah blushed and Dylan slid his arm over her shoulder, pulling her into his side. "All good, I assure you."

"Of course. But we're still tryin' to figure out what you see in this old, rusty cowboy."

Dylan chuckled.

"He has his moments," Sarah said sweetly.

"That he does."

Trent chose that moment to walk up, quickly greeting him and Sarah. Once again, Sarah seemed nervous, which amused Dylan.

"You taking them on a tour?" Luke questioned, sipping his drink.

"That's the plan."

Luke turned back to Dylan. "Congrats, by the way. I heard you're goin' into business with this crazy fuck."

Dylan laughed. "You heard right."

"Good. He needs someone to keep him in line. Maybe his own club will keep him out of my hair."

"Don't count on it." Trent smirked. "I live to interfere."

"Ain't that the damn truth." Luke glanced down at Sarah. "It was great to meet you."

"You, too."

"I've gotta go find Cole before he gets in too much trouble."

With that, Luke sauntered off, leaving the three of them standing there.

"You ready for this?" Trent directed his question at Sarah.

"As ready as I'll ever be."

Her actions belied her words, so Dylan nudged Sarah forward, falling into step with Trent.

"The main floor is relatively tame," Trent noted.

"Tame?" Sarah scoffed. "There are naked people and a woman with a... I don't even know what that is."

"It's a crop," Dylan added helpfully.

Trent chuckled. "Let me rephrase that. It's relatively tame compared to what you'll see upstairs. Thankfully, there is more privacy up there."

"Thankfully? For who?"

Trent smiled down at Sarah. "You'll see."

True to his word, it didn't take long for Trent to prove to Sarah that privacy was sometimes the way to go. After making a quick trip through the business end of the building where the offices were, Trent led the way down the narrow hall that overlooked the main floor. This side of the building held the recreational rooms. Unlike the three glass rooms on the main floor, which allowed onlookers to see from all angles, all of the rooms on the second floor had doors. Some people utilized them, marking the rooms as occupied.

Not surprisingly, most of the people who visited Devotion were there to watch or be watched, so it was rare that the room was completely dark—meaning the occupants inside weren't visible to the voyeurs who lingered. Some were looking for participants to join them, others simply to be watched doing whatever it was that struck their fancy.

Trent continued on, leading the way to the largest of the rooms at the end of the hall.

"This is more how I envision my entire club looking," he noted as they stepped inside.

It was unoccupied at the moment, which allowed them the opportunity to look around. There were several pieces of equipment, including a Saint Andrew's cross, a spanking bench, and plenty of other "torture" devices.

"I envision your club being classy," Sarah said, her eyes roaming the room before landing on Trent. "Similar to downstairs but on a grander scale. That's what I'm really trying to say." She smiled shyly. "When I look at you, I think of platinum and gold. That should carry over into your club. And aside from that, everything is clean and crisp and white. Rugged, sand-colored leather would be utilized, as well as dark hardwood." She nodded toward his booted feet. "A balance between the two sides to you. Glitter and diamonds versus rustic and warm. A dichotomy, I guess you could say."

"So you've given this some thought," Trent noted.

"A little." Sarah's cheeks reddened.

"Keep going," Trent urged, crossing his arms over his chest and leaning against the Saint Andrew's cross.

"When I think about your club, I see a main floor with a central bar and various seating areas. That would be the glitter and gold part. Similar to the VIP area at Devil's Playground. Only, more like a high-end hotel lobby, but bigger, more spread out. Then, instead of a second floor, yours will have a basement. A dungeon, I guess you would call it. That'll still be classy, but darker, edgier. Sexy."

It was obvious to Dylan that Trent was completely enthralled with Sarah. He couldn't necessarily blame him. The woman had clearly given this some serious thought.

"Now, don't get me wrong. I'm not a designer."

Trent grinned. "I've got one of those."

"Of course you do," she said teasingly.

Sarah glanced to Dylan. He smiled at her.

"Unfortunately, I haven't come up with a name. I gave some thought to Sinners and Saints, but I don't really like it. Then I had the idea of Sinful Shadows, but again, I just didn't see it. So, I'm sorry I can't help on that front."

"Oh, you helped more than you know," Trent said, standing to his full height.

"Yeah? Did you come up with a name?"

Trent shook his head. "No, you did."

"I did?" Sarah's eyes widened. "What are you thinking?"

"The one word that described it all."

Sarah frowned.

Dylan had already picked up on exactly what Trent was thinking. He'd seen the man's face when she said the one single word that really did describe it perfectly.

"Which is?"

"Dichotomy," Trent said, grinning as he moved toward the door. "It's perfect."

Yep, just what Dylan thought.

CHAPTER TWENTY-SIX

THE BEST PART ABOUT TOURING DEVOTION WITH Trent was that Sarah hadn't thought about where she was or what might happen later for the past two hours. Keeping her mind occupied was probably the only reason she'd made it this far into the night without having an honest-to-goodness panic attack.

Granted, now that the tour was over and Trent was off doing God knows what, Sarah was once again completely focused on Dylan and what his intentions were with her. After confirming that she didn't want something stronger, Dylan had ordered 7-Up from a waitress, and then they'd wandered around for a few minutes, ending up right back where they started, on the second floor overlooking the main-floor activities.

"Quit thinking so hard," Dylan whispered, pulling her in close as they stood at the railing.

His body was warm against hers as he pressed into her back.

"I'm trying my best," she told him truthfully.

It wasn't easy, all things considered.

Dylan turned her so that she was facing him, her butt against the wrought iron rail. In a moment of panic, she briefly wondered if anyone could see beneath her skirt. If they could, they were getting an eyeful right about now since she wasn't wearing panties.

Of course, that thought flittered right out of her head the instant Dylan's lips descended on hers. His mouth was firm, his lips warm, his hands gentle as he urged her closer. She leaned into him, loving how easily he could distract her from her thoughts. Apparently she'd gotten a little too lost in the kiss, because the next thing she knew, they were in one of the private rooms. She hardly remembered moving, inching out of the hallway bit by bit.

And here they were.

Sarah tried not to think about what came next. Would a stranger walk in any second now? Was this other person not a stranger? Did she know him? Would this be awkward and weird?

"I've waited for this moment," Dylan mumbled against her lips, his hands trailing down to her thighs. "Two hours with Trent was hell. I've been counting down the seconds until I could get my hands on you."

Sarah giggled. "I guess you better make up for that lost time."

"I can do that." He pulled back and looked at her, his gaze imploring hers. "I can definitely do that."

She knew what he was thinking, so before he could voice his question, she beat him to the punch. "I'm good, Dylan. With everything." Sarah pulled his head back down so she could reach his mouth. "I've been waiting all night, too. I want nothing more than to feel you inside me."

A rough growl escaped him as he settled his mouth over hers once more. Sarah slipped her arms around his neck, bringing her body closer to his as their tongues explored. When he pulled her farther into the room, she moved with him, refusing to let go.

She was overwhelmed by this man. The warmth of his body, the rich, intoxicating scent of his cologne, the sexy rumble coming from his chest. Dylan Thomas did it for her in so many ways. Ways she never thought possible. Sarah could feel her body heating, her desire intensifying. She hadn't been lying when she said she was ready for this. Her pussy clenched with the need to be filled. Her clit pulsed with an ache that she knew Dylan would sate eventually.

He wasn't moving fast though. He seemed to be taking his time, his hands trailing over her hips, then down to her thighs. His rough fingertips sensually scraped across her skin, back and forth. When he pulled his mouth from hers, Sarah met his eyes and what she saw stole her breath. There was so much passion, a burning need that mirrored her own, glittering in his dark eyes.

"I want this." Dylan's words were said softly, his hand cupping her face. "I can't explain why, but it's all I can think about."

Sarah nodded. "And I want to give you this," she assured him.

It was only then that she realized they weren't alone.

Sarah sucked in a breath when she mentally calculated the number of hands that were on her body. There weren't only two, there were four. And the warmth at her back was coming from another person.

"Tell me you want to see where this goes," Dylan urged, his thumb brushing over her bottom lip. "Tell me that you want us to pleasure you, to make you feel things you've never imagined."

"Yes," she rasped. Her body had a mind of its own, impulsively leaning into the hard body behind her as those big, work-roughened hands gently slipped around to her chest.

Dylan's eyes left her face, his gaze sliding to the person behind her. "Christian, you remember Sarah." Dylan peered down at her again. "Sarah, Christian."

"Chris," the man voiced. "You can call me Chris."

She couldn't form words because she was now caught up in the sensations that were assaulting her body as she processed the fact that she had gone to high school with this man. She'd spent days thinking about this, wondering how awkward it would be. But it wasn't. Yet. And that was surprising because she had yet to see Chris's face. She knew what he'd looked like in high school, but now...

Dylan took a step back. "I want him to undress you while I watch."

Sucking in a deep breath, Sarah willed the rioting butterflies in her belly to chill out.

When Dylan moved farther back, perching on the edge of the mattress, the strong arms around her relaxed slightly. She kept her eyes locked with Dylan's as the man—Chris—slowly tugged on the string at her side. He clearly knew how this worked. Once it was freed, the wrap-dress slid open. His hand dipped inside and tugged on the other string, then slid the dress from her shoulders, allowing it to fall to the floor.

She felt every bit as naked as she was thanks to Dylan's slow perusal of her body.

Dylan tilted his chin. Obviously a silent command for Chris, because he unhooked her bra and it too fell to the floor.

"Take his shirt off, Sarah."

She faltered for a moment, not sure she wanted to turn around. Since she had yet to see Chris's face, she could easily pretend this never happened. But once she did...

Chris clearly was on to her hesitancy, because his hands gently cupped her arms and guided her around until she was facing him.

She was eye level with the man's chest, which meant she had to look up—way up—to see his face. Sarah stared up into the steel-blue eyes of the man she was allowing to touch her. Aside from being older, he looked a lot like he had in high school. He was tall, a few inches taller than Dylan. He had dark hair and a scruffy jaw, like Dylan. The similarities ended there though. Where Dylan's face was ruggedly handsome, Chris's was less chiseled, smoother. He looked younger than Dylan, but she knew they were the same age.

"Very nice to see you again." Chris's deep, gravelly voice slid over her nerve-endings, making her entire body pulse.

"His shirt," Dylan reminded.

Sarah slowly slid her hand up Chris's torso, working each button open slowly. Her fingers trembled, but she managed.

As she revealed sun-bronzed skin, she admired every inch. He was in great shape. All solid muscle. It was obvious he worked outdoors because even in the winter he had the evidence of a tan.

Once she had the shirt unbuttoned, Chris shook it off, then his hands did a slow glide from her shoulders down to her elbows. He turned her once more so that she was facing Dylan. This time when he pressed his chest to her back, she felt the warmth of his skin.

Dylan got to his feet and moved toward them.

"Oh, God," Sarah moaned when Chris's mouth trailed over her neck at the same time Dylan leaned in and pressed his lips to hers.

Two men.

There were two men kissing her, touching her. It was surreal and she didn't want it to end. She forced her brain to decipher between the various sensations, but it was nearly impossible. Her senses were overwhelmed.

Sarah had no idea how long the kiss lasted, but she was still reeling when Dylan pulled her toward the bed and settled her on his thighs, facing away from him. He brushed her hair off her neck, his lips trailing over the skin he exposed. His hands roamed slowly, gently over her chest, her breasts, her belly. All the while, she was watching Chris as he inched closer to them.

Chris didn't say a word, but his eyes said more than words could have. He looked at her as though she was the most tempting woman he'd ever met. It did something strange to her insides, a warmth curling through her belly, extending lower.

"Spread your legs," Dylan whispered, his big hands urging her thighs apart. "I want Chris to taste you."

Oh, geez. Sarah knew what that meant, and though a touch of modesty skirted the edge of her mind, she allowed Dylan's hands to spread her legs, to glide up her thighs, his fingers separating the slick lips of her pussy and baring her to this man's gaze.

Chris dropped to his knees as though he were going to worship her.

A rough growl reverberated from Chris as his mouth trailed over the inside of her thigh, then slid to the other. Sarah realized she was gripping Dylan's forearms, holding on to him tightly.

"Taste her," Dylan ordered. "Put your mouth on her pussy."

Dylan groaned, his lips skimming her neck when Chris's head lowered between her thighs.

The instant his hot breath stroked her sensitive flesh, Sarah flinched. And when his lips grazed her clit, she nearly fell off Dylan's legs.

"How does it feel, Sarah? To have his tongue on your clit?"

Sarah moaned. No way could she speak. It felt incredible, even if she knew this was wrong. No, wait. It wasn't wrong. More like taboo. Uncommon, definitely. But that didn't change the fact that she was overwhelmed by heat from this man's mouth as he gently licked her, tormenting her. He was teasing more than anything, driving her higher and higher with every leisurely stroke of his tongue.

Dylan's hands trailed over her. Her thighs, her hips, her belly. They worked their way up to her shoulders, slid down her back, and once again around to her thighs. Her skin tingled. Her nipples puckered.

When Dylan's hands cupped her breasts, his fingers lightly tugging her nipples, she leaned into him more. Her eyes were locked on Chris as he sat back, his big hands on her thighs. He was watching what Dylan was doing.

With her hands clutching Dylan's wrists, Sarah watched as Chris leaned in and wrapped his lips around her nipple, his tongue thrashing against the sensitive peak. Lightning bolted from her nipple to her clit.

"Touch him," Dylan instructed.

Sarah reluctantly released Dylan's wrists and slipped her fingers into Chris's silky dark hair. She pulled him closer, trying to assuage the ache that had taken up residence in her body.

She was briefly aware of Dylan shifting, of her butt hitting the mattress, of being lowered to her back while Chris continued to torment her with delicate pulls of his mouth on her breast.

And then there were two mouths on her and Sarah went up in flames. Dylan's mouth fastened to her other nipple and Sarah cried out from the sheer ecstasy of it. They worked in tandem, driving her higher and higher. She felt someone's fingers separating the oversensitive flesh between her thighs, but she wasn't sure who it was. One finger dipped inside her and she bowed up off the bed.

"Oh, God!" An orgasm streaked through her, surprising her.

"Damn, she's sweet," Chris whispered. "So fucking hot. I want to watch her come at least a dozen times."

A dozen. Sarah wouldn't survive a dozen.

She tried to breathe, her eyes traveling from one man to the other, then back again until Dylan's eyes were locked with hers.

"Are you okay?" Dylan inquired.

Sarah shook her head. "No ... I need ... more..."

The pure sensuality that darkened Dylan's face sent a tremor skittering up her spine.

DYLAN WAS DOING HIS DAMNEDEST TO MAKE this good for Sarah. From the second Chris's hands touched her, Dylan had wanted to bury himself deep in her body and watch her come apart between them. He couldn't explain what it was about this that turned him on, but it did. Seeing Chris's hands stroking her, his mouth feasting on her, the way Sarah writhed and moaned, begging for more. Knowing that they were turning her on, bringing her pleasure... It made him so hard it fucking hurt.

But they weren't done with her yet.

Not by a long shot.

Crawling over her, Dylan found Sarah's mouth with his. He kissed her slowly, sweetly while Chris got ready for the next part of the evening. Dylan trailed his lips over her jaw, her neck.

"What do you think so far?" he asked, keeping his voice low.

"So far?"

He lifted his head and looked into her eyes.

"You mean there's more?"

"Baby, we're just getting started." He didn't tell her how true that statement was.

"Well, don't stop now. I'm looking forward to whatever you've got in store for me." She pulled his head back down and he kissed her. This time he deepened the kiss, stroking her tongue with his, nipping her lower lip.

He heard the sound of a door open, then close, but he didn't stop kissing Sarah. She didn't question what was going on, but he figured she'd heard it, too. Only when the bed dipped on both sides of him did Dylan pull back. He watched her face as she peered over at Chris, who was on her left, then turned her head to the right. Her eyes widened as she acknowledged the newcomer.

"You remember Tristan," Chris introduced. "My identical twin brother."

Dylan held his breath, wondering if Sarah would panic now that she was in bed with three men. She seemed to ponder the addition, her eyes raking over Tristan's face.

"Do you trust me, Sarah?" Dylan asked, needing her to say something.

Her blue eyes slowly moved to his face.

And she smiled.

"I trust you."

Swallowing hard, Dylan leaned down and crushed his mouth to hers. This was what he wanted. To share her. He knew deep down that Sarah belonged to him. Her heart, her soul, those were what he wanted for himself. The fact that she trusted him with her pleasure meant so much to him. It'd been a gamble to take this this far.

"Stay right there," Dylan instructed when he released her mouth.

He got to his feet and watched the three of them on the bed. Chris didn't hesitate, leaning in and brushing his lips over Sarah's before trailing down her chest and once again latching on to one beautiful tit. Tristan did the same, mirroring his brother. Dylan quickly disposed of his clothes, then reached for Sarah's legs, pulling her toward the edge of the bed. When she was right where he wanted her, he knelt between her thighs.

Tristan reached for one leg, hooking her knee over his arm, and Chris did the same, spreading her wide while Dylan licked her. He could see Sarah watching him, her eyes glazing over as he worked her with his lips and tongue.

Chris and Tristan feasted on her breasts again, making sure she felt the warring sensations throughout her body. The point was to give her more pleasure than she ever thought possible. No single man would ever be able to provide her with this. It wasn't physically possible.

Dylan dipped two fingers inside her, gently at first, then fucking her deeper while he flicked her clit with his tongue. He watched as she grabbed on to both men at her sides, her body arching as she cried out.

"Fuck, yes, beautiful girl," Tristan growled. "Come for us, Sarah."

Watching, waiting, desperate to see her fly off the cliff, Dylan continued to plunge his fingers into her. He latched on to her clit and sucked...

"Oh, God, yes!" Sarah screamed, her clit pulsing against his lips as she came.

He willed himself to relax. All he wanted to do was to pounce on her, to bury his cock into the wet, warm depths of her body and fuck her until neither of them knew their names. His dick was iron-hard and desperate for her, but he knew not to rush this. It would be over before they knew it anyway. No reason for him to race to the finish line.

Getting to his feet, he watched as Chris and Tristan gently soothed her, their hands roaming over her body, fingertips caressing her nipples, gliding over her navel, sliding down to graze the glistening folds of her pussy. It took him longer than normal to grab a condom because he was transfixed by the sight.

Right or wrong, this was what he enjoyed.

More so because Sarah made him feel secure enough to explore with her.

In every way imaginable.

Chapter Twenty-Seven

Sarah wasn't sure she could endure another orgasm like that. She'd been consumed by pleasure. Three mouths on her...

It was still hard to believe that this was happening.

"Come here, baby," Dylan crooned against her ear.

She hadn't realized anyone else had moved, but Dylan had somehow appeared at her side, and when he pulled her onto him, she went willingly. Straddling his hips, she draped herself over his chest, her bones like jelly.

"I need to be inside you," Dylan said. "Need to feel your sweet pussy milking me."

His words had tingles dancing beneath her skin.

Sarah managed to sit up, allowing him to nestle his cock against her folds. That was when she realized he'd put on a condom. Maybe she had passed out from the intensity of her orgasm. Honestly, she couldn't remember the past few minutes.

"Sit on my cock, Sarah," Dylan commanded.

Without waiting, she took him deep into her body, his cock brushing sensitive nerve endings.

She felt the bed shift, knew someone was behind her. She wasn't sure who it was because she didn't know Chris or Tristan well enough to tell them apart. Whoever it was pulled her back against his chest, his arms slipping around to cup her breasts. The other one knelt on the mattress beside Dylan.

Meeting Dylan's eyes again, she smiled reassuringly, letting him know she was still good with this. Hell, she was more than good with this and that was the biggest kicker of all. Sarah wanted to spend the rest of the night crushed between these three men, their hands and mouths driving her out of her mind.

"Ahh, yeah." Dylan gripped her hips, pulling her down on him so that he was lodged balls deep inside her. "Feels so damn good."

He lifted her slightly, then thrust his hips upward, fucking her, filling her, giving her just what she needed. A mouth was on her breast, licking, sucking, nipping momentarily, but then he was gone. A firm hand on her back pushed her forward until she was once again lying on Dylan.

"Give me your tongue," he urged.

Sarah kissed Dylan, allowing her tongue to stroke his. Dylan clearly had other plans. He sucked on her tongue, mimicking the way he was fucking her. It was enough of a distraction to keep her from noticing the warmth against her anus.

"What's he doing?" Dylan asked when Sarah shifted, her body grinding against him as the foreign sensations whipped through her.

She didn't answer. Couldn't.

"Is he licking your ass?"

Sarah nodded.

"Does it feel good?"

She nodded again. It felt ... amazing.

Dylan's hips rocked, fucking into her while that devious tongue fucked her asshole, making her body hum.

But soon it was over when the man behind her shifted and she felt his fingers slide down the crack of her ass. She wasn't naïve. She knew what was going to happen. There were three of them and one of her. It was simple math.

"Relax, sweet girl." She was pretty sure that was Chris behind her, teasing her ass with his finger.

She tried to relax; she really did.

"Open your eyes. Focus on me," Dylan instructed. "Let it feel good, Sarah."

Sarah opened her eyes and shifted her position. The move caused her clit to press against Dylan, and she rocked into him, enjoying the feeling. She pressed her hands to the mattress beside Dylan's head, her eyes focused on him.

"I want to watch you suck Tristan's dick," he told her softly. "Take him in your mouth."

Sarah turned her head, realizing Tristan was kneeling there, his cock in his hand. He was big, probably far too big to fit in her mouth. Another thought took over. If he was that big … and Chris was his twin brother…

"Relax, sweetheart," Chris called from behind her.

There was pressure against her ass and something pushed inside. She could only assume it was one finger because there wasn't any pain. Sarah focused on Dylan, on the way he continued to move inside her, his hands now fondling her breasts as she opened her mouth and wrapped her lips around the head of Tristan's cock.

"Fuck, yes," Dylan hissed.

She knew he liked this. Even if she didn't understand that aspect of it, she realized he truly did want to watch as these men pleasured her. No way could she give that too much thought because then she'd have to wonder why she liked it so much, too. When she had realized there was one man in the room with her and Dylan, she'd been surprised. But when she'd realized there were *two* men … Sarah hadn't been sure what to expect.

But the truth was, she was enjoying this. The way they looked at her, the sexy words, the rough growls. Although she was at the center of it all, and they were in total control, she felt empowered.

Tristan's hand cupped the top of her head, and he held her still while he began feeding his cock deeper into her mouth. Sarah tried to focus on that, but she was having a hard time. Her body was overstimulated. Dylan fucking her pussy, Chris moving behind her, Tristan fucking her mouth.

Suddenly, all of the movements intensified and she felt Chris pushing into her. This time she knew it wasn't his fingers. He was guiding his dick into her ass. Every muscle in her body tightened, but so did Dylan's grip on her nipples. She cried out from the pleasure-pain that shot through her.

"So fucking tight," Chris groaned behind her. "That's it, Sarah. Let me fuck that sweet ass."

Her pussy clenched around Dylan's dick, making him growl.

"Fuck, yes," Tristan groaned. "Such a sweet mouth. That's it, sweet girl, suck me. Just like that."

Sarah had no choice but to allow these three men to take over and they did. She couldn't focus on any one thing because they were all fucking into her, filling her. It was an incredible feeling, being this full. The erotic friction of Dylan's cock tunneling in and out of her pussy warred with the overwhelming pressure of Chris fucking her ass. It was too much but not enough at the same time.

The biggest concern she had...

Whether or not she would be able to come because she couldn't seem to focus.

DYLAN WAS HANGING BY A THREAD. HE could feel Chris's shaft sliding against his inside Sarah's body. She was so fucking tight, her muscles clutching his dick, her body pulling him deeper, and there was only a thin membrane separating him from Chris. Thanks to the combined weight of Sarah and Chris, Dylan couldn't move, other than to thrust up into her while Chris fucked her from behind. He allowed Chris's momentum to drive them while he focused on the way Tristan fucked her mouth.

The woman was driving him to the brink of insanity. Her soft moans, sexy mewls, and the way her fingernails dug into his chest now that she'd planted her hands flat against him were too much. There was no denying that she was hovering right there on the brink with him.

Tristan pulled his cock from her mouth but stroked himself against her lips while Dylan watched. He wished he could've seen both men fucking her, but he wouldn't trade this spot for his life. Being inside Sarah, watching as she writhed and moaned, her body splintering from the sensations... Best spot in the house.

"Fuck me," Sarah begged. "Harder. Need ... more..."

Dylan gripped her hips, holding her still while Chris began pounding against her ass. Dylan thrust deeper inside her, retreating slightly, slamming in again while she rocked above him.

Chris's hand slipped around, sliding down her stomach toward the apex of her thighs. Dylan watched Sarah's face as Chris fondled the tiny bundle of nerves.

"Yes ... yes ... yes... Oh, God. Oh, God... Dylan! It's too much... I'm gonna..." Sarah screamed.

Sarah's orgasm triggered his. Dylan's release slammed into him as he came with a growl at the same time Chris impaled her one last time, his groan echoing in the room.

And then it was Tristan's turn. He guided his cock back into Sarah's mouth as Dylan lay there and watched. He couldn't look away as Tristan used her for his own pleasure. He knew how good her mouth was.

"Gonna come, sweet girl... Oh, fuck, yes." Before he came, Tristan pulled out of her mouth, cum spurting onto her back as she locked eyes with Dylan.

When it was over, Dylan pulled Sarah down on him, cradling her head to his chest as he fought to breathe. The bed shifted; Chris and Tristan disappeared. He could hear them moving around.

As they lay there, Tristan quickly cleaned Sarah, using a washcloth on her back and her ass. Dylan would've thanked him for the thoughtfulness if he could have woven at least a couple of words together. As it was, he was emotionally and physically drained.

While he lay there with his eyes closed, his arms around Sarah, he listened to the sounds in the room. Cleaning up, getting dressed. Then the sound of the door opening and shutting, leaving them in silence.

Dylan realized Sarah had fallen asleep on him. He didn't want to wake her, so he settled on holding her for a little while.

He tried not to think, not to worry.

It was a hell of a lot harder than it should've been.

His thoughts were all over the place.

"I remember them," Sarah said softly.

"Who?"

"Christian and Tristan. From high school."

Dylan didn't say anything.

"It's safe to assume y'all still keep in touch."

Dylan smiled to himself. Yeah, that was a good assumption. "So, what did you think?"

"About?"

"Being fucked by three men."

Sarah sighed. "It was ... an experience."

"Did you enjoy it?"

"I did. Immensely."

"Would you be willing to do it again?"

"Tonight?"

Dylan chuckled at the concern in her voice.

"Not tonight, baby. You need to rest."

"I do need to rest," she confirmed. "But yes, I'd be willing to do it again."

He liked that she would. Although it had seemed she'd enjoyed herself, he hadn't known for sure. Hearing the words from her mouth settled him somewhat.

Sarah eased off him, but she didn't move far, her head resting on his chest, her body beside his. "Tell me something."

"Hmm."

"Did you do that with Meghan?"

Just the mention of Meghan's name had Dylan's body tensing. Before he could even think about what he was doing, he was out of the bed and grabbing for his clothes. When he looked over at Sarah, her eyes were wide.

"Get dressed," he commanded. Realizing he sounded like a dick, he tacked on, "Please."

Without another word, Sarah grabbed her clothes and disappeared into the adjoining bathroom. He heard the toilet flush, the water in the sink come on. Fifteen minutes later, Sarah wandered out into the room, but Dylan noticed she wasn't looking at him.

When he moved toward her, she took a step back.

"I'm sorry," he told her.

Sarah's eyes lifted to his. "No, you're not."

Dylan frowned.

"Every time I try to talk about anything personal, you close up on me, Dylan. Have you ever wondered about my past? About my loss? You've never asked, so I assume you haven't. Well, I wonder about that with you. But it's clear that you're not ready to talk about her yet. And that means that this thing between us"—she motioned with her hands—"no matter how intimate it gets, is going nowhere."

Dylan disagreed, but he kept his mouth shut because, after all, she did have a good point.

Chapter Twenty-Eight

By the time Dylan pulled into her driveway, Sarah was a bundle of emotions ready to implode. She couldn't believe the way Dylan had acted when she'd tried to talk to him. Who knew that mentioning Meghan would've had him shutting completely down? Then again, it had been the first time Sarah had tried talking about her and mentioning her name. Suggesting Dylan talk hadn't led him to bringing up the subject. And after what they'd shared tonight...

Well, Sarah had mistakenly believed that they were making strides.

Apparently she'd been wrong.

Without waiting for Dylan to get out of the truck, Sarah opened her door and made a beeline for the porch. She didn't look back, but she knew Dylan was following her because she heard his door open and shut. She wasn't sure why he even bothered, because if they tried to talk tonight, things would likely backfire in her face.

As much as she wanted to rail at him, to insist that he talk about things that mattered, she knew now was not the time to do that. She wasn't in the right frame of mind and neither was he. There was no way she could accurately express how much he'd hurt her by shutting down like that.

When she opened the door, she didn't bother asking if he wanted to come in. It was evident that he did or he wouldn't have followed her to her door.

"We need to talk," Dylan said when he closed the front door.

Sarah spun around and glared at him. "Now?"

"Yes, now."

"Oh, so it's okay when *you're* ready to talk. But when I'm trying to make conversation, you can bolt on me? I don't think that's how this is supposed to work."

"You wanted to talk about Meghan," Dylan barked. "That's a topic of conversation that's off-limits."

Sarah stepped back as though he'd slapped her. His words were certainly the equivalent.

"I'm sorry, I wasn't aware of the off-limits rule," she countered. "I thought we'd moved past that."

"Past what, Sarah?"

She couldn't believe they were having this conversation. "Remember earlier? When you asked me if I trusted you?"

Dylan stared at her as though she'd lost her mind.

"I said yes. *Because I trust you*, Dylan. And I thought you trusted me."

"I do."

"Bullshit. You trust me with sex, but that's it. That's all this is, right? Sex? No different than three years ago. I'm a distraction and you got what you wanted. So what the fuck are you sticking around for?"

Sarah could tell she'd hit a sore spot with him.

"You want to talk about Meghan?" he yelled. "Fine. Let's talk about her. Let's talk about how I spent the last eleven years of my life getting over the fact that she died in my fucking arms, Sarah. That's what you want to hear, right? That I'm over it. That I'm not broken."

"Fuck you," she hissed. That wasn't at all what she'd wanted to hear.

"But it's what you want, right?" Dylan taunted her. "You want me to come crawling on my hands and knees, providing you the opportunity to fix me. Right, Sarah? It's what you do best? You put everyone else before yourself so you can fix them?"

What the hell was Dylan talking about? He was delusional was what he was.

"Fuck you!" Sarah exclaimed, turning away from him and walking toward the kitchen. She tried to control her breathing. This conversation wasn't going to go anywhere, so hashing it out was pointless.

"You fix people," he continued. "Ashleigh told me how she'd reached out to you and you wanted to help fix me. Is that why you're with me? To make sure I don't relapse? Did my sister talk you into this?"

Sarah pivoted around to face him. "Are you serious? That was three fucking years ago, Dylan. And, yes, maybe the old Sarah had wanted to try and help you back then. That's what friends do, right? They help each other. They listen. They *talk*."

"Then why didn't you?"

"Why didn't I what?"

"That night I came over ... when we fucked... I didn't hear you trying to stop me from leaving. You didn't reach out."

"You're pinning that on me?" The anger surged in her veins. "If I recall correctly, you called me that night. Not the other way around."

Dylan exhaled sharply. "You didn't try to get in touch. Why is that, Sarah?"

He knew damn well why she hadn't. Because he'd fucked her and run. Not that she was going to mention that.

"Tell me, Sarah. Why now? Why are you willing to be with me now? I'm no different than I was then."

Knowing she had to think before she spoke, Sarah turned and went into the kitchen.

He was wrong about not being different. The man she'd known had been beyond help at the time. Her help, anyway. He'd needed professional help to deal with the depression. She hadn't known about the alcoholism, but he'd needed professional help for that, too. Until he'd decided to come out of his decade-long coma, there hadn't been a single person on the face of the earth who could've helped him. Which was a complete shame because she'd known the real Dylan at one point.

Placing her hands on her hips, Sarah turned to face him and was stunned to see him standing with his palms planted against the wall, his head hanging between his arms, not moving.

"Dylan?" Sarah couldn't help but feel the pain radiating from him, although moments before he'd been all but ready to rip her a new one for simply wanting to talk to him.

"I'm sorry, Sarah," he whispered.

"For what?" God, she really shouldn't do this. She knew she shouldn't. "For walking in here and going all caveman on me? Or for inviting me into your life in the first place? Or for having some off-the-wall notion that you need to try and protect me from you?"

"All of the above." Dylan turned to face her. Those dark brown eyes no longer held the heat she had seen in them earlier.

She was still pissed, though there was a ribbon of concern twined in there, too. "I'm a grown woman. I can make my own decisions, but you don't have to worry—I'm not interested in doing this anymore." *Like hell.*

Dylan's head snapped toward her. "You're lying."

He stood up tall, an imposing figure in her house.

"You're wrong about me wanting to fix you, Dylan. In fact, I grew tired of trying to fix everyone else a long damn time ago." She gestured toward herself. "Why do you think I changed so much of myself? I didn't want to be that girl anymore. It turned out that while I was so focused on helping everyone else, I forgot to think about myself. I don't have that problem anymore."

There was chemistry between them, Sarah felt it, but aside from some incredibly good sex, Dylan hadn't promised her anything. It was her own fault for getting in over her head with this man. These past few weeks had been the best of her life. She hadn't remembered feeling so free, so completely uninhibited. She liked that feeling. In fact, she liked who she was when she was with Dylan.

But she honestly didn't think she was strong enough to compete with Meghan's memory. She didn't want to wonder every single day whether or not Dylan was hers or if he was going to fall back into the past, thinking of all that he'd missed out on. Would she wake one morning to find him gone from her life like everyone else? She couldn't take that.

She was all for trying new things. But getting her heart broken definitely wasn't in the plan. Been there, done that. The T-shirt no longer fit.

DYLAN HAD NO IDEA WHAT THE FUCK had come over him. He felt like a jackass, and that was probably exactly how he should feel. First of all, they'd just spent the last few hours together in the most intimate way possible. The woman had rocked his fucking world.

But the first time she tried to talk to him, he'd freaked the fuck out.

It was almost as though he was intentionally trying to push her, trying to hurt her so she could feel some of what he was feeling.

"Look, I really should go," he finally said, though he didn't need to. Sarah should've kicked him out on his ass long ago, told him to go to hell, because she certainly didn't deserve the shit he was dishing out.

Truth was, he was scared.

No, that wasn't the right word. He was fucking terrified.

He knew what he felt for Sarah was love. But knowing and accepting, at least for him, were two different things. As much as he wanted to commit to her, he didn't know how. He'd spent so many years living in the past, holding himself back, not allowing any happiness to seep into his life… It had turned him into a coward.

Turning to go, he didn't look at her, but he stopped in his tracks the second she spoke.

"Dylan, wait." Her voice was but a whisper in the silence of her living room. "Don't go."

He didn't want to go, but he needed to. He was prepared to take those few steps to reach the door, but then Sarah's small hand touched his arm, and Dylan fought the emotion that surged in his chest.

"Look at me," she said firmly. "That's what you always tell me, right? When we make love. You want me to look at you."

He did. He wanted that connection, to know that she saw him and only him. He had needed that connection with her. Reluctantly, Dylan turned to face her.

She was staring up at him, her eyes sad. He hated that he'd been the one to put that look on her face. It tore him up inside to know that he couldn't give her what she needed.

"Sarah…" He wasn't sure what he wanted to say to her, but he knew he needed to say something.

Staring back at him was a woman so sweet, and so damn beautiful, sometimes it hurt to look at her. Just like he remembered her from high school. He would never compare her to Meghan because that wasn't fair to either woman, but he would admit that never in his life had another woman touched him as deeply as Sarah. She saw through him, to the heart of him, and if anyone had the ability to fix him, he wanted it to be her.

Only he wasn't broken in the way that she thought. In the past few weeks, Sarah had changed him. She'd healed a part of him he'd believed would be a painful ache for the rest of his life. The emptiness inside him was gone when he was with her. He wanted that in his life. He wanted *her* in his life.

And he didn't want her to merely be a distraction.

No.

She wasn't.

Sarah was so much more than that. She was…

Everything.

Sarah moved closer and Dylan fought the urge to move backward, to put more space between them, because she lured him in with the innocence he saw in those navy blue eyes, though he knew the strong, capable woman who lurked beneath them. The beautiful woman who'd lived through as much pain, if not more, than he had, and she'd come out the other side even stronger. She was a survivor.

"I'm sorry for bringing up Meghan. My timing sucked and I—"

"You shouldn't be apologizing to me. You weren't wrong, Sarah. I was. And I owe you an apology. Despite what you think, I do trust you. And even though I acted like a complete and total jackass, I'm not willing to give up on us," he told her, glancing down at his hands, then back up at her. "Not now. Not ever."

"Me, neither."

A hot ball of emotion clogged his throat.

One thing he'd learned about Sarah these past few weeks was that she didn't do something half-ass. If she gave a little, she gave all, and he fucking admired that about her.

"You're stronger than I am," he whispered.

"That's what you think," she replied quickly. "Do you know why I spent so much time and energy changing my entire life? I mean, seriously, Dylan. I quit a perfectly good job so I could try and find myself. And I did it all so I could make it through another day and another after that. I didn't like who I'd become. And yes, I spent so much time blaming Paul for killing himself... I hated him with a passion because he left me alone. Does that sound strong to you?"

"Yes. Actually it does. You know how to get through it."

Her broken laugh startled him. "I wish that were true."

Shit.

Dylan glanced at the floor, not wanting to say the wrong thing. They did need to talk, and more importantly, he needed to open up, to tell her how he truly felt. For weeks, they'd gotten by, distracting one another, but it wasn't enough. He needed to know that this was going somewhere. And maybe that made him needy, but he couldn't change the fact.

"Would you like a cup of coffee?" she asked, mentally pulling him up short.

When he looked at her, a small smile tipped her lips.

Had he heard her right? "Coffee?"

"Yes."

"We're not gonna talk?"

"We will," she clarified. "But right now, we need a distraction."

"Sarah..."

"No, Dylan. Hear me out."

Dylan nodded, encouraging her to continue.

"Living in the moment is good and fine," she began. "For some people. But for you and me, our past isn't something we can let go of. And maybe that'll never be the case, but if we take a few minutes to ground ourselves, pull ourselves out of that past that haunts us, we can try to move forward again."

Dylan understood what she was saying.

"We are who we are and we have to accept that. It might take us a few more tries than other people, but we can get to the same place. But we don't have to rush it, either."

"So we're gonna distract ourselves with coffee?" he asked, still stunned.

"It worked, didn't it?"

His brows furrowed. "What worked?"

Sarah took a step closer. "It no longer feels tight right here," she said, placing her hand on his chest over his heart.

She was right, it didn't. The panic he'd been consumed by had faded and the only thing left was...

Dylan cupped her face in his hands. "Sarah..."

Her eyes widened and his heart rate picked up.

"I..." Dylan had to say it. He had to get it out there. "I love you."

Her face softened and her eyes searched his face as though she didn't believe the words he'd said. A tear slid down her cheek, and that sense of panic set in again, threatening to strangle him. Before he could pull his hands away from her face, Sarah's fingers curled around his wrists, holding him in place.

"I love you, too."

The weight that had been resting on his chest lifted, and for a minute, Dylan thought his legs might buckle beneath him. The last thing he'd expected was for her to love him back.

"Stop thinking," she said hurriedly.

Dylan nodded, smiling down at her as he wiped the tear away with his thumb.

"Coffee?" she asked and he couldn't help but laugh.

"I don't want coffee, Sarah." He wanted her.

All of her.

CHAPTER TWENTY-NINE

"IF YOU DON'T WANT COFFEE, WHAT DO you want?" Sarah asked, still holding Dylan's wrists as he cupped her face.

Her heart was pounding a million miles a second from the three little words that had come out of Dylan's mouth. She still couldn't believe he'd said them.

"You. I want all of you. Now and forever."

She tried not to focus on the forever part. Admittedly, it wasn't so easy. But that was her eternal hope winning out.

"Show me your bedroom, Sarah."

Smiling, Sarah choked back the emotion that was overwhelming her. Once again, she was going to allow this man to distract her. She didn't mind it this time because she knew what was coming.

Sarah led him down the hall to her bedroom, but Dylan didn't stop there. He turned toward the bathroom and he tugged on her arm until she followed. Several minutes later, they were naked and in the shower, the warm water sluicing over her skin as Dylan soaped her up.

"This is not very spontaneous, Mr. Thomas," she teased.

His eyes softened as he looked at her. "Priorities, baby."

Honestly, she thought he would've made love to her right there, but he was clearly on a mission. It didn't take long before they were both cleaned and dried.

"Eep!" Sarah squealed when Dylan lifted her into his arms and carried her back to the bedroom, gently lowering her to the bed.

He came down over her, his eyes locked with hers. There was so much emotion in his eyes, she was tempted to look away, scared that she was getting caught up in the moment. She wanted this to be real. She didn't want to find out that Dylan's proclamation had been based on the emotional upheaval that the day had caused.

"God, Sarah." He brushed his lips against hers. "I love you."

She reached between them and fisted his cock, stroking him slowly while he kissed her. His mouth was so gentle she wanted to cry. He was making love to her, and she could feel every ounce of the emotion behind his kiss.

This wasn't a distraction. This was the real thing.

"Wrap your legs around me."

Sarah did as instructed, releasing him from her grip.

"Do I need a condom, Sarah?"

She shook her head. "I can't have children."

His eyes stayed locked on hers.

"I had a hysterectomy years ago." It had been medically necessary, but at the time, she hadn't cared, because she'd long ago given up on having children of her own when Paul died.

"Let me love you."

Sarah nodded.

Dylan pushed in deep. She was wet and ready, her body desperate to feel his.

They made love for what felt like hours but was probably only minutes. Never once did they look away from one another. Sarah could feel Dylan in her soul. This man she'd loved for so long. She wondered if their paths had crossed all those years ago—back when they were naïve teenagers—for a reason. Perhaps a higher power had known how their lives would turn out, the loss they would suffer.

And somehow they would find themselves again in each other's arms.

It was a happy thought, one Sarah wanted to hold on to forever.

"I love you," Dylan whispered, his hand caressing her cheek. "I'm not good at this, but you probably already know that."

Sarah smiled. "I'm not, either."

He rocked into her again and again, her body humming with every thrust until she was nothing more than a bundle of overstimulated nerves.

"Let me love you forever, Sarah. Since the day you let me into your house three years ago, I've known who owned my heart. But I wasn't looking for you to fix me, so I had to fix myself. For you. I wanted to be worthy of you."

Sarah couldn't stop the tears streaming down her face. "Dylan..."

"Marry me, Sarah."

Her heart slammed against her ribs, then stopped beating completely. She had to remember to breathe. Not an easy task when he kissed her so sweetly.

"Marry me," he repeated when he pulled his mouth from hers. "Say yes, please."

"Yes. Definitely yes."

ASKING A WOMAN TO MARRY YOU WHILE having sex probably wasn't the best way to go, but Dylan hadn't wanted to wait any longer. He had royally fucked up, and he didn't want to risk losing Sarah forever. She had forgiven him, but that didn't matter.

Now, as he lay in the dark, holding her against him, he thought about Meghan. He smiled to himself, wondering if this was her handiwork. If he had to guess, Meghan had put Sarah in his path. She'd always been trying to take care of him, and even in the afterlife, she was reaching out to him.

Oddly enough, he wasn't sad when he thought of her now. He was thankful for the time he'd had with her.

"What are you thinking about?"

Dylan turned his head, brushing his lips across Sarah's forehead. "Meghan."

"Yeah?"

"She always liked you," he told her.

"Me?"

"Yeah. Back in high school. When you and I were dating, Meghan and I were just friends. She thought you were good for me because you were so sassy and smart."

"I had to be in order to keep you from steamrolling right over me."

"She actually got mad at me when I told her that I had to break up with you."

"But you were going off to college," Sarah said. "It only made sense."

Dylan tried to see her face in the dark.

"What? You think I didn't know that's why you broke up with me?"

"I figured you thought it was Meghan."

"No. I didn't think you were that kind of guy."

"I wasn't."

"I know. Hence the reason I didn't egg your truck like my friends wanted me to."

Dylan smiled into the dark. "And to answer your question earlier ... about Meghan." He sighed. "Yes, I did share her before we were married. She wasn't into it, so I shut that side of myself down."

"Did it bother you that you had to?"

"No. After a while, I never thought about it."

"You loved her, Dylan. It makes sense that you did what you could to make her happy." Sarah turned. "I want you to know you can talk about her with me. I'd like to be able to talk about Paul."

He kissed her forehead again. "I'd like that. I want to be able to talk to you."

"Good. And as long as you do, I won't have to withhold sex from you."

Dylan laughed, pulling her tighter to him. "Were you serious when you said you'd marry me?"

"Yes." Her hand slid over his chest. "Were you serious when you asked?"

"Yes."

"Do you want to talk to your kids first?" she asked.

Dylan kissed her forehead. "I'll talk to them. They'll be thrilled, I'm sure. But the bigger question is, where are we gonna live? My place or yours?"

"Where do you wanna live?" she asked. "I'm not married to this house, just so you know. In a fit of rage, I sold my house because Paul had lived there, and like I said, I was mad at him for so long. So, I bought this one so I didn't have to live with my mother."

"Well, you've got one up on me then, because I live in the guest house on my grandfather's ranch. I didn't want the commitment of buying another house."

"It looks like we've got options then."

"Options." Dylan rolled over so that he was hovering over Sarah. "I like options."

CHAPTER THIRTY

Tuesday, January 31

"I'M GETTING MARRIED," SARAH BLURTED.

Elaine stared back, a small smile on her lips. Sarah waited patiently for her to say something. "I assume from the fact that you're glowing that this is something that you want?"

Sarah clasped her hands together, fighting the urge to fidget. "It is."

"You love him."

It was obvious that wasn't a question, but Elaine surely knew her well enough by now to know that Sarah wouldn't even dream of getting married unless it was for love.

"This is happy news, Sarah. Are you having any second thoughts?"

"Not at all."

"Have you told your mother?"

Sarah smiled. "I did. She was the first person I called."

"And what did she say?"

Chuckling, Sarah looked up and met Elaine's gaze. "She told me that I'm taking my New Year's resolution rather seriously. And then she told me that I better bring Dylan by so she can talk to him. That should be interesting."

"And have you talked to Jake?"

"No, not yet. I called and left him a message. He called me a little while ago and I asked him to meet me for lunch."

"How do you think he'll take it?"

"I think he wants me to be happy."

"You think?"

"He's going through some issues of his own right now."

"Something you can help him with?"

Sarah knew that was a trick question. "No. And I haven't been sticking my nose in. I told him I'm here to talk whenever he needs me. I'm not trying to fix him."

Elaine smiled. "But you want to."

"No," Sarah admitted. "I don't want to fix *him*. I wish I could make the situation better for him, but I can't. And since he's not in danger, I know I can't project my feelings on him. So, I've offered an ear and when he's ready, I know he'll talk to me."

"I'm proud of you, Sarah. I think you've come a long way over the years."

"I think I have, too. It took some time, but I've made some progress."

"And Dylan? How's he doing?"

"He's good. He's in control of his life. He told me that was the reason he didn't contact me after ... you know."

Elaine nodded.

"He said he had to fix himself in order to be worthy of me." Her heart melted a little more as she said the words aloud.

"And you believe him?"

"I do."

"It sounds like things are working out."

"I think they are." Sarah glanced at her watch.

"Well, I won't keep you since you've got a lunch date."

"Dylan's joining us," Sarah noted.

"He is?"

"Yes. And he's asked his kids to come as well. So we can tell them together."

"Are you nervous?"

Sarah shook her head but then laughed. "Of course I'm nervous. These are his children. I want them to like me."

Elaine's smile was so warm Sarah could practically feel it. "You're a strong, independent, highly intelligent woman. You've got a good heart, Sarah. I don't think you have anything to worry about. Doesn't mean you won't." Elaine chuckled. "But you've come through this stronger. I know you can handle anything that crosses your path."

Sarah got to her feet when Elaine did. "That means a lot," she told her therapist. "But I hope you know you're not off the hook. I have every intention of continuing these sessions. Dylan even mentioned he'd like to come with me."

"I'd like that," Elaine said. "And I'll still be here. Ready to listen whenever you need me."

"Thank you."

"For what?" Elaine's eyebrows slanted.

"For listening, for guiding me in the right direction."

"Oh, honey, I might've listened, but your heart led you in the right direction. Now you have to simply follow it."

Swallowing hard, Sarah hugged Elaine and then turned on her heel and headed for her car.

Now, if she could make it through lunch, she might just be all right.

DYLAN SHOULD'VE REALIZED THAT PUTTING NATE AND Jake at the same table was going to cause some friction. Thankfully, they had Stacey to keep things moving. She hadn't stopped talking since she took a seat between the boys.

"So, why'd you bring us here?" Nate asked, his forehead creased. He was clearly uncomfortable as he glanced between Dylan and Sarah.

"We wanted to tell you that we're getting married."

Yes, well, that was one way to get his children to be quiet. Even Stacey didn't seem to know what to say. Granted, Dylan assumed by the smile on her face that she wasn't completely horrified by the idea.

"You love him?" Jake asked Sarah.

"I do," she confirmed without missing a beat.

Jake peered over at Dylan briefly, then back to his aunt. "Then I'm happy for you." A small smile curved his mouth. "You deserve to be happy, Aunt Sarah."

"Thank you."

Dylan could see the tears forming in her eyes.

"Well, I had absolutely no idea you were in love," Stacey announced. "But I only have one thing to say."

Dylan waited and he felt Sarah stiffen beside him.

"It's about damn time."

They both choked out a laugh.

"Nate? Do you have any questions?" Dylan prompted his son.

Nate seemed to consider that for a moment, then met Dylan's eyes. "Only one."

"What's that?"

A smile formed on his son's face and Dylan's chest constricted at the sight. It had been so long since he'd seen Nate smile.

"Does this mean that the guest house will be vacant?"

Dylan chuckled and Sarah squeezed his hand. "It's possible."

"Cool."

"Have you told Aunt Ashleigh yet?" Stacey asked.

"Not yet. But I'm sure she'll know before the day is out."

"She will," Stacey confirmed. "Because I already texted her."

Dylan shook his head. His daughter was something else. He glanced from one face to the next. Stacey, Nate, Jake. "Y'all are really okay with this?"

Nate nodded, Stacey said, "Of course," and Jake smiled.

"Are you gonna tell them about the new job?" Sarah asked, her voice barely above a whisper.

"New job? Where?" Stacey asked, her attention fully on Dylan now.

"I'm going to be working for … Trent Ramsey."

Three pairs of eyes widened as all the kids stared back at him. Dylan was pretty sure they wouldn't remember the part about him and Sarah getting married.

"Do we get to meet him?"

"Oh, my God! Trent Ramsey from the Dillon Chronicles. Are you serious?"

"Wow. That's cool."

And just like that, the three kids were now talking amongst themselves, chattering on about Trent freaking Ramsey.

Dylan glanced at Sarah.

"I told you we should've led with that," she teased.

For the first time in his life, Dylan felt completely at peace with himself. It had taken a long time to get to this point, but as he stared at the woman he loved, he knew that this was a new beginning.

One he was definitely looking forward to.

Epilogue

Eleven months later

Sarah felt as though she was living on an entirely different plane than she had just a few months ago. Ever since the night she'd run into Dylan at the CISS party, her world had been turned upside down. And that had been only the beginning. These days, she felt ... different.

She wasn't sure what the difference was though. Aside from the fact that she was now married, living in a cute little four-bedroom house not too far from Trent Ramsey's new BDSM club with her husband and her two cats. Okay, so maybe the fact she was working at a BDSM club was what felt so different. The very same BDSM club that was officially opening tonight.

And yes, all was in place. She'd assured Trent of that on the phone, when he called her for the tenth time this morning. That was another big thing that had changed. She talked to Trent freaking Ramsey damn near every single day on the phone or in person.

Seriously, how could she not? The man had offered her a job. A fantastic one making good money. But more importantly, she got to work alongside her husband. Trent hadn't only wanted her to co-manage the place with Dylan—something she and Dylan had talked about long before she finally accepted the position—but he'd also wanted her to work with his designer, who just so happened to be married to Luke McCoy, the owner of Devotion.

Apparently, Trent had liked Sarah's design ideas so much he had scrapped his own and implemented the changes. Needless to say, for the nine months it took for them to complete the club, Sarah hadn't had much time to sit around and think.

Which was a good thing.

"Are you ready for this?" Dylan asked, moving up behind her as they stood near the main bar at ... yes, you guessed it ... Dichotomy.

Trent had loved the idea. Not only because it defined him so perfectly but because it also defined the club.

"As ready as I'll ever be," she told him, going on her toes to kiss him. "I mean, we are in a BDSM club, so who knows what's gonna happen when those doors open."

Dylan chuckled. "Good news is there aren't people waiting on the other side of those doors. But they'll be arriving soon."

Through the garage, Sarah knew. The front doors were simply for show. If someone wandered up to that part of the building, they'd be greeted by a receptionist, who would handle their issue and send them on their way.

The paying clientele were given individual pass codes that would let them in through the underground parking garage. Their anonymity was of the utmost concern, and the club had been built with that in mind.

"So, maybe we can sneak off later?" Dylan suggested. "Try out one of those spanking benches."

Sarah laughed. "Are Christian and Tristan gonna stop by?"

Dylan turned to face her fully. "I asked them to. Why?"

"Well, if they do show up, then maybe you'll get your wish."

"Why's that?"

"Because they'll be a good distraction, don't you know?"

Dylan jerked her to him, making her giggle as he kissed her hard. "Woman, whatever am I gonna do with you?"

"Whatever you want. Don't you know that by now?"

Trent Ramsey felt as though he'd been waiting for this night all his life. The grand opening of Dichotomy. He still had a hard time believing it was finally here. Everything was perfect. The place looked spectacular—far better than he'd ever imagined. He knew he owed his gratitude to Sarah and Dylan. They'd worked diligently getting it all in order, paying attention to every little detail.

Now, the only thing left to do was wait to see who showed up.

More importantly, he was waiting to see if *she* showed up.

She was a submissive looking for a Dom, after all.

And Trent was more than ready to fill the position.

Which was why he'd sent her an invitation. A personal one.

One he couldn't imagine she could turn down.

Want Trent Ramsey's story?

Keep reading for an excerpt from

THEIR *Famous* **DOMINANT**

ONE

Trent

"Master Ramsey?"

Turning at the sound of my name, I noticed the blushing submissive staring at me, flanked on both sides by her tuxedo-wearing Doms. While her light blue eyes were wide with what could only pass as star-struck wonder, her Dominants' identical hazel eyes were filled with amusement.

Langston Moore and his twin brother, Landon, had just claimed their submissive in an official collaring ceremony in front of their friends and family. And I'd be lying if I said I wasn't completely honored that they'd thought to include me.

My mind snapshotted the image of the threesome, a memory of this day etched in my mind for future reference.

"Luci," I greeted, smiling at the young woman who was the star of today's festivities. While it was evident Luciana Moore wanted to say something, no words fell from her lips as she stared back at me with eyes as round as saucers.

"Go on, pet," Landon urged his beaming bride.

"I ... uh..." Luci's voice chirped on the last word.

Langston chuckled. "What our tongue-tied submissive wants to say is thank you for bein' here today."

"The pleasure is all mine." I shook hands with Langston, then Landon. "The ceremony was beautiful."

"As is our submissive," Landon noted with pride.

I peered down at the petite submissive, who looked like an erotic fairy princess clad in an elegantly designed white corset, a platinum and diamond collar gracing her neck, and little else. "I'd have to agree. It's been a memorable day."

"With no small thanks to you for the venue," Langston added.

"The location was merely the backdrop," I told him, my gaze stopping on Luci once more. "You, young lady, are even more beautiful now that you've been officially collared."

Luci blushed as she usually did when she was around me. "Thank you, Master Ramsey."

"I still remember the first night I met you at Dichotomy." My gaze shot to Landon. "She came with you that night."

He grinned from ear to ear. "She did."

"And I'm sure she was just as star-struck then as she is now," Langston noted.

"She was," I agreed. "In fact, if I recall, that response broke one of Landon's rules and you spent most of the night walking around naked."

"*Mostly* naked," Landon corrected. "I allowed her to keep on the G-string."

I grinned, and Luci blushed again.

Needless to say, it had been interesting to witness, as it was any time a new submissive was introduced into our world.

"Thank you for overlooking my blunder that night, Master Ramsey," Luci replied, her voice husky and soft.

"You were quite sweet."

"But seriously," Landon said, his tone sobering. "We're honored that you attended."

"Don't be honored," I told him with a smirk. "I have every intention of drinking my weight in champagne. It won't be cheap."

Landon laughed. "I don't doubt that."

"Truth is," Langston said, "I didn't think you were that easy, Ramsey. You didn't even put up a fight when I invited you."

He was right. I wasn't easy. Usually.

"I'm only easy for you, my friend," I told him, grinning.

In the past year and a half, Langston and his three partners at his PR firm—his twin brother, Landon, along with Justin Parker and Benjamin Snowden—had become good friends of mine. We met through Dichotomy, the BDSM club I opened in Chicago roughly two years ago. The four men were part of the first wave of members who had joined the club and I'd gotten well acquainted with them.

Partially because of them, I'd been spending more and more time here in Chicago in recent months, needing a break from the monotony that had become my life.

"Probably not wise to let word get out that you'll roll over with very little persuasion." Langston chuckled, his gaze darting to the people milling about behind us. "Those subs following you around like lost puppies might think twice."

I didn't bother looking back at the submissives I knew were mingling nearby. I had yet to show any interest whatsoever, however they still trailed close behind. It was something I despised, and any submissive who hoped for even a small amount of my attention knew that.

"One could only be so lucky," I told him.

Langston's gaze slid to the far side of the room and mine followed.

"Your assistant looks a little out of sorts," he said with a grin.

I allowed my eyes to rake over the handsome man donning a designer tux and a wild-eyed expression as he took in everything around him.

"This is a first for him," I told them.

"Well, you wouldn't know it," Langston said facetiously.

"What gave it away?"

"Probably the fact that his jaw is dragging the floor," Langston said with a laugh.

At least the boy had the sense to keep his tongue in his mouth.

"Give him time," Landon chimed in. "He'll get used to it."

I had to wonder whether that was true or not. While I had purposely kept my assistant out of this side of my life, something had compelled me to invite him today. I was glad that I had because I enjoyed his company. He was one of the few people in the world I trusted implicitly. It had taken three years to get to that point, but I knew he had my best interests at heart.

I turned my attention back to the triad before me. "Is King around?"

Langston's eyes scanned the area behind me, obviously seeking out his father. "He's around here somewhere. Probably tryin' to keep a tight leash on our mother." Langston looked back at me and grinned. "You know how parents can be. I'm not sure anything is good enough for her boys and our mother's been flutterin' around, tryin' to ensure everything is perfect."

"Well, someone should tell her she accomplished her goal," I informed Langston, choosing to slide right over the reference to mothers.

If anyone wanted parental advice, I was the last person they should come to. My own mother had put me up for adoption when she was a whopping fourteen years old. I didn't know who she was, much less who had sired me. Nor did I care.

A nice couple had adopted me when I was a newborn, but a fire in our home had taken their lives when I was seven. The neighbor had managed to get me out, but by the time he did, the house was fully engulfed. According to the medical examiner, they died of smoke inhalation.

At that point, without any family who could care for me, I ended up back in foster care—where I was obviously destined to be. I spent several years in and out of homes, largely due to my age, along with my inability to behave. When I was fourteen, Rosa and Daniel Singer had come into my life. Although they never officially adopted me, they did foster me through most of my formative years.

While it hadn't been a childhood grounded in routine or consistency, I couldn't complain too much. I wasn't broken in the sense I'd had a shitty childhood, and I damn sure didn't want anyone's pity.

However, I did attribute the lack of control to my innate need to be in control now. It was one of the reasons I'd ventured into the realm of BDSM and then practically built my life around it.

I noticed several others lining up, probably hoping to give their congratulations to the threesome. "Well, I should stop monopolizing your time."

Langston smirked. "You headin' back to Texas after this?"

"Actually, I'm off to California to meet with my agent."

Landon cleared his throat. "Official business?"

I met the other man's curious hazel eyes. "We've got a few things to discuss."

"We're still considerin' your proposal," he admitted quickly.

I shook my head and huffed a laugh. "While I'm a businessman first, today is not for that. We'll catch up in a couple of weeks when you're back from your honeymoon."

Landon nodded, but I could see his reluctance. While I was eager to find out whether or not the partners had come to a decision regarding the proposal I'd made, I wasn't going to allow that to interfere with the festivities today.

"Well, thank you again for handlin' the venue," Landon said, motioning toward our surroundings. "We couldn't have asked for a better place."

"Even if I remember specifically tellin' you we weren't lookin' for anything fancy," Langston tacked on. The significant stress on *fancy* did not go unnoticed. "I should've known how you rich boys work."

I laughed. With a net worth of 750 million dollars, I could hold my own, sure. However, I happened to know that Langston and his partners weren't doing too bad in the finance department. In fact, they were in the process of expanding an already outrageously profitable business. Chatter PR Global was officially the third-ranked public relations firm in the world.

Granted, my side ventures were quickly increasing my wealth and I could credit that to good business decisions on my part. Not only was I one of, if not *the* highest-paid actor in Hollywood, I was also a venture capitalist and I had my hand in many pies. Along with the dozens of start-ups I'd helped fund, I was a silent partner in many things, owned some impressive real estate that was turning nice profits. I'd learned to diversify early on and it had paid off. Even more so since I'd invested in a technology company that was in the process of launching a software platform that would change the way most people did business.

In a word, I was rich. No sense denying it. However, I was also pragmatic.

"I promised you wouldn't be disappointed, Moore," I reminded Langston.

"That you did," he agreed. "You were true to your word."

Admittedly, this had been the perfect venue for a formal collaring ceremony. In fact, it was a place I'd considered for myself should I ever find a submissive of my own. Unfortunately, at the rate I was going, I wasn't sure that would ever happen.

"All right," I told them firmly. "I'm off to see if I can get my assistant to relax a little."

"Maybe offer him some champagne," Landon suggested. "Or bourbon."

I glanced over at Troy. I wasn't sure any amount of alcohol was going to help.

"Thanks again for comin'," Langston said.

"My pleasure." I turned my attention to Luci one last time. "You keep these boys in line."

"I will, Master Ramsey," she answered, still slightly bewildered.

With a smile, I turned and ambled away, my gaze landing on my assistant.

Troy Shelton—my personal assistant for the past three years—looked as though he wanted to crawl into a hole and hide. Even in spite of that, he was a very attractive man. He took good care of himself, which I found ridiculously appealing. Well-built with his sculpted chest and narrow waist, tall. He filled out a tuxedo nicely.

His shoulder-length, dark brown hair hung loosely in that style that said he didn't care what it looked like but he spent plenty of time getting it to do what he wanted it to do. His jaw had that purposeful stubble, his cheekbones were high, his nose perfectly proportioned to his face, and his mocha-brown eyes didn't look tired or strung out. In my world, that was not the norm. Considering my demanding schedule and my equally demanding personality, that was a wonder, really.

The thought made me smile.

There was something inexplicably masculine about him, but underneath, there was something innately submissive.

When a waiter offered champagne, I took two glasses from his tray.

"You all right?" I asked when I approached Troy, handing over one of the glasses.

Uncertain brown eyes flew up to my face as Troy nodded. "Of course, boss."

I smiled to myself as I scanned the crowd, taking note of the numerous bodyguards strategically placed throughout. While security of this magnitude wasn't usually necessary at a function such as this, I'd had to come up with a backup plan when word leaked that I was going to be attending today's ceremony. Luckily, I had friends in high places and it had only taken one phone call to ensure the press wasn't going to sneak into the party without an invitation.

"By the way, boss, Ken called. Twice. Said he needs an answer."

I frowned. "Ignore his calls," I instructed. "I'll discuss with him in person on Monday."

"Have you made a decision?" he inquired.

"Yeah," I told him. I'd known from the beginning of the unnecessary negotiations that I was turning down the part I was being offered. Although the movie would no doubt be a success, I was taking fewer and fewer roles these days for personal reasons. The only person who didn't seem to get it was my agent.

"Is there anything I can get you?" Troy offered.

Casting a sideways glance his way, I kept my initial response to myself. There was something I wanted from him, but we had a long way to go before we ever got to that place.

"I'm good for now," I replied. "We're here to relax, not work."

"Right, boss." His eyes widened as a Domme walked by, leading her scantily clad submissive around with a leash.

While Troy was otherwise preoccupied ogling the people around us, I let my gaze trail over him momentarily. I had no idea what I was doing checking him out, but I found something uniquely appealing about the man. Although my mind had been set on one particular woman for so long, I couldn't deny the fact that I had an overwhelming urge to dominate Troy.

Better yet, both of them together.

At the same time.

For those who knew me, that was an important detail that would come into play one day.

I just had no idea that *one day* would come quite so soon.

Their Famous Dominant is part of the Office Intrigue series but can be read as a standalone.

Available now!

ACKNOWLEDGMENTS

Writing this book has been bittersweet. When I first started writing this book three years ago, I didn't know where it would lead me. Never did I dream that it would take me to the end of the Club Destiny series, yet here we are. CONVICTION was the very first book that I published as Nicole Edwards back in 2012, and I have to thank all of the readers who took a chance on me. The fact that it has become such a beloved series has surpassed all of my wildest dreams

Okay, now on to the acknowledgments. I know that I will likely leave out someone important, but here goes.

First of all, I have to say thank you to my amazing husband who puts up with me every single day. If it wasn't for him and his belief that I could do this, I wouldn't be writing this today. He has been my backbone.

I need to say a huge thank you to Jennifer Greeff. It is because you have stepped in to help me out as my assistant that I was even able to finish this book. Thank you. For everything.

I have to give a huge shout out to Carla Rogers. Carla, you were the very first person to ever email me in an author capacity and it so happened to be about the Club Destiny series. I had no idea what was in store for me at the time, but I thank you for opening my eyes and allowing me to see the great big Indie book world that is out there.

And Chancy Powley … you've been here with me since 2013. I'm pretty sure you were slightly disappointed (maybe more than slightly) with one of my books, and you wanted to offer feedback. Since then, you've beta read every single one of my books. I am grateful in ways I can never explain. And more importantly, I am honored to call you friend.

I have to thank my new beta readers – Amber Willis, Allison Holzapfel, and Karen DiGaetano. Ladies, I look forward to what the future has in store for us. Thank you for coming along for the ride.

A huge thank you to my proofreaders. Jenna Underwood, Annette Elens, Theresa Martin, and Sara Gross. It's your attention to detail that has allowed this book to be the best that it can be.

I also have to thank my street team – Naughty (and nice) Girls – which has expanded in recent weeks. Traci Hyland and Maureen Ames, you have been with me for so long and I know there are times I don't show you the appreciation you deserve, but I want you to know that your desire to get my name out there means everything. And a huge welcome to Cindy Rockey-Bocz, Michelle Nageldinger, Erin Lewis, Jackie Wright, Chris Geier, Kara Hildebrand, Shannon Thompson, Tracy Barbour, Nadine Hunter, Toni Thompson, and Rachelle Newham.

I can't forget my copyeditor, Amy at Blue Otter Editing. Thank goodness I've got you to catch all my punctuation, grammar, and tense errors.

A huge shout out to Alfie Gordillo because, man, you've given me one seriously hot cover. The instant I saw that picture, I messaged you because I knew it was perfect for this book. It so happens that it took more than a year after that before I published the book, but I'm honored to have you on the cover. And a big thank you to Cassie Roop with Pink Ink Designs for making the picture possible. You're a rock star behind the camera, and I hope you never stop doing what you're doing.

Nicole Nation 2.0 for the constant support and love. You've been there for me from almost the beginning. This group of ladies has kept me going for so long, I'm not sure I'd know what to do without them.

And, of course, YOU, the reader. Your emails, messages, posts, comments, tweets… they mean more to me than you can imagine. I thrive on hearing from you, knowing that my characters and my stories have touched you in some way keeps me going. I've been known to shed a tear or two when reading an email because you simply bring so much joy to my life with your support. I thank you for that.

ABOUT NICOLE EDWARDS

New York Times and *USA Today* bestselling author Nicole Edwards lives in the suburbs of Austin, Texas with her husband and their youngest of three children. The two older ones have flown the coup, while the youngest is in high school. When Nicole is not writing about sexy alpha males and sassy, independent women, she can often be found with a book in hand or attempting to keep the dogs happy. You can find her hanging out on social media and interacting with her readers - even when she's supposed to be writing.

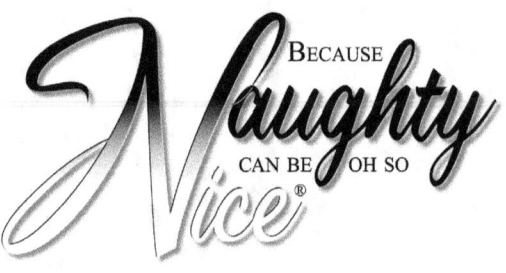

CONNECT WITH NICOLE

I hope you're as eager to get the information as I am to give it. Any one of these things is worth signing up for, or feel free to sign up for all. I promise to keep each one unique and interesting.

NIC NEWS: If you haven't signed up for my newsletter and you want to get notifications regarding preorders, new releases, giveaways, sales, etc., then you'll want to sign up. I promise not to spam your email, just get you the most important updates.

NICOLE'S HOT SHEET: A couple of years ago I produced a weekly hot sheet that gave a summary of what I'd done and what I had in the works, and I have decided to bring it back. This is a more personal newsletter that I send out for those who are curious about me, my family, my dogs, and all that goes along with the daily author life.

NICOLE'S BLOG: My blog is used for writer ramblings, which I am known to do from time to time. I will keep these separate from the newsletter updates or what I post in the Hot Sheet so that I don't duplicate in your inbox.

NICOLE NATION: I created Nicole Nation on my website to provide exclusive content to my readers including, First Look notifications, sneak peeks, A Day in the Life character stories, exclusive giveaways, cards from Nicole, Join Nicole's review team. It's free and gets you access to exclusive content you won't find anywhere else!

NN ON FACEBOOK: Join my reader group to interact with other readers, ask me questions, play fun weekly games, celebrate during release week, and enter exclusive giveaways!

INSTAGRAM: Basically, Instagram is where I post pictures of my dogs, so if you want to see epic cuteness, you should follow me.

TEXT: Want a simple, fast way to get updates on new releases? Sign up for text messaging. If you are in the U.S. simply text NICOLE to 64600. I promise not to spam your phone. This is just my way of letting you know what's happening because I know you're busy, but if you're anything like me, you always have your phone on you.

Website:	NicoleEdwardsAuthor.com
Facebook:	/Author.Nicole.Edwards
Instagram:	NicoleEdwardsAuthor
BookBub:	/NicoleEdwardsAuthor

By Nicole Edwards

The Walkers

Alluring Indulgence
Kaleb
Zane
Travis
Holidays with The Walker Brothers
Ethan
Braydon
Sawyer
Brendon

The Walkers Of Coyote Ridge
Curtis
Jared
Hard to Hold
Hard to Handle
Beau
Rex
A Coyote Ridge Christmas
Mack
Kaden & Keegan

Brantley Walker: Off The Books
All In
Without A Trace
Hide & Seek

AUSTIN ARROWS
Rush
Kaufman

CLUB DESTINY
Conviction
Temptation
Addicted
Seduction
Infatuation
Captivated
Devotion
Perception
Entrusted
Adored
Distraction

DEAD HEAT RANCH
Boots Optional
Betting on Grace
Overnight Love

DEVIL'S BEND
Chasing Dreams
Vanishing Dreams

MISPLACED HALOS
Protected in Darkness
Salvation in Darkness
Bound in Darkness

OFFICE INTRIGUE
Office Intrigue
Intrigued Out of The Office
Their Rebellious Submissive
Their Famous Dominant
Their Ruthless Sadist
Their Naughty Student
Their Fairy Princess
Owned

PIER 70
Reckless
Fearless
Speechless
Harmless
Clueless

SNIPER 1 SECURITY
Wait for Morning
Never Say Never
Tomorrow's Too Late

SOUTHERN BOY MAFIA/DEVIL'S PLAYGROUND
Beautifully Brutal
Without Regret
Beautifully Loyal
Without Restraint

STANDALONE NOVELS
Unhinged Trilogy
A Million Tiny Pieces
Inked on Paper
Bad Reputation
Bad Business

NAUGHTY HOLIDAY EDITIONS
2015
2016

www.ingramcontent.com/pod-product-compliance
Lightning Source LLC
Chambersburg PA
CBHW072127250626
47159CB00007B/2589